MAY -- 2015

D0477813

NO LONGER PROPERTY OF
SEATTLE PUBLIC LIBRARY

BATMAN
LI'L GOTHAM

Dustin Nguyen Derek Fridolfs Writers **Dustin Nguyen** Artist & Collection Cover Artist
Saida Temofonte Letterer BATMAN Created by **BOB KANE**

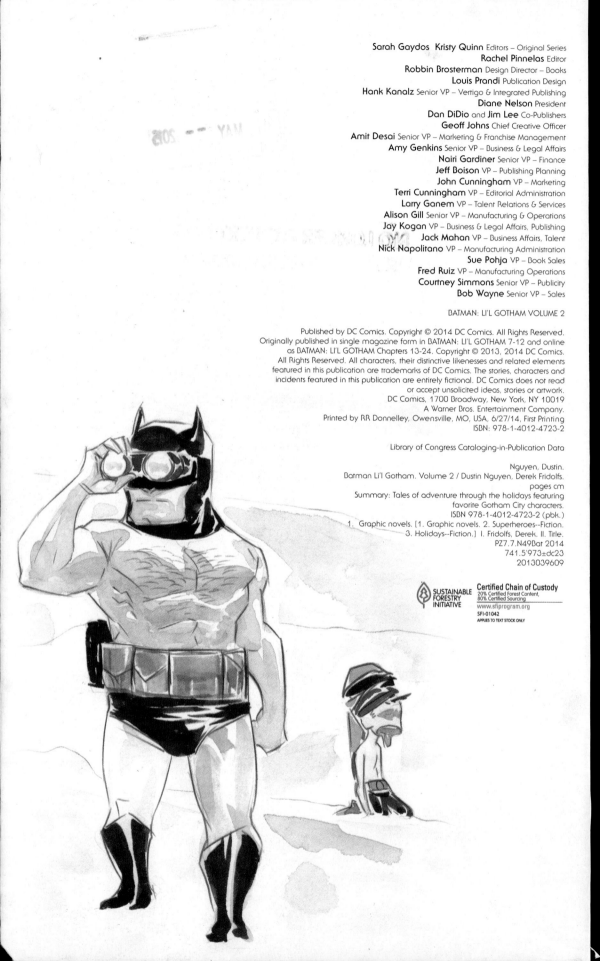

Sarah Gaydos Kristy Quinn Editors – Original Series
Rachel Pinnelas Editor
Robbin Brosterman Design Director – Books
Louis Prandi Publication Design
Hank Kanalz Senior VP – Vertigo & Integrated Publishing
Diane Nelson President
Dan DiDio and Jim Lee Co-Publishers
Geoff Johns Chief Creative Officer
Amit Desai Senior VP – Marketing & Franchise Management
Amy Genkins Senior VP – Business & Legal Affairs
Nairi Gardiner Senior VP – Finance
Jeff Boison VP – Publishing Planning
John Cunningham VP – Marketing
Terri Cunningham VP – Editorial Administration
Larry Ganem VP – Talent Relations & Services
Alison Gill Senior VP – Manufacturing & Operations
Jay Kogan VP – Business & Legal Affairs, Publishing
Jack Mahan VP – Business Affairs, Talent
Nick Napolitano VP – Manufacturing Administration
Sue Pohja VP – Book Sales
Fred Ruiz VP – Manufacturing Operations
Courtney Simmons Senior VP – Publicity
Bob Wayne Senior VP – Sales

BATMAN: LI'L GOTHAM VOLUME 2

Published by DC Comics. Copyright © 2014 DC Comics. All Rights Reserved.
Originally published in single magazine form in BATMAN: LI'L GOTHAM 7-12 and online
as BATMAN: LI'L GOTHAM Chapters 13-24. Copyright © 2013, 2014 DC Comics.
All Rights Reserved. All characters, their distinctive likenesses and related elements
featured in this publication are trademarks of DC Comics. The stories, characters and
incidents featured in this publication are entirely fictional. DC Comics does not read
or accept unsolicited ideas, stories or artwork.
DC Comics, 1700 Broadway, New York, NY 10019
A Warner Bros. Entertainment Company.
Printed by RR Donnelley, Owensville, MO, USA, 6/27/14, First Printing
ISBN: 978-1-4012-4723-2

Library of Congress Cataloging-in-Publication Data

Nguyen, Dustin.
Batman Li'l Gotham. Volume 2 / Dustin Nguyen, Derek Fridolfs.
pages cm
Summary: Tales of adventure through the holidays featuring
favorite Gotham City characters.
ISBN 978-1-4012-4723-2 (pbk.)
1. Graphic novels. [1. Graphic novels. 2. Superheroes--Fiction.
3. Holidays--Fiction.] I. Fridolfs, Derek. II. Title.
PZ7.7.N49Bat 2014
741.5'973±dc23
2013039609

SUSTAINABLE
FORESTRY
INITIATIVE
Certified Chain of Custody
20% Certified Forest Content,
80% Certified Sourcing
www.sfiprogram.org
SFI-01042
APPLIES TO TEXT STOCK ONLY

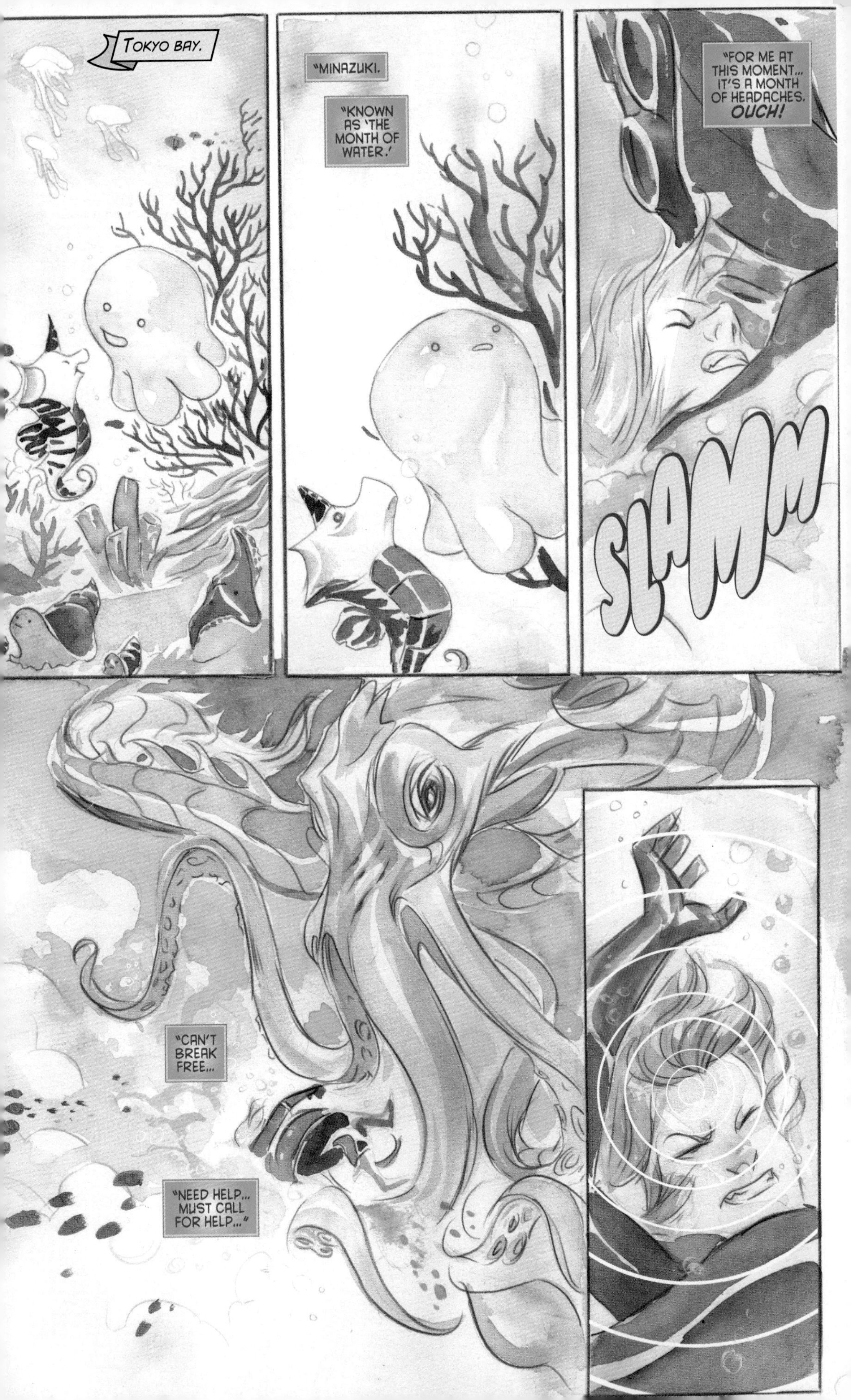
TOKYO BAY.
"MINAZUKI.
"KNOWN AS 'THE MONTH OF WATER.'
"FOR ME AT THIS MOMENT... IT'S A MONTH OF HEADACHES. OUCH!
SLAMMM
"CAN'T BREAK FREE...
"NEED HELP... MUST CALL FOR HELP..."

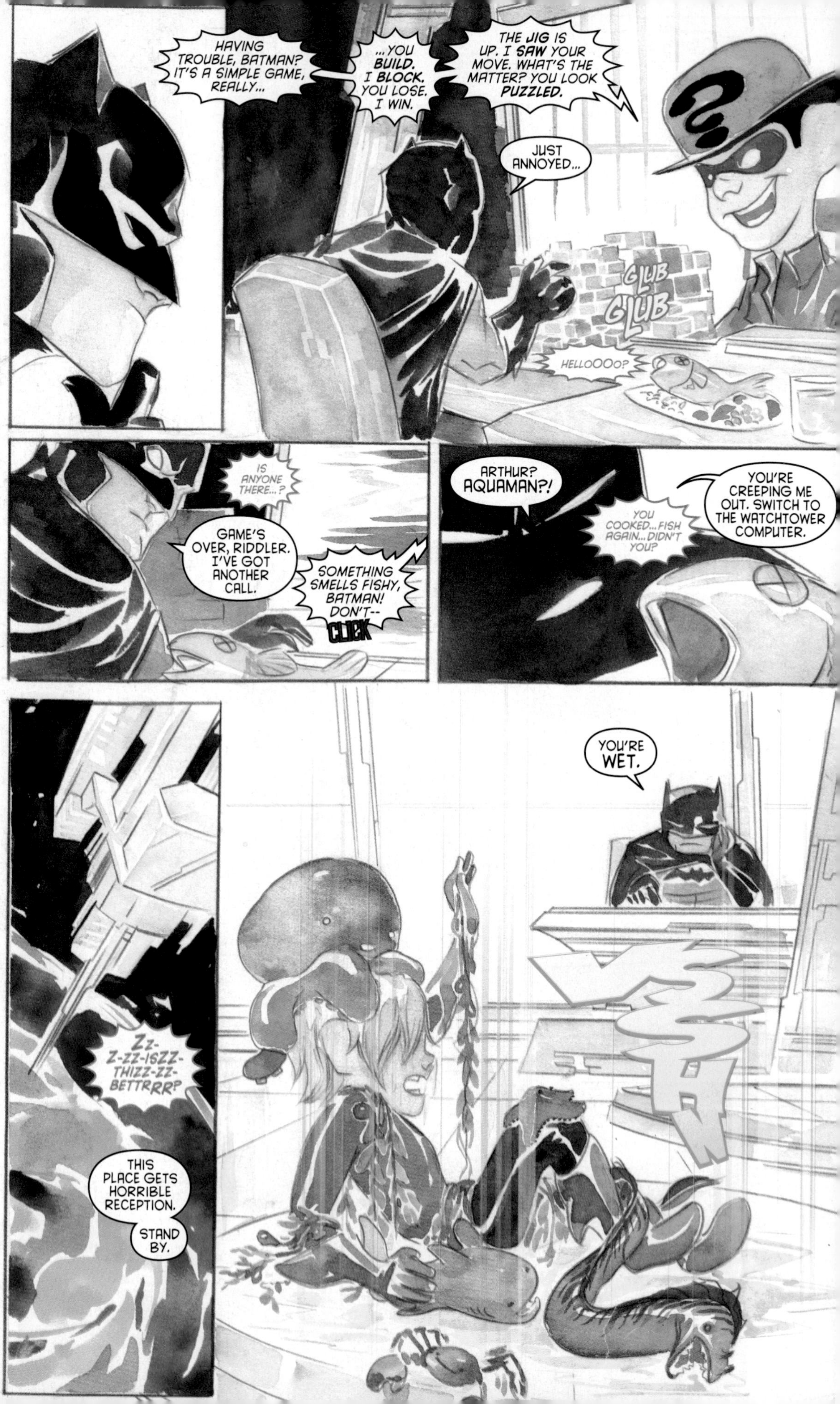
HAVING TROUBLE, BATMAN? IT'S A SIMPLE GAME, REALLY...
...YOU BUILD. I BLOCK. YOU LOSE. I WIN.
THE JIG IS UP. I SAW YOUR MOVE. WHAT'S THE MATTER? YOU LOOK PUZZLED.
JUST ANNOYED...
GLUB GLUB
HELLOOOO?
IS ANYONE THERE...?
GAME'S OVER, RIDDLER. I'VE GOT ANOTHER CALL.
SOMETHING SMELLS FISHY, BATMAN! DON'T--
CLICK
ARTHUR? AQUAMAN?!
YOU COOKED...FISH AGAIN...DIDN'T YOU?
YOU'RE CREEPING ME OUT. SWITCH TO THE WATCHTOWER COMPUTER.
ZZ-Z-ZZ-ISZZ-THIZZ-ZZ-BETTRRR?
THIS PLACE GETS HORRIBLE RECEPTION.
STAND BY.
YOU'RE WET.

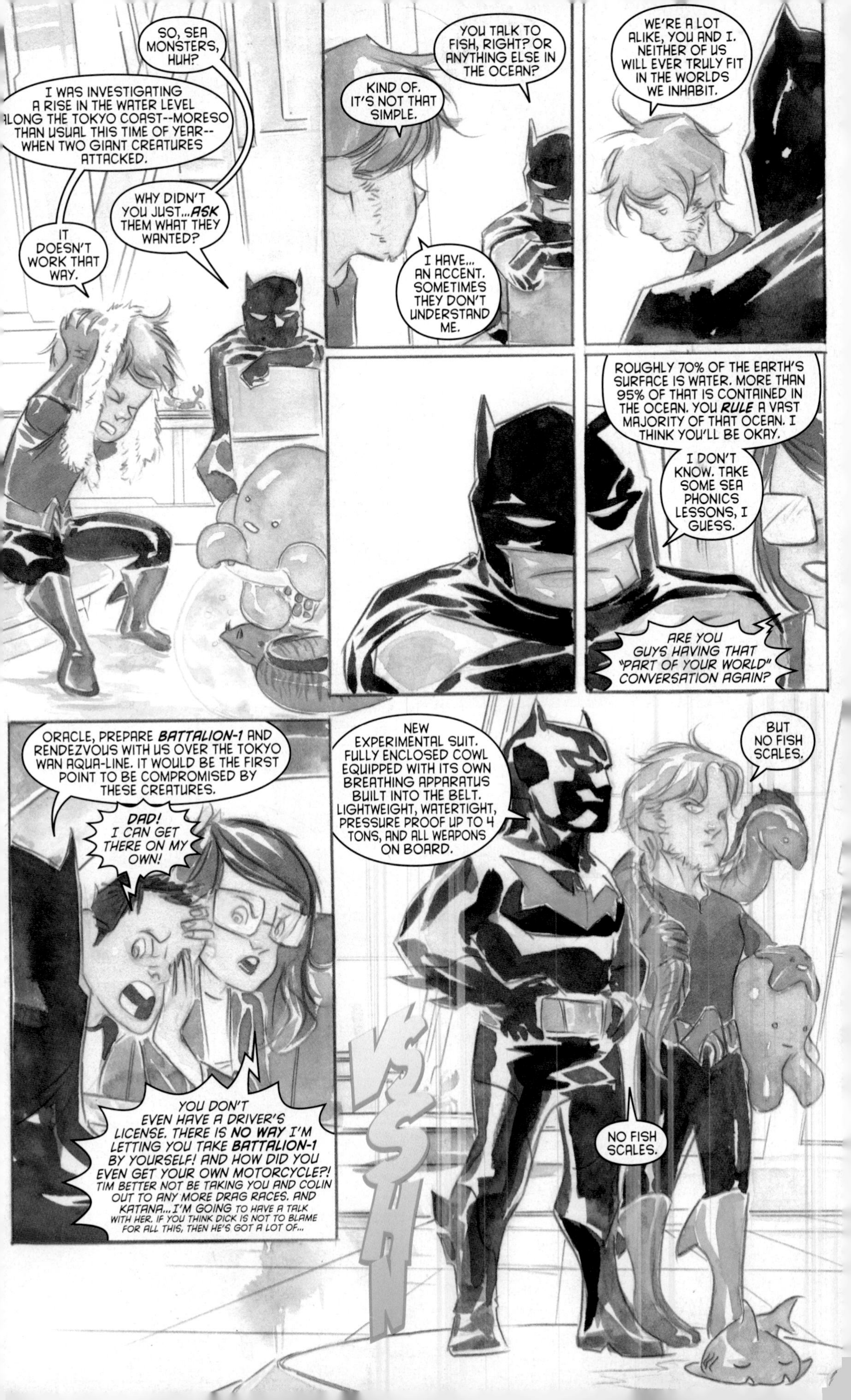

SO, SEA MONSTERS, HUH?
I WAS INVESTIGATING A RISE IN THE WATER LEVEL ALONG THE TOKYO COAST--MORESO THAN USUAL THIS TIME OF YEAR--WHEN TWO GIANT CREATURES ATTACKED.
WHY DIDN'T YOU JUST...ASK THEM WHAT THEY WANTED?
IT DOESN'T WORK THAT WAY.
YOU TALK TO FISH, RIGHT? OR ANYTHING ELSE IN THE OCEAN?
KIND OF. IT'S NOT THAT SIMPLE.
I HAVE... AN ACCENT. SOMETIMES THEY DON'T UNDERSTAND ME.
WE'RE A LOT ALIKE, YOU AND I. NEITHER OF US WILL EVER TRULY FIT IN THE WORLDS WE INHABIT.
ROUGHLY 70% OF THE EARTH'S SURFACE IS WATER. MORE THAN 95% OF THAT IS CONTAINED IN THE OCEAN. YOU RULE A VAST MAJORITY OF THAT OCEAN. I THINK YOU'LL BE OKAY.
I DON'T KNOW. TAKE SOME SEA PHONICS LESSONS, I GUESS.
ARE YOU GUYS HAVING THAT "PART OF YOUR WORLD" CONVERSATION AGAIN?
ORACLE, PREPARE BATTALION-1 AND RENDEZVOUS WITH US OVER THE TOKYO WAN AQUA-LINE. IT WOULD BE THE FIRST POINT TO BE COMPROMISED BY THESE CREATURES.
DAD! I CAN GET THERE ON MY OWN!
YOU DON'T EVEN HAVE A DRIVER'S LICENSE. THERE IS NO WAY I'M LETTING YOU TAKE BATTALION-1 BY YOURSELF! AND HOW DID YOU EVEN GET YOUR OWN MOTORCYCLE?! TIM BETTER NOT BE TAKING YOU AND COLIN OUT TO ANY MORE DRAG RACES. AND KATANA... I'M GOING TO HAVE A TALK WITH HER. IF YOU THINK DICK IS NOT TO BLAME FOR ALL THIS, THEN HE'S GOT A LOT OF...
NEW EXPERIMENTAL SUIT. FULLY ENCLOSED COWL EQUIPPED WITH ITS OWN BREATHING APPARATUS BUILT INTO THE BELT. LIGHTWEIGHT, WATERTIGHT, PRESSURE PROOF UP TO 4 TONS, AND ALL WEAPONS ON BOARD.
BUT NO FISH SCALES.
NO FISH SCALES.
VSSHH

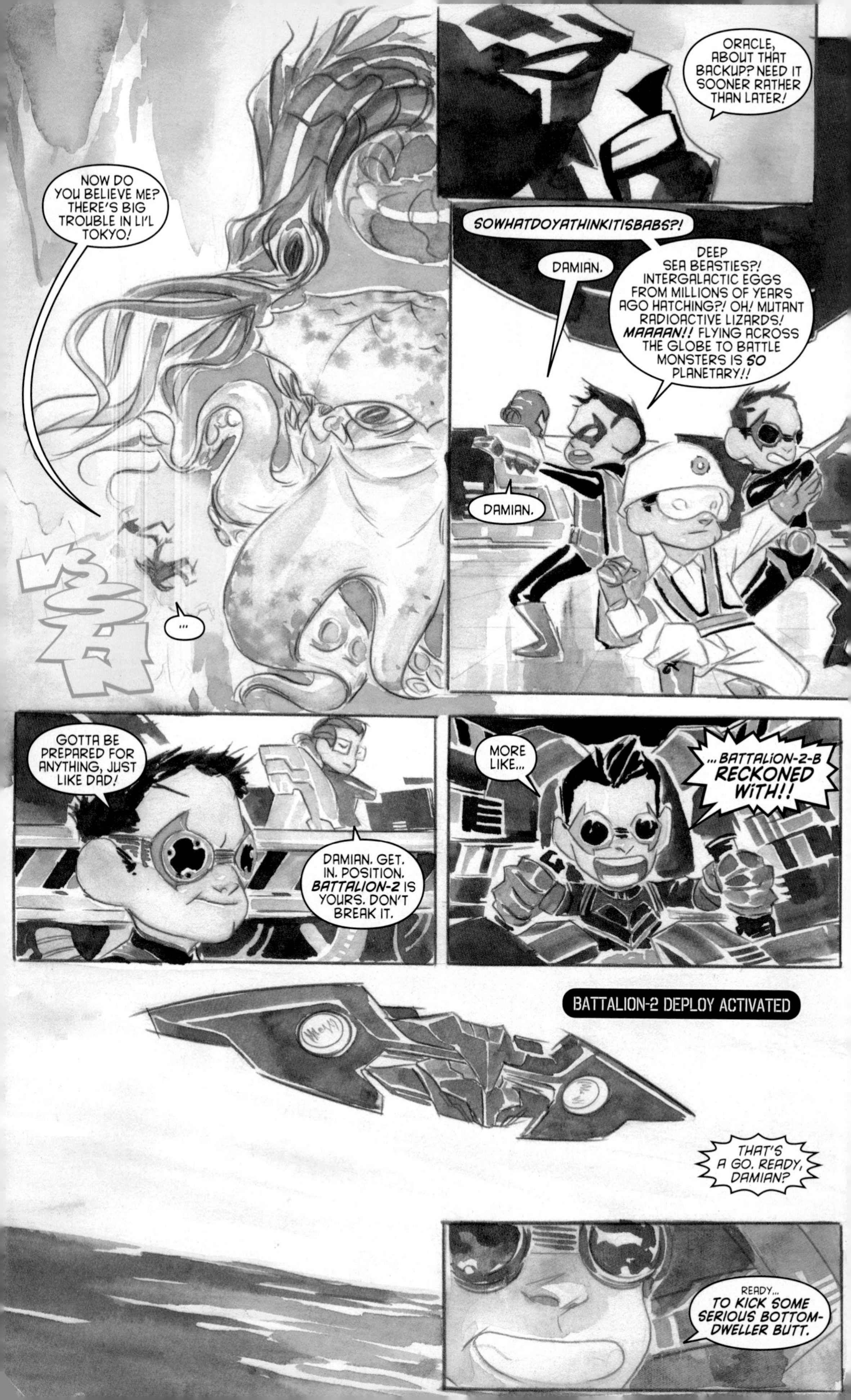
NOW DO YOU BELIEVE ME? THERE'S BIG TROUBLE IN LI'L TOKYO!
VS
...
ORACLE, ABOUT THAT BACKUP? NEED IT SOONER RATHER THAN LATER!
SOWHATDOYATHINKITISBABS?!
DAMIAN.
DEEP SEA BEASTIES?! INTERGALACTIC EGGS FROM MILLIONS OF YEARS AGO HATCHING?! OH! MUTANT RADIOACTIVE LIZARDS! MAAAAN!! FLYING ACROSS THE GLOBE TO BATTLE MONSTERS IS SO PLANETARY!!
DAMIAN.
GOTTA BE PREPARED FOR ANYTHING, JUST LIKE DAD!
DAMIAN. GET. IN. POSITION. BATTALION-2 IS YOURS. DON'T BREAK IT.
MORE LIKE...
...BATTALION-2-B RECKONED WITH!!
BATTALION-2 DEPLOY ACTIVATED
THAT'S A GO. READY, DAMIAN?
READY... TO KICK SOME SERIOUS BOTTOM-DWELLER BUTT.

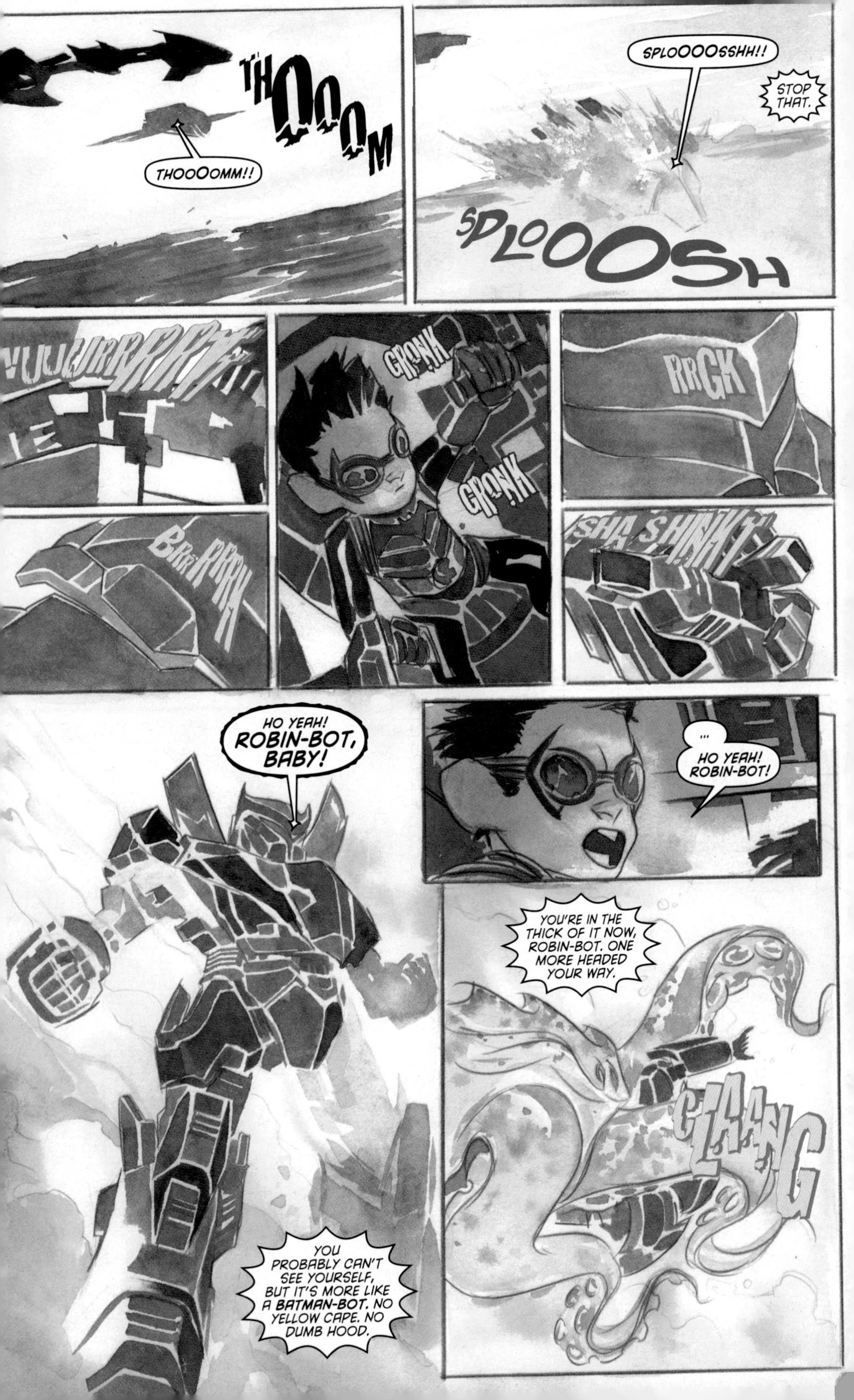
THOOOOM
THOOOOMM!!
SPLOOOOSSHH!!
STOP THAT.
SPLOOOOSH
VUUUURRRRRKK
GRONK
GRONK
RRGK
BRRRRRK
SHA SHINK
HO YEAH! ROBIN-BOT, BABY!
... HO YEAH! ROBIN-BOT!
YOU'RE IN THE THICK OF IT NOW, ROBIN-BOT. ONE MORE HEADED YOUR WAY.
CLAANG
YOU PROBABLY CAN'T SEE YOURSELF, BUT IT'S MORE LIKE A BATMAN-BOT. NO YELLOW CAPE. NO DUMB HOOD.

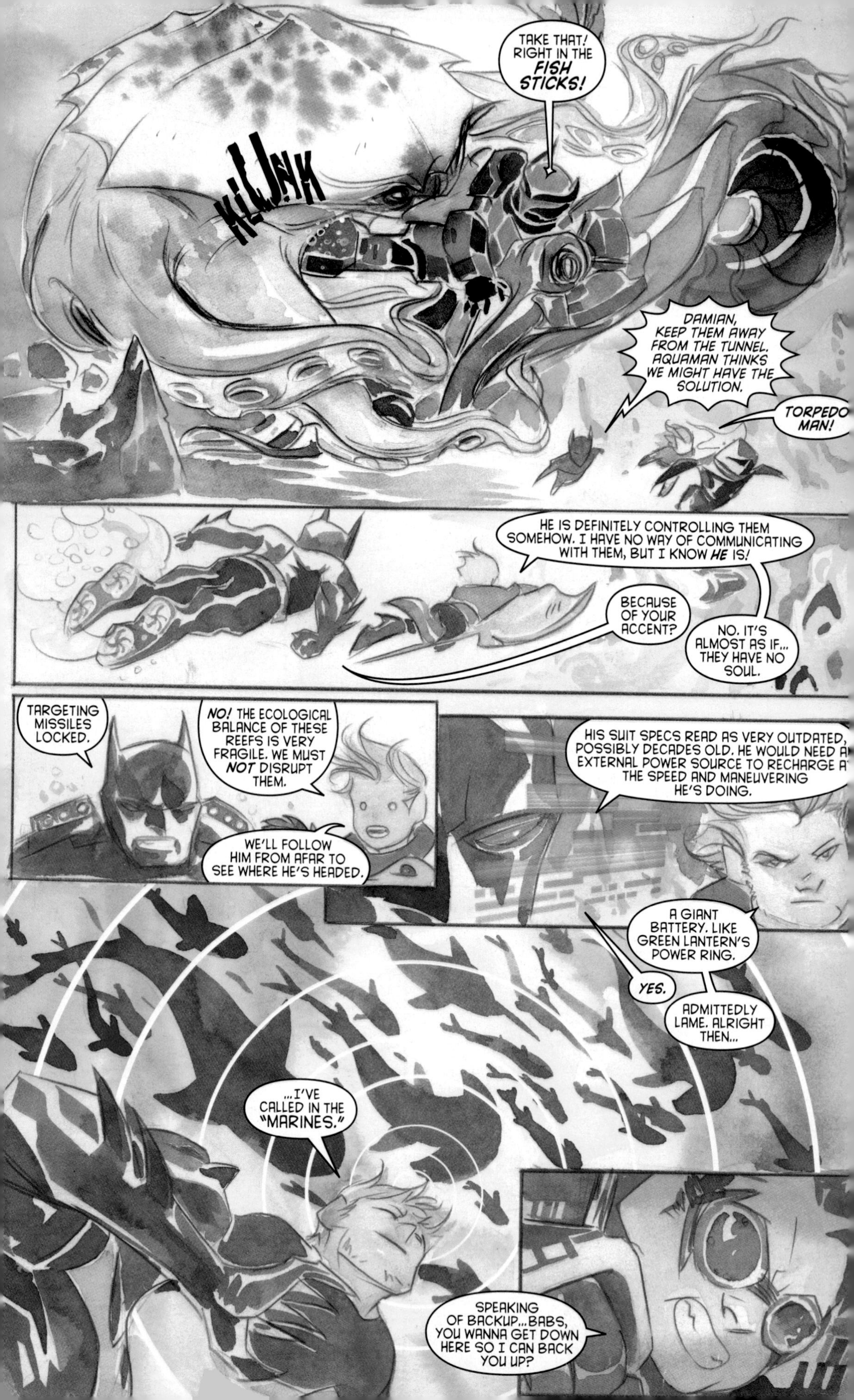
TAKE THAT! RIGHT IN THE FISH STICKS!
KLUNK
DAMIAN, KEEP THEM AWAY FROM THE TUNNEL. AQUAMAN THINKS WE MIGHT HAVE THE SOLUTION.
TORPEDO MAN!
HE IS DEFINITELY CONTROLLING THEM SOMEHOW. I HAVE NO WAY OF COMMUNICATING WITH THEM, BUT I KNOW HE IS!
BECAUSE OF YOUR ACCENT?
NO. IT'S ALMOST AS IF... THEY HAVE NO SOUL.
TARGETING MISSILES LOCKED.
NO! THE ECOLOGICAL BALANCE OF THESE REEFS IS VERY FRAGILE. WE MUST NOT DISRUPT THEM.
WE'LL FOLLOW HIM FROM AFAR TO SEE WHERE HE'S HEADED.
HIS SUIT SPECS READ AS VERY OUTDATED, POSSIBLY DECADES OLD. HE WOULD NEED AN EXTERNAL POWER SOURCE TO RECHARGE AT THE SPEED AND MANEUVERING HE'S DOING.
A GIANT BATTERY. LIKE GREEN LANTERN'S POWER RING.
YES.
ADMITTEDLY LAME. ALRIGHT THEN...
...I'VE CALLED IN THE "MARINES."
SPEAKING OF BACKUP...BABS, YOU WANNA GET DOWN HERE SO I CAN BACK YOU UP?

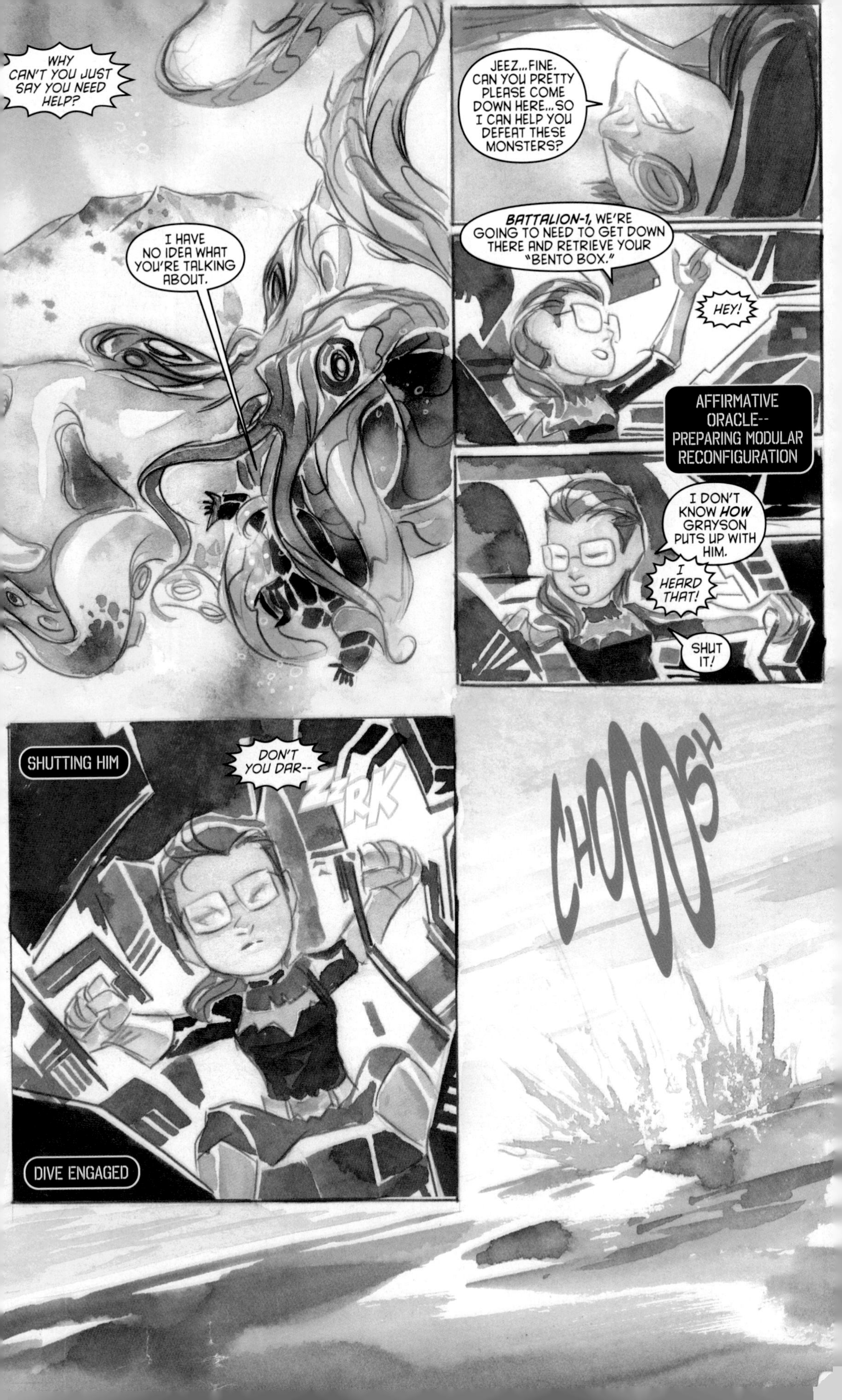
WHY CAN'T YOU JUST SAY YOU NEED HELP?
JEEZ...FINE. CAN YOU PRETTY PLEASE COME DOWN HERE...SO I CAN HELP YOU DEFEAT THESE MONSTERS?
I HAVE NO IDEA WHAT YOU'RE TALKING ABOUT.
BATTALION-1, WE'RE GOING TO NEED TO GET DOWN THERE AND RETRIEVE YOUR "BENTO BOX."
HEY!
AFFIRMATIVE ORACLE-- PREPARING MODULAR RECONFIGURATION
I DON'T KNOW HOW GRAYSON PUTS UP WITH HIM.
I HEARD THAT!
SHUT IT!
SHUTTING HIM
DON'T YOU DAR--
ZZRK
DIVE ENGAGED
CHOOOSH

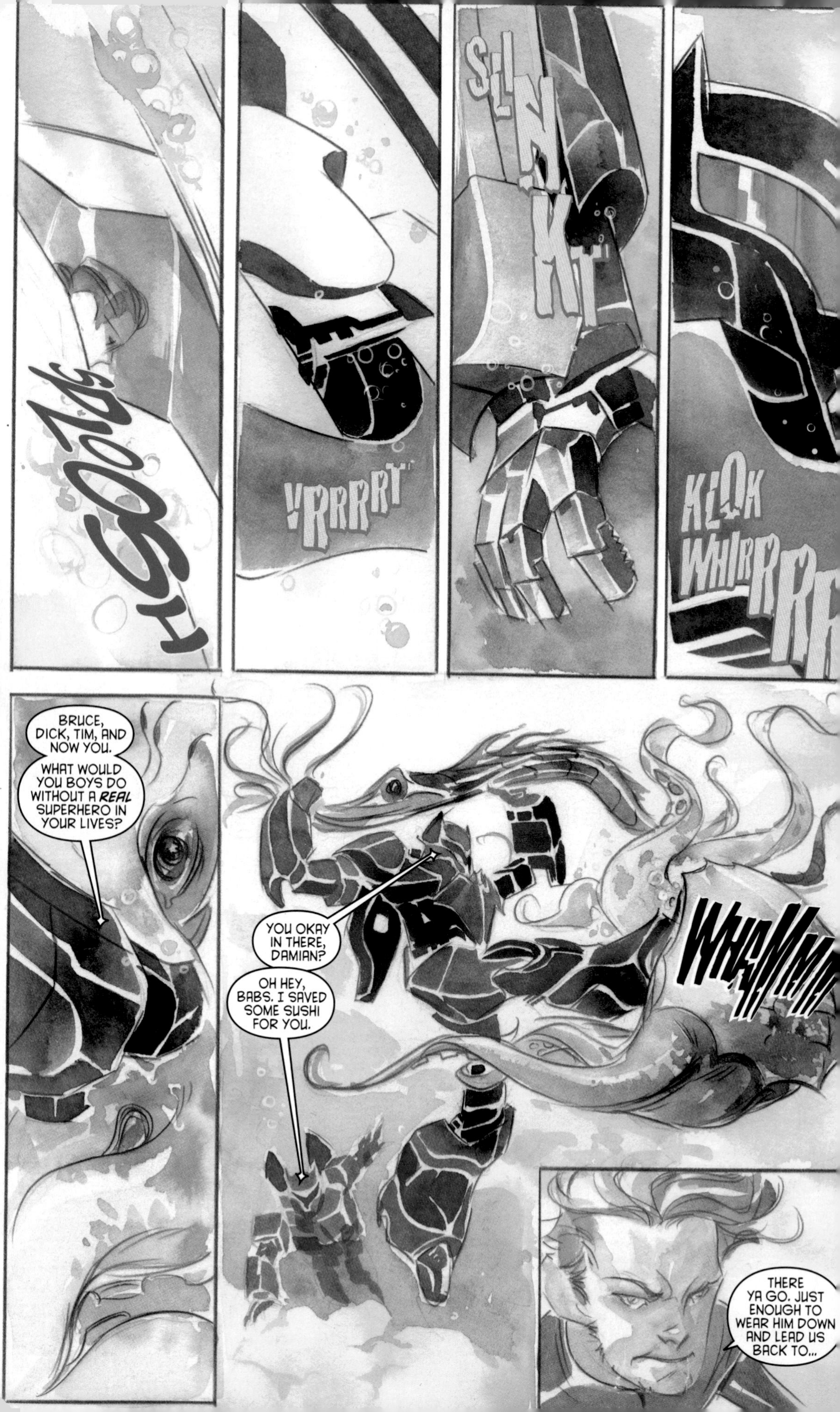
HOOSH
VRRRRT
SLINKT
KLOK WHIRRRR
BRUCE, DICK, TIM, AND NOW YOU.
WHAT WOULD YOU BOYS DO WITHOUT A *REAL* SUPERHERO IN YOUR LIVES?
YOU OKAY IN THERE, DAMIAN?
OH HEY, BABS. I SAVED SOME SUSHI FOR YOU.
THERE YA GO. JUST ENOUGH TO WEAR HIM DOWN AND LEAD US BACK TO...

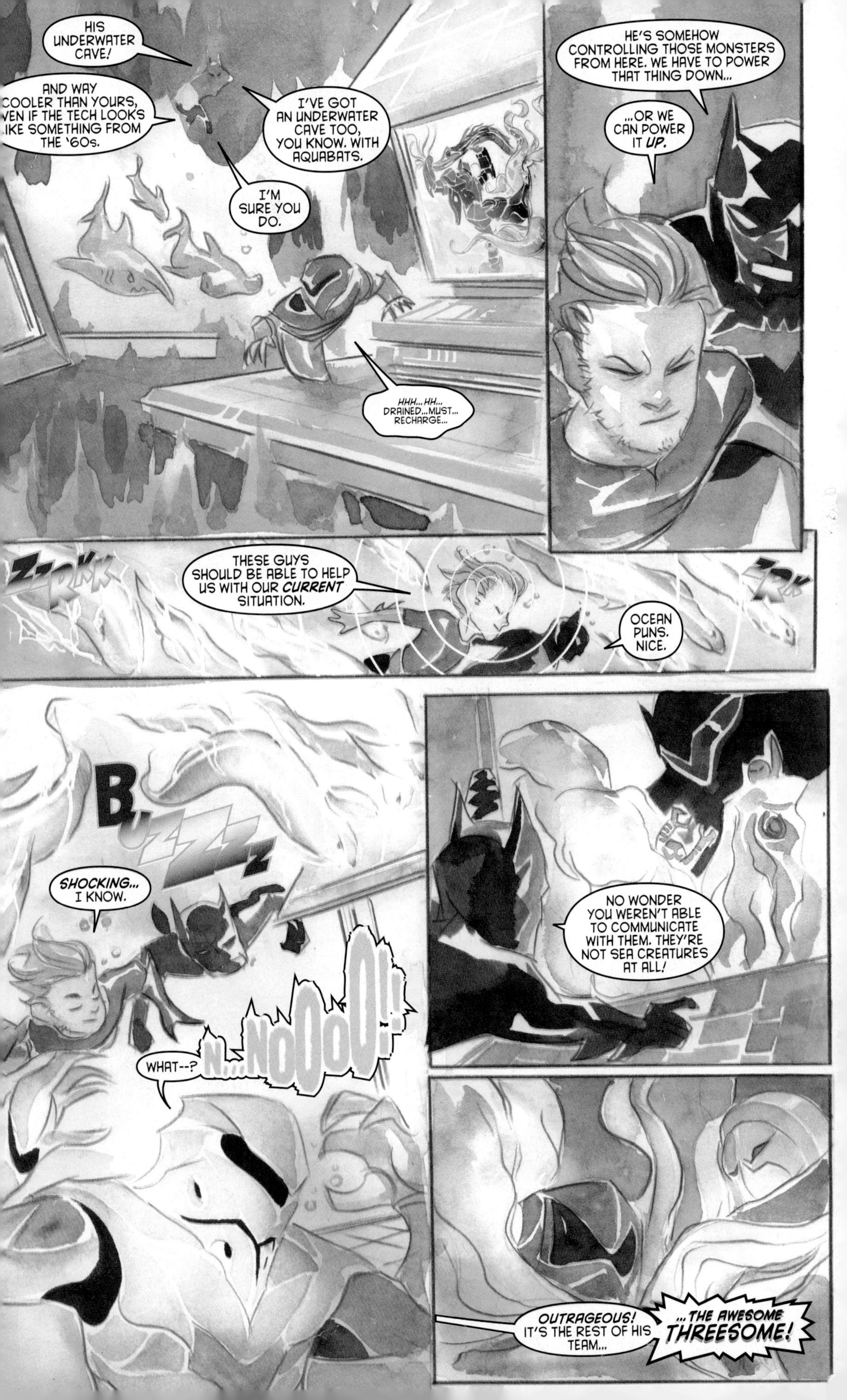
HIS UNDERWATER CAVE!
AND WAY COOLER THAN YOURS, EVEN IF THE TECH LOOKS LIKE SOMETHING FROM THE '60s.
I'VE GOT AN UNDERWATER CAVE TOO, YOU KNOW. WITH AQUABATS.
I'M SURE YOU DO.
HHH...HH... DRAINED...MUST... RECHARGE...
HE'S SOMEHOW CONTROLLING THOSE MONSTERS FROM HERE. WE HAVE TO POWER THAT THING DOWN...
...OR WE CAN POWER IT UP.
ZZZRK
THESE GUYS SHOULD BE ABLE TO HELP US WITH OUR CURRENT SITUATION.
OCEAN PUNS. NICE.
BUZZZZ
SHOCKING... I KNOW.
WHAT--?
N...NOOOO!!
NO WONDER YOU WEREN'T ABLE TO COMMUNICATE WITH THEM. THEY'RE NOT SEA CREATURES AT ALL!
OUTRAGEOUS! IT'S THE REST OF HIS TEAM...
...THE AWESOME THREESOME!

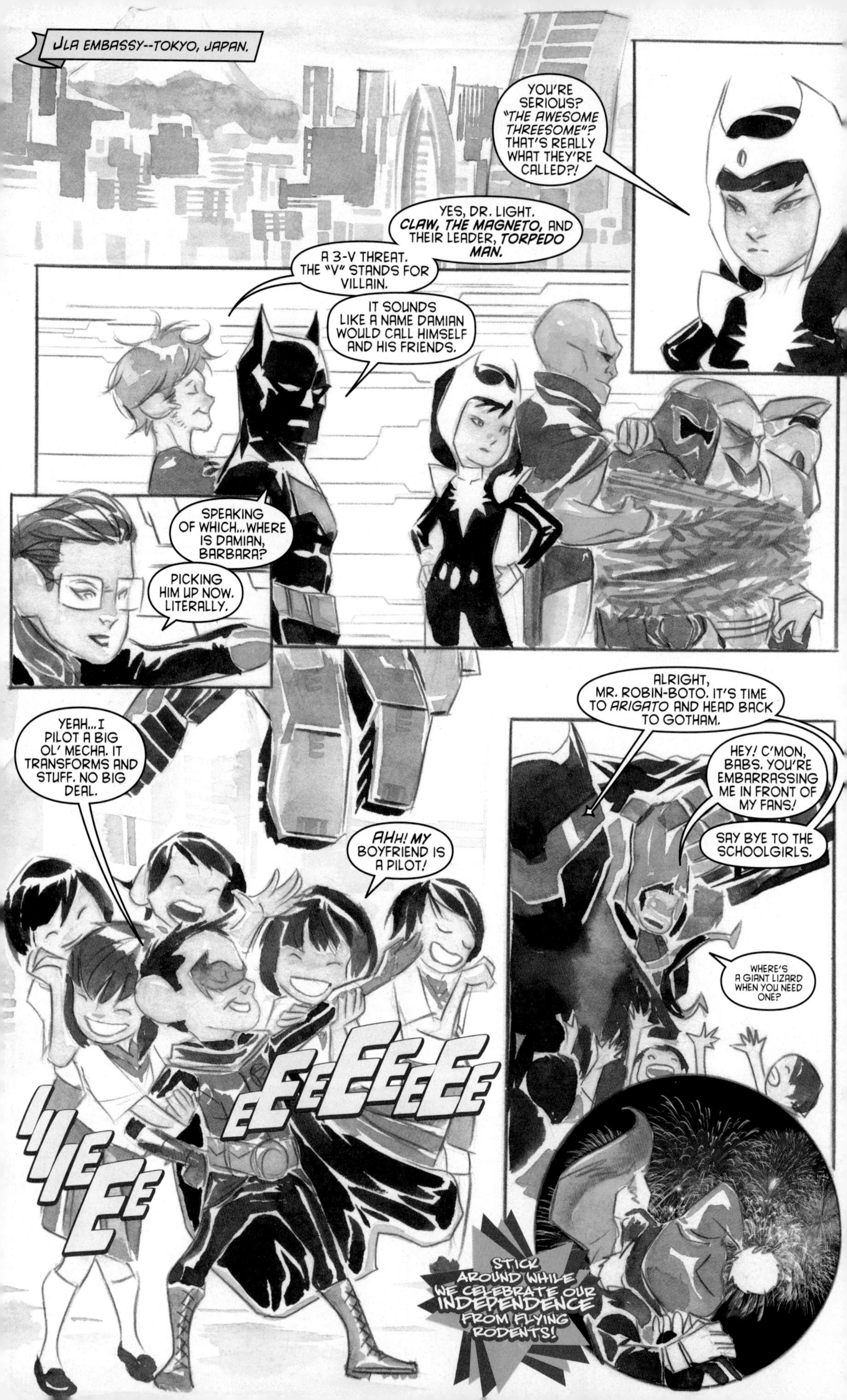
JLA EMBASSY--TOKYO, JAPAN.
YOU'RE SERIOUS? "THE AWESOME THREESOME"? THAT'S REALLY WHAT THEY'RE CALLED?!
YES, DR. LIGHT. CLAW, THE MAGNETO, AND THEIR LEADER, TORPEDO MAN.
A 3-V THREAT. THE "V" STANDS FOR VILLAIN.
IT SOUNDS LIKE A NAME DAMIAN WOULD CALL HIMSELF AND HIS FRIENDS.
SPEAKING OF WHICH... WHERE IS DAMIAN, BARBARA?
PICKING HIM UP NOW. LITERALLY.
YEAH... I PILOT A BIG OL' MECHA. IT TRANSFORMS AND STUFF. NO BIG DEAL.
AHH! MY BOYFRIEND IS A PILOT!
IIIIEEE EEEEEEEEEE
ALRIGHT, MR. ROBIN-BOTO. IT'S TIME TO ARIGATO AND HEAD BACK TO GOTHAM.
HEY! C'MON, BABS. YOU'RE EMBARRASSING ME IN FRONT OF MY FANS!
SAY BYE TO THE SCHOOLGIRLS.
WHERE'S A GIANT LIZARD WHEN YOU NEED ONE?
STICK AROUND WHILE WE CELEBRATE OUR INDEPENDENCE FROM FLYING RODENTS!

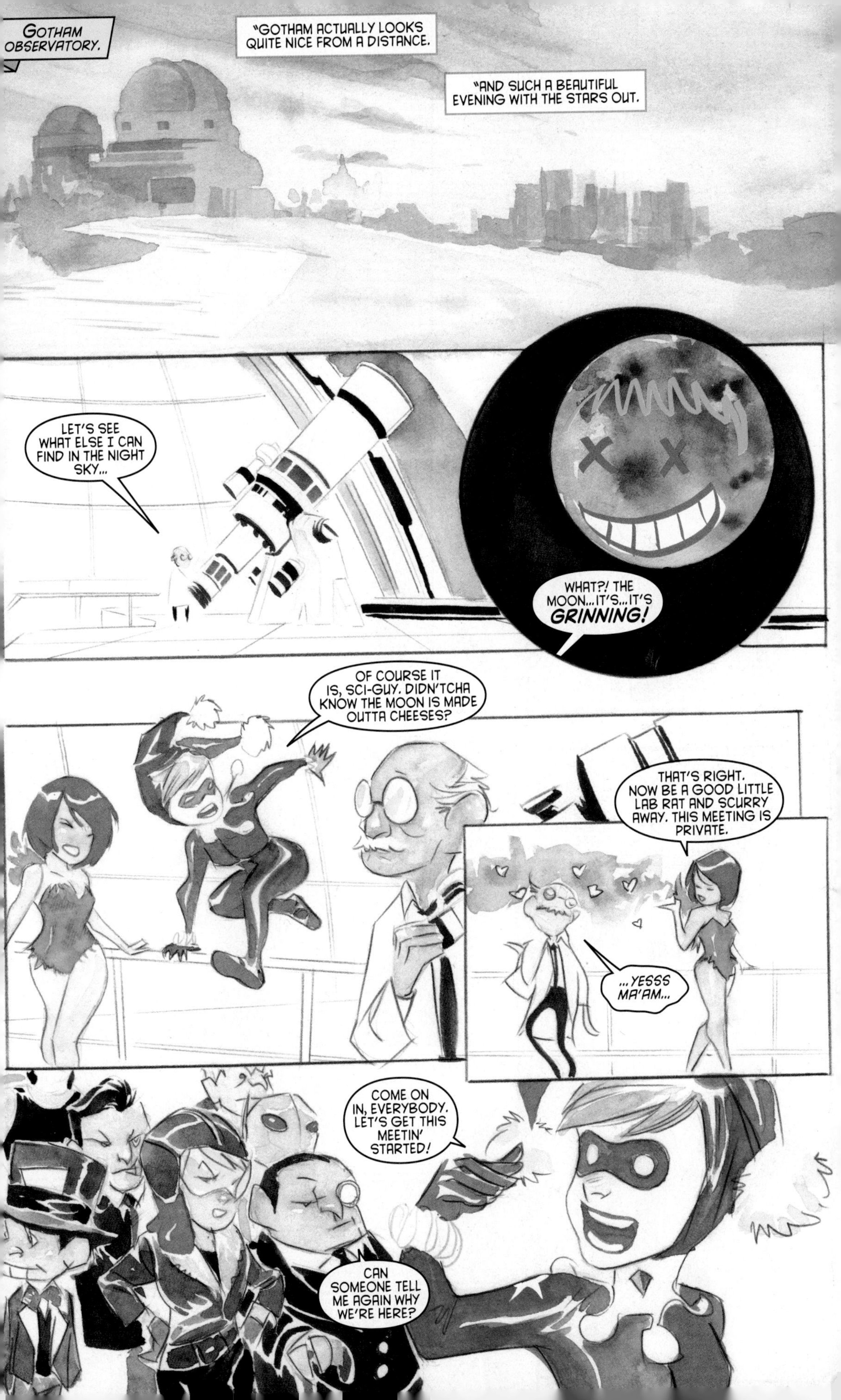

GOTHAM OBSERVATORY.
"GOTHAM ACTUALLY LOOKS QUITE NICE FROM A DISTANCE.
"AND SUCH A BEAUTIFUL EVENING WITH THE STARS OUT.
LET'S SEE WHAT ELSE I CAN FIND IN THE NIGHT SKY...
WHAT?! THE MOON...IT'S...IT'S GRINNING!
OF COURSE IT IS, SCI-GUY. DIDN'TCHA KNOW THE MOON IS MADE OUTTA CHEESES?
THAT'S RIGHT. NOW BE A GOOD LITTLE LAB RAT AND SCURRY AWAY. THIS MEETING IS PRIVATE.
...YESSS MA'AM...
COME ON IN, EVERYBODY. LET'S GET THIS MEETIN' STARTED!
CAN SOMEONE TELL ME AGAIN WHY WE'RE HERE?

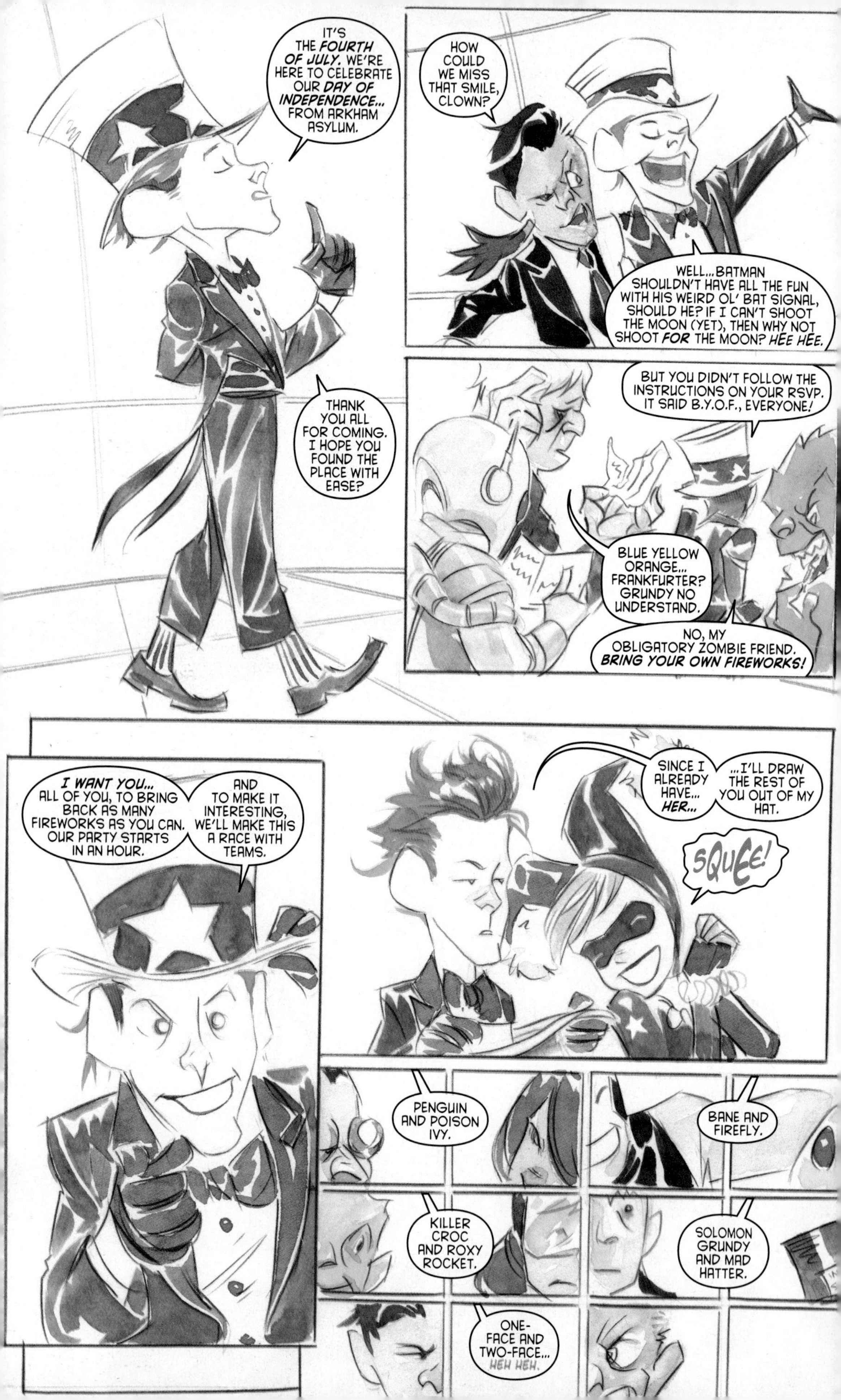
IT'S THE FOURTH OF JULY. WE'RE HERE TO CELEBRATE OUR DAY OF INDEPENDENCE... FROM ARKHAM ASYLUM.
THANK YOU ALL FOR COMING. I HOPE YOU FOUND THE PLACE WITH EASE?
HOW COULD WE MISS THAT SMILE, CLOWN?
WELL...BATMAN SHOULDN'T HAVE ALL THE FUN WITH HIS WEIRD OL' BAT SIGNAL, SHOULD HE? IF I CAN'T SHOOT THE MOON (YET), THEN WHY NOT SHOOT FOR THE MOON? HEE HEE.
BUT YOU DIDN'T FOLLOW THE INSTRUCTIONS ON YOUR RSVP. IT SAID B.Y.O.F., EVERYONE!
BLUE YELLOW ORANGE... FRANKFURTER? GRUNDY NO UNDERSTAND.
NO, MY OBLIGATORY ZOMBIE FRIEND. BRING YOUR OWN FIREWORKS!
I WANT YOU... ALL OF YOU, TO BRING BACK AS MANY FIREWORKS AS YOU CAN. OUR PARTY STARTS IN AN HOUR.
AND TO MAKE IT INTERESTING, WE'LL MAKE THIS A RACE WITH TEAMS.
SINCE I ALREADY HAVE... HER...
...I'LL DRAW THE REST OF YOU OUT OF MY HAT.
SQUEE!
PENGUIN AND POISON IVY.
BANE AND FIREFLY.
KILLER CROC AND ROXY ROCKET.
SOLOMON GRUNDY AND MAD HATTER.
ONE-FACE AND TWO-FACE... HEH HEH.

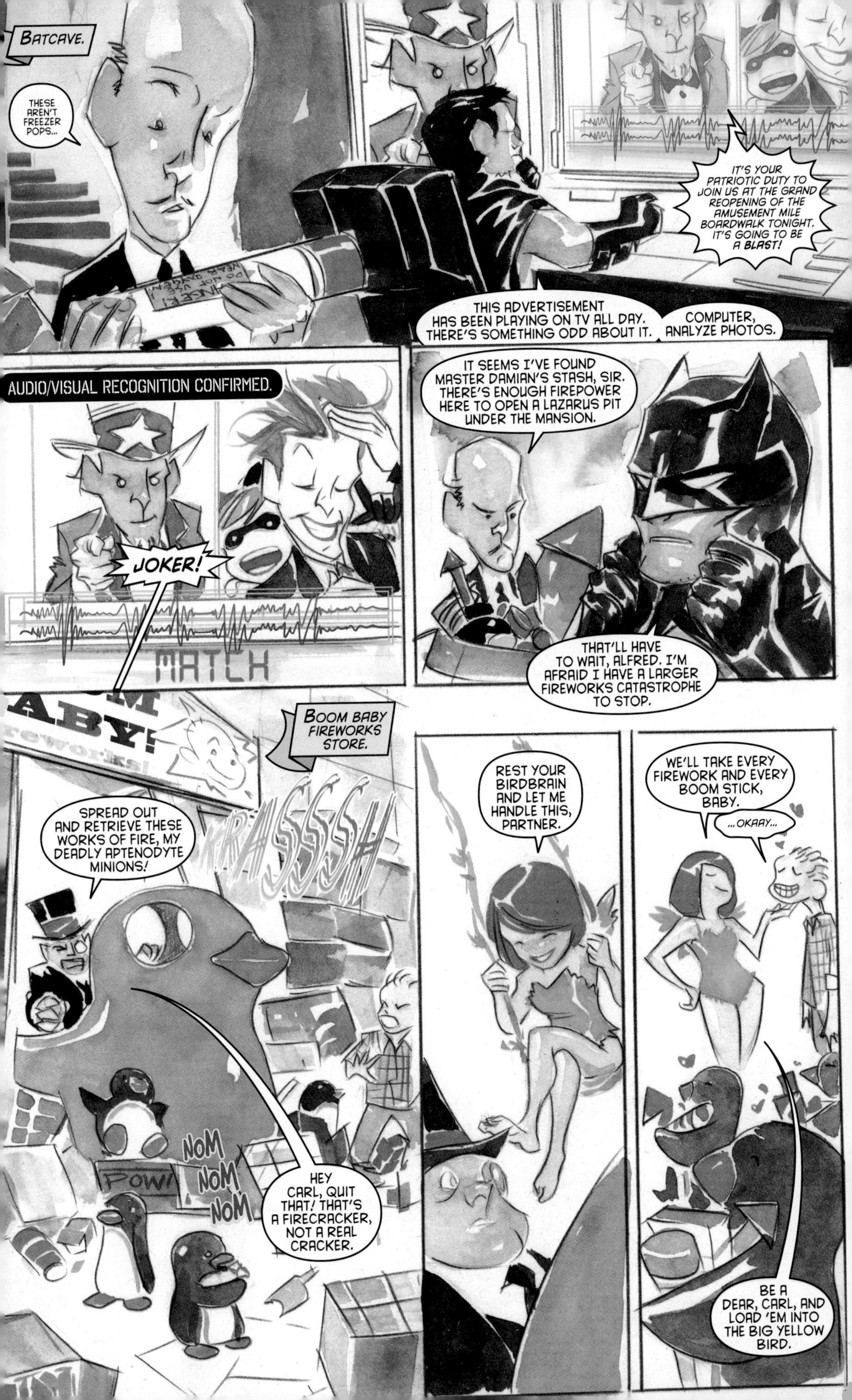
BATCAVE.
THESE AREN'T FREEZER POPS...
IT'S YOUR PATRIOTIC DUTY TO JOIN US AT THE GRAND REOPENING OF THE AMUSEMENT MILE BOARDWALK TONIGHT. IT'S GOING TO BE A BLAST!
THIS ADVERTISEMENT HAS BEEN PLAYING ON TV ALL DAY. THERE'S SOMETHING ODD ABOUT IT.
COMPUTER, ANALYZE PHOTOS.
AUDIO/VISUAL RECOGNITION CONFIRMED.
JOKER!
MATCH
IT SEEMS I'VE FOUND MASTER DAMIAN'S STASH, SIR. THERE'S ENOUGH FIREPOWER HERE TO OPEN A LAZARUS PIT UNDER THE MANSION.
THAT'LL HAVE TO WAIT, ALFRED. I'M AFRAID I HAVE A LARGER FIREWORKS CATASTROPHE TO STOP.
BOOM BABY FIREWORKS STORE.
SPREAD OUT AND RETRIEVE THESE WORKS OF FIRE, MY DEADLY APTENODYTE MINIONS!
KRASSSSH
NOM NOM NOM
POW
HEY CARL, QUIT THAT! THAT'S A FIRECRACKER, NOT A REAL CRACKER.
REST YOUR BIRDBRAIN AND LET ME HANDLE THIS, PARTNER.
WE'LL TAKE EVERY FIREWORK AND EVERY BOOM STICK, BABY.
...OKAAY...
BE A DEAR, CARL, AND LOAD 'EM INTO THE BIG YELLOW BIRD.

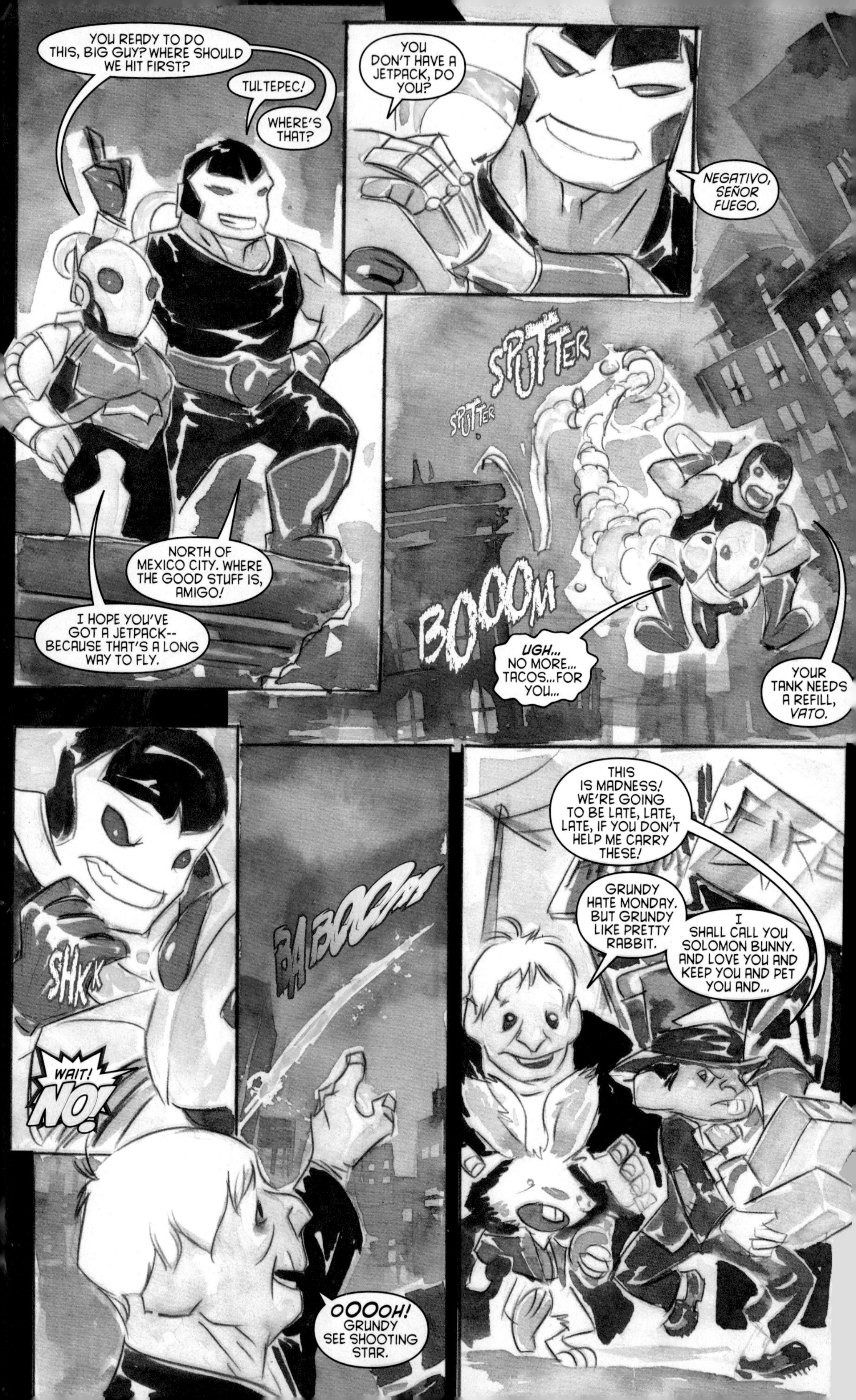
YOU READY TO DO THIS, BIG GUY? WHERE SHOULD WE HIT FIRST?
TULTEPEC!
WHERE'S THAT?
NORTH OF MEXICO CITY. WHERE THE GOOD STUFF IS, AMIGO!
I HOPE YOU'VE GOT A JETPACK-- BECAUSE THAT'S A LONG WAY TO FLY.
YOU DON'T HAVE A JETPACK, DO YOU?
NEGATIVO, SEÑOR FUEGO.
SPUTTER
SPUTTER
BOOOM
UGH... NO MORE... TACOS...FOR YOU...
YOUR TANK NEEDS A REFILL, VATO.
SHKK
WAIT! NO!
BABOOM
OOOOH! GRUNDY SEE SHOOTING STAR.
THIS IS MADNESS! WE'RE GOING TO BE LATE, LATE, LATE, IF YOU DON'T HELP ME CARRY THESE!
GRUNDY HATE MONDAY. BUT GRUNDY LIKE PRETTY RABBIT.
I SHALL CALL YOU SOLOMON BUNNY. AND LOVE YOU AND KEEP YOU AND PET YOU AND...
FIRE

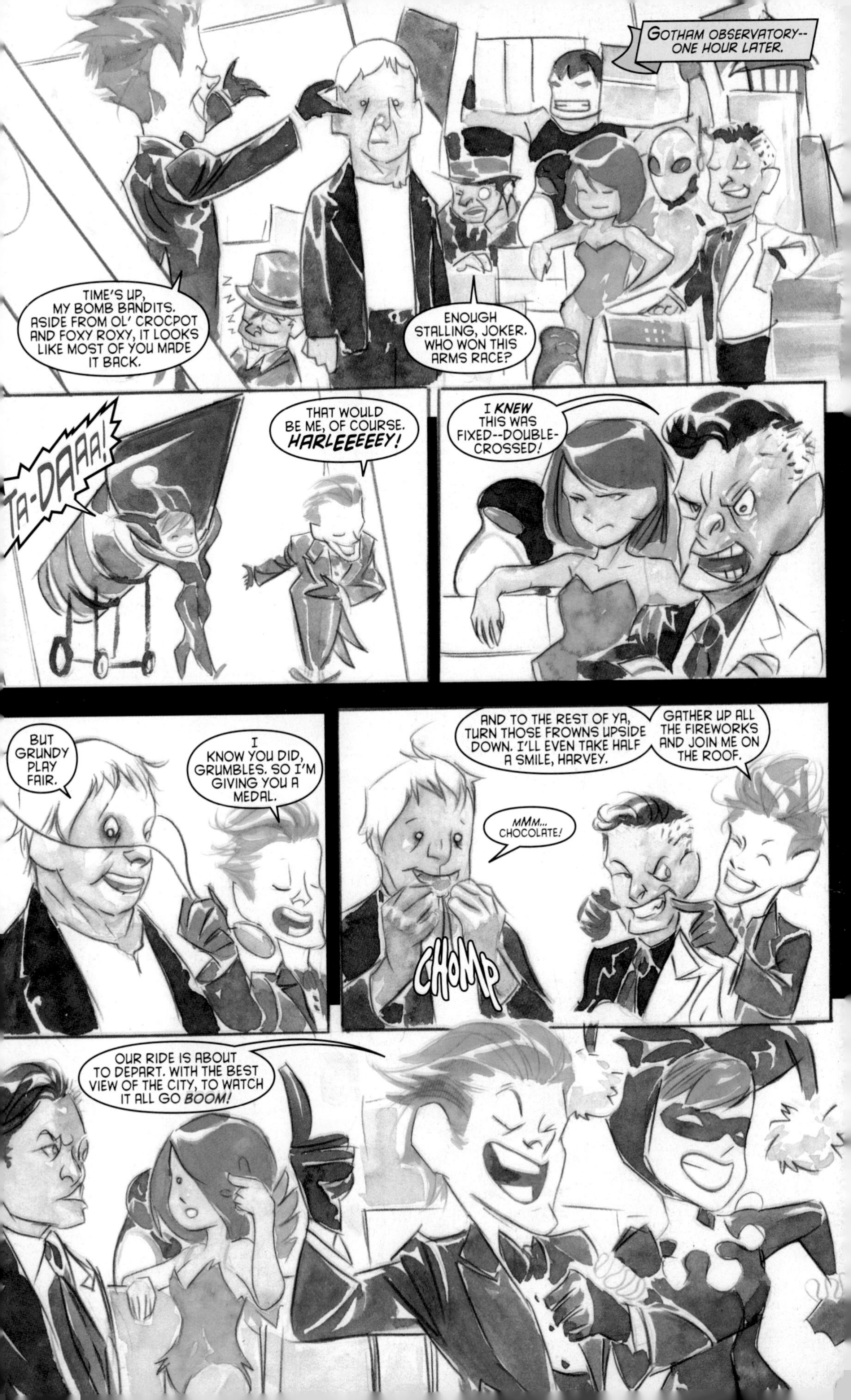

GOTHAM OBSERVATORY--ONE HOUR LATER.
TIME'S UP, MY BOMB BANDITS. ASIDE FROM OL' CROCPOT AND FOXY ROXY, IT LOOKS LIKE MOST OF YOU MADE IT BACK.
ENOUGH STALLING, JOKER. WHO WON THIS ARMS RACE?
TA-DAAA!
THAT WOULD BE ME, OF COURSE. HARLEEEEEY!
I KNEW THIS WAS FIXED--DOUBLE-CROSSED!
BUT GRUNDY PLAY FAIR.
I KNOW YOU DID, GRUMBLES. SO I'M GIVING YOU A MEDAL.
AND TO THE REST OF YA, TURN THOSE FROWNS UPSIDE DOWN. I'LL EVEN TAKE HALF A SMILE, HARVEY.
GATHER UP ALL THE FIREWORKS AND JOIN ME ON THE ROOF.
MMM... CHOCOLATE!
CHOMP
OUR RIDE IS ABOUT TO DEPART. WITH THE BEST VIEW OF THE CITY, TO WATCH IT ALL GO BOOM!

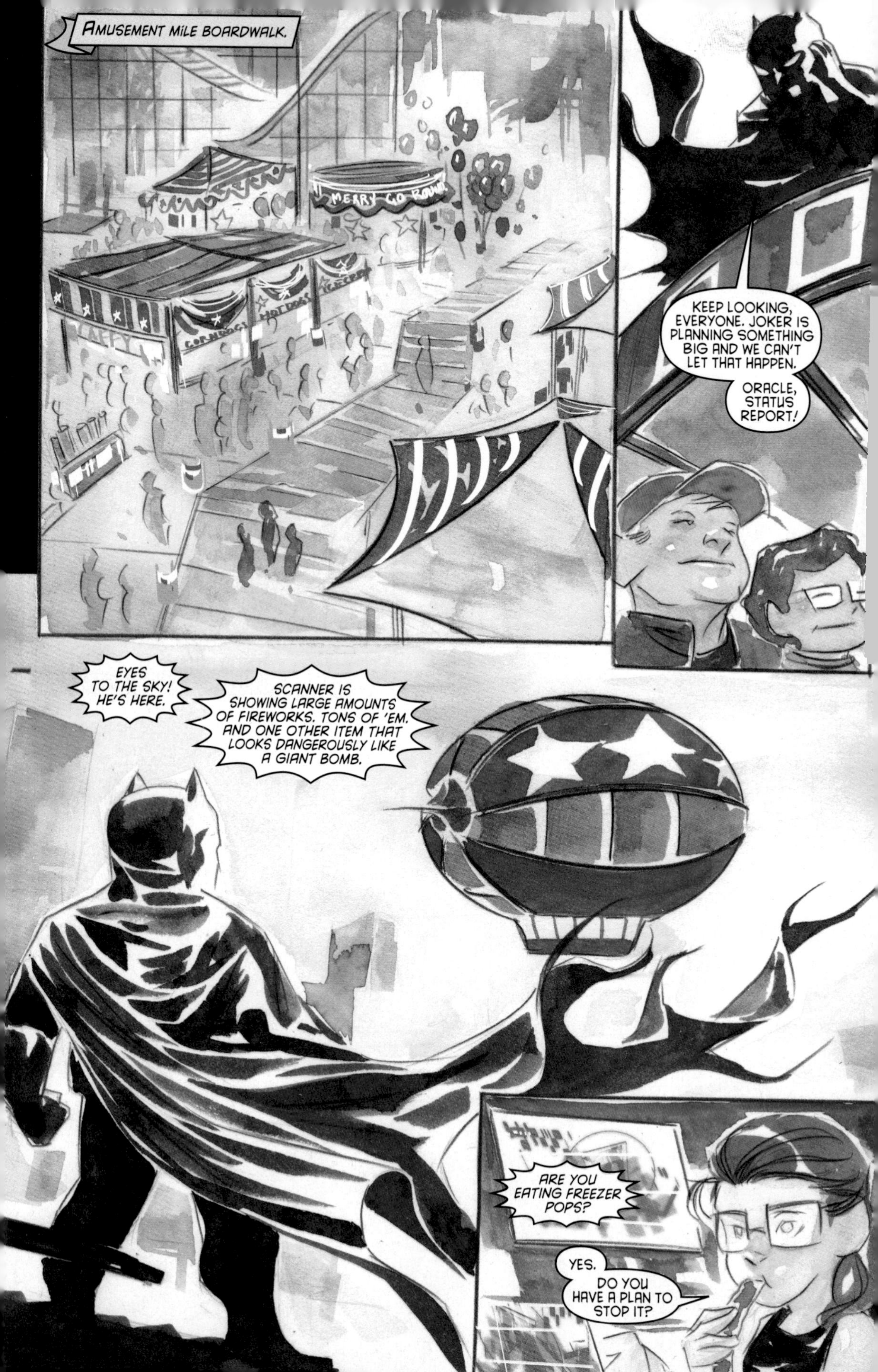
AMUSEMENT MILE BOARDWALK.
MERRY GO ROUND
CORNDOGS
HOT DOGS
KEEP LOOKING, EVERYONE. JOKER IS PLANNING SOMETHING BIG AND WE CAN'T LET THAT HAPPEN.
ORACLE, STATUS REPORT!
EYES TO THE SKY! HE'S HERE.
SCANNER IS SHOWING LARGE AMOUNTS OF FIREWORKS. TONS OF 'EM. AND ONE OTHER ITEM THAT LOOKS DANGEROUSLY LIKE A GIANT BOMB.
ARE YOU EATING FREEZER POPS?
YES.
DO YOU HAVE A PLAN TO STOP IT?

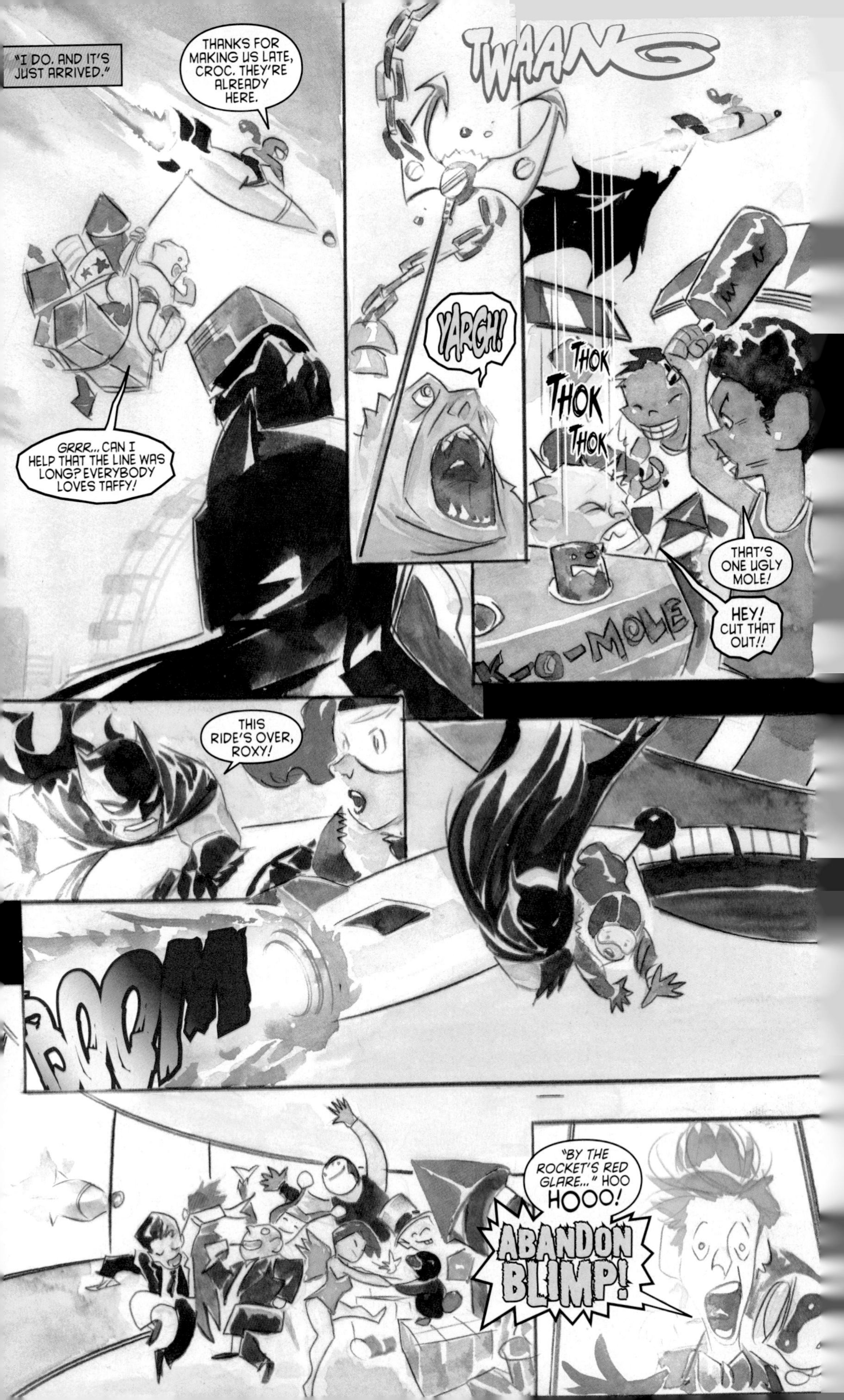

"I DO. AND IT'S JUST ARRIVED."
THANKS FOR MAKING US LATE, CROC. THEY'RE ALREADY HERE.
GRRR... CAN I HELP THAT THE LINE WAS LONG? EVERYBODY LOVES TAFFY!
TWAANG
YARGH!
THOK
THOK
THOK
THAT'S ONE UGLY MOLE!
HEY! CUT THAT OUT!!
K-O-MOLE
THIS RIDE'S OVER, ROXY!
BOOM
"BY THE ROCKET'S RED GLARE..." HOO HOOO!
ABANDON BLIMP!

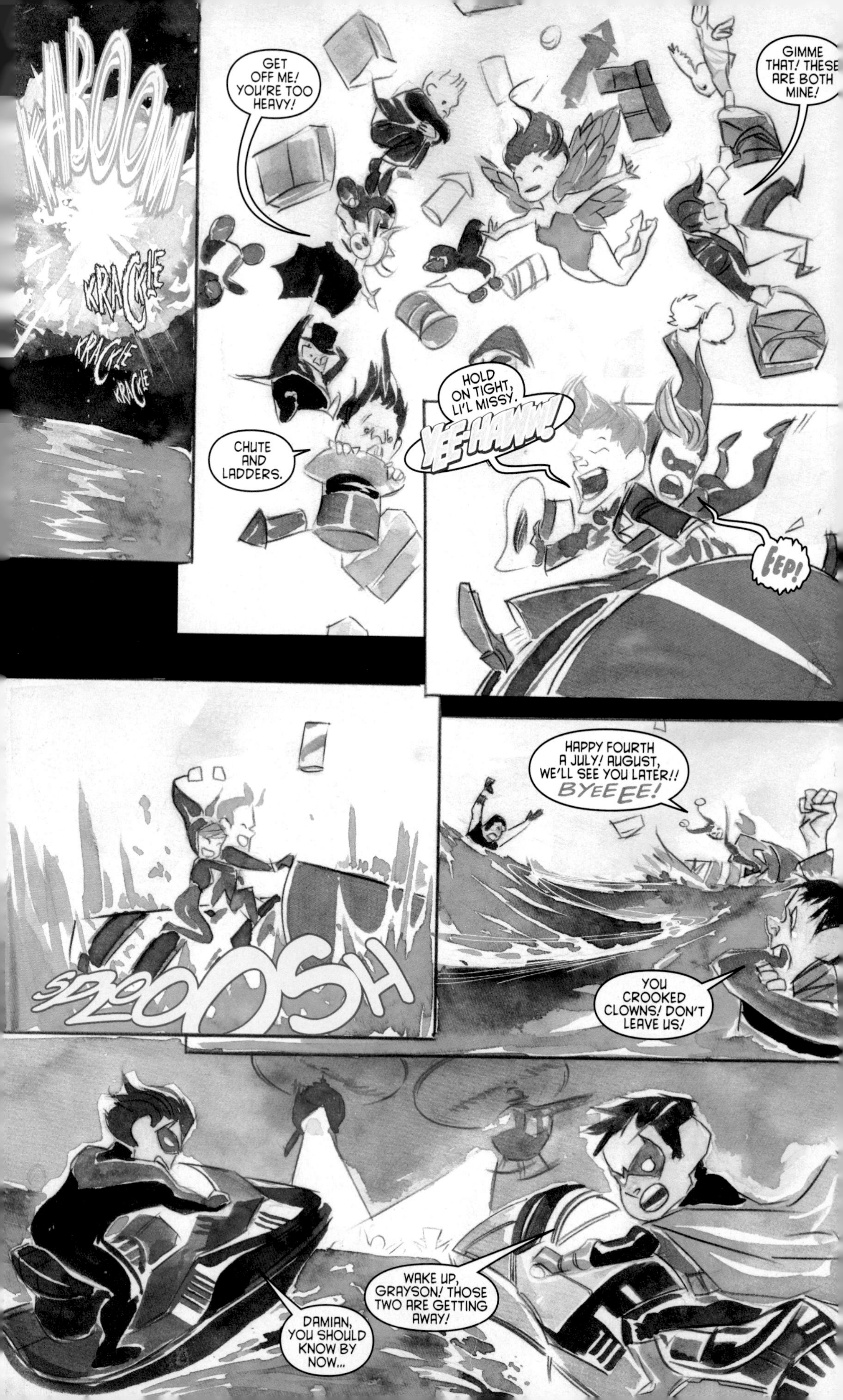

KABOOM
KRACKLE
KRACKLE
KRACKLE
GET OFF ME! YOU'RE TOO HEAVY!
GIMME THAT! THESE ARE BOTH MINE!
CHUTE AND LADDERS.
HOLD ON TIGHT, LI'L MISSY.
YEE-HAWW!
EEP!
SPLOOOSH
HAPPY FOURTH A JULY! AUGUST, WE'LL SEE YOU LATER!! BYEEEE!
YOU CROOKED CLOWNS! DON'T LEAVE US!
WAKE UP, GRAYSON! THOSE TWO ARE GETTING AWAY!
DAMIAN, YOU SHOULD KNOW BY NOW...

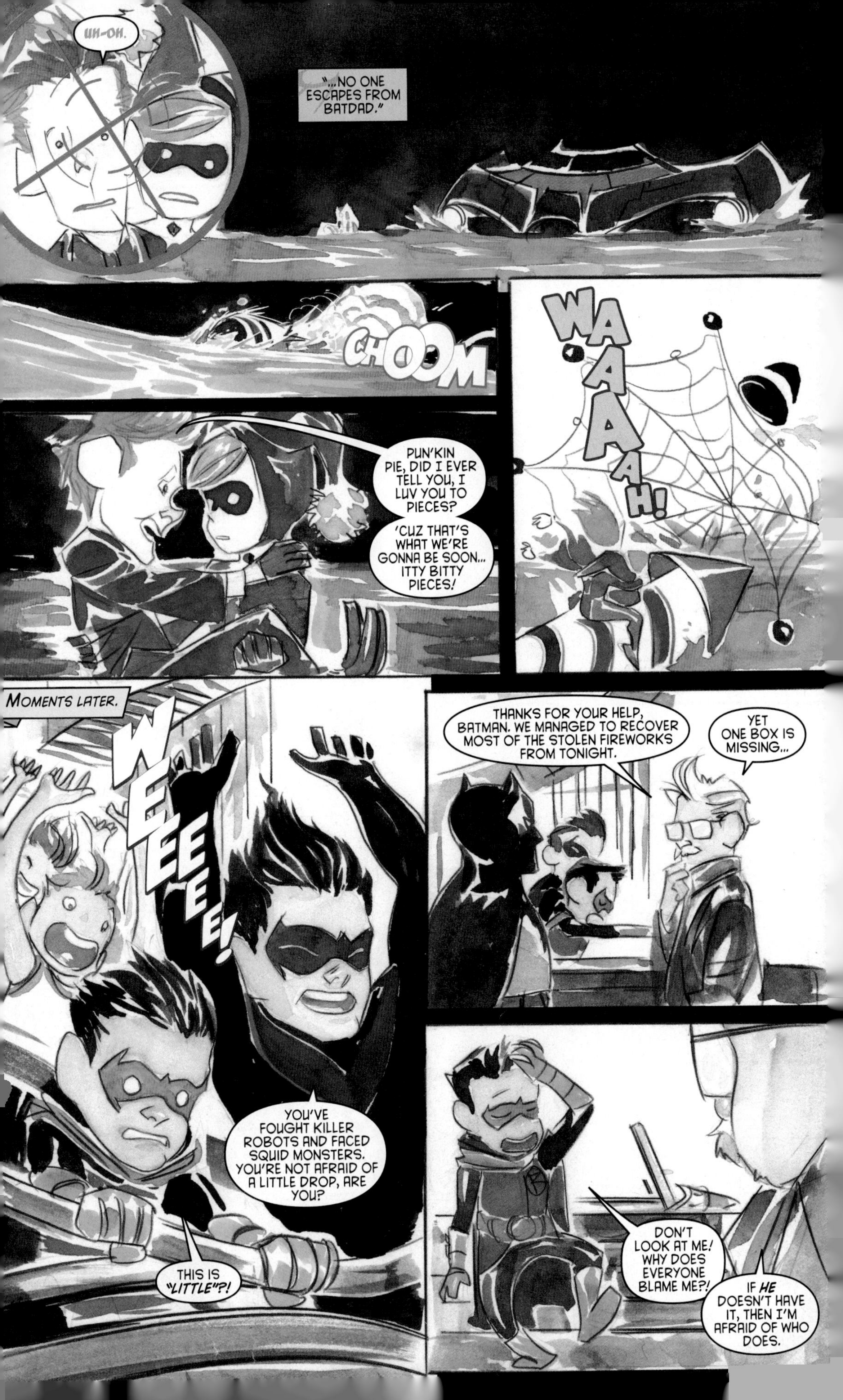
UH-OH.
"...NO ONE ESCAPES FROM BATDAD."
CHOOM
WAAAAH!
PUN'KIN PIE, DID I EVER TELL YOU, I LUV YOU TO PIECES?
'CUZ THAT'S WHAT WE'RE GONNA BE SOON... ITTY BITTY PIECES!
MOMENTS LATER.
WEEEEE!
YOU'VE FOUGHT KILLER ROBOTS AND FACED SQUID MONSTERS. YOU'RE NOT AFRAID OF A LITTLE DROP, ARE YOU?
THIS IS "LITTLE"?!
THANKS FOR YOUR HELP, BATMAN. WE MANAGED TO RECOVER MOST OF THE STOLEN FIREWORKS FROM TONIGHT.
YET ONE BOX IS MISSING...
DON'T LOOK AT ME! WHY DOES EVERYONE BLAME ME?!
IF HE DOESN'T HAVE IT, THEN I'M AFRAID OF WHO DOES.

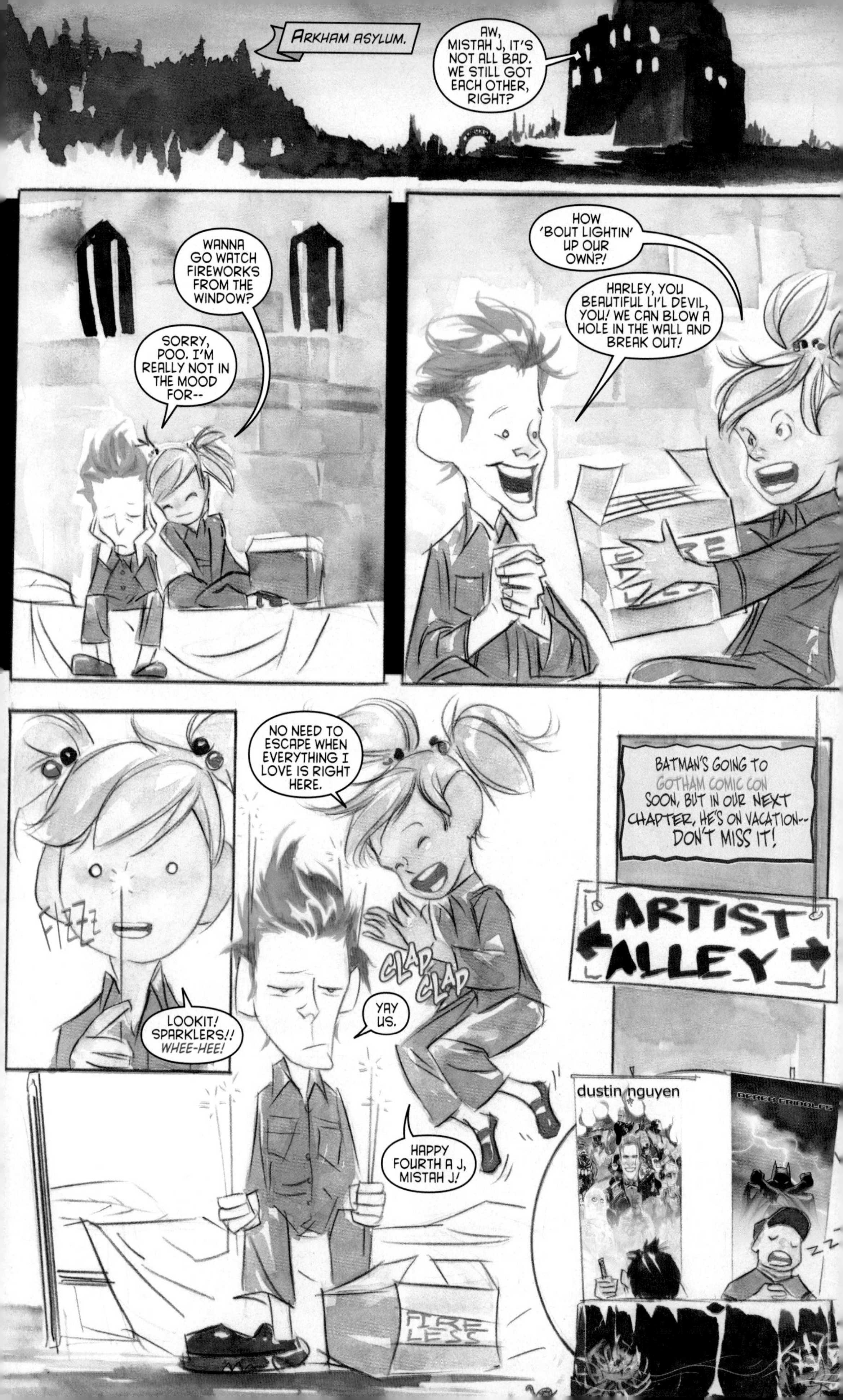
ARKHAM ASYLUM.
AW, MISTAH J, IT'S NOT ALL BAD. WE STILL GOT EACH OTHER, RIGHT?
WANNA GO WATCH FIREWORKS FROM THE WINDOW?
SORRY, POO. I'M REALLY NOT IN THE MOOD FOR--
HOW 'BOUT LIGHTIN' UP OUR OWN?!
HARLEY, YOU BEAUTIFUL LI'L DEVIL, YOU! WE CAN BLOW A HOLE IN THE WALL AND BREAK OUT!
FIZZZ
LOOKIT! SPARKLERS!! WHEE-HEE!
NO NEED TO ESCAPE WHEN EVERYTHING I LOVE IS RIGHT HERE.
CLAP CLAP
YAY US.
HAPPY FOURTH A J, MISTAH J!
FIRE LESS
BATMAN'S GOING TO GOTHAM COMIC CON SOON, BUT IN OUR NEXT CHAPTER, HE'S ON VACATION-- DON'T MISS IT!
ARTIST ALLEY
dustin nguyen
DEREK FRIDOLFS
Z Z

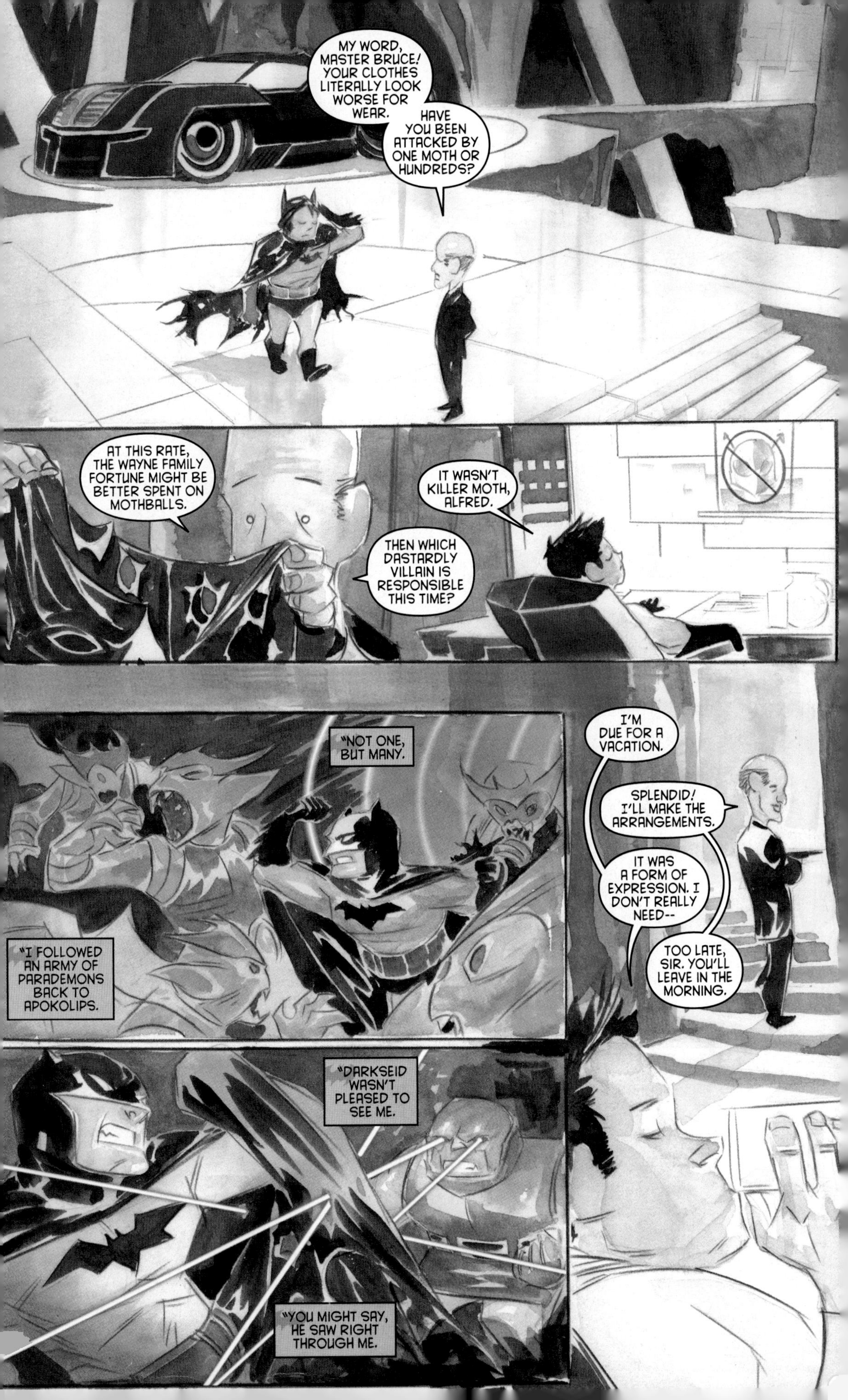
MY WORD, MASTER BRUCE! YOUR CLOTHES LITERALLY LOOK WORSE FOR WEAR.
HAVE YOU BEEN ATTACKED BY ONE MOTH OR HUNDREDS?
AT THIS RATE, THE WAYNE FAMILY FORTUNE MIGHT BE BETTER SPENT ON MOTHBALLS.
IT WASN'T KILLER MOTH, ALFRED.
THEN WHICH DASTARDLY VILLAIN IS RESPONSIBLE THIS TIME?
"NOT ONE, BUT MANY.
"I FOLLOWED AN ARMY OF PARADEMONS BACK TO APOKOLIPS.
"DARKSEID WASN'T PLEASED TO SEE ME.
"YOU MIGHT SAY, HE SAW RIGHT THROUGH ME.
I'M DUE FOR A VACATION.
SPLENDID! I'LL MAKE THE ARRANGEMENTS.
IT WAS A FORM OF EXPRESSION. I DON'T REALLY NEED--
TOO LATE, SIR. YOU'LL LEAVE IN THE MORNING.

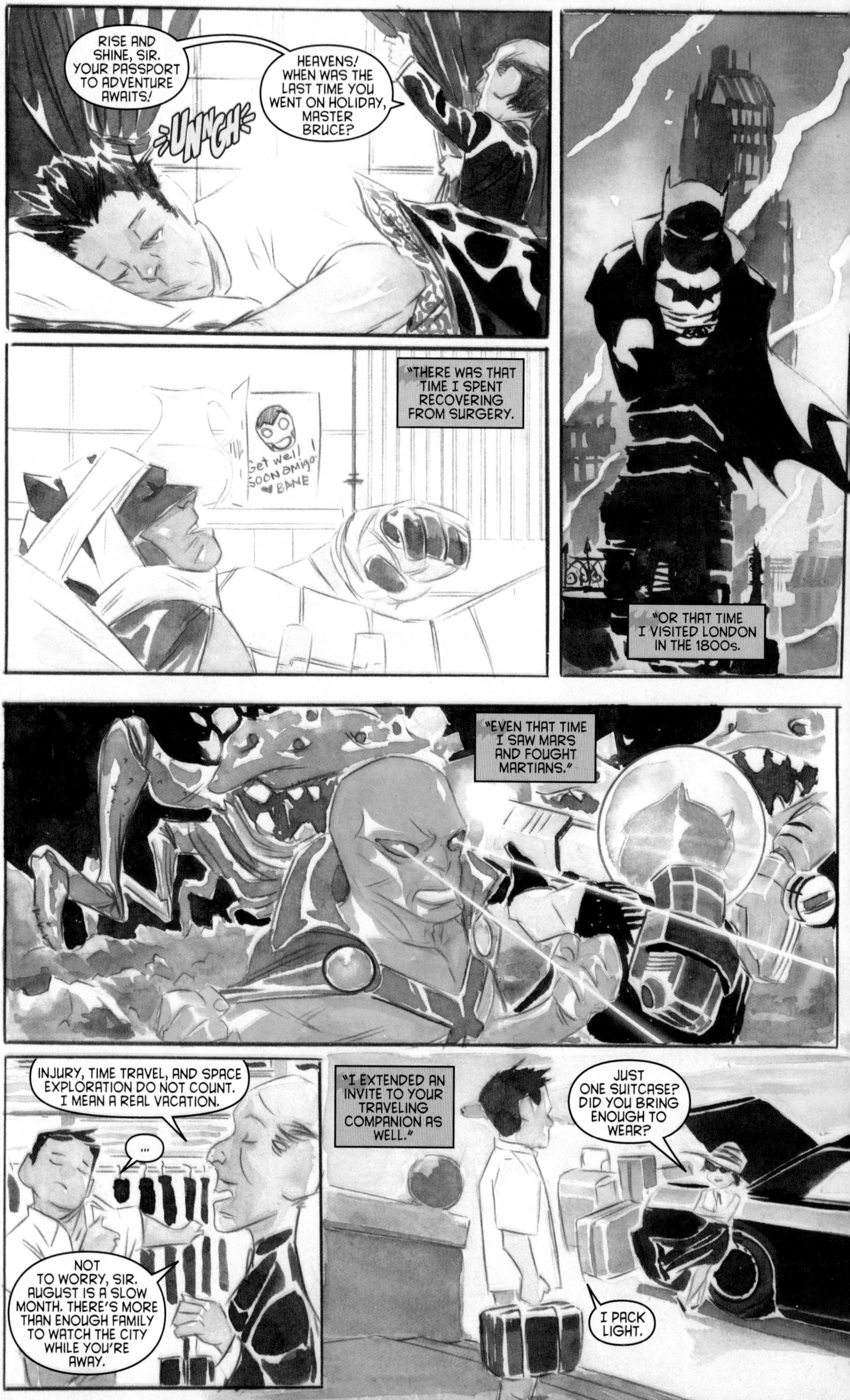
RISE AND SHINE, SIR. YOUR PASSPORT TO ADVENTURE AWAITS!
UNNGH
HEAVENS! WHEN WAS THE LAST TIME YOU WENT ON HOLIDAY, MASTER BRUCE?
"THERE WAS THAT TIME I SPENT RECOVERING FROM SURGERY.
Get well soon amigo BANE
"OR THAT TIME I VISITED LONDON IN THE 1800s.
"EVEN THAT TIME I SAW MARS AND FOUGHT MARTIANS."
INJURY, TIME TRAVEL, AND SPACE EXPLORATION DO NOT COUNT. I MEAN A REAL VACATION.
...
NOT TO WORRY, SIR. AUGUST IS A SLOW MONTH. THERE'S MORE THAN ENOUGH FAMILY TO WATCH THE CITY WHILE YOU'RE AWAY.
"I EXTENDED AN INVITE TO YOUR TRAVELING COMPANION AS WELL."
JUST ONE SUITCASE? DID YOU BRING ENOUGH TO WEAR?
I PACK LIGHT.

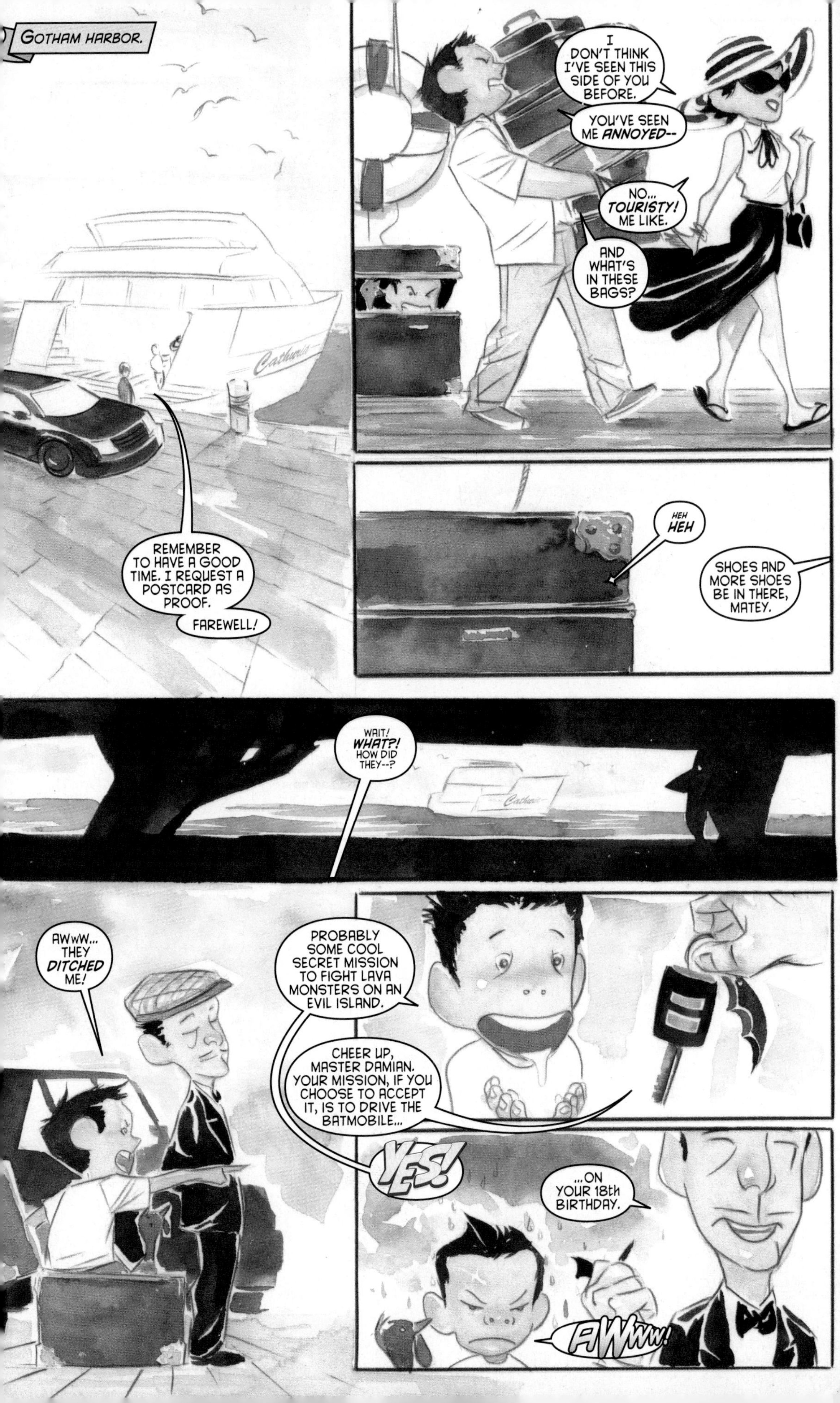
GOTHAM HARBOR.
I DON'T THINK I'VE SEEN THIS SIDE OF YOU BEFORE.
YOU'VE SEEN ME ANNOYED--
NO... TOURISTY! ME LIKE.
AND WHAT'S IN THESE BAGS?
REMEMBER TO HAVE A GOOD TIME. I REQUEST A POSTCARD AS PROOF.
FAREWELL!
HEH HEH
SHOES AND MORE SHOES BE IN THERE, MATEY.
WAIT! WHAT?! HOW DID THEY--?
AWWW... THEY DITCHED ME!
PROBABLY SOME COOL SECRET MISSION TO FIGHT LAVA MONSTERS ON AN EVIL ISLAND.
CHEER UP, MASTER DAMIAN. YOUR MISSION, IF YOU CHOOSE TO ACCEPT IT, IS TO DRIVE THE BATMOBILE...
YES!
...ON YOUR 18th BIRTHDAY.
AWWW!

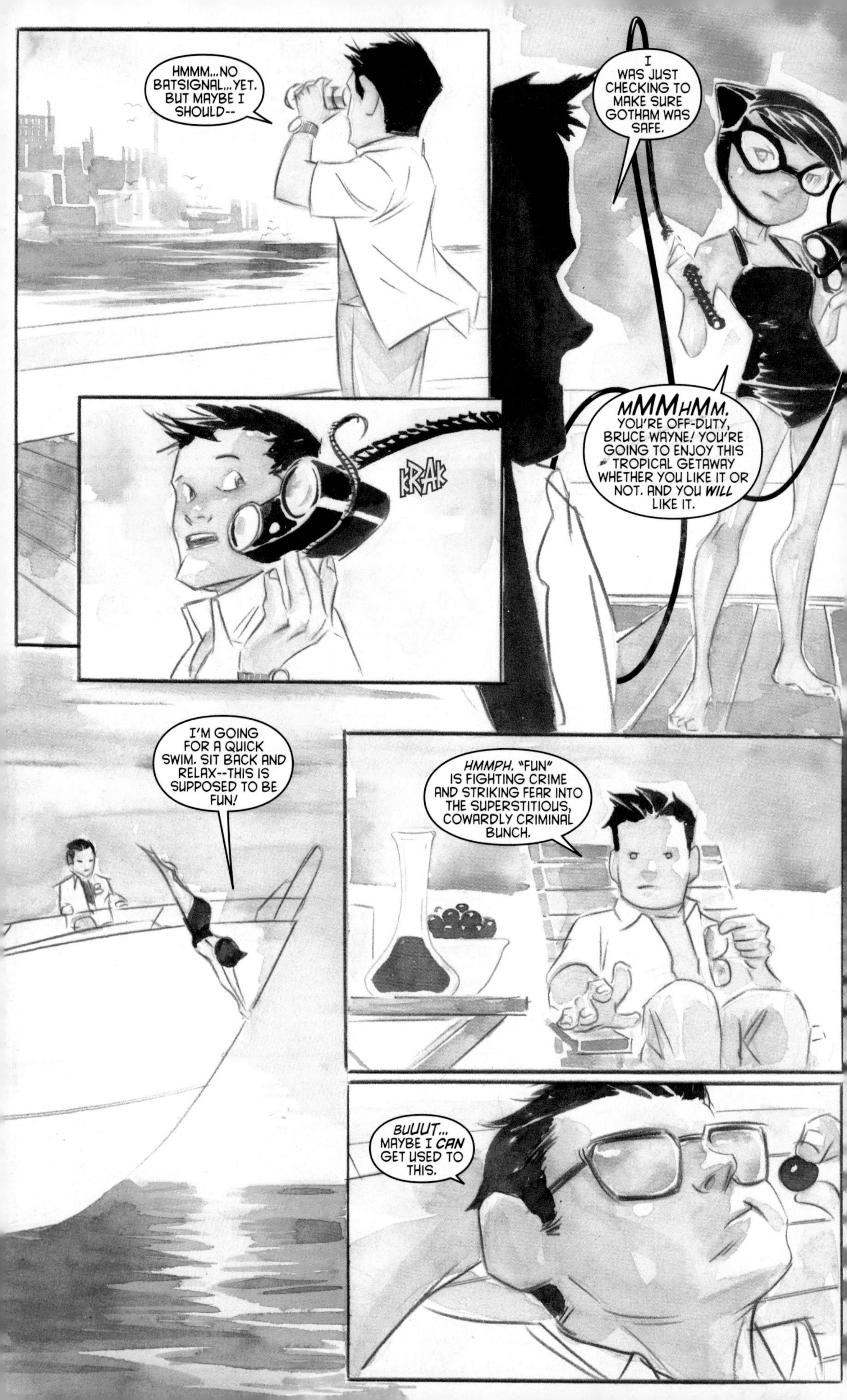
HMMM...NO BATSIGNAL...YET. BUT MAYBE I SHOULD--
I WAS JUST CHECKING TO MAKE SURE GOTHAM WAS SAFE.
KRAK
MMMHMM. YOU'RE OFF-DUTY, BRUCE WAYNE! YOU'RE GOING TO ENJOY THIS TROPICAL GETAWAY WHETHER YOU LIKE IT OR NOT. AND YOU WILL LIKE IT.
I'M GOING FOR A QUICK SWIM. SIT BACK AND RELAX--THIS IS SUPPOSED TO BE FUN!
HMMPH. "FUN" IS FIGHTING CRIME AND STRIKING FEAR INTO THE SUPERSTITIOUS, COWARDLY CRIMINAL BUNCH.
BUUUT... MAYBE I CAN GET USED TO THIS.

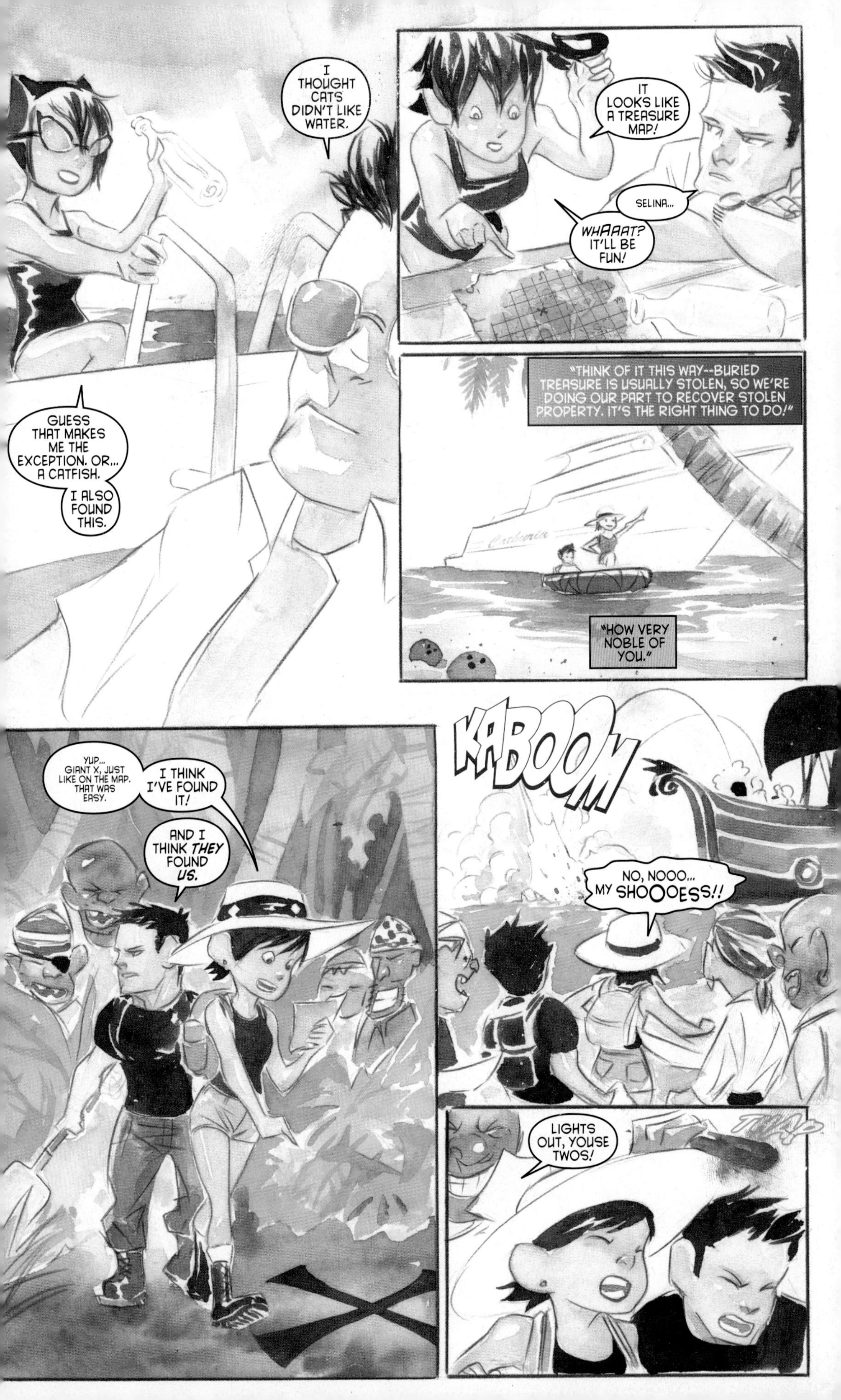

I THOUGHT CATS DIDN'T LIKE WATER.
GUESS THAT MAKES ME THE EXCEPTION. OR... A CATFISH.
I ALSO FOUND THIS.
IT LOOKS LIKE A TREASURE MAP!
SELINA...
WHAAAT? IT'LL BE FUN!
"THINK OF IT THIS WAY--BURIED TREASURE IS USUALLY STOLEN, SO WE'RE DOING OUR PART TO RECOVER STOLEN PROPERTY. IT'S THE RIGHT THING TO DO!"
"HOW VERY NOBLE OF YOU."
I THINK I'VE FOUND IT!
YUP... GIANT X, JUST LIKE ON THE MAP. THAT WAS EASY.
AND I THINK THEY FOUND US.
KABOOM
NO, NOOO... MY SHOOOESS!!
LIGHTS OUT, YOUSE TWOS!

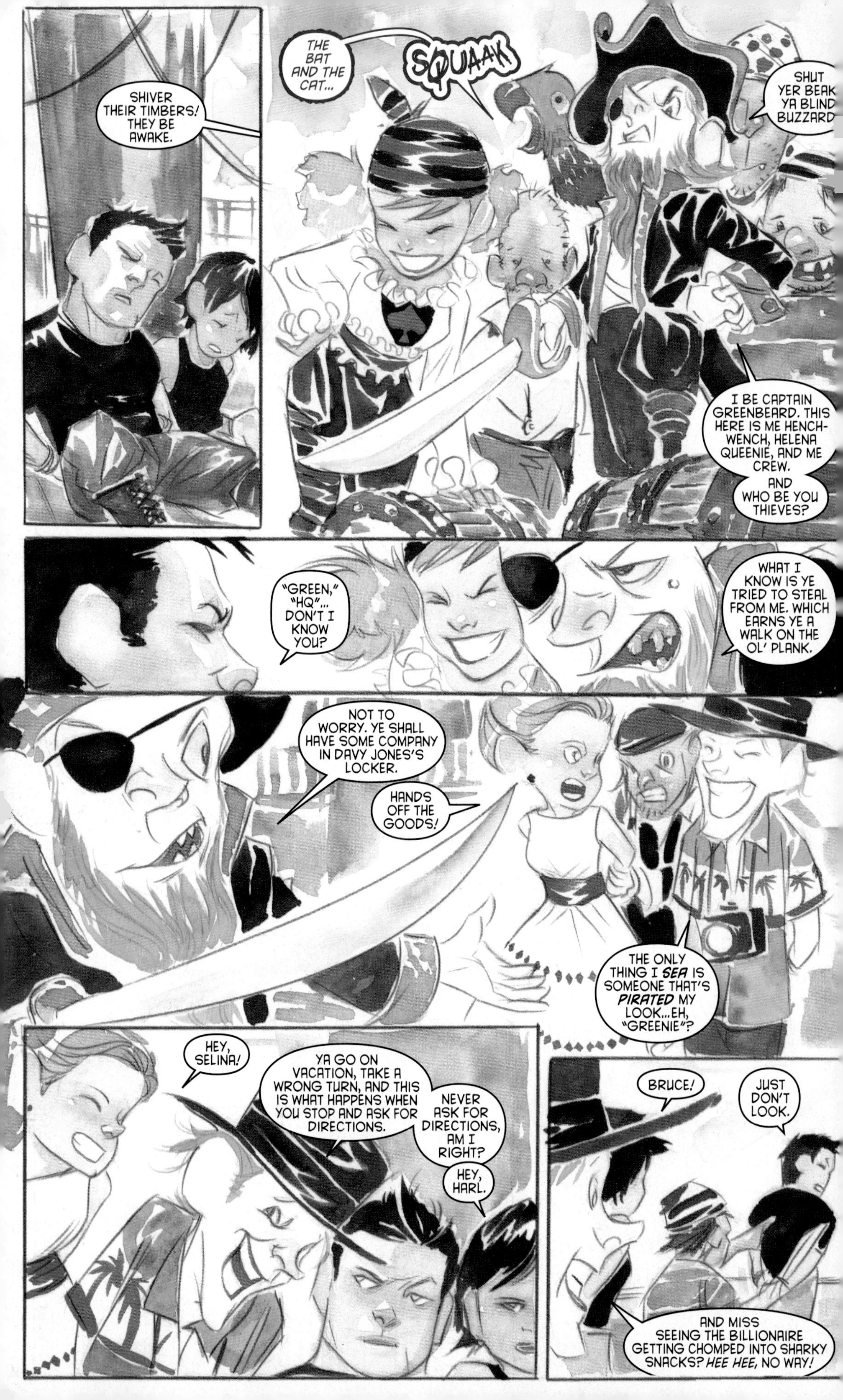
SHIVER THEIR TIMBERS! THEY BE AWAKE.
THE BAT AND THE CAT...
SQUAAK
SHUT YER BEAK YA BLIND BUZZARD
I BE CAPTAIN GREENBEARD. THIS HERE IS ME HENCH-WENCH, HELENA QUEENIE, AND ME CREW.
AND WHO BE YOU THIEVES?
"GREEN," "HQ"... DON'T I KNOW YOU?
WHAT I KNOW IS YE TRIED TO STEAL FROM ME. WHICH EARNS YE A WALK ON THE OL' PLANK.
NOT TO WORRY. YE SHALL HAVE SOME COMPANY IN DAVY JONES'S LOCKER.
HANDS OFF THE GOODS!
THE ONLY THING I SEA IS SOMEONE THAT'S PIRATED MY LOOK...EH, "GREENIE"?
HEY, SELINA!
YA GO ON VACATION, TAKE A WRONG TURN, AND THIS IS WHAT HAPPENS WHEN YOU STOP AND ASK FOR DIRECTIONS.
NEVER ASK FOR DIRECTIONS, AM I RIGHT?
HEY, HARL.
BRUCE!
JUST DON'T LOOK.
AND MISS SEEING THE BILLIONAIRE GETTING CHOMPED INTO SHARKY SNACKS? HEE HEE, NO WAY!

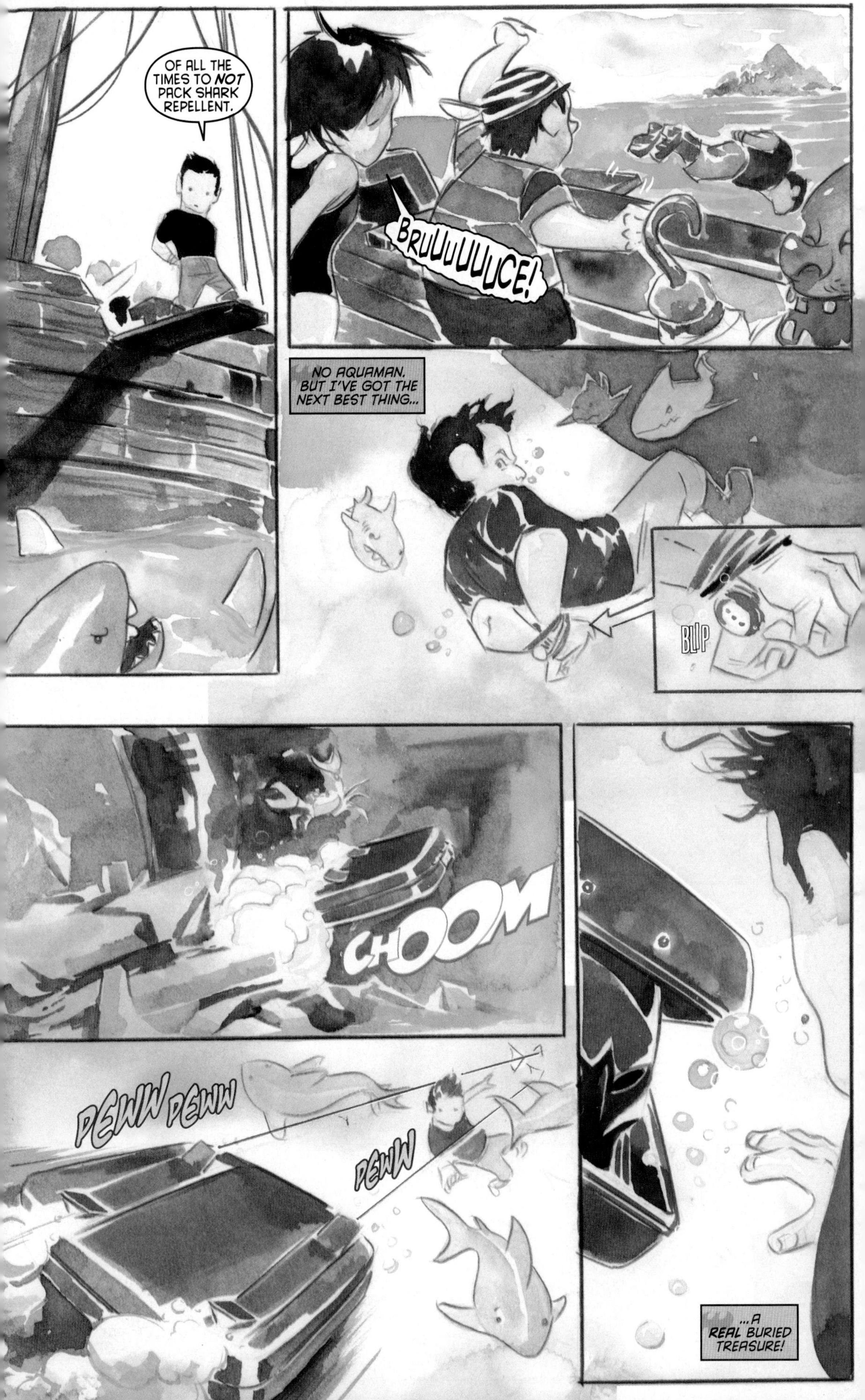
OF ALL THE TIMES TO NOT PACK SHARK REPELLENT.
BRUUUUUUCE!
NO AQUAMAN. BUT I'VE GOT THE NEXT BEST THING...
BLIP
CHOOM
PEWW PEWW
PEWW
...A REAL BURIED TREASURE!

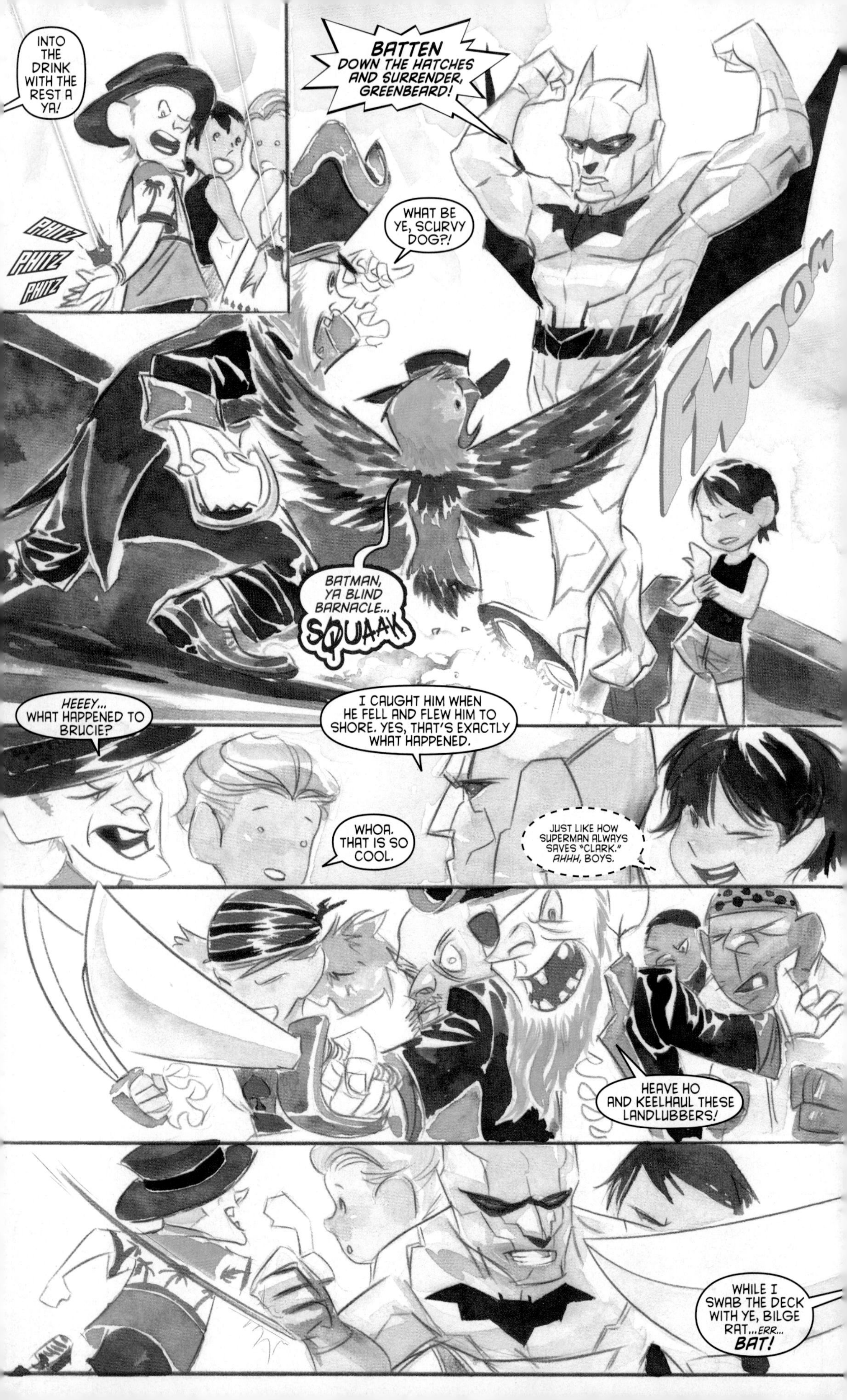
INTO THE DRINK WITH THE REST A YA!
PHITZ
PHITZ
PHITZ
BATTEN DOWN THE HATCHES AND SURRENDER, GREENBEARD!
WHAT BE YE, SCURVY DOG?!
FWOOM
BATMAN, YA BLIND BARNACLE...
SQUAAK
HEEEY... WHAT HAPPENED TO BRUCIE?
I CAUGHT HIM WHEN HE FELL AND FLEW HIM TO SHORE. YES, THAT'S EXACTLY WHAT HAPPENED.
WHOA. THAT IS SO COOL.
JUST LIKE HOW SUPERMAN ALWAYS SAVES "CLARK." AHHH, BOYS.
HEAVE HO AND KEELHAUL THESE LANDLUBBERS!
WHILE I SWAB THE DECK WITH YE, BILGE RAT...ERR... BAT!

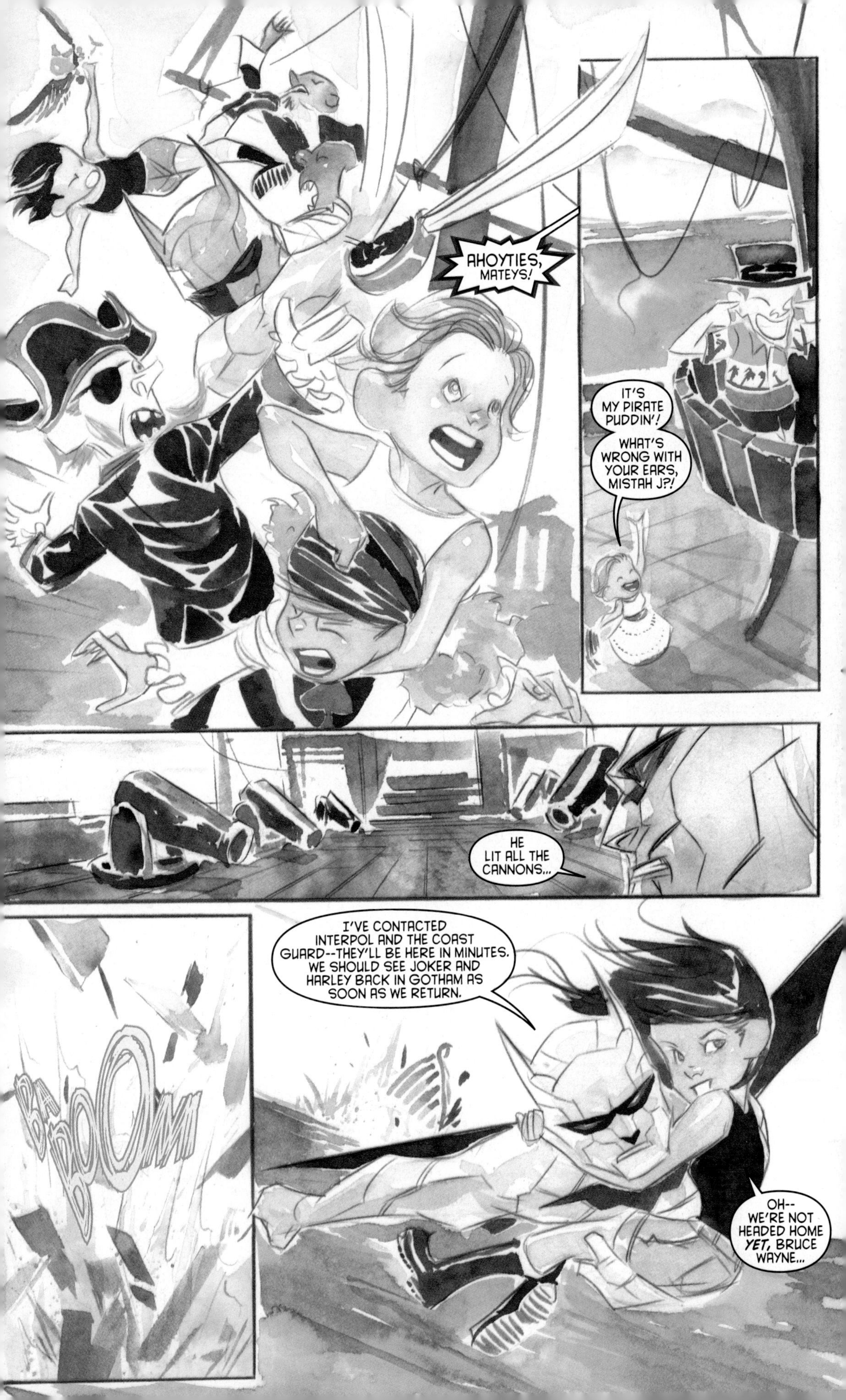

AHOYTIES, MATEYS!
IT'S MY PIRATE PUDDIN'!
WHAT'S WRONG WITH YOUR EARS, MISTAH J?!
HE LIT ALL THE CANNONS...
I'VE CONTACTED INTERPOL AND THE COAST GUARD--THEY'LL BE HERE IN MINUTES. WE SHOULD SEE JOKER AND HARLEY BACK IN GOTHAM AS SOON AS WE RETURN.
OH-- WE'RE NOT HEADED HOME *YET,* BRUCE WAYNE...

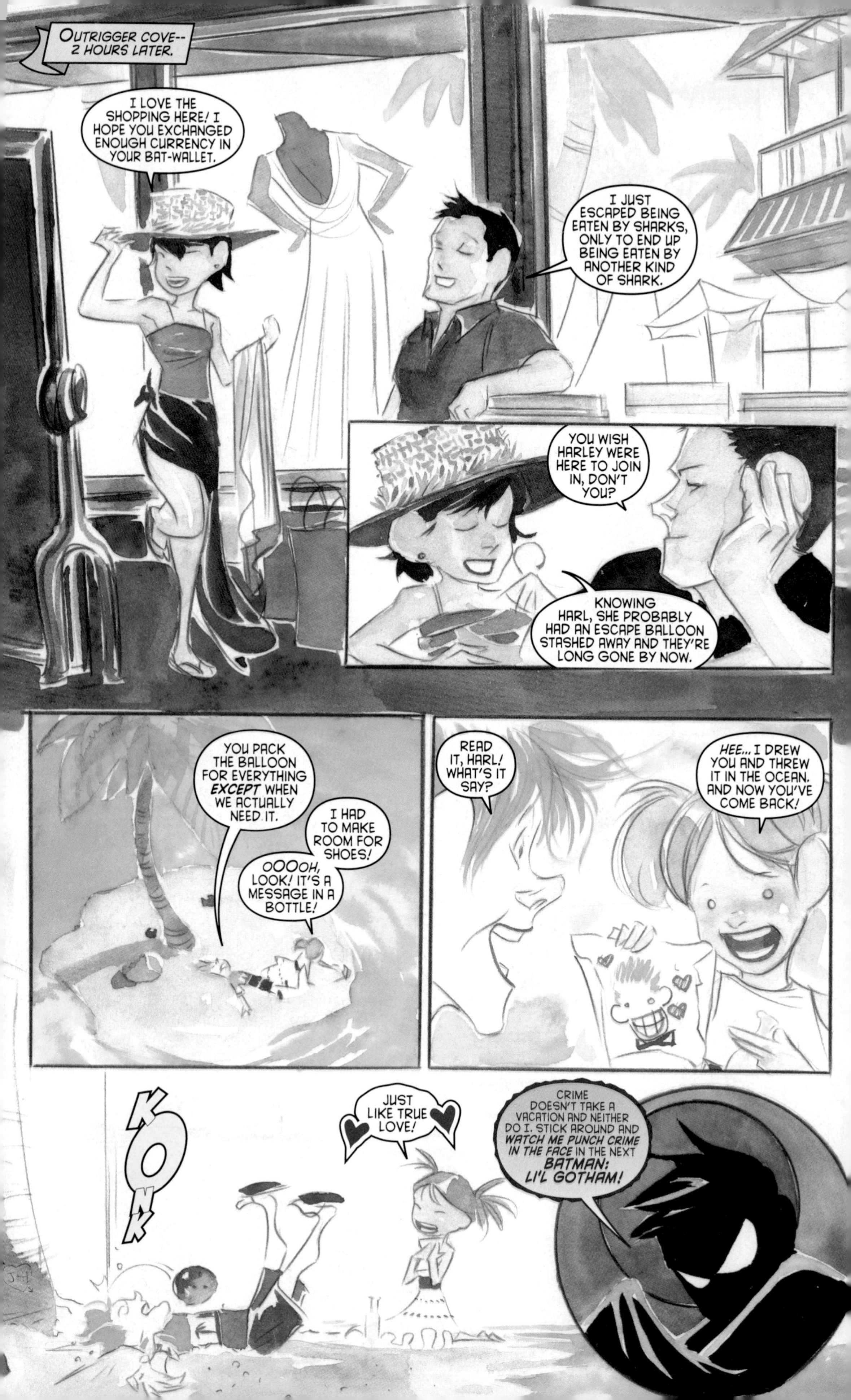
OUTRIGGER COVE--
2 HOURS LATER.
I LOVE THE SHOPPING HERE! I HOPE YOU EXCHANGED ENOUGH CURRENCY IN YOUR BAT-WALLET.
I JUST ESCAPED BEING EATEN BY SHARKS, ONLY TO END UP BEING EATEN BY ANOTHER KIND OF SHARK.
YOU WISH HARLEY WERE HERE TO JOIN IN, DON'T YOU?
KNOWING HARL, SHE PROBABLY HAD AN ESCAPE BALLOON STASHED AWAY AND THEY'RE LONG GONE BY NOW.
YOU PACK THE BALLOON FOR EVERYTHING EXCEPT WHEN WE ACTUALLY NEED IT.
I HAD TO MAKE ROOM FOR SHOES!
OOOOH, LOOK! IT'S A MESSAGE IN A BOTTLE!
READ IT, HARL! WHAT'S IT SAY?
HEE... I DREW YOU AND THREW IT IN THE OCEAN. AND NOW YOU'VE COME BACK!
KONK
JUST LIKE TRUE LOVE!
CRIME DOESN'T TAKE A VACATION AND NEITHER DO I. STICK AROUND AND WATCH ME PUNCH CRIME IN THE FACE IN THE NEXT BATMAN: LI'L GOTHAM!

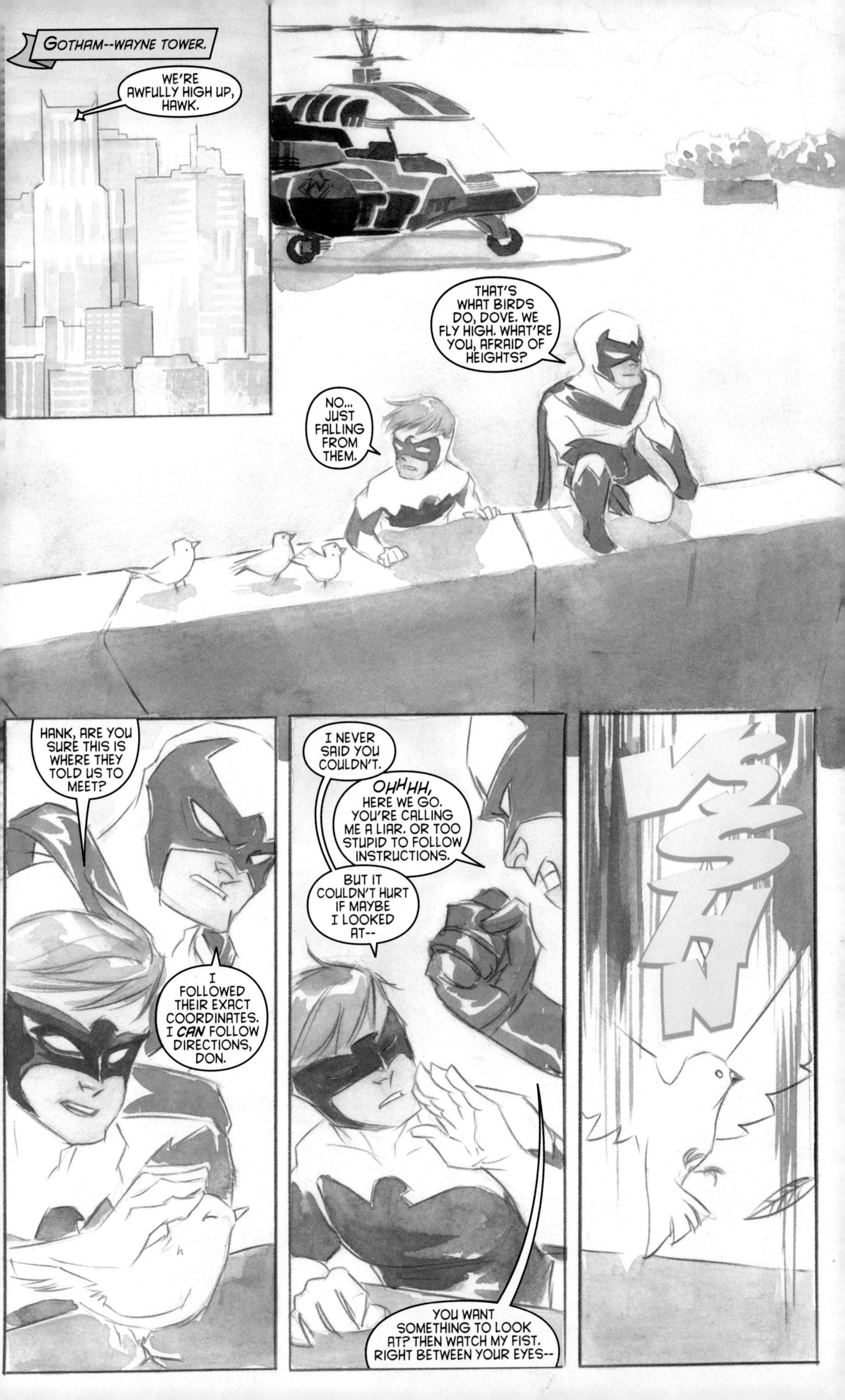
GOTHAM--WAYNE TOWER.
WE'RE AWFULLY HIGH UP, HAWK.
THAT'S WHAT BIRDS DO, DOVE. WE FLY HIGH. WHAT'RE YOU, AFRAID OF HEIGHTS?
NO... JUST FALLING FROM THEM.
HANK, ARE YOU SURE THIS IS WHERE THEY TOLD US TO MEET?
I FOLLOWED THEIR EXACT COORDINATES. I CAN FOLLOW DIRECTIONS, DON.
I NEVER SAID YOU COULDN'T.
OHHHH, HERE WE GO. YOU'RE CALLING ME A LIAR. OR TOO STUPID TO FOLLOW INSTRUCTIONS.
BUT IT COULDN'T HURT IF MAYBE I LOOKED AT--
YOU WANT SOMETHING TO LOOK AT? THEN WATCH MY FIST. RIGHT BETWEEN YOUR EYES--

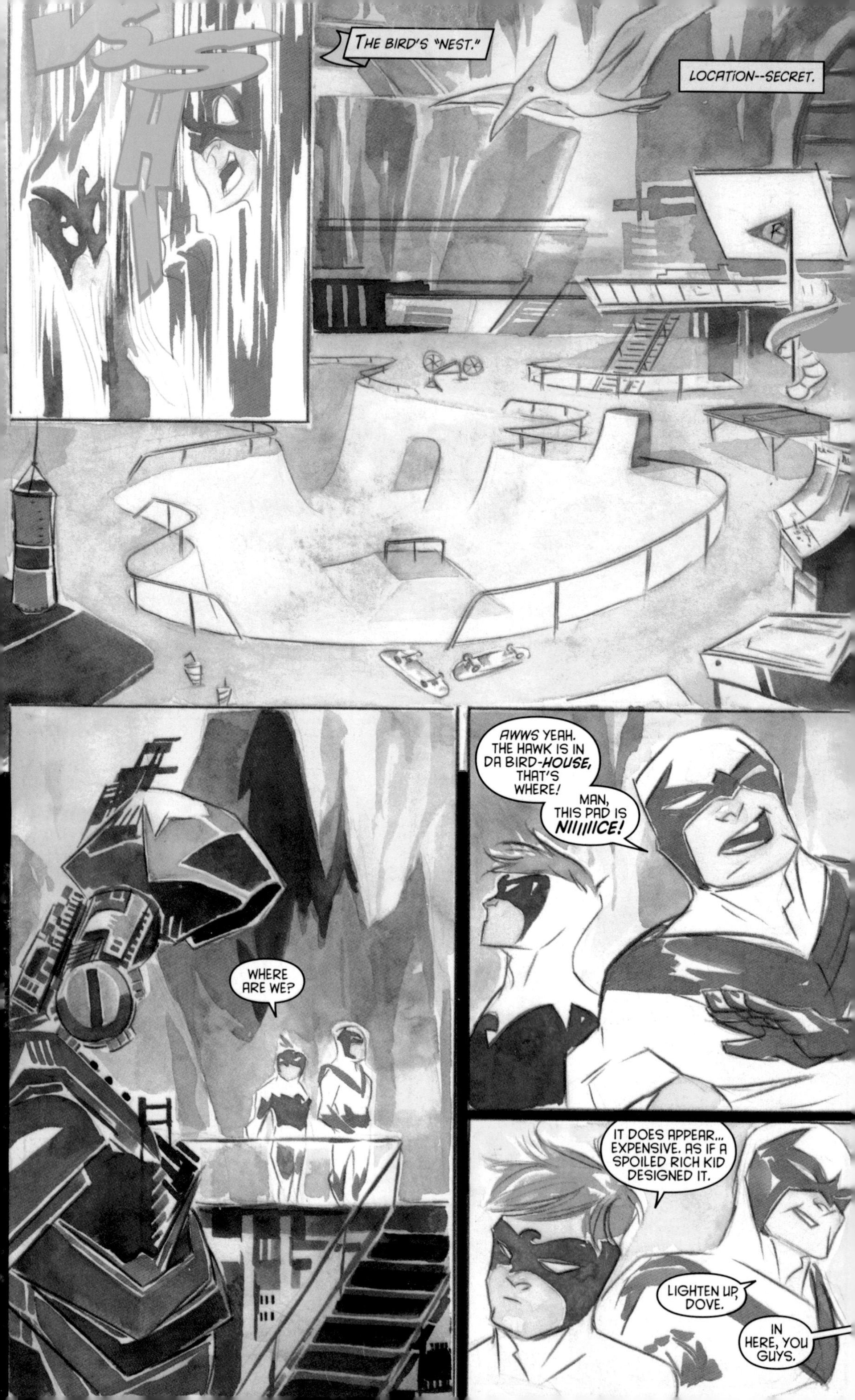
SHHH
THE BIRD'S "NEST."
LOCATION--SECRET.
WHERE ARE WE?
AWWS YEAH. THE HAWK IS IN DA BIRD-HOUSE, THAT'S WHERE!
MAN, THIS PAD IS NIIIIIICE!
IT DOES APPEAR... EXPENSIVE. AS IF A SPOILED RICH KID DESIGNED IT.
LIGHTEN UP, DOVE.
IN HERE, YOU GUYS.

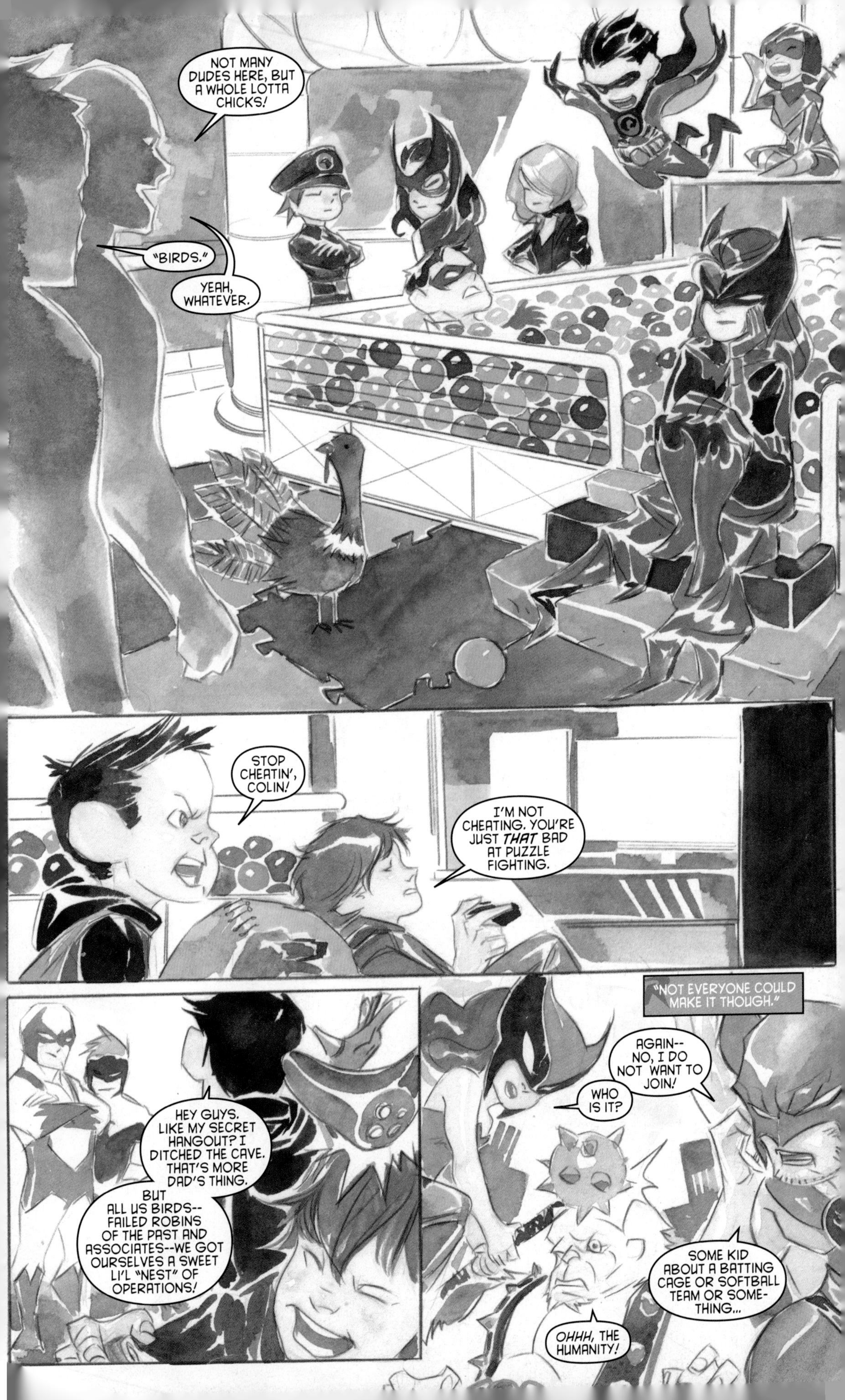
NOT MANY DUDES HERE, BUT A WHOLE LOTTA CHICKS!
"BIRDS."
YEAH, WHATEVER.
STOP CHEATIN', COLIN!
I'M NOT CHEATING. YOU'RE JUST *THAT* BAD AT PUZZLE FIGHTING.
HEY GUYS. LIKE MY SECRET HANGOUT? I DITCHED THE CAVE. THAT'S MORE DAD'S THING.
BUT ALL US BIRDS-- FAILED ROBINS OF THE PAST AND ASSOCIATES--WE GOT OURSELVES A SWEET LI'L "NEST" OF OPERATIONS!
"NOT EVERYONE COULD MAKE IT THOUGH."
AGAIN-- NO, I DO NOT WANT TO JOIN!
WHO IS IT?
SOME KID ABOUT A BATTING CAGE OR SOFTBALL TEAM OR SOME-THING...
OHHH, THE HUMANITY!

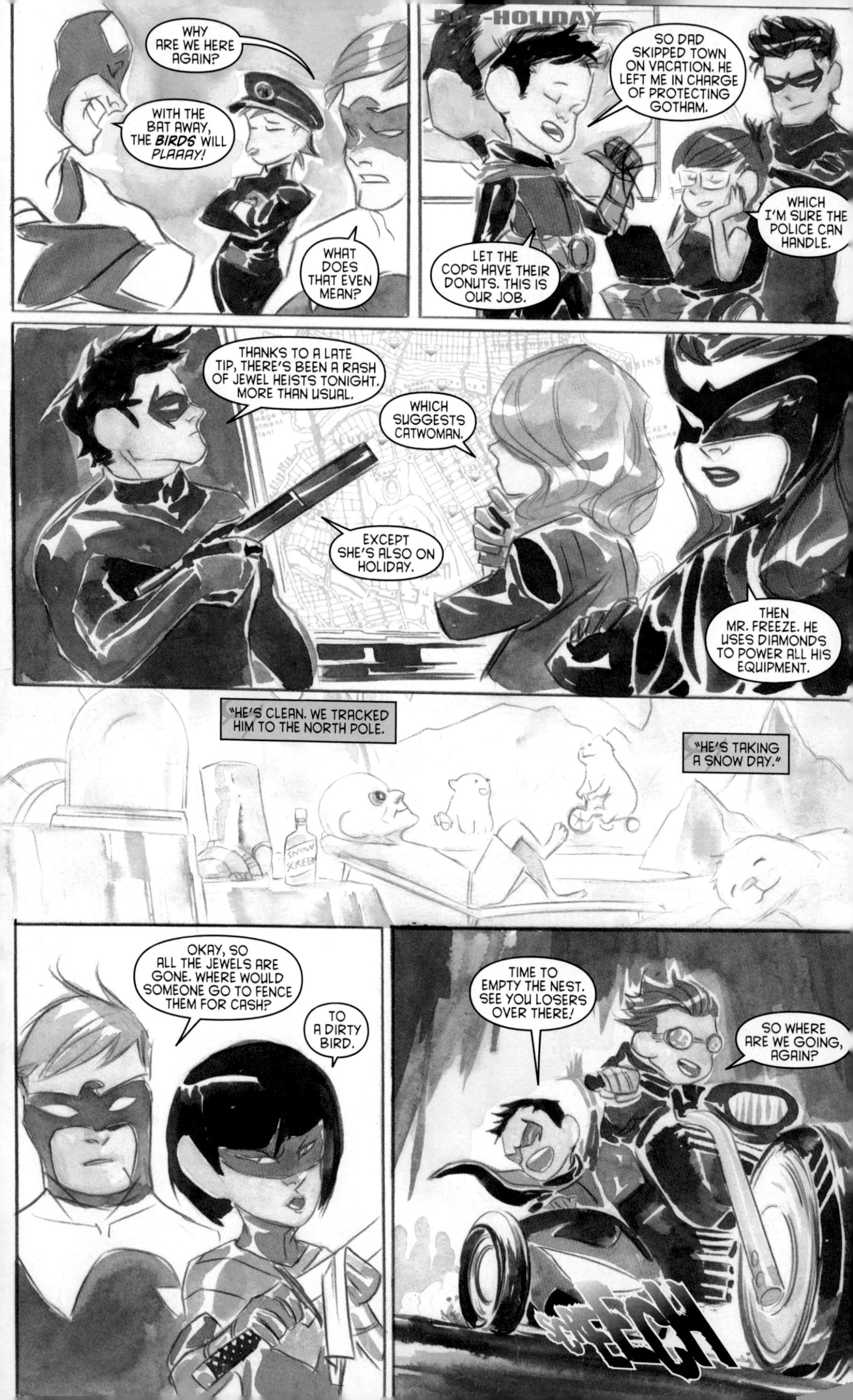

WHY ARE WE HERE AGAIN?
WITH THE BAT AWAY, THE *BIRDS* WILL *PLAAAY!*
WHAT DOES THAT EVEN MEAN?
-HOLIDAY
SO DAD SKIPPED TOWN ON VACATION. HE LEFT ME IN CHARGE OF PROTECTING GOTHAM.
WHICH I'M SURE THE POLICE CAN HANDLE.
LET THE COPS HAVE THEIR DONUTS. THIS IS OUR JOB.
THANKS TO A LATE TIP, THERE'S BEEN A RASH OF JEWEL HEISTS TONIGHT. MORE THAN USUAL.
WHICH SUGGESTS CATWOMAN.
EXCEPT SHE'S ALSO ON HOLIDAY.
THEN MR. FREEZE. HE USES DIAMONDS TO POWER ALL HIS EQUIPMENT.
"HE'S CLEAN. WE TRACKED HIM TO THE NORTH POLE.
"HE'S TAKING A SNOW DAY."
SNOW SCREEN
OKAY, SO ALL THE JEWELS ARE GONE. WHERE WOULD SOMEONE GO TO FENCE THEM FOR CASH?
TO A DIRTY BIRD.
TIME TO EMPTY THE NEST. SEE YOU LOSERS OVER THERE!
SO WHERE ARE WE GOING, AGAIN?
SCREECH

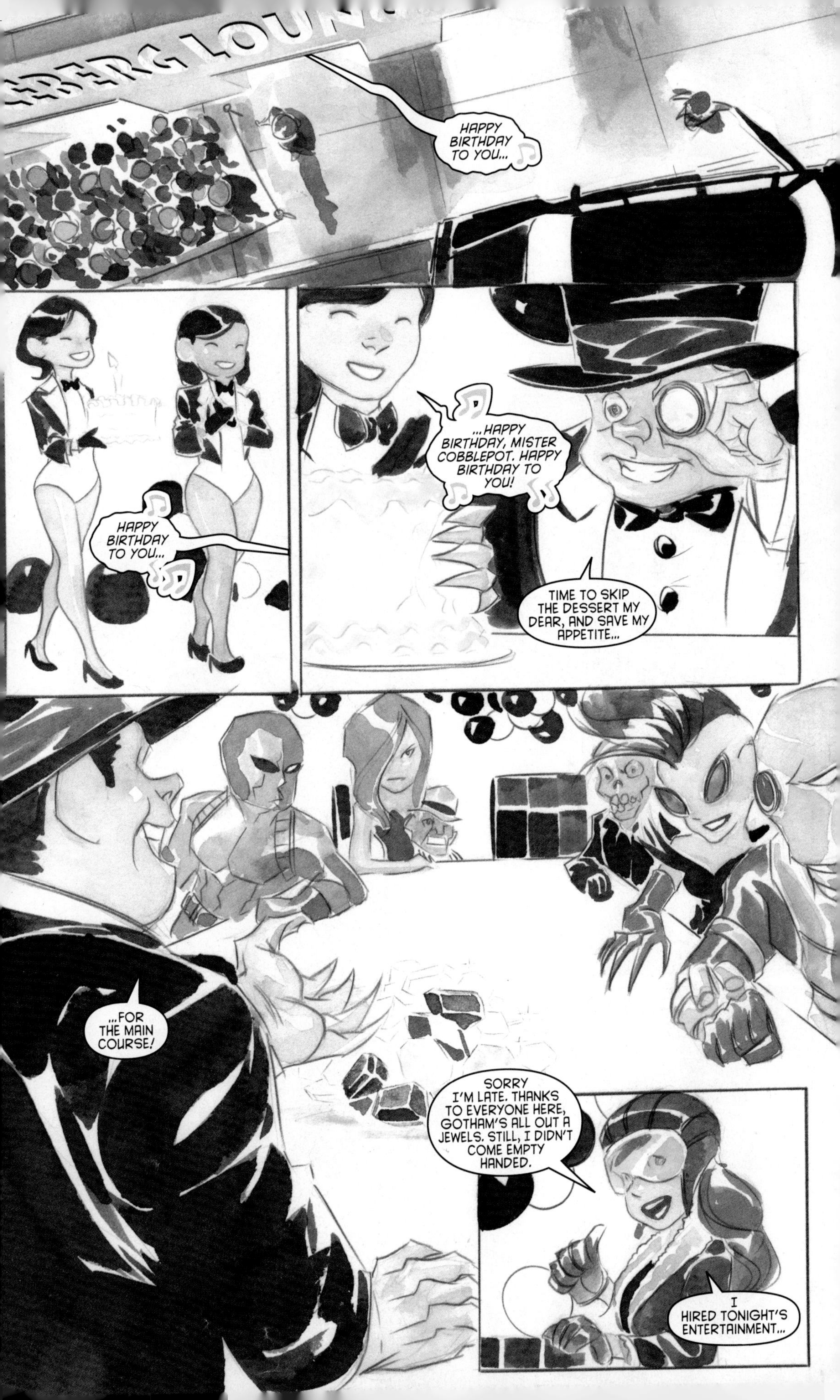

HAPPY BIRTHDAY TO YOU...
HAPPY BIRTHDAY TO YOU...
...HAPPY BIRTHDAY, MISTER COBBLEPOT. HAPPY BIRTHDAY TO YOU!
TIME TO SKIP THE DESSERT MY DEAR, AND SAVE MY APPETITE...
...FOR THE MAIN COURSE!
SORRY I'M LATE. THANKS TO EVERYONE HERE, GOTHAM'S ALL OUT A JEWELS. STILL, I DIDN'T COME EMPTY HANDED.
I HIRED TONIGHT'S ENTERTAINMENT...

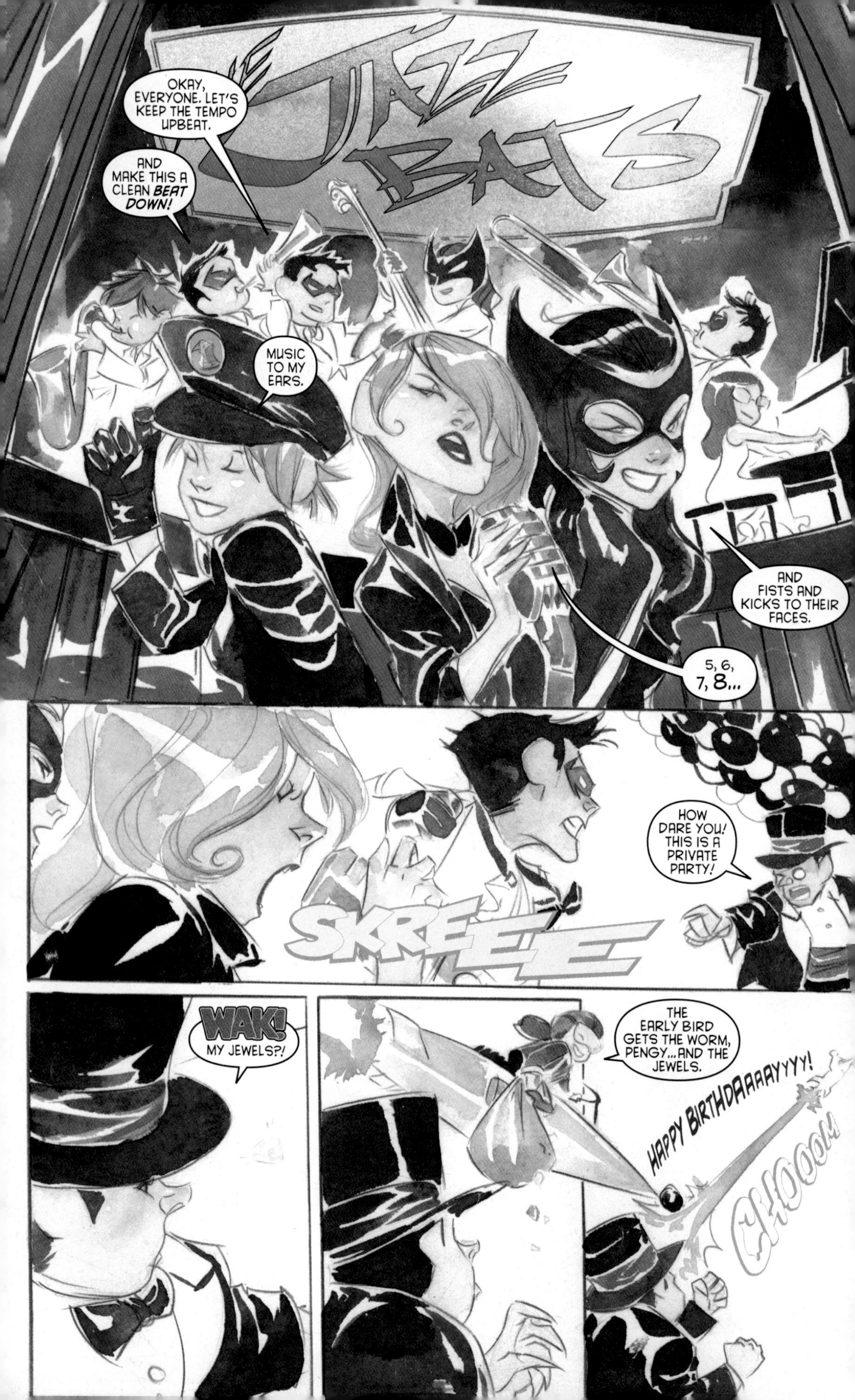
JAZZ BATS
OKAY, EVERYONE. LET'S KEEP THE TEMPO UPBEAT.
AND MAKE THIS A CLEAN *BEAT DOWN!*
MUSIC TO MY EARS.
AND FISTS AND KICKS TO THEIR FACES.
5, 6, 7, 8...
HOW DARE YOU! THIS IS A PRIVATE PARTY!
SKREEEE
WAK! MY JEWELS?!
THE EARLY BIRD GETS THE WORM, PENGY...AND THE JEWELS.
HAPPY BIRTHDAAAAAYYYY!
CHOOOM

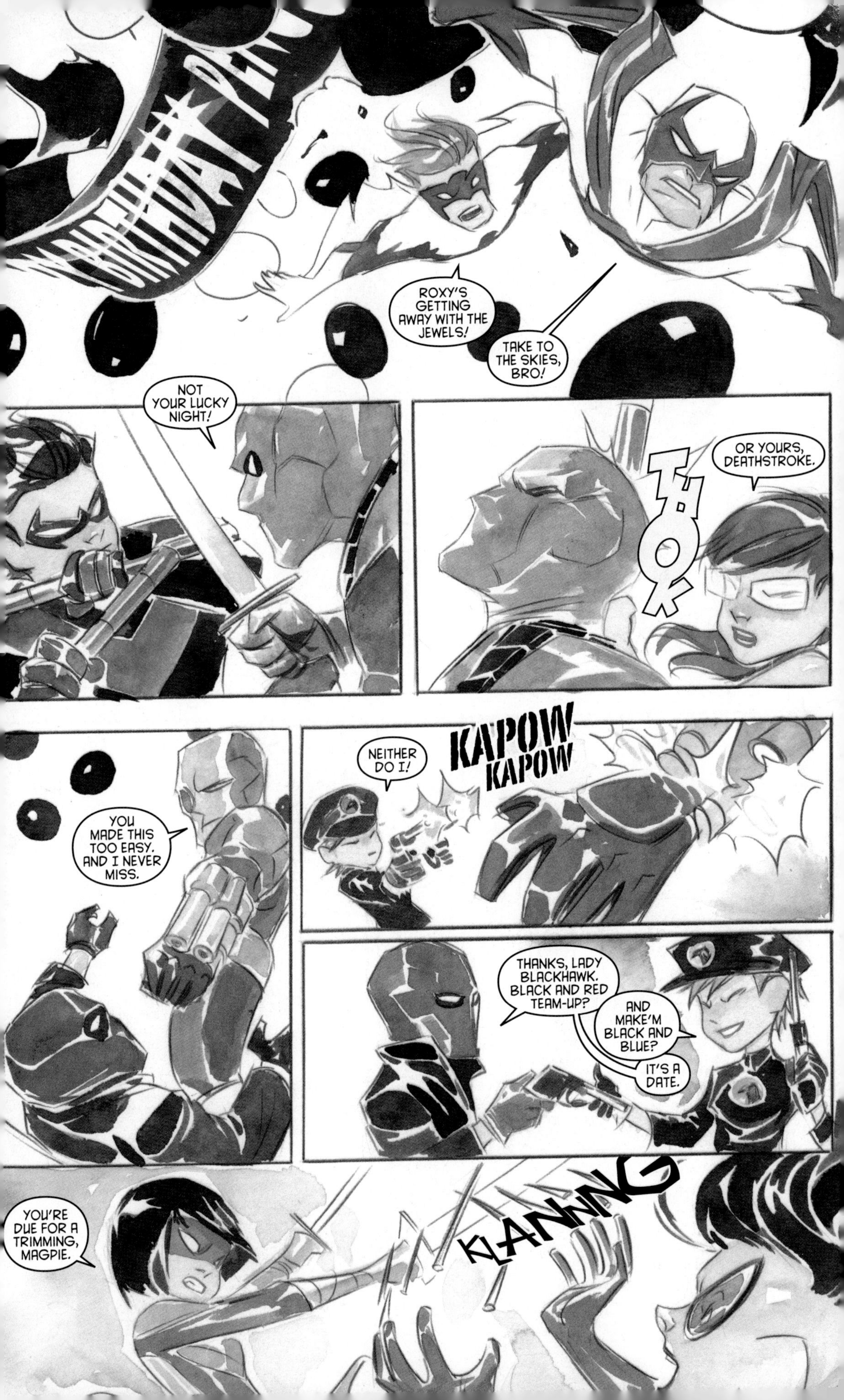
ROXY'S GETTING AWAY WITH THE JEWELS!
TAKE TO THE SKIES, BRO!
NOT YOUR LUCKY NIGHT!
OR YOURS, DEATHSTROKE.
THOK
YOU MADE THIS TOO EASY. AND I NEVER MISS.
NEITHER DO I!
KAPOW
KAPOW
THANKS, LADY BLACKHAWK. BLACK AND RED TEAM-UP?
AND MAKE'M BLACK AND BLUE?
IT'S A DATE.
YOU'RE DUE FOR A TRIMMING, MAGPIE.
KLANNNG

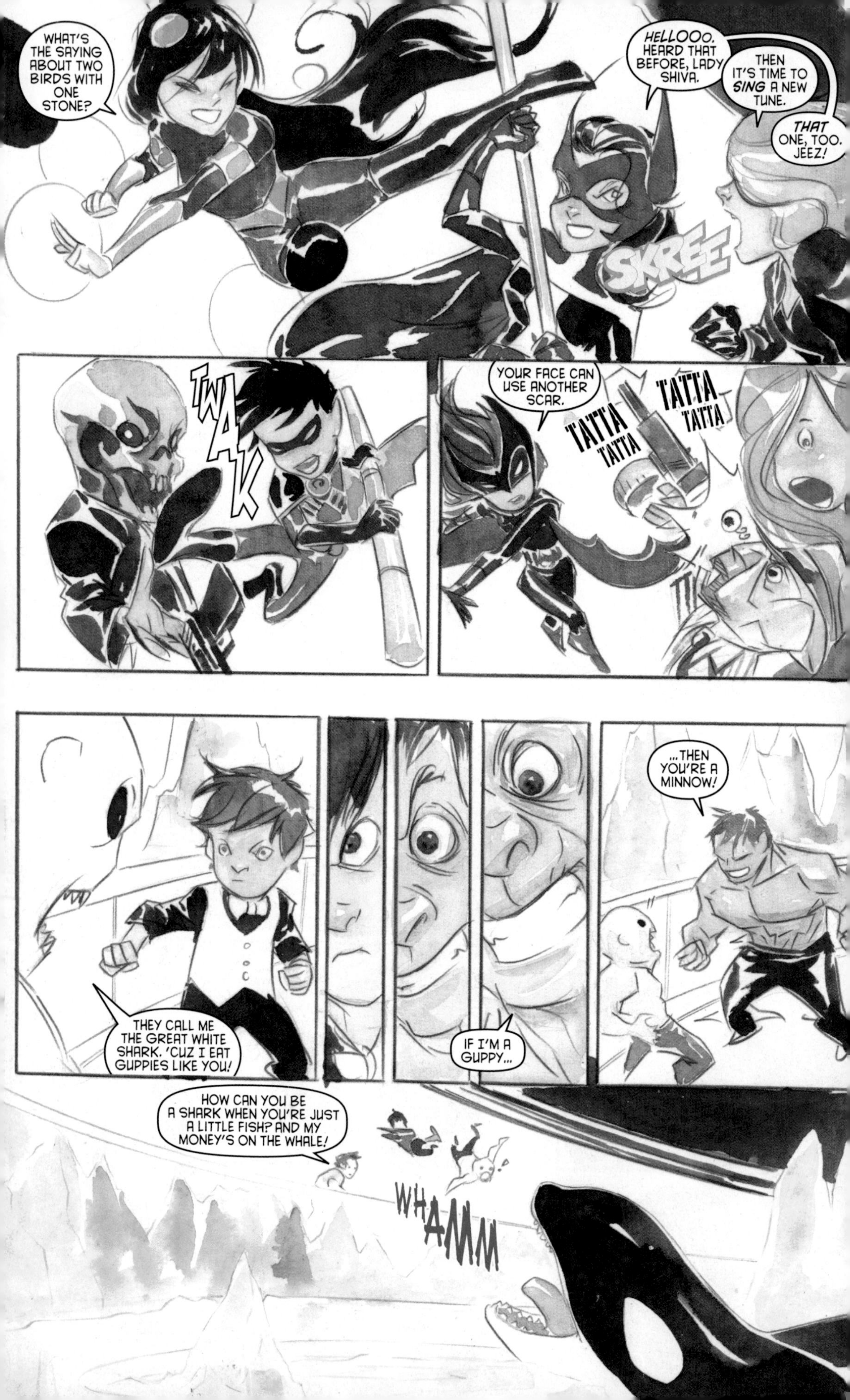
WHAT'S THE SAYING ABOUT TWO BIRDS WITH ONE STONE?
HELLOOo. HEARD THAT BEFORE, LADY SHIVA.
THEN IT'S TIME TO SING A NEW TUNE.
THAT ONE, TOO. JEEZ!
SKREE
TWAK
YOUR FACE CAN USE ANOTHER SCAR.
TATTA TATTA
TATTA TATTA
THEY CALL ME THE GREAT WHITE SHARK. 'CUZ I EAT GUPPIES LIKE YOU!
IF I'M A GUPPY...
...THEN YOU'RE A MINNOW!
HOW CAN YOU BE A SHARK WHEN YOU'RE JUST A LITTLE FISH? AND MY MONEY'S ON THE WHALE!
WHAMM

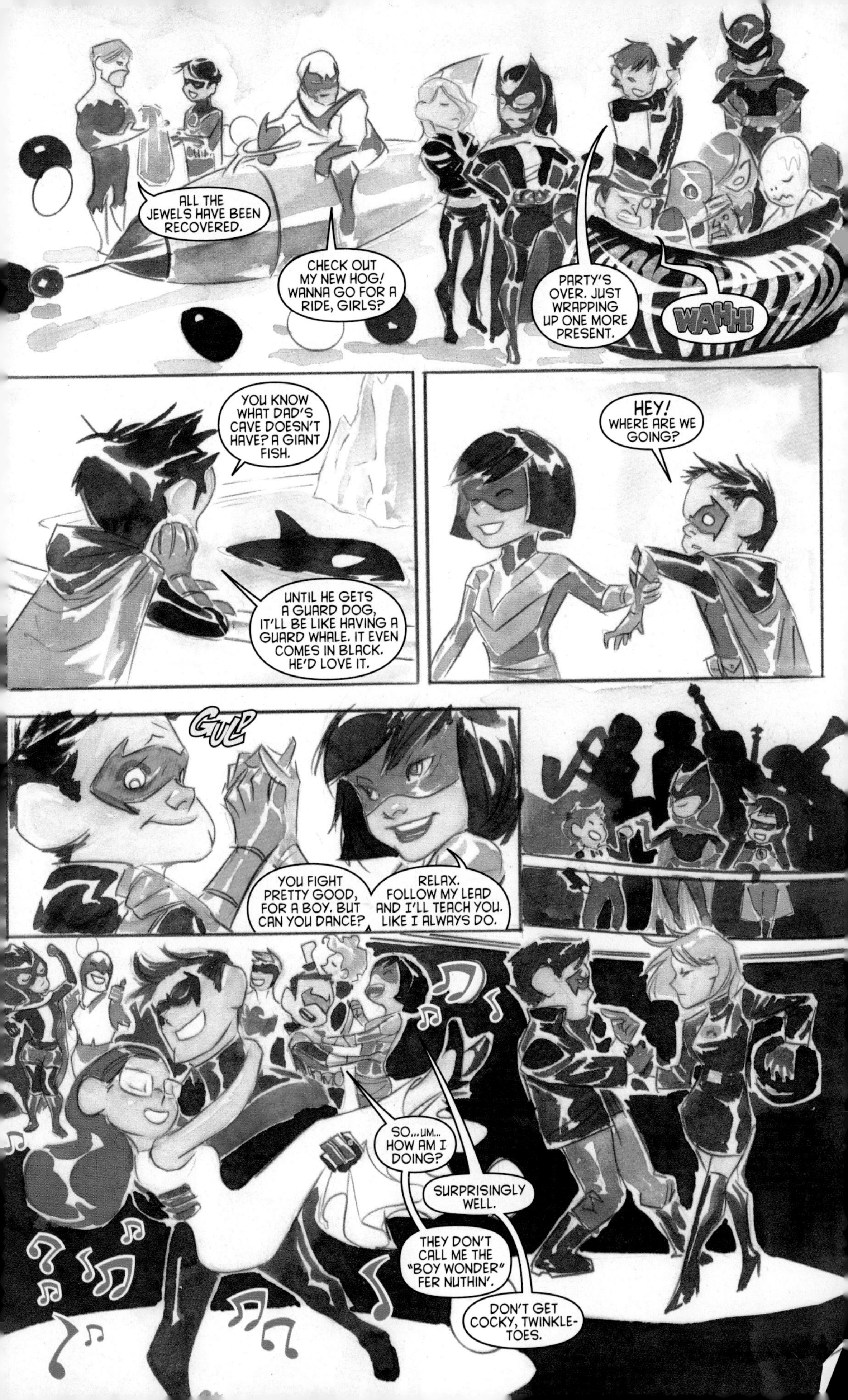
ALL THE JEWELS HAVE BEEN RECOVERED.
CHECK OUT MY NEW HOG! WANNA GO FOR A RIDE, GIRLS?
PARTY'S OVER. JUST WRAPPING UP ONE MORE PRESENT.
WAHH!
YOU KNOW WHAT DAD'S CAVE DOESN'T HAVE? A GIANT FISH.
UNTIL HE GETS A GUARD DOG, IT'LL BE LIKE HAVING A GUARD WHALE. IT EVEN COMES IN BLACK. HE'D LOVE IT.
HEY! WHERE ARE WE GOING?
GULP
YOU FIGHT PRETTY GOOD, FOR A BOY. BUT CAN YOU DANCE?
RELAX. FOLLOW MY LEAD AND I'LL TEACH YOU. LIKE I ALWAYS DO.
SO...UM... HOW AM I DOING?
SURPRISINGLY WELL.
THEY DON'T CALL ME THE "BOY WONDER" FER NUTHIN'.
DON'T GET COCKY, TWINKLE-TOES.

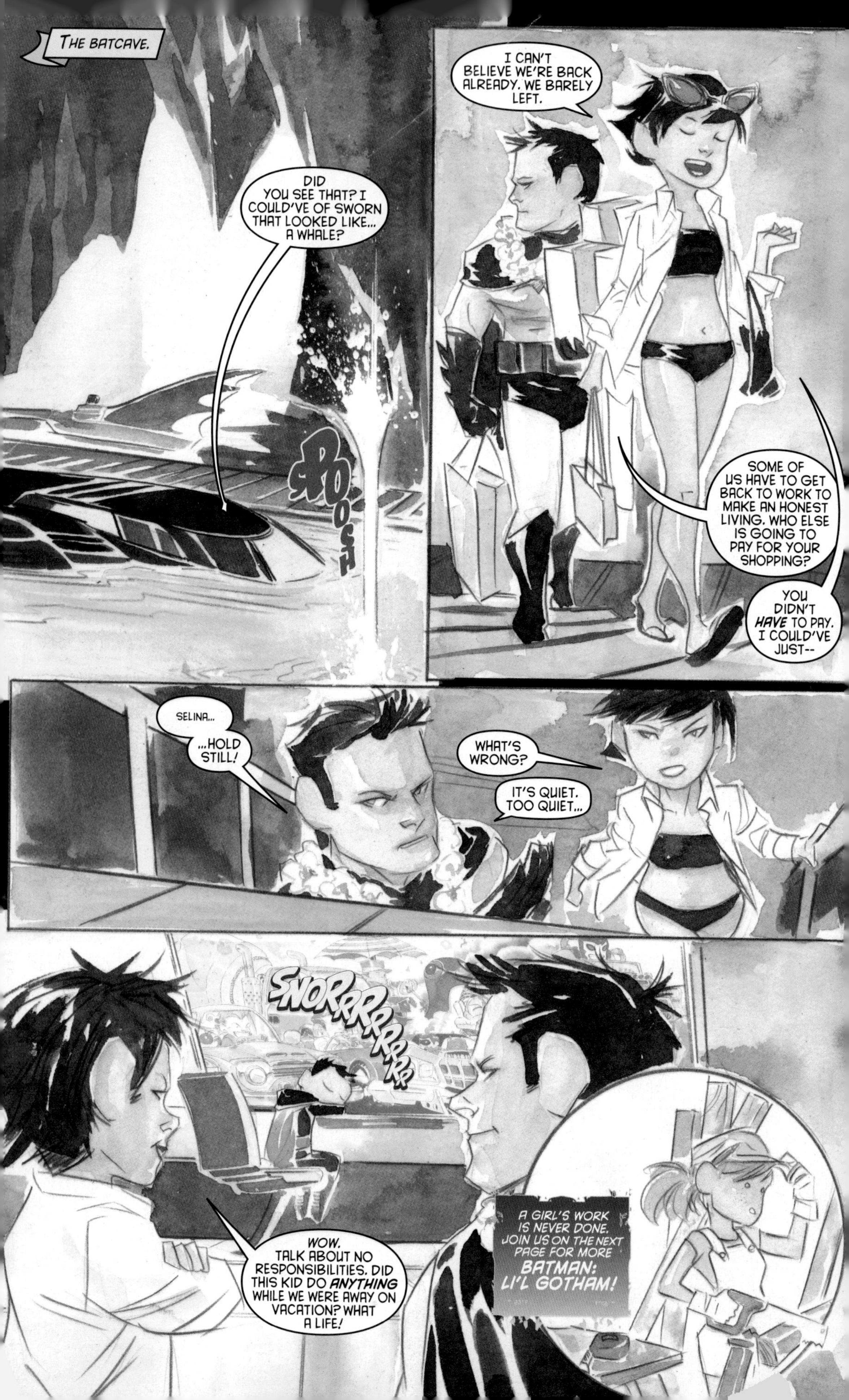
THE BATCAVE.
DID YOU SEE THAT? I COULD'VE OF SWORN THAT LOOKED LIKE... A WHALE?
SPLOOOSH
I CAN'T BELIEVE WE'RE BACK ALREADY. WE BARELY LEFT.
SOME OF US HAVE TO GET BACK TO WORK TO MAKE AN HONEST LIVING. WHO ELSE IS GOING TO PAY FOR YOUR SHOPPING?
YOU DIDN'T *HAVE* TO PAY. I COULD'VE JUST--
SELINA...
...HOLD STILL!
WHAT'S WRONG?
IT'S QUIET. TOO QUIET...
SNORRRRRRRR
WOW. TALK ABOUT NO RESPONSIBILITIES. DID THIS KID DO *ANYTHING* WHILE WE WERE AWAY ON VACATION? WHAT A LIFE!
A GIRL'S WORK IS NEVER DONE. JOIN US ON THE NEXT PAGE FOR MORE BATMAN: LI'L GOTHAM!

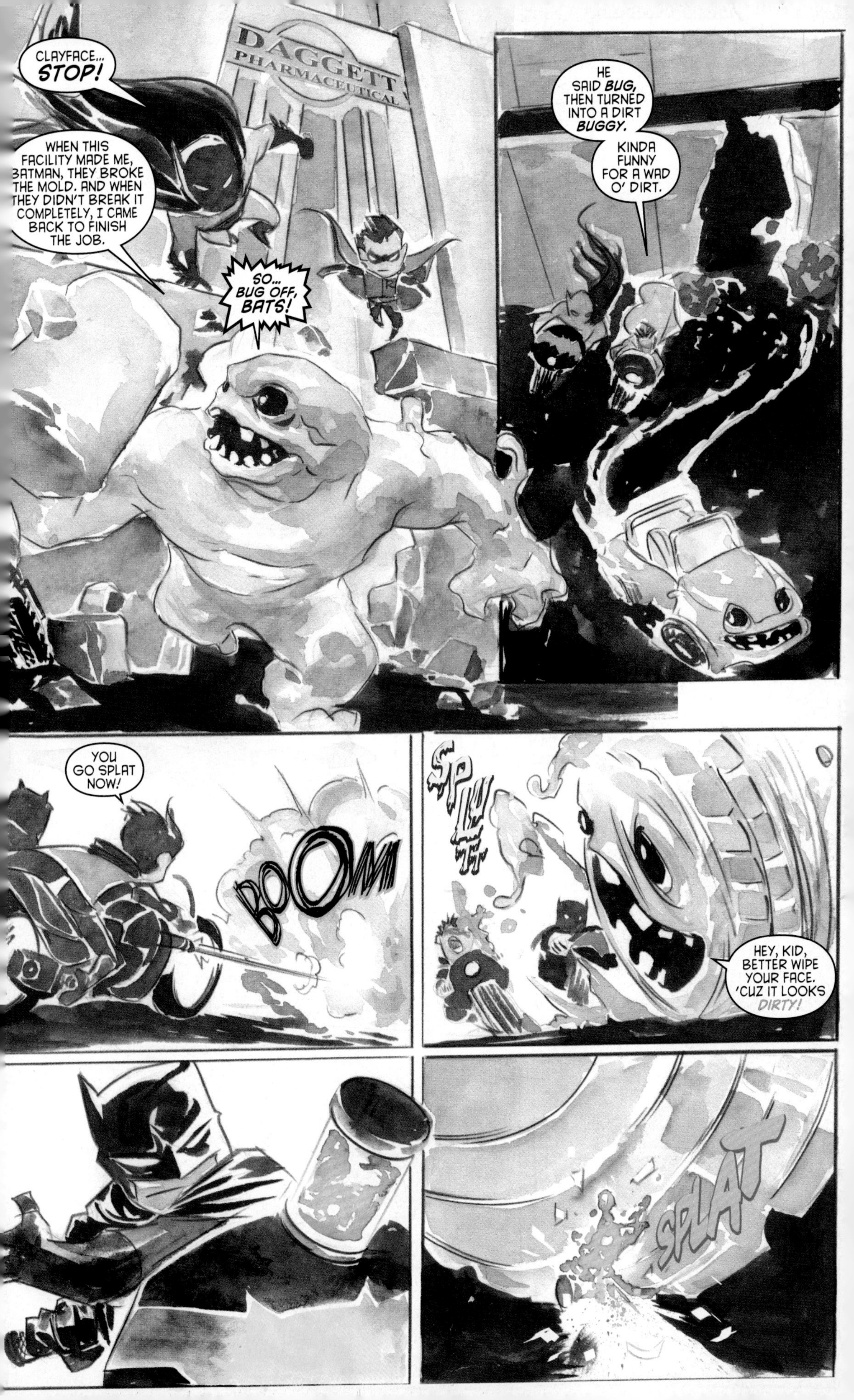
DAGGETT PHARMACEUTICAL
CLAYFACE... STOP!
WHEN THIS FACILITY MADE ME, BATMAN, THEY BROKE THE MOLD. AND WHEN THEY DIDN'T BREAK IT COMPLETELY, I CAME BACK TO FINISH THE JOB.
SO... BUG OFF, BATS!
HE SAID BUG, THEN TURNED INTO A DIRT BUGGY.
KINDA FUNNY FOR A WAD O' DIRT.
YOU GO SPLAT NOW!
BOOM
HEY, KID, BETTER WIPE YOUR FACE. 'CUZ IT LOOKS DIRTY!
SPLAT

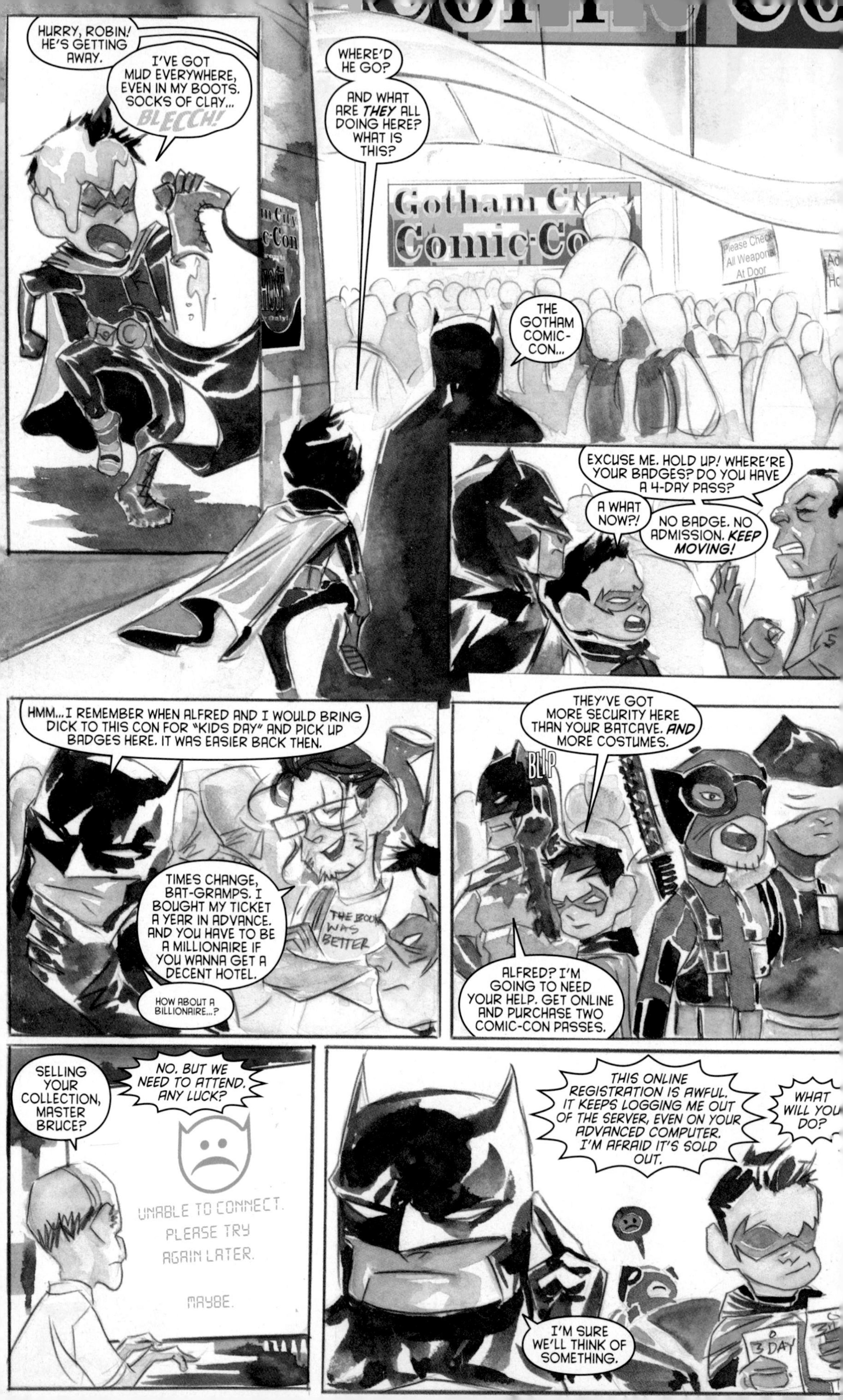
HURRY, ROBIN! HE'S GETTING AWAY.
I'VE GOT MUD EVERYWHERE, EVEN IN MY BOOTS. SOCKS OF CLAY... BLECCH!
WHERE'D HE GO?
AND WHAT ARE THEY ALL DOING HERE? WHAT IS THIS?
Gotham City Comic-Con
Please Check All Weapons At Door
THE GOTHAM COMIC-CON...
EXCUSE ME. HOLD UP! WHERE'RE YOUR BADGES? DO YOU HAVE A 4-DAY PASS?
A WHAT NOW?!
NO BADGE. NO ADMISSION. KEEP MOVING!
HMM...I REMEMBER WHEN ALFRED AND I WOULD BRING DICK TO THIS CON FOR "KIDS DAY" AND PICK UP BADGES HERE. IT WAS EASIER BACK THEN.
TIMES CHANGE, BAT-GRAMPS. I BOUGHT MY TICKET A YEAR IN ADVANCE. AND YOU HAVE TO BE A MILLIONAIRE IF YOU WANNA GET A DECENT HOTEL.
THE BOOK WAS BETTER
HOW ABOUT A BILLIONAIRE...?
THEY'VE GOT MORE SECURITY HERE THAN YOUR BATCAVE. AND MORE COSTUMES.
BLIP
ALFRED? I'M GOING TO NEED YOUR HELP. GET ONLINE AND PURCHASE TWO COMIC-CON PASSES.
SELLING YOUR COLLECTION, MASTER BRUCE?
NO. BUT WE NEED TO ATTEND. ANY LUCK?
UNABLE TO CONNECT. PLEASE TRY AGAIN LATER.
MAYBE.
THIS ONLINE REGISTRATION IS AWFUL. IT KEEPS LOGGING ME OUT OF THE SERVER, EVEN ON YOUR ADVANCED COMPUTER. I'M AFRAID IT'S SOLD OUT.
WHAT WILL YOU DO?
I'M SURE WE'LL THINK OF SOMETHING.
3 DAY

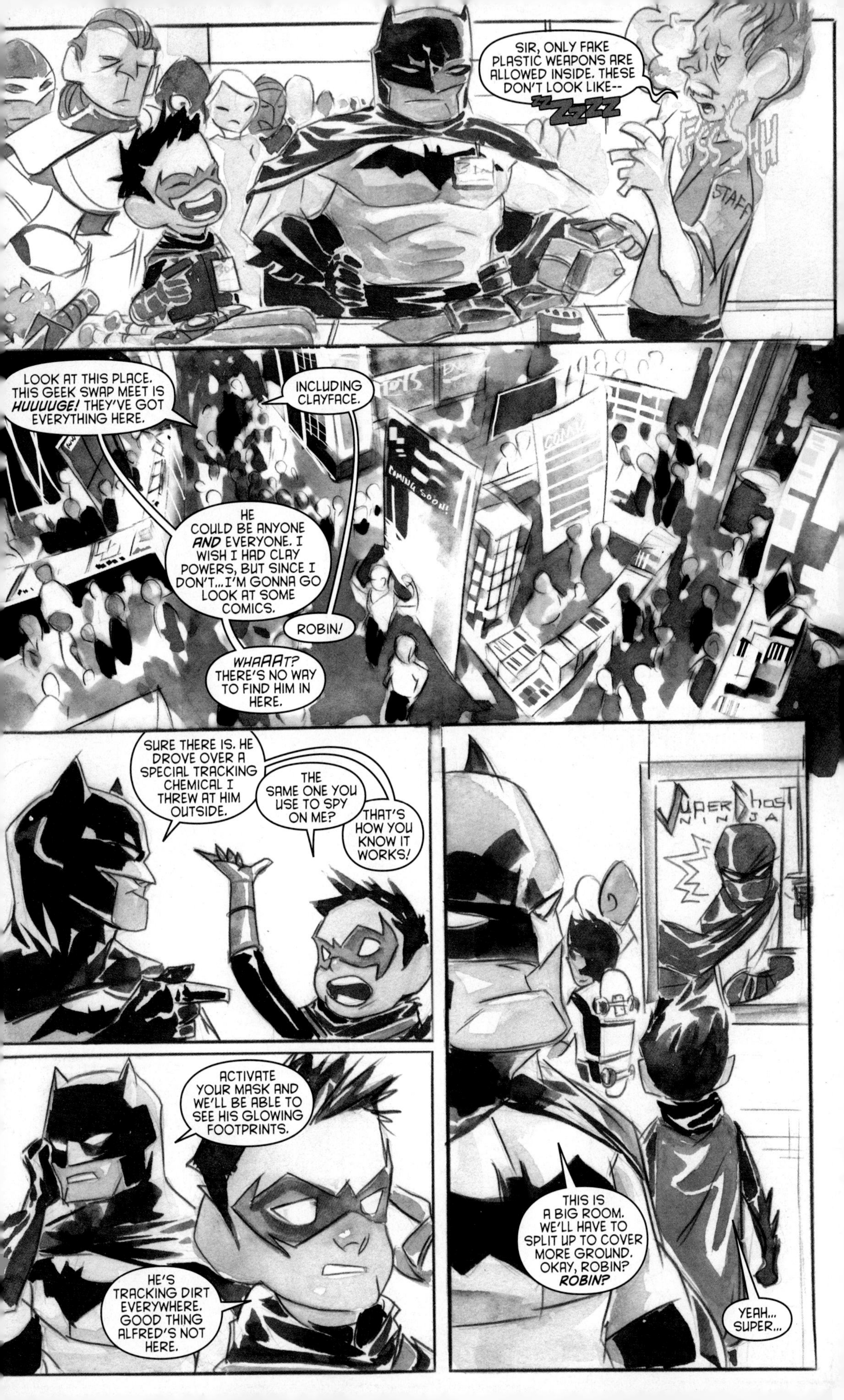
SIR, ONLY FAKE PLASTIC WEAPONS ARE ALLOWED INSIDE. THESE DON'T LOOK LIKE--
ZZZZZ
FSSSHH
STAFF
LOOK AT THIS PLACE. THIS GEEK SWAP MEET IS HUUUUGE! THEY'VE GOT EVERYTHING HERE.
INCLUDING CLAYFACE.
HE COULD BE ANYONE AND EVERYONE. I WISH I HAD CLAY POWERS, BUT SINCE I DON'T...I'M GONNA GO LOOK AT SOME COMICS.
ROBIN!
WHAAAT? THERE'S NO WAY TO FIND HIM IN HERE.
COMING SOON!
SURE THERE IS. HE DROVE OVER A SPECIAL TRACKING CHEMICAL I THREW AT HIM OUTSIDE.
THE SAME ONE YOU USE TO SPY ON ME?
THAT'S HOW YOU KNOW IT WORKS!
ACTIVATE YOUR MASK AND WE'LL BE ABLE TO SEE HIS GLOWING FOOTPRINTS.
HE'S TRACKING DIRT EVERYWHERE. GOOD THING ALFRED'S NOT HERE.
SUPER GHOST NINJA
THIS IS A BIG ROOM. WE'LL HAVE TO SPLIT UP TO COVER MORE GROUND. OKAY, ROBIN? ROBIN?
YEAH... SUPER...

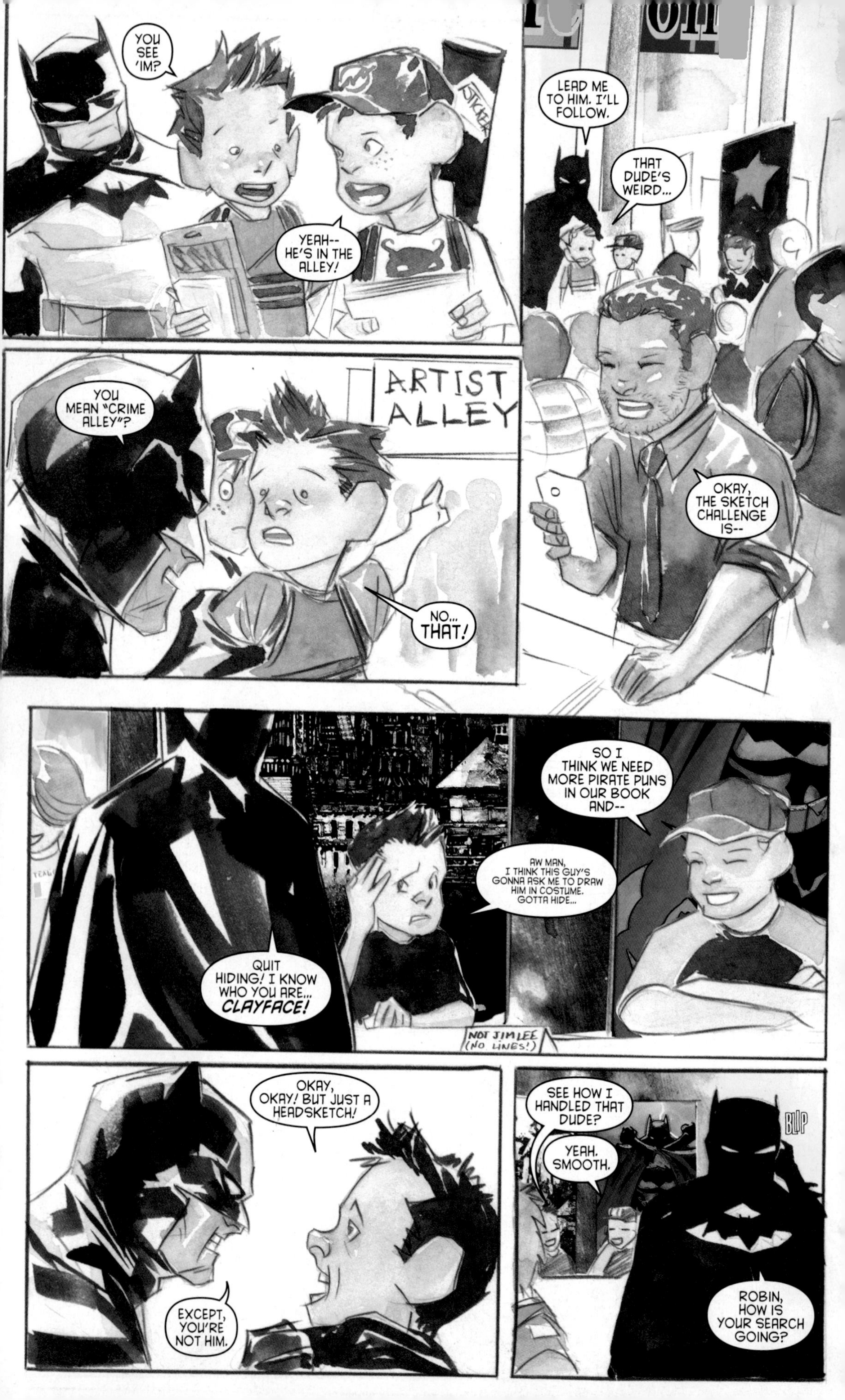
YOU SEE 'IM?
YEAH-- HE'S IN THE ALLEY!
LEAD ME TO HIM. I'LL FOLLOW.
THAT DUDE'S WEIRD...
YOU MEAN "CRIME ALLEY"?
ARTIST ALLEY
NO... THAT!
OKAY, THE SKETCH CHALLENGE IS--
AW MAN, I THINK THIS GUY'S GONNA ASK ME TO DRAW HIM IN COSTUME. GOTTA HIDE...
QUIT HIDING! I KNOW WHO YOU ARE... CLAYFACE!
NOT JIM LEE (NO LINES!)
SO I THINK WE NEED MORE PIRATE PUNS IN OUR BOOK AND--
OKAY, OKAY! BUT JUST A HEADSKETCH!
EXCEPT, YOU'RE NOT HIM.
SEE HOW I HANDLED THAT DUDE?
YEAH. SMOOTH.
BLIP
ROBIN, HOW IS YOUR SEARCH GOING?

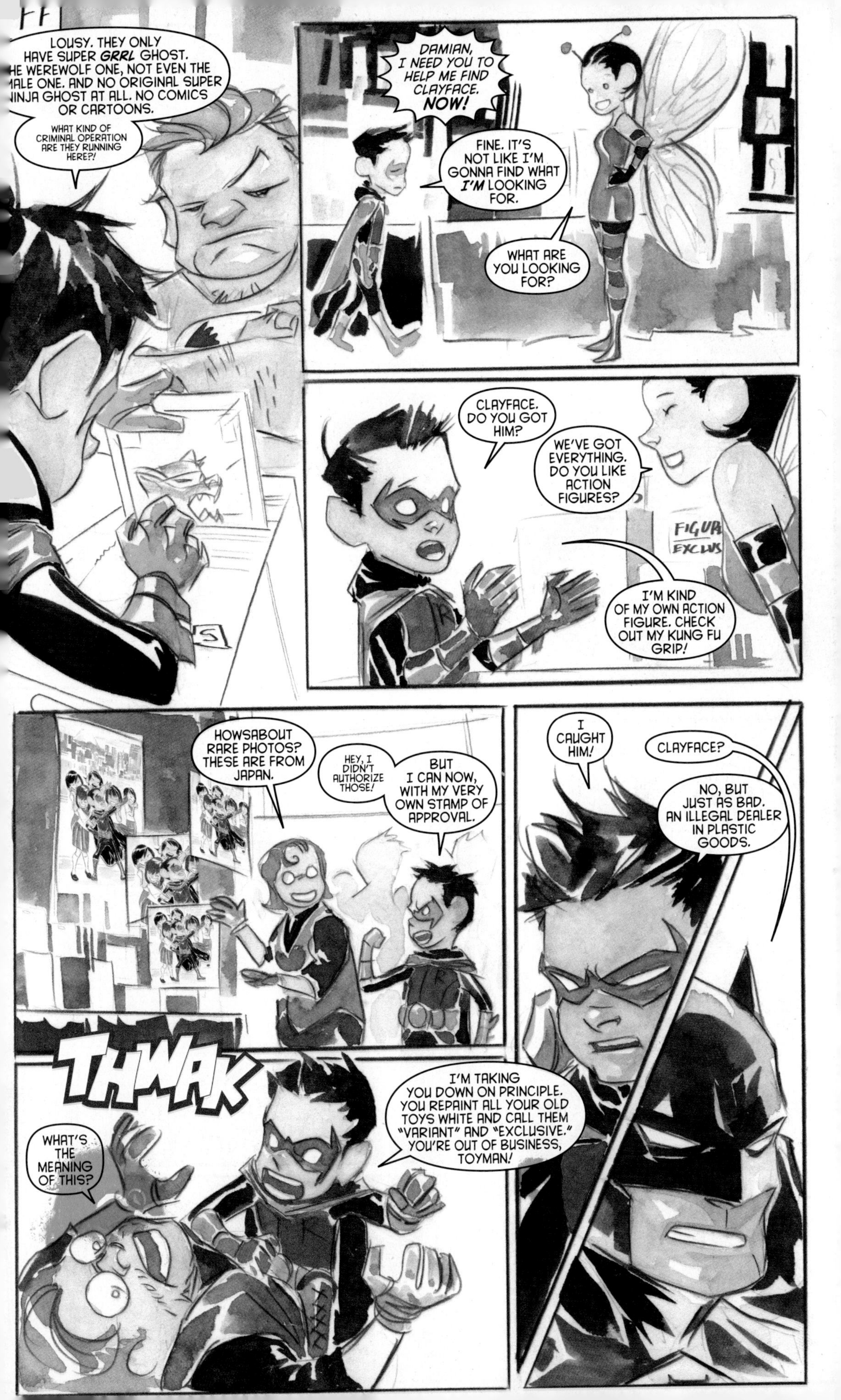
LOUSY. THEY ONLY HAVE SUPER GRRL GHOST. THE WEREWOLF ONE, NOT EVEN THE MALE ONE. AND NO ORIGINAL SUPER NINJA GHOST AT ALL. NO COMICS OR CARTOONS.
WHAT KIND OF CRIMINAL OPERATION ARE THEY RUNNING HERE?!
DAMIAN, I NEED YOU TO HELP ME FIND CLAYFACE. NOW!
FINE. IT'S NOT LIKE I'M GONNA FIND WHAT I'M LOOKING FOR.
WHAT ARE YOU LOOKING FOR?
CLAYFACE. DO YOU GOT HIM?
WE'VE GOT EVERYTHING. DO YOU LIKE ACTION FIGURES?
I'M KIND OF MY OWN ACTION FIGURE. CHECK OUT MY KUNG FU GRIP!
HOWSABOUT RARE PHOTOS? THESE ARE FROM JAPAN.
HEY, I DIDN'T AUTHORIZE THOSE!
BUT I CAN NOW, WITH MY VERY OWN STAMP OF APPROVAL.
THWAK
WHAT'S THE MEANING OF THIS?
I'M TAKING YOU DOWN ON PRINCIPLE. YOU REPAINT ALL YOUR OLD TOYS WHITE AND CALL THEM "VARIANT" AND "EXCLUSIVE." YOU'RE OUT OF BUSINESS, TOYMAN!
I CAUGHT HIM!
CLAYFACE?
NO, BUT JUST AS BAD. AN ILLEGAL DEALER IN PLASTIC GOODS.

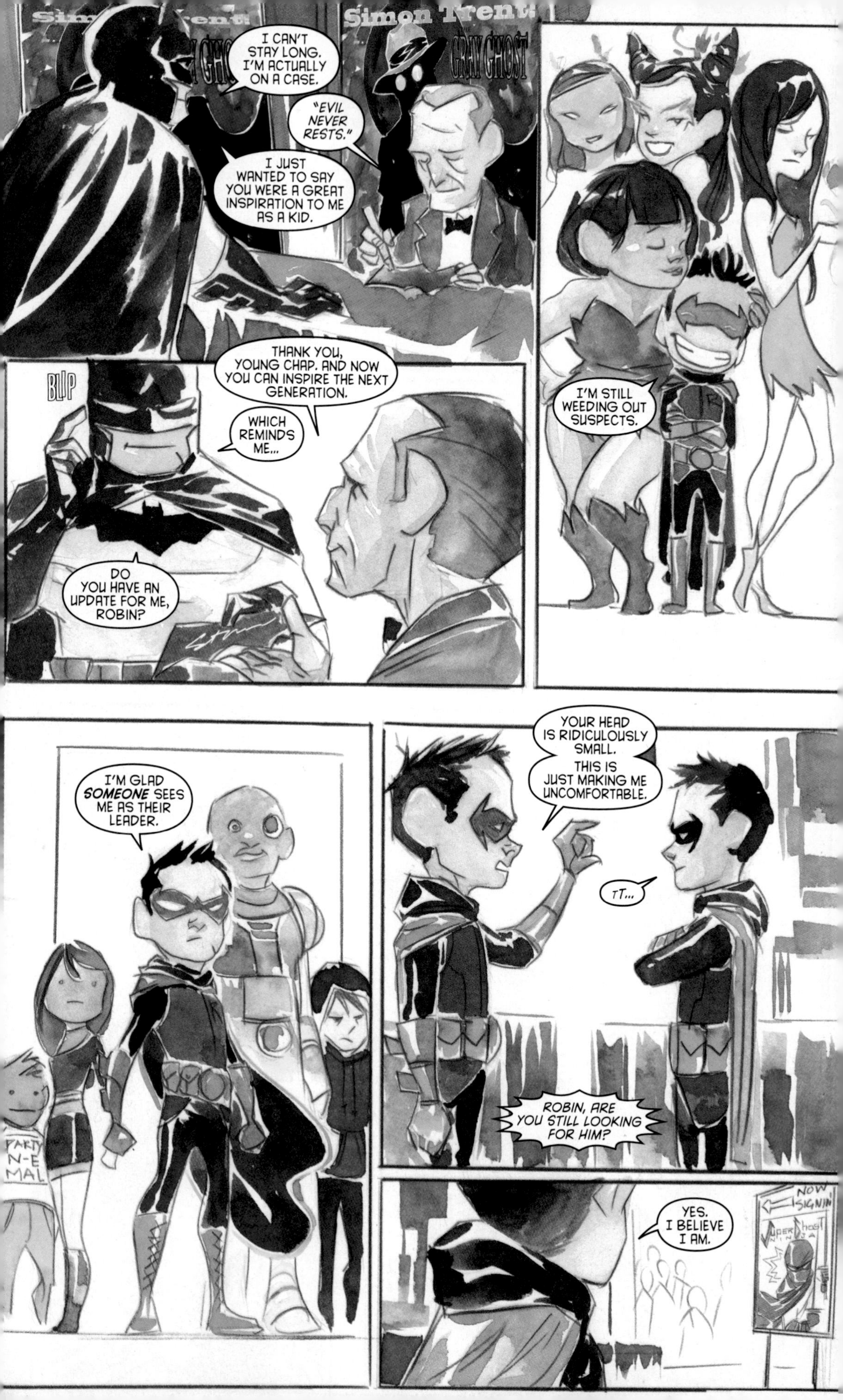
Simon Trent
GRAY GHOST
I CAN'T STAY LONG. I'M ACTUALLY ON A CASE.
"EVIL NEVER RESTS."
I JUST WANTED TO SAY YOU WERE A GREAT INSPIRATION TO ME AS A KID.
BLIP
THANK YOU, YOUNG CHAP. AND NOW YOU CAN INSPIRE THE NEXT GENERATION.
WHICH REMINDS ME...
DO YOU HAVE AN UPDATE FOR ME, ROBIN?
I'M STILL WEEDING OUT SUSPECTS.
I'M GLAD *SOMEONE* SEES ME AS THEIR LEADER.
PARTY N-E MAL
YOUR HEAD IS RIDICULOUSLY SMALL.
THIS IS JUST MAKING ME UNCOMFORTABLE.
TT...
ROBIN, ARE YOU STILL LOOKING FOR HIM?
YES. I BELIEVE I AM.
NOW SIGNIN

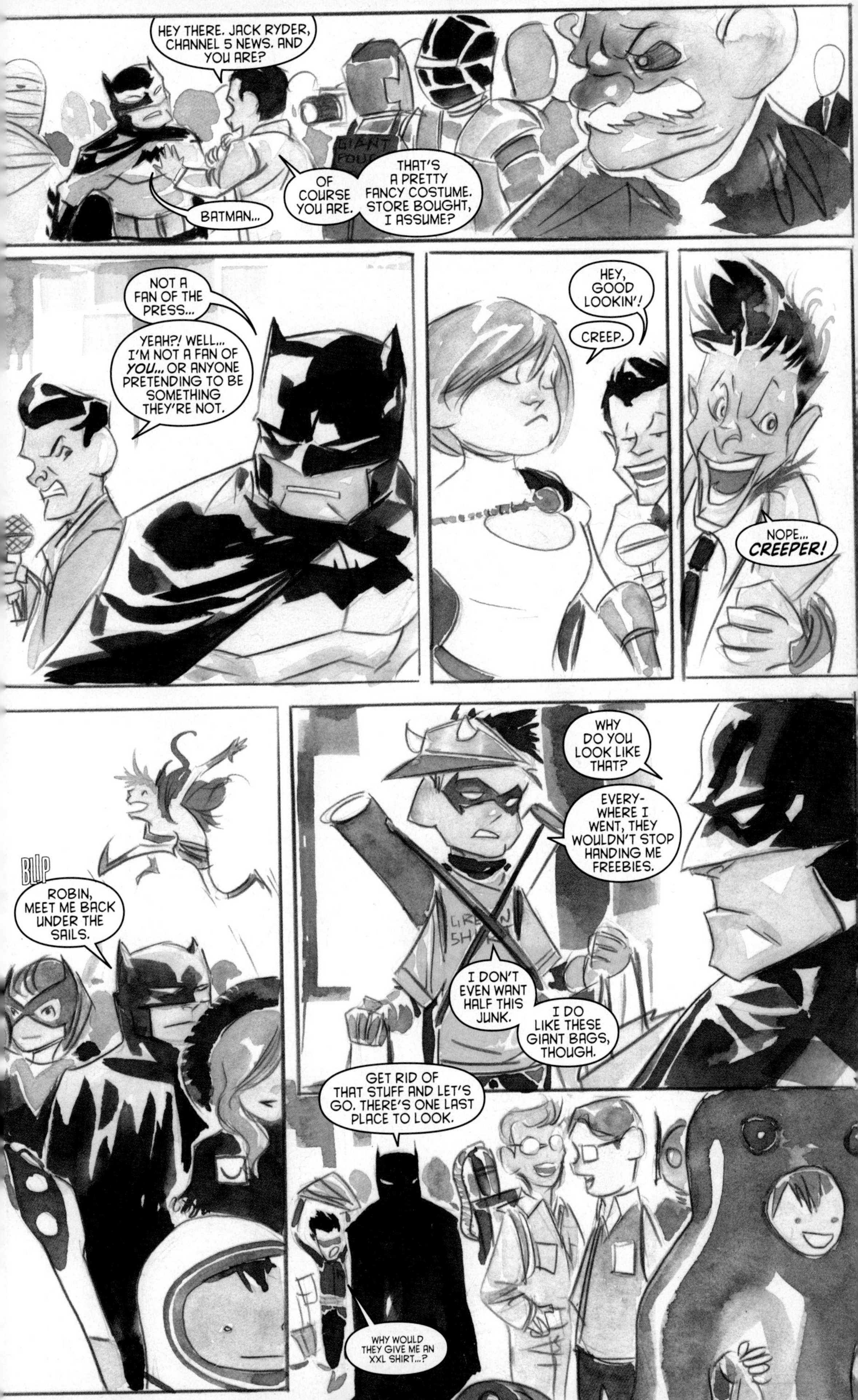
HEY THERE. JACK RYDER, CHANNEL 5 NEWS. AND YOU ARE?
BATMAN...
OF COURSE YOU ARE.
THAT'S A PRETTY FANCY COSTUME. STORE BOUGHT, I ASSUME?
NOT A FAN OF THE PRESS...
YEAH?! WELL... I'M NOT A FAN OF *YOU...* OR ANYONE PRETENDING TO BE SOMETHING THEY'RE NOT.
HEY, GOOD LOOKIN'!
CREEP.
NOPE... *CREEPER!*
BLIP
ROBIN, MEET ME BACK UNDER THE SAILS.
WHY DO YOU LOOK LIKE THAT?
EVERY-WHERE I WENT, THEY WOULDN'T STOP HANDING ME FREEBIES.
I DON'T EVEN WANT HALF THIS JUNK.
I DO LIKE THESE GIANT BAGS, THOUGH.
GET RID OF THAT STUFF AND LET'S GO. THERE'S ONE LAST PLACE TO LOOK.
WHY WOULD THEY GIVE ME AN XXL SHIRT...?

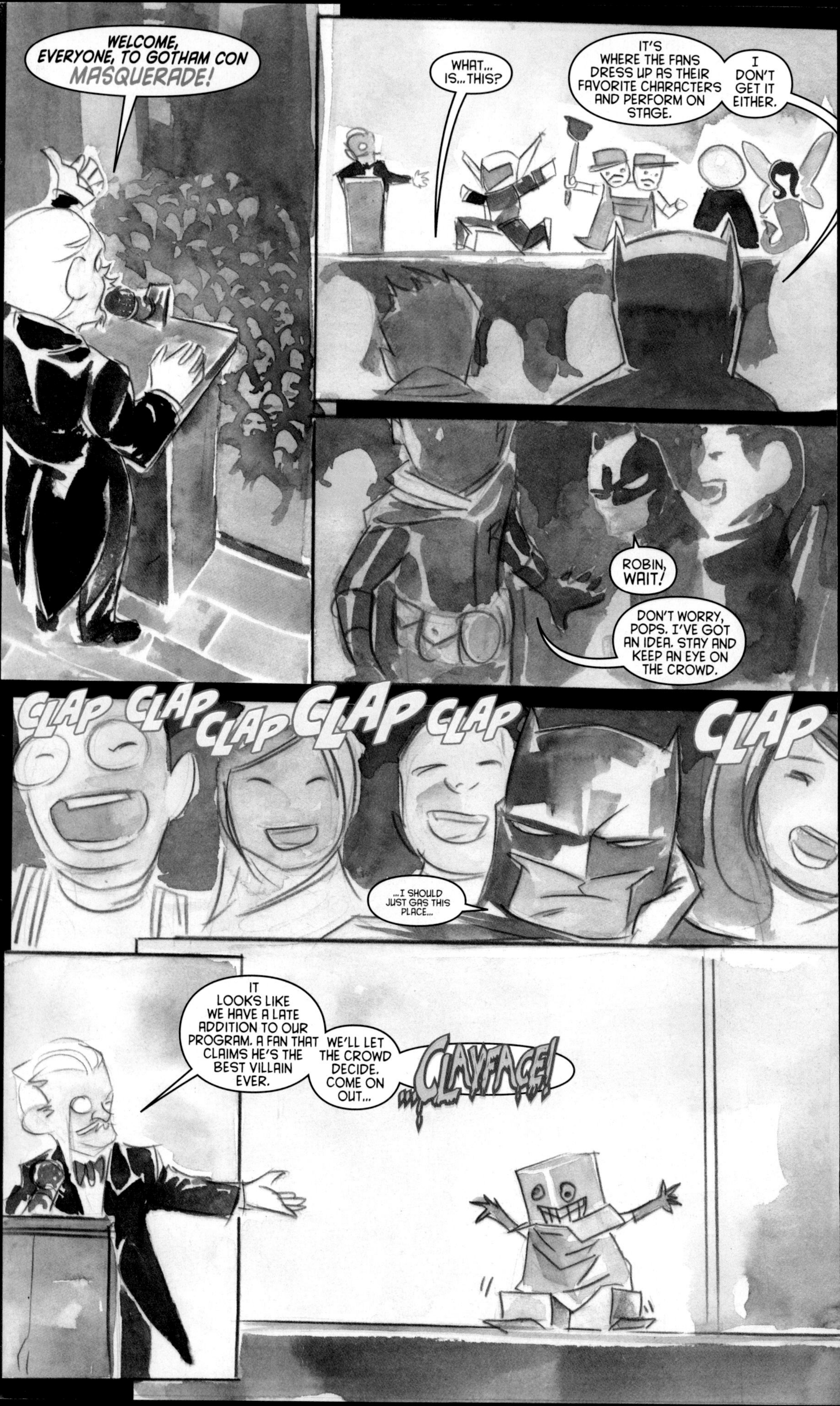

WELCOME, EVERYONE, TO GOTHAM CON MASQUERADE!
WHAT... IS...THIS?
IT'S WHERE THE FANS DRESS UP AS THEIR FAVORITE CHARACTERS AND PERFORM ON STAGE.
I DON'T GET IT EITHER.
ROBIN, WAIT!
DON'T WORRY, POPS. I'VE GOT AN IDEA. STAY AND KEEP AN EYE ON THE CROWD.
CLAP CLAP CLAP CLAP CLAP
CLAP
...I SHOULD JUST GAS THIS PLACE...
IT LOOKS LIKE WE HAVE A LATE ADDITION TO OUR PROGRAM. A FAN THAT CLAIMS HE'S THE BEST VILLAIN EVER.
WE'LL LET THE CROWD DECIDE. COME ON OUT...
...CLAYFACE!

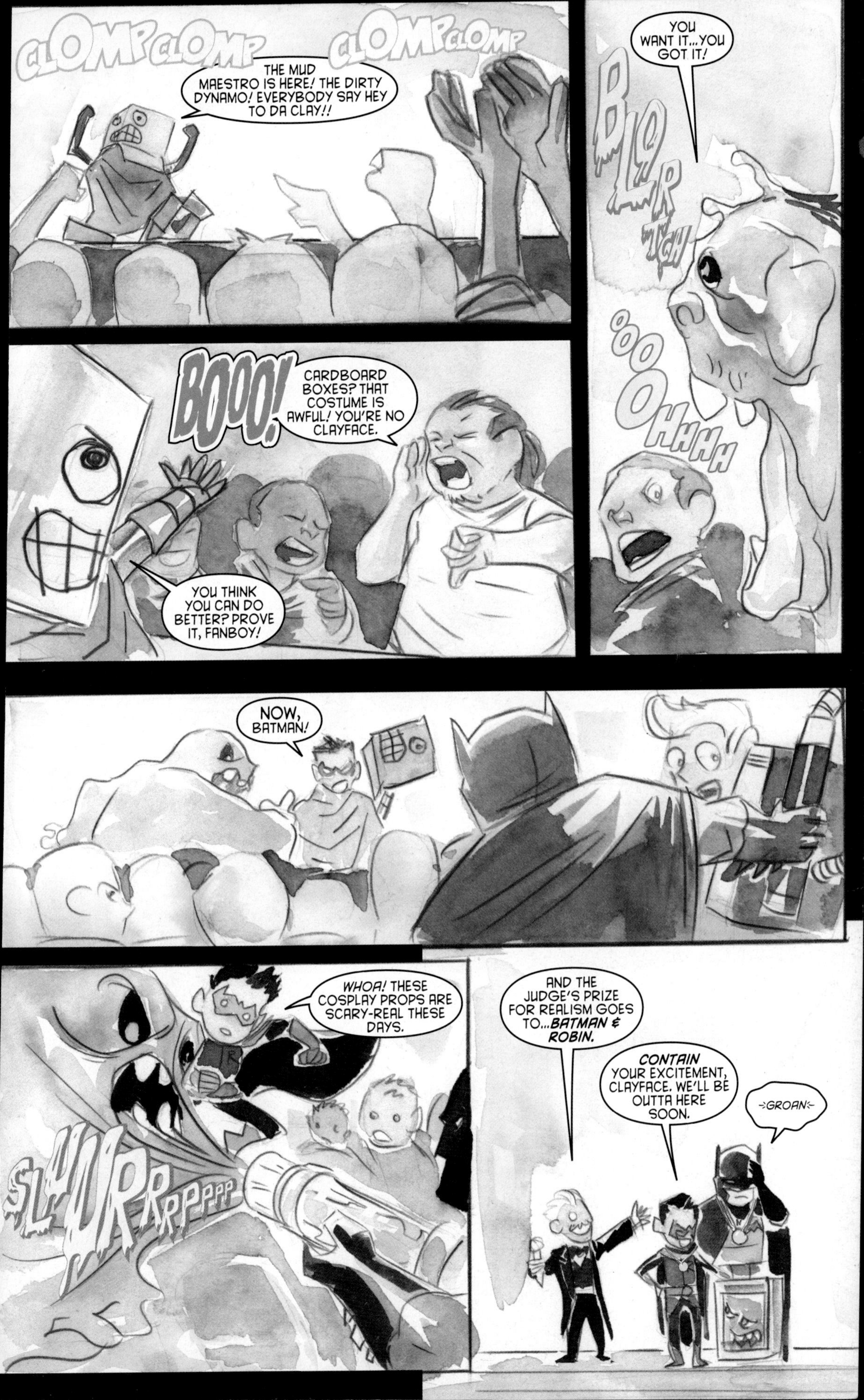
CLOMP CLOMP CLOMP CLOMP
THE MUD MAESTRO IS HERE! THE DIRTY DYNAMO! EVERYBODY SAY HEY TO DA CLAY!!
YOU WANT IT...YOU GOT IT!
BLORTCH
OOOOHHHHH
BOOO!
CARDBOARD BOXES? THAT COSTUME IS AWFUL! YOU'RE NO CLAYFACE.
YOU THINK YOU CAN DO BETTER? PROVE IT, FANBOY!
NOW, BATMAN!
WHOA! THESE COSPLAY PROPS ARE SCARY-REAL THESE DAYS.
SLURRRPPPP
AND THE JUDGE'S PRIZE FOR REALISM GOES TO...BATMAN & ROBIN.
CONTAIN YOUR EXCITEMENT, CLAYFACE. WE'LL BE OUTTA HERE SOON.
GROAN

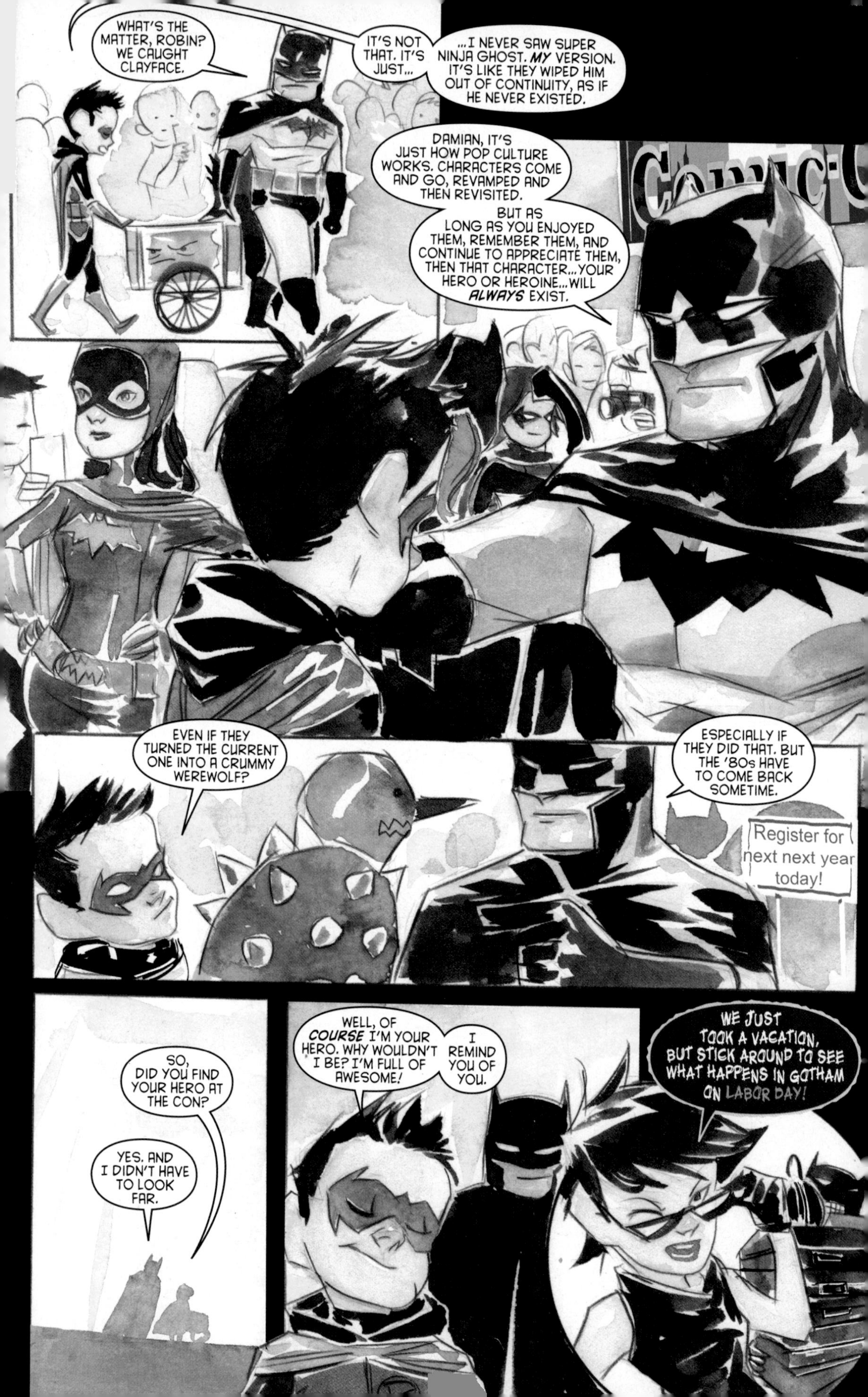
WHAT'S THE MATTER, ROBIN? WE CAUGHT CLAYFACE.
IT'S NOT THAT. IT'S JUST...
...I NEVER SAW SUPER NINJA GHOST. MY VERSION. IT'S LIKE THEY WIPED HIM OUT OF CONTINUITY, AS IF HE NEVER EXISTED.
DAMIAN, IT'S JUST HOW POP CULTURE WORKS. CHARACTERS COME AND GO, REVAMPED AND THEN REVISITED.
BUT AS LONG AS YOU ENJOYED THEM, REMEMBER THEM, AND CONTINUE TO APPRECIATE THEM, THEN THAT CHARACTER...YOUR HERO OR HEROINE...WILL ALWAYS EXIST.
EVEN IF THEY TURNED THE CURRENT ONE INTO A CRUMMY WEREWOLF?
ESPECIALLY IF THEY DID THAT. BUT THE '80s HAVE TO COME BACK SOMETIME.
Register for next next year today!
SO, DID YOU FIND YOUR HERO AT THE CON?
YES. AND I DIDN'T HAVE TO LOOK FAR.
WELL, OF COURSE I'M YOUR HERO. WHY WOULDN'T I BE? I'M FULL OF AWESOME!
I REMIND YOU OF YOU.
WE JUST TOOK A VACATION, BUT STICK AROUND TO SEE WHAT HAPPENS IN GOTHAM ON LABOR DAY!

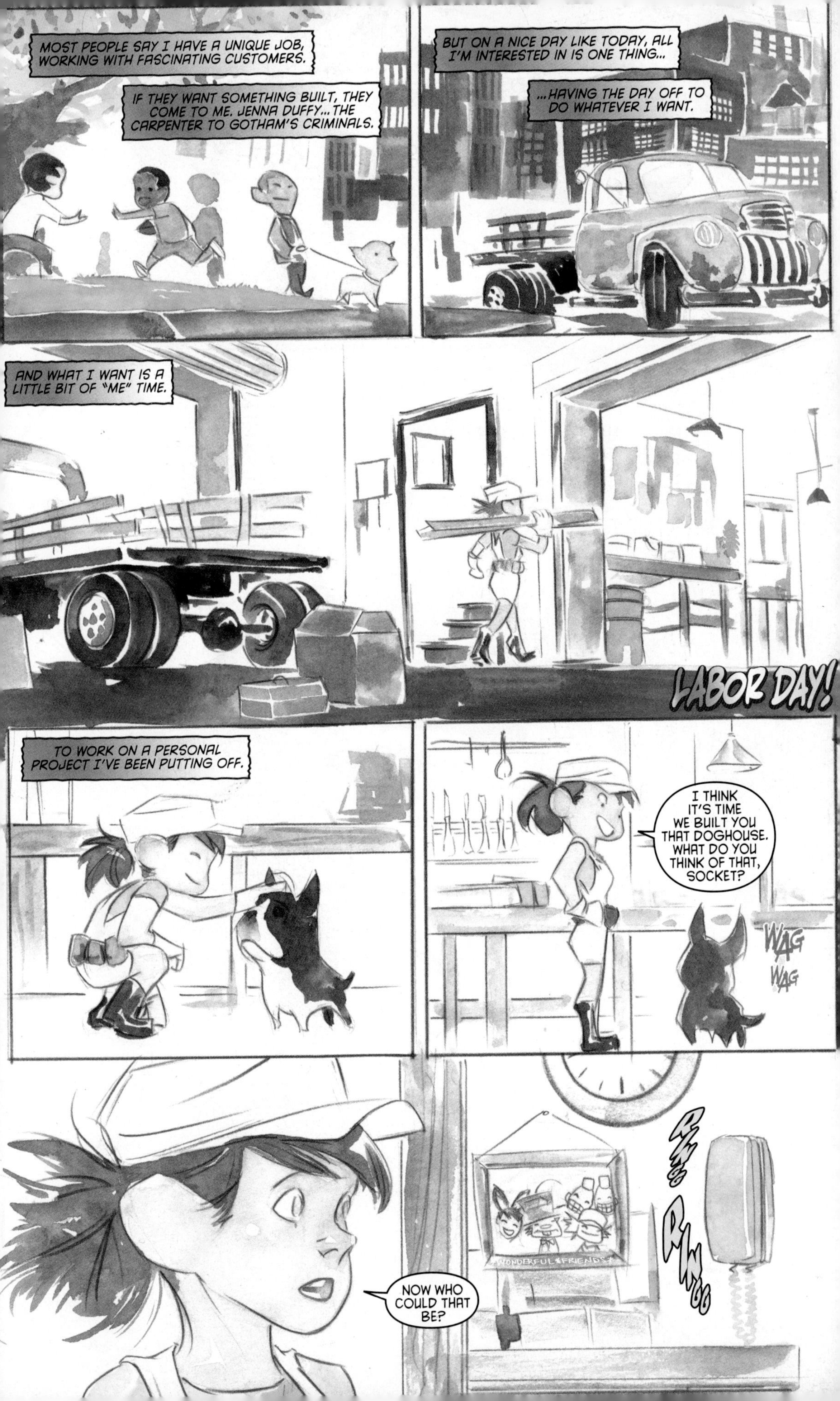
MOST PEOPLE SAY I HAVE A UNIQUE JOB, WORKING WITH FASCINATING CUSTOMERS.
IF THEY WANT SOMETHING BUILT, THEY COME TO ME. JENNA DUFFY... THE CARPENTER TO GOTHAM'S CRIMINALS.
BUT ON A NICE DAY LIKE TODAY, ALL I'M INTERESTED IN IS ONE THING...
...HAVING THE DAY OFF TO DO WHATEVER I WANT.
AND WHAT I WANT IS A LITTLE BIT OF "ME" TIME.
LABOR DAY!
TO WORK ON A PERSONAL PROJECT I'VE BEEN PUTTING OFF.
I THINK IT'S TIME WE BUILT YOU THAT DOGHOUSE. WHAT DO YOU THINK OF THAT, SOCKET?
WAG
WAG
NOW WHO COULD THAT BE?
WONDERFUL FRIENDS
RING
RING

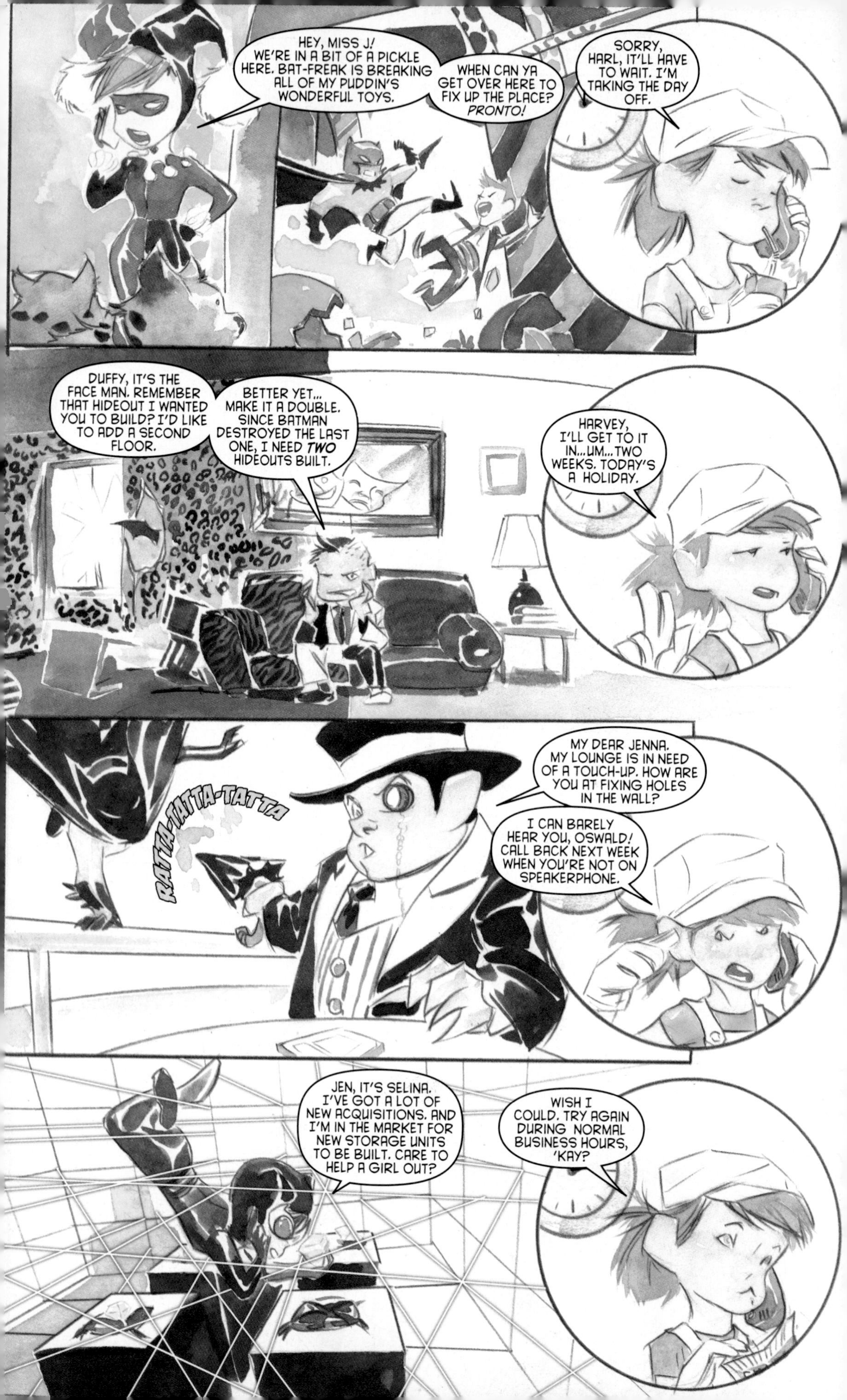
HEY, MISS J! WE'RE IN A BIT OF A PICKLE HERE. BAT-FREAK IS BREAKING ALL OF MY PUDDIN'S WONDERFUL TOYS.
WHEN CAN YA GET OVER HERE TO FIX UP THE PLACE? *PRONTO!*
SORRY, HARL, IT'LL HAVE TO WAIT. I'M TAKING THE DAY OFF.
DUFFY, IT'S THE FACE MAN. REMEMBER THAT HIDEOUT I WANTED YOU TO BUILD? I'D LIKE TO ADD A SECOND FLOOR.
BETTER YET... MAKE IT A DOUBLE. SINCE BATMAN DESTROYED THE LAST ONE, I NEED ***TWO*** HIDEOUTS BUILT.
HARVEY, I'LL GET TO IT IN...UM...TWO WEEKS. TODAY'S A HOLIDAY.
MY DEAR JENNA. MY LOUNGE IS IN NEED OF A TOUCH-UP. HOW ARE YOU AT FIXING HOLES IN THE WALL?
RATTA-TATTA-TATTA
I CAN BARELY HEAR YOU, OSWALD! CALL BACK NEXT WEEK WHEN YOU'RE NOT ON SPEAKERPHONE.
JEN, IT'S SELINA. I'VE GOT A LOT OF NEW ACQUISITIONS. AND I'M IN THE MARKET FOR NEW STORAGE UNITS TO BE BUILT. CARE TO HELP A GIRL OUT?
WISH I COULD. TRY AGAIN DURING NORMAL BUSINESS HOURS, 'KAY?

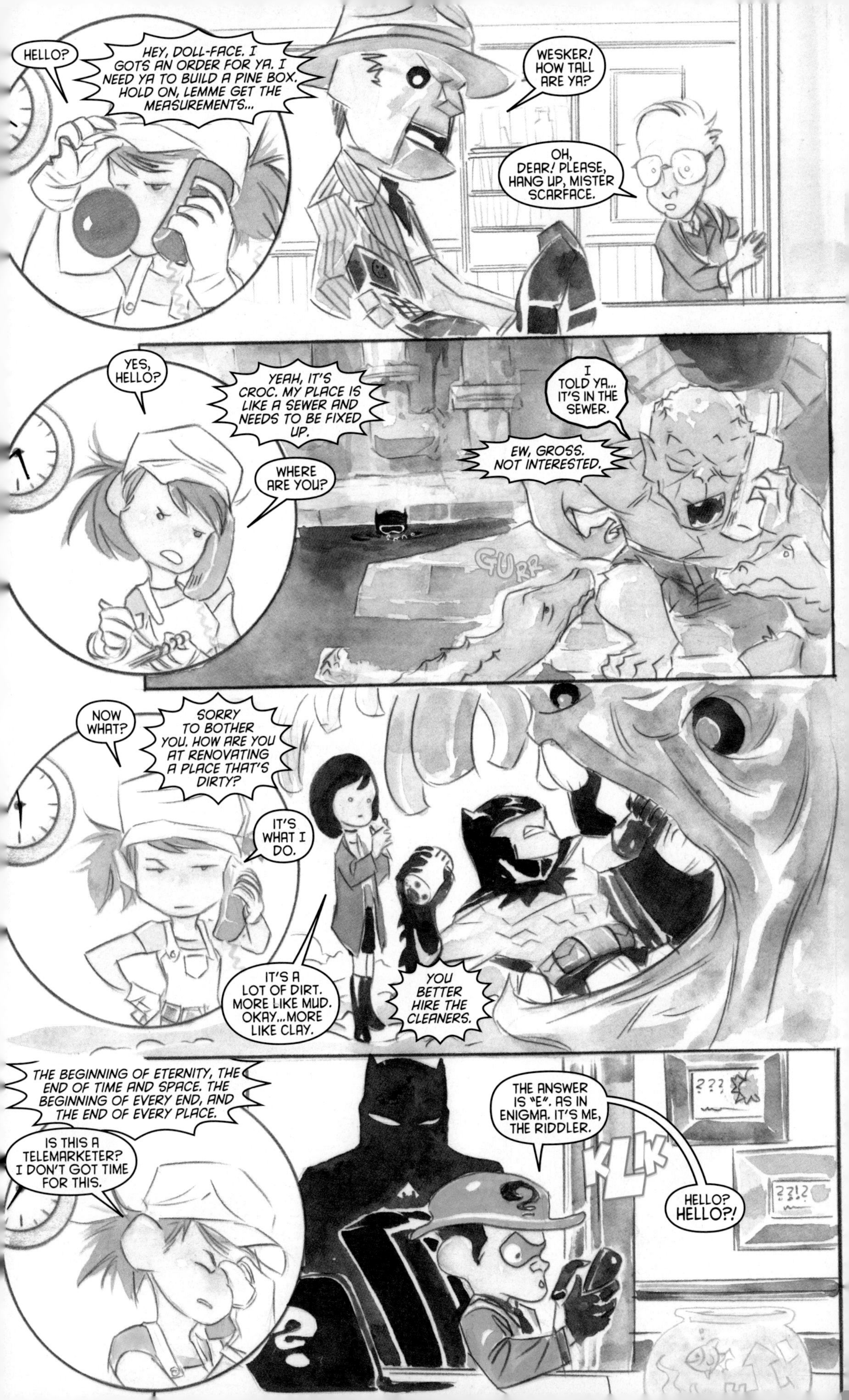
HELLO?
HEY, DOLL-FACE. I GOTS AN ORDER FOR YA. I NEED YA TO BUILD A PINE BOX. HOLD ON, LEMME GET THE MEASUREMENTS...
WESKER! HOW TALL ARE YA?
OH, DEAR! PLEASE, HANG UP, MISTER SCARFACE.
YES, HELLO?
YEAH, IT'S CROC. MY PLACE IS LIKE A SEWER AND NEEDS TO BE FIXED UP.
WHERE ARE YOU?
I TOLD YA... IT'S IN THE SEWER.
EW, GROSS. NOT INTERESTED.
GURR
NOW WHAT?
SORRY TO BOTHER YOU. HOW ARE YOU AT RENOVATING A PLACE THAT'S DIRTY?
IT'S WHAT I DO.
IT'S A LOT OF DIRT. MORE LIKE MUD. OKAY...MORE LIKE CLAY.
YOU BETTER HIRE THE CLEANERS.
THE BEGINNING OF ETERNITY, THE END OF TIME AND SPACE. THE BEGINNING OF EVERY END, AND THE END OF EVERY PLACE.
IS THIS A TELEMARKETER? I DON'T GOT TIME FOR THIS.
THE ANSWER IS "E". AS IN ENIGMA. IT'S ME, THE RIDDLER.
KLIK
HELLO? HELLO?!

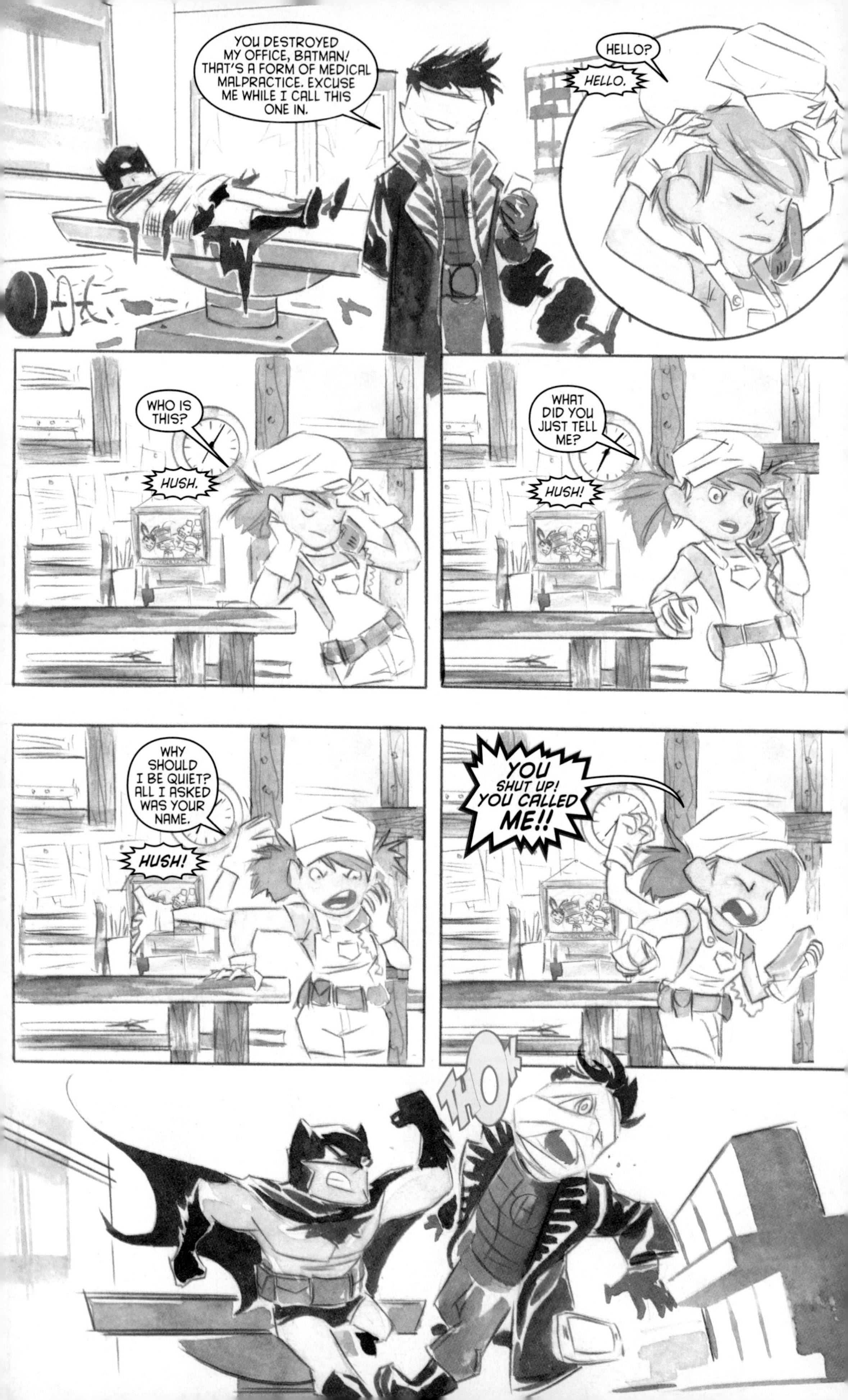
YOU DESTROYED MY OFFICE, BATMAN! THAT'S A FORM OF MEDICAL MALPRACTICE. EXCUSE ME WHILE I CALL THIS ONE IN.
HELLO?
HELLO.
WHO IS THIS?
HUSH.
WHAT DID YOU JUST TELL ME?
HUSH!
WHY SHOULD I BE QUIET? ALL I ASKED WAS YOUR NAME.
HUSH!
YOU SHUT UP! YOU CALLED ME!!
THOK

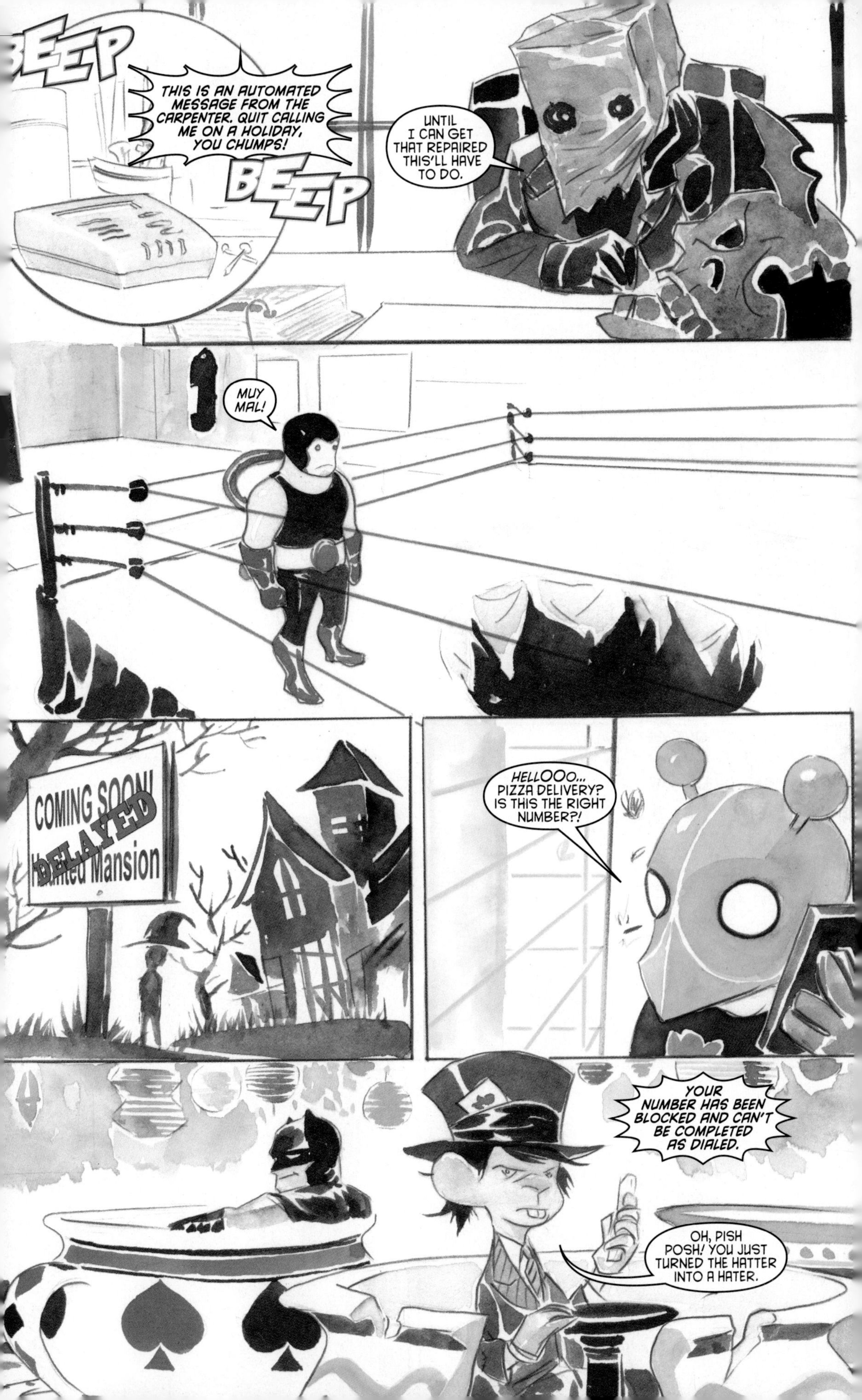
BEEP
THIS IS AN AUTOMATED MESSAGE FROM THE CARPENTER. QUIT CALLING ME ON A HOLIDAY, YOU CHUMPS!
BEEP
UNTIL I CAN GET THAT REPAIRED THIS'LL HAVE TO DO.
MUY MAL!
COMING SOON!
DELAYED
Haunted Mansion
HELLOOo... PIZZA DELIVERY? IS THIS THE RIGHT NUMBER?!
YOUR NUMBER HAS BEEN BLOCKED AND CAN'T BE COMPLETED AS DIALED.
OH, PISH POSH! YOU JUST TURNED THE HATTER INTO A HATER.

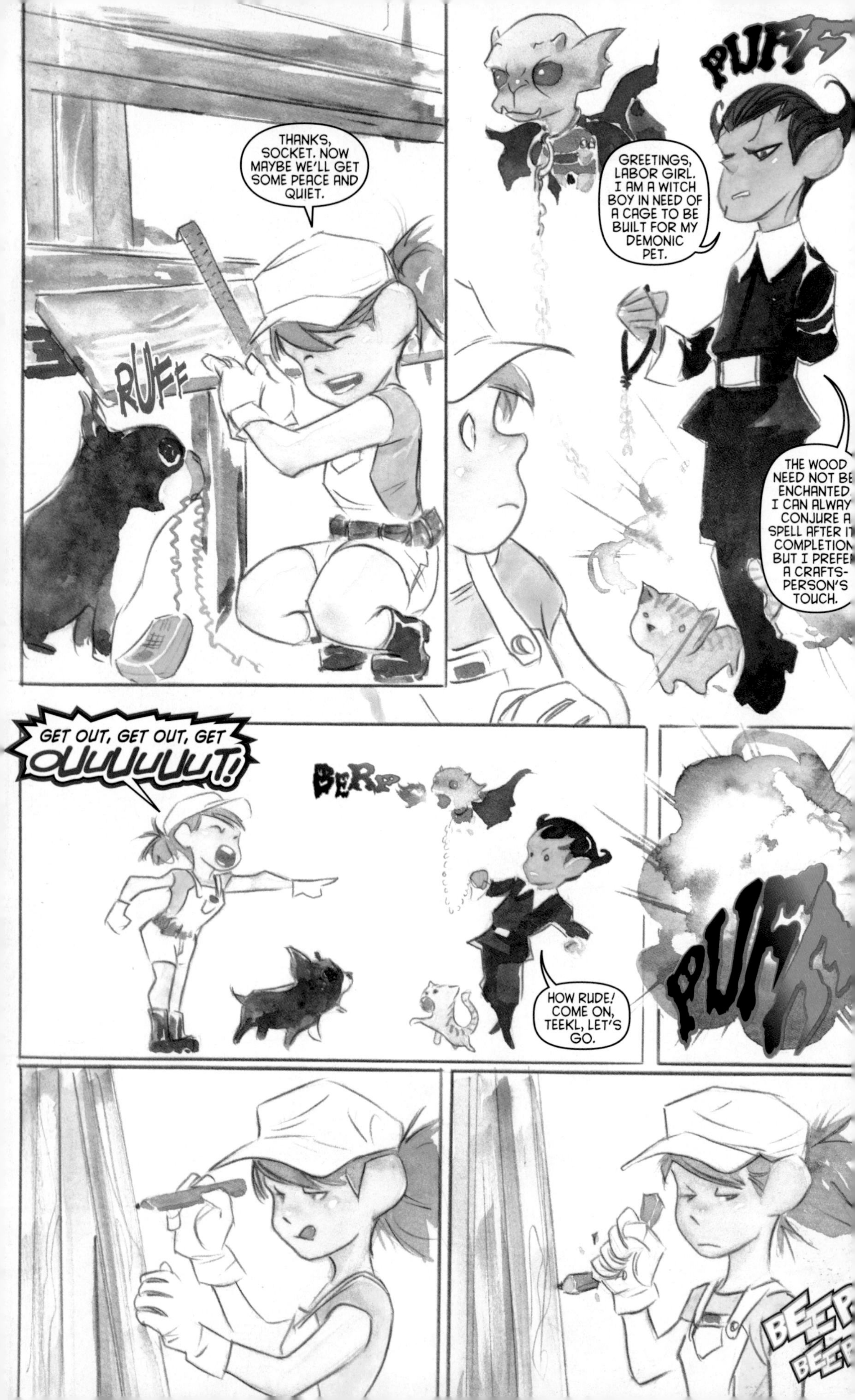
THANKS, SOCKET. NOW MAYBE WE'LL GET SOME PEACE AND QUIET.
RUFF
PUFF
GREETINGS, LABOR GIRL. I AM A WITCH BOY IN NEED OF A CAGE TO BE BUILT FOR MY DEMONIC PET.
THE WOOD NEED NOT BE ENCHANTED. I CAN ALWAYS CONJURE A SPELL AFTER ITS COMPLETION, BUT I PREFER A CRAFTS-PERSON'S TOUCH.
GET OUT, GET OUT, GET OUUUUUUT!
BERP
HOW RUDE! COME ON, TEEKL, LET'S GO.
PUFF
BEEP BEEP

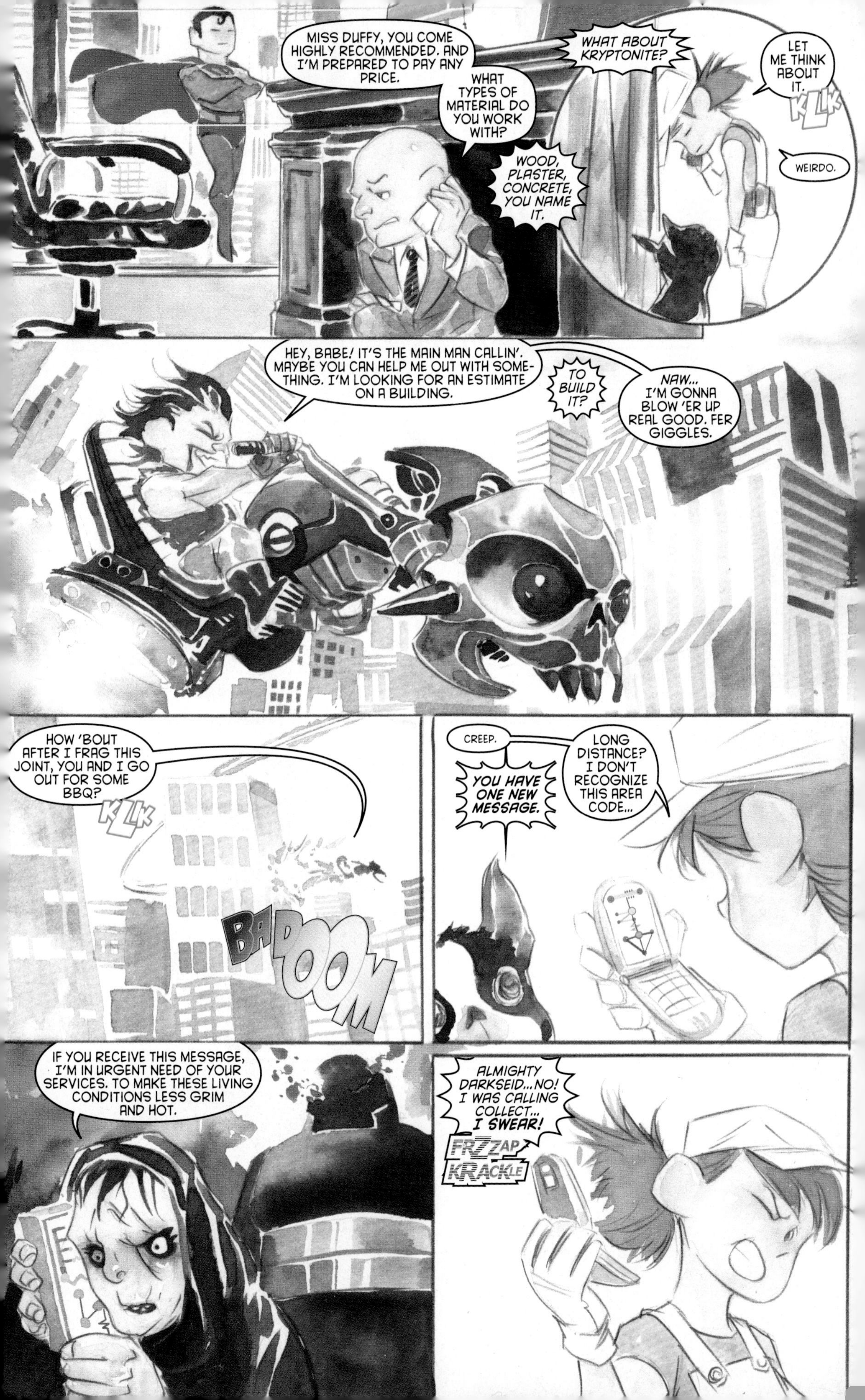
MISS DUFFY, YOU COME HIGHLY RECOMMENDED. AND I'M PREPARED TO PAY ANY PRICE.
WHAT TYPES OF MATERIAL DO YOU WORK WITH?
WOOD, PLASTER, CONCRETE, YOU NAME IT.
WHAT ABOUT KRYPTONITE?
LET ME THINK ABOUT IT.
KLIK
WEIRDO.
HEY, BABE! IT'S THE MAIN MAN CALLIN'. MAYBE YOU CAN HELP ME OUT WITH SOMETHING. I'M LOOKING FOR AN ESTIMATE ON A BUILDING.
TO BUILD IT?
NAW... I'M GONNA BLOW 'ER UP REAL GOOD. FER GIGGLES.
HOW 'BOUT AFTER I FRAG THIS JOINT, YOU AND I GO OUT FOR SOME BBQ?
KLIK
BADOOM
CREEP.
LONG DISTANCE? I DON'T RECOGNIZE THIS AREA CODE...
YOU HAVE ONE NEW MESSAGE.
IF YOU RECEIVE THIS MESSAGE, I'M IN URGENT NEED OF YOUR SERVICES. TO MAKE THESE LIVING CONDITIONS LESS GRIM AND HOT.
ALMIGHTY DARKSEID... NO! I WAS CALLING COLLECT... I SWEAR!
FRZZAP
KRACKLE

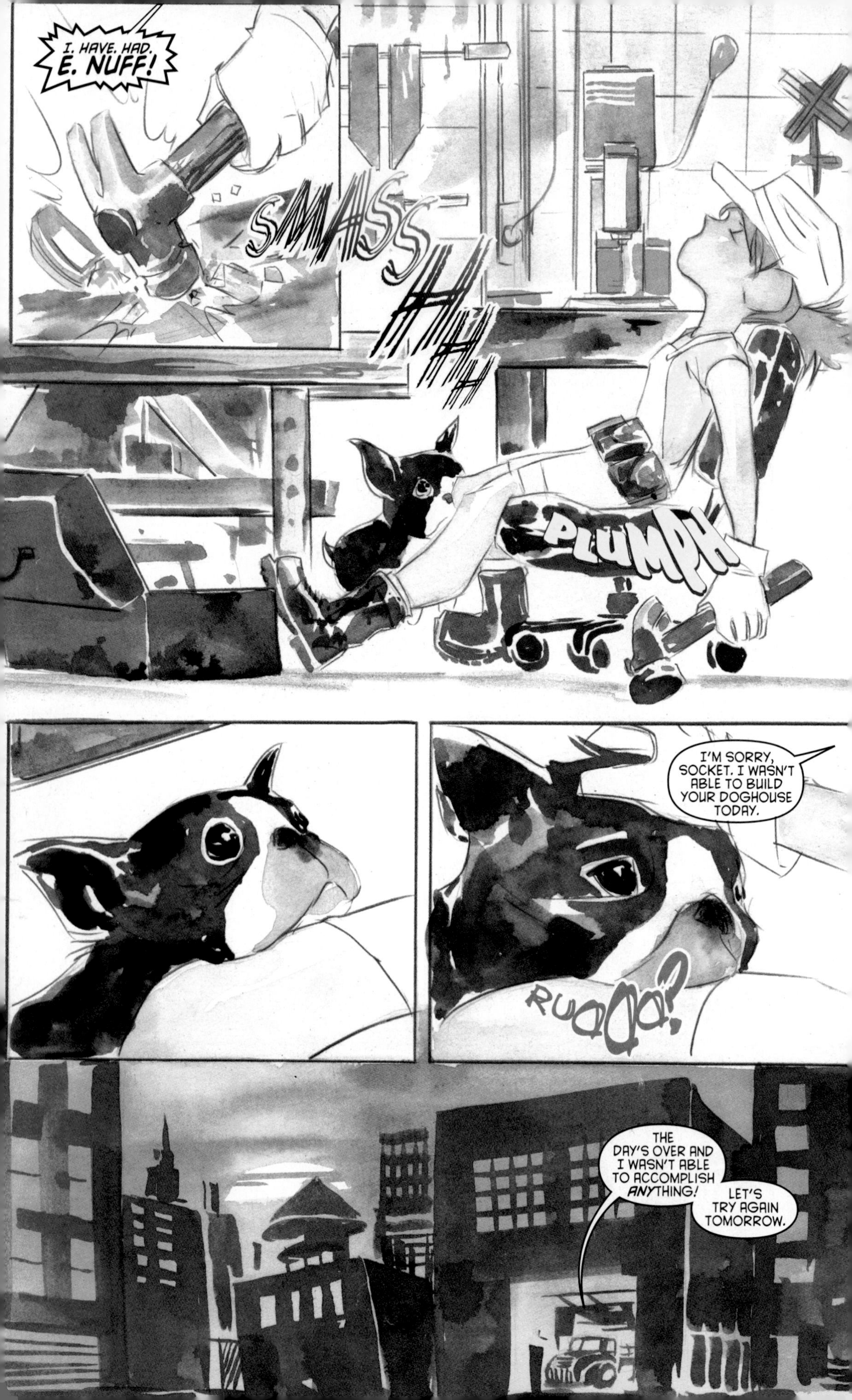
I. HAVE. HAD. E. NUFF!
SMASSHHH
PLUMPH
I'M SORRY, SOCKET. I WASN'T ABLE TO BUILD YOUR DOGHOUSE TODAY.
RUAAA?
THE DAY'S OVER AND I WASN'T ABLE TO ACCOMPLISH ANYTHING!
LET'S TRY AGAIN TOMORROW.

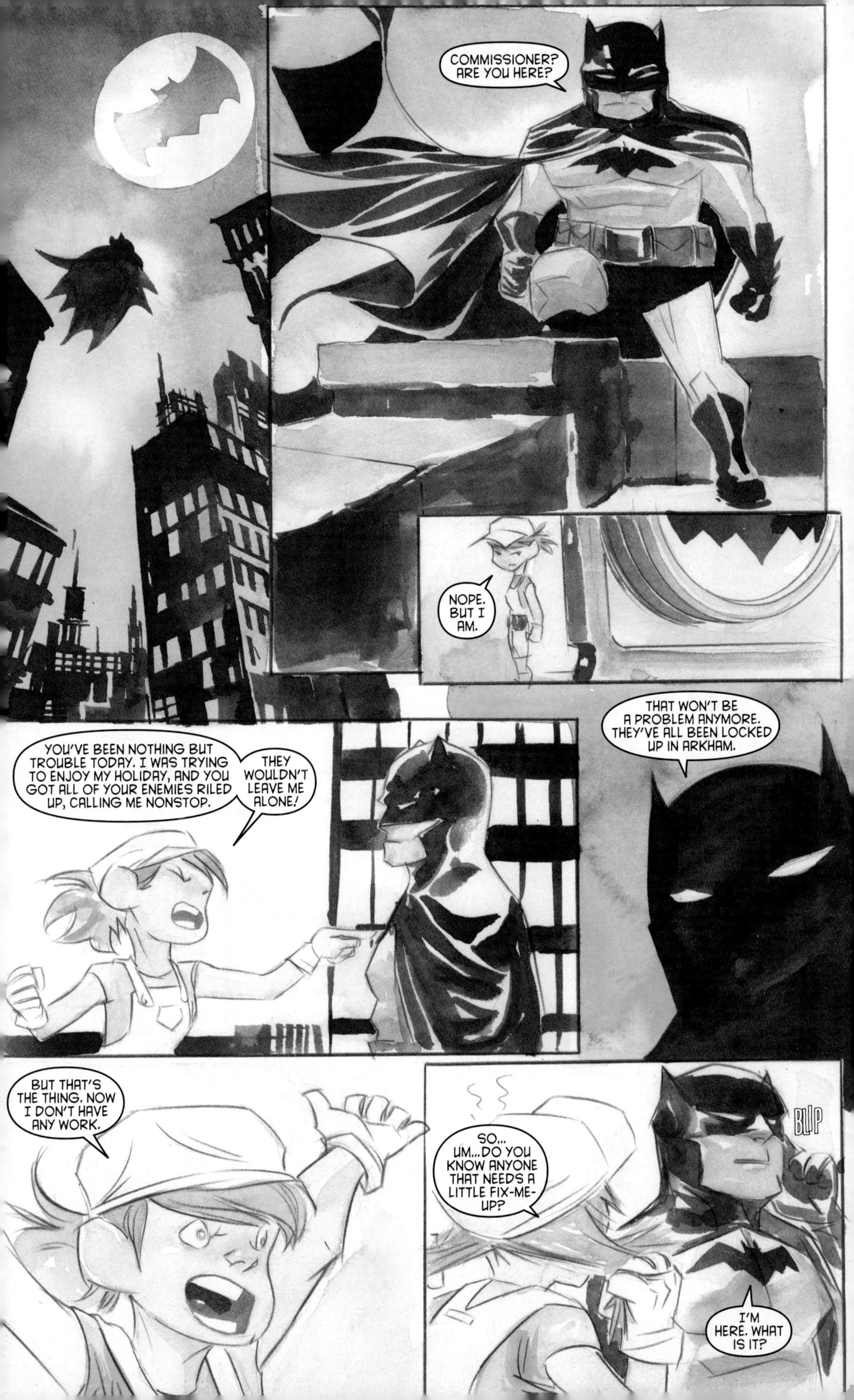
COMMISSIONER? ARE YOU HERE?
NOPE. BUT I AM.
YOU'VE BEEN NOTHING BUT TROUBLE TODAY. I WAS TRYING TO ENJOY MY HOLIDAY, AND YOU GOT ALL OF YOUR ENEMIES RILED UP, CALLING ME NONSTOP.
THEY WOULDN'T LEAVE ME ALONE!
THAT WON'T BE A PROBLEM ANYMORE. THEY'VE ALL BEEN LOCKED UP IN ARKHAM.
BUT THAT'S THE THING. NOW I DON'T HAVE ANY WORK.
SO... UM...DO YOU KNOW ANYONE THAT NEEDS A LITTLE FIX-ME-UP?
BLIP
I'M HERE. WHAT IS IT?

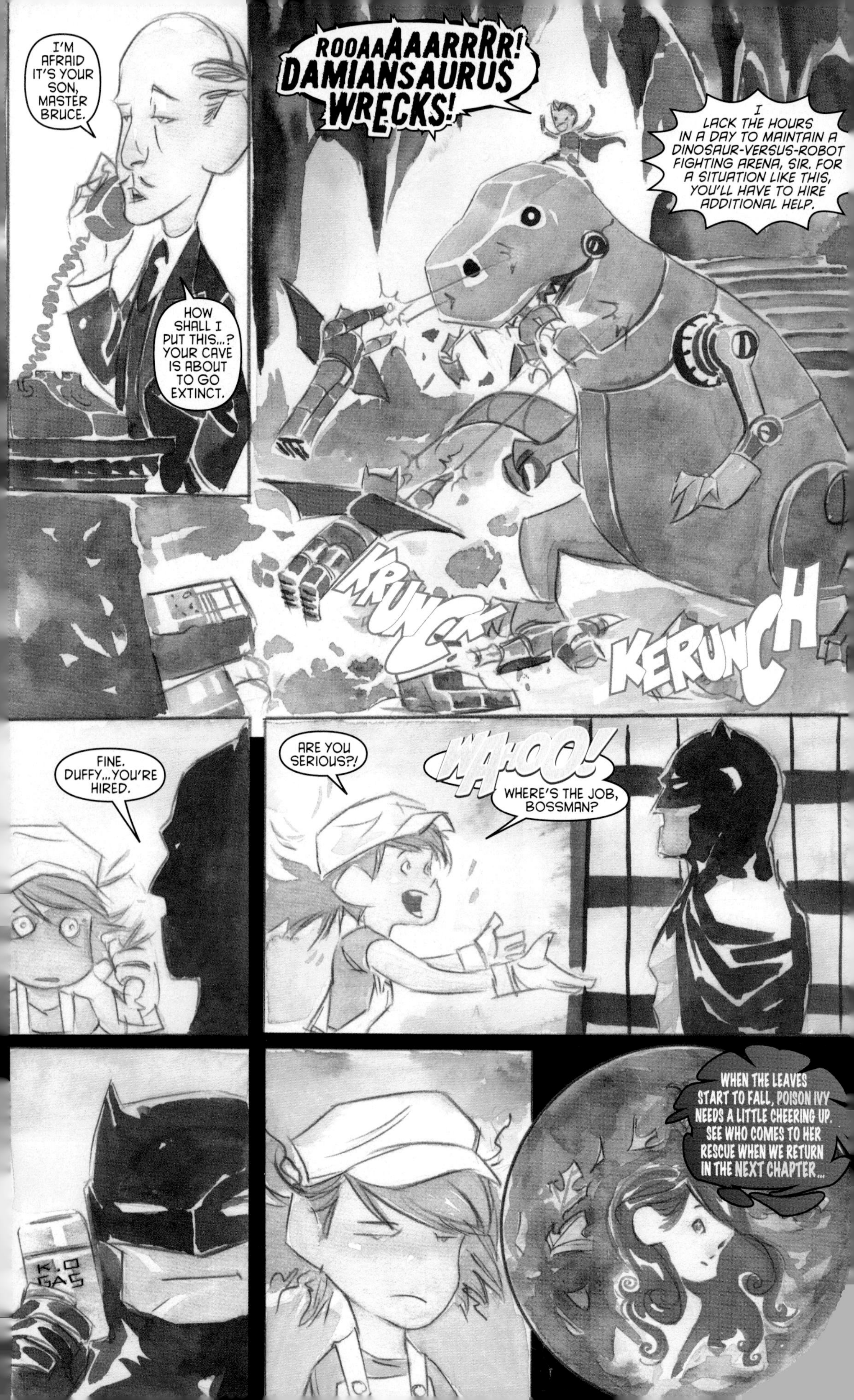
I'M AFRAID IT'S YOUR SON, MASTER BRUCE.
ROOOAAAAARRRRR! DAMIANSAURUS WRECKS!
I LACK THE HOURS IN A DAY TO MAINTAIN A DINOSAUR-VERSUS-ROBOT FIGHTING ARENA, SIR. FOR A SITUATION LIKE THIS, YOU'LL HAVE TO HIRE ADDITIONAL HELP.
HOW SHALL I PUT THIS...? YOUR CAVE IS ABOUT TO GO EXTINCT.
KRUNCH
KERUNCH
FINE. DUFFY... YOU'RE HIRED.
ARE YOU SERIOUS?!
WAHOO!
WHERE'S THE JOB, BOSSMAN?
K.O GAS
WHEN THE LEAVES START TO FALL, POISON IVY NEEDS A LITTLE CHEERING UP. SEE WHO COMES TO HER RESCUE WHEN WE RETURN IN THE NEXT CHAPTER...

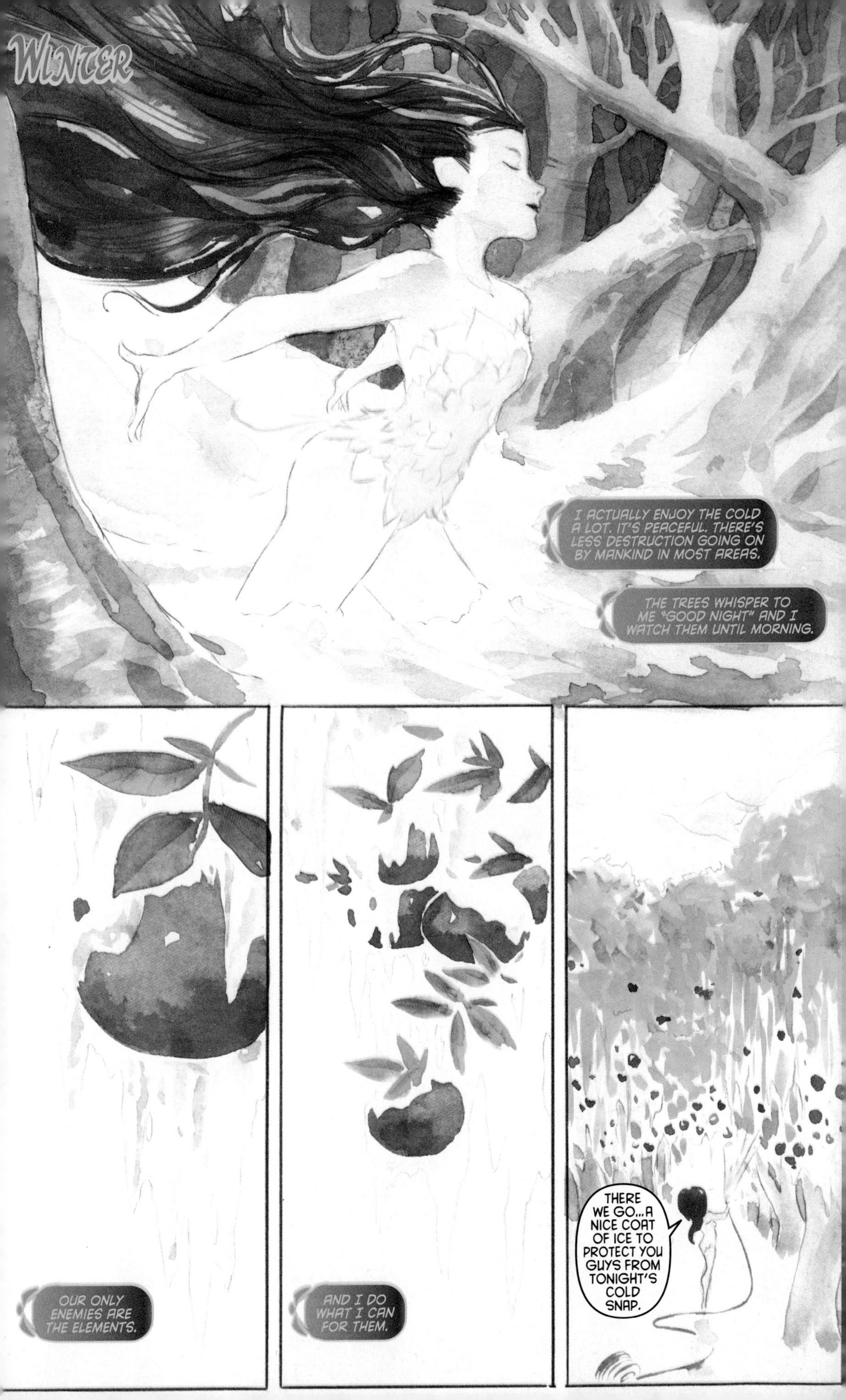
WINTER
I ACTUALLY ENJOY THE COLD A LOT. IT'S PEACEFUL. THERE'S LESS DESTRUCTION GOING ON BY MANKIND IN MOST AREAS.
THE TREES WHISPER TO ME "GOOD NIGHT" AND I WATCH THEM UNTIL MORNING.
OUR ONLY ENEMIES ARE THE ELEMENTS.
AND I DO WHAT I CAN FOR THEM.
THERE WE GO...A NICE COAT OF ICE TO PROTECT YOU GUYS FROM TONIGHT'S COLD SNAP.

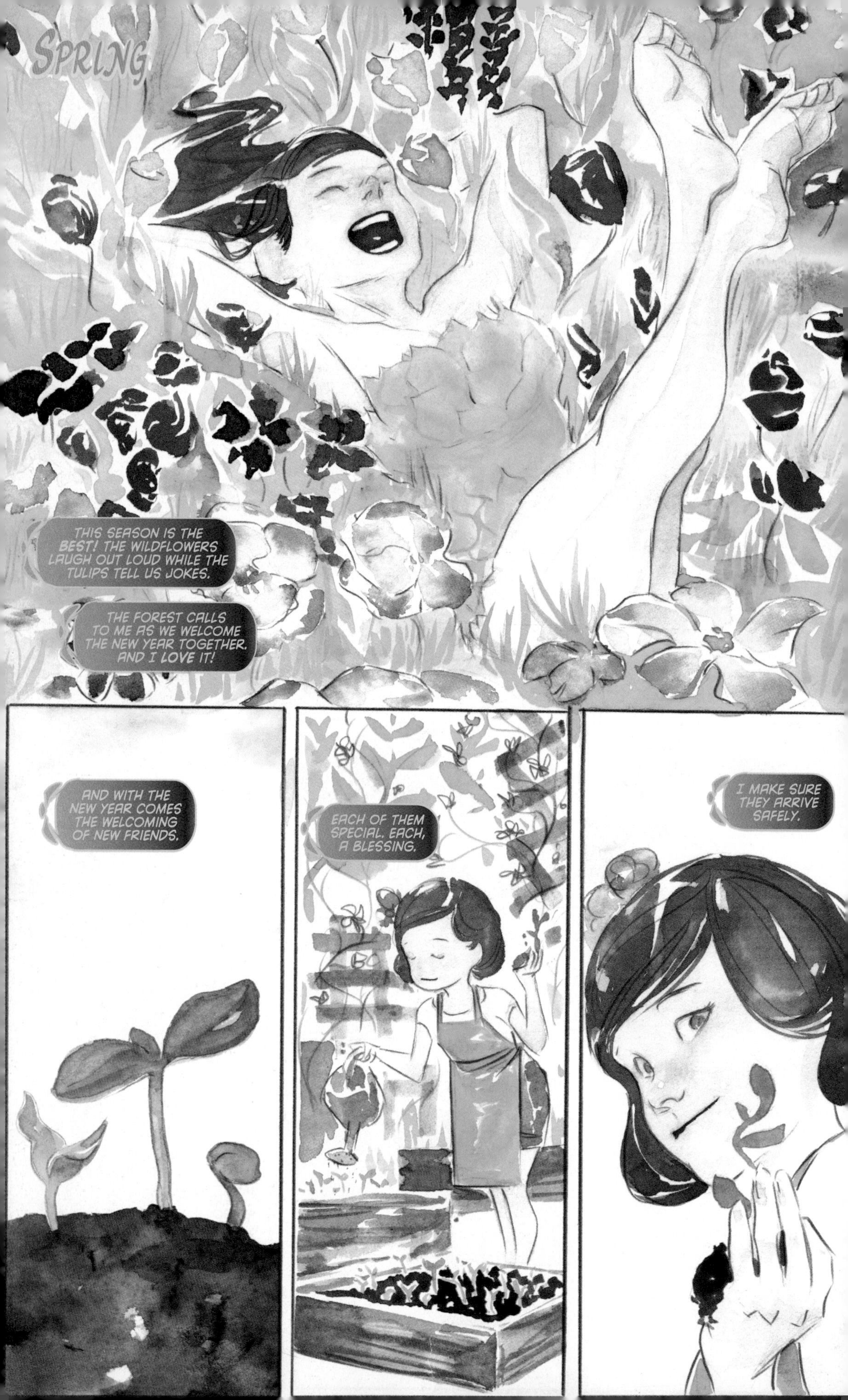
SPRING
THIS SEASON IS THE BEST! THE WILDFLOWERS LAUGH OUT LOUD WHILE THE TULIPS TELL US JOKES.
THE FOREST CALLS TO ME AS WE WELCOME THE NEW YEAR TOGETHER. AND I LOVE IT!
AND WITH THE NEW YEAR COMES THE WELCOMING OF NEW FRIENDS.
EACH OF THEM SPECIAL. EACH, A BLESSING.
I MAKE SURE THEY ARRIVE SAFELY.

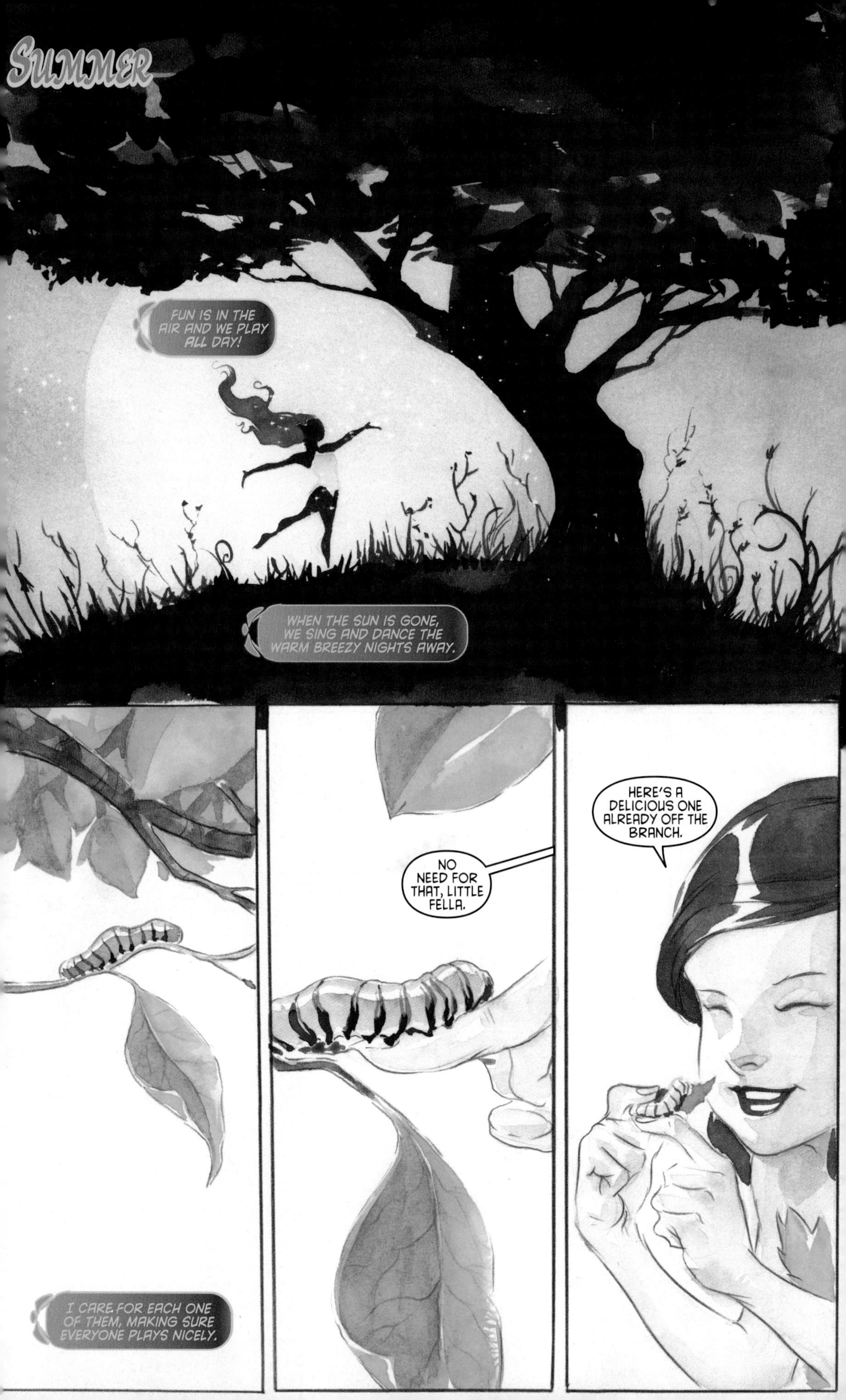
SUMMER
FUN IS IN THE AIR AND WE PLAY ALL DAY!
WHEN THE SUN IS GONE, WE SING AND DANCE THE WARM BREEZY NIGHTS AWAY.
I CARE FOR EACH ONE OF THEM, MAKING SURE EVERYONE PLAYS NICELY.
NO NEED FOR THAT, LITTLE FELLA.
HERE'S A DELICIOUS ONE ALREADY OFF THE BRANCH.

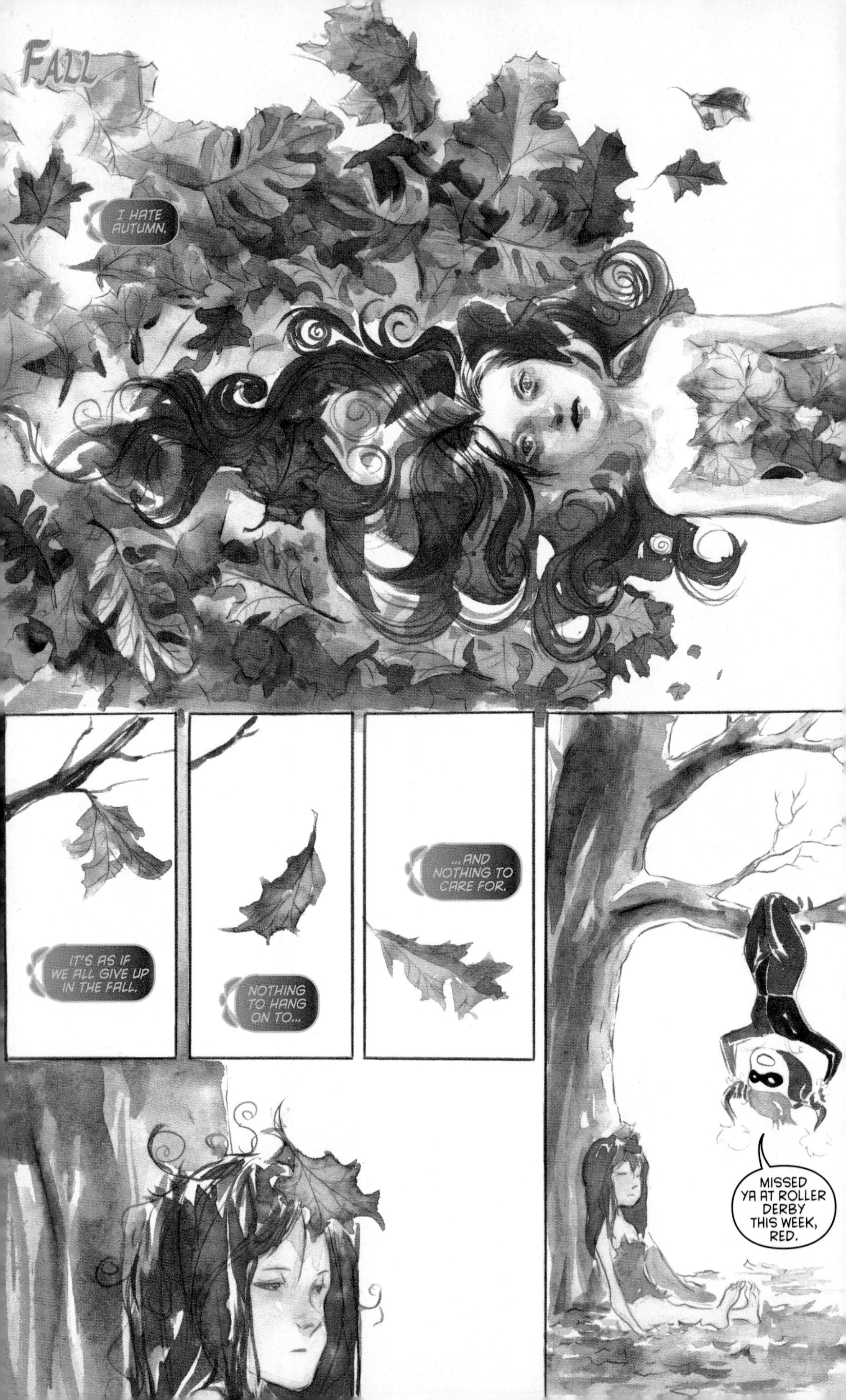
FALL
I HATE AUTUMN.
IT'S AS IF WE ALL GIVE UP IN THE FALL.
NOTHING TO HANG ON TO...
...AND NOTHING TO CARE FOR.
MISSED YA AT ROLLER DERBY THIS WEEK, RED.

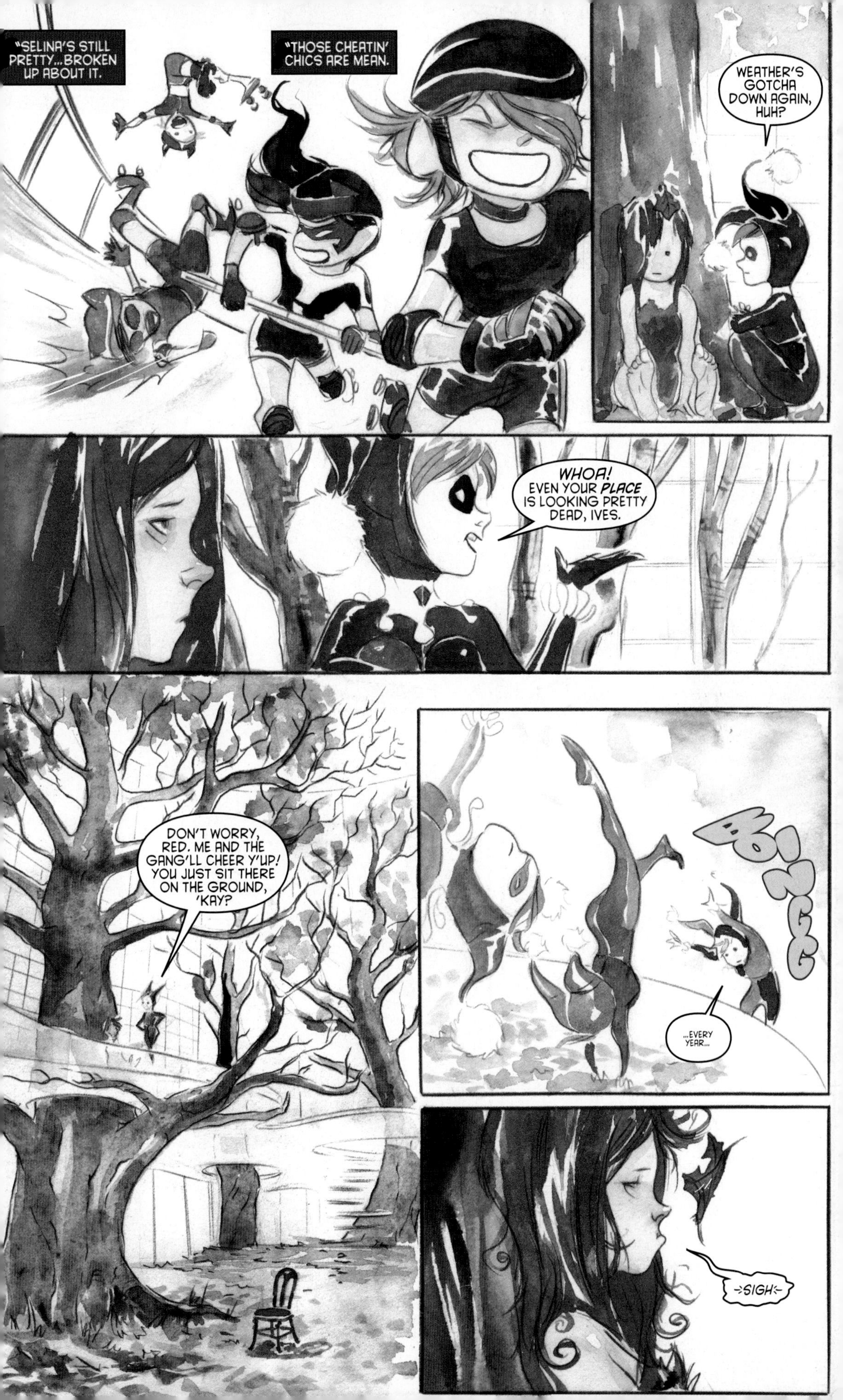
"SELINA'S STILL PRETTY...BROKEN UP ABOUT IT.
"THOSE CHEATIN' CHICS ARE MEAN.
WEATHER'S GOTCHA DOWN AGAIN, HUH?
WHOA! EVEN YOUR PLACE IS LOOKING PRETTY DEAD, IVES.
DON'T WORRY, RED. ME AND THE GANG'LL CHEER Y'UP! YOU JUST SIT THERE ON THE GROUND, 'KAY?
BOINGG
...EVERY YEAR...
SIGH

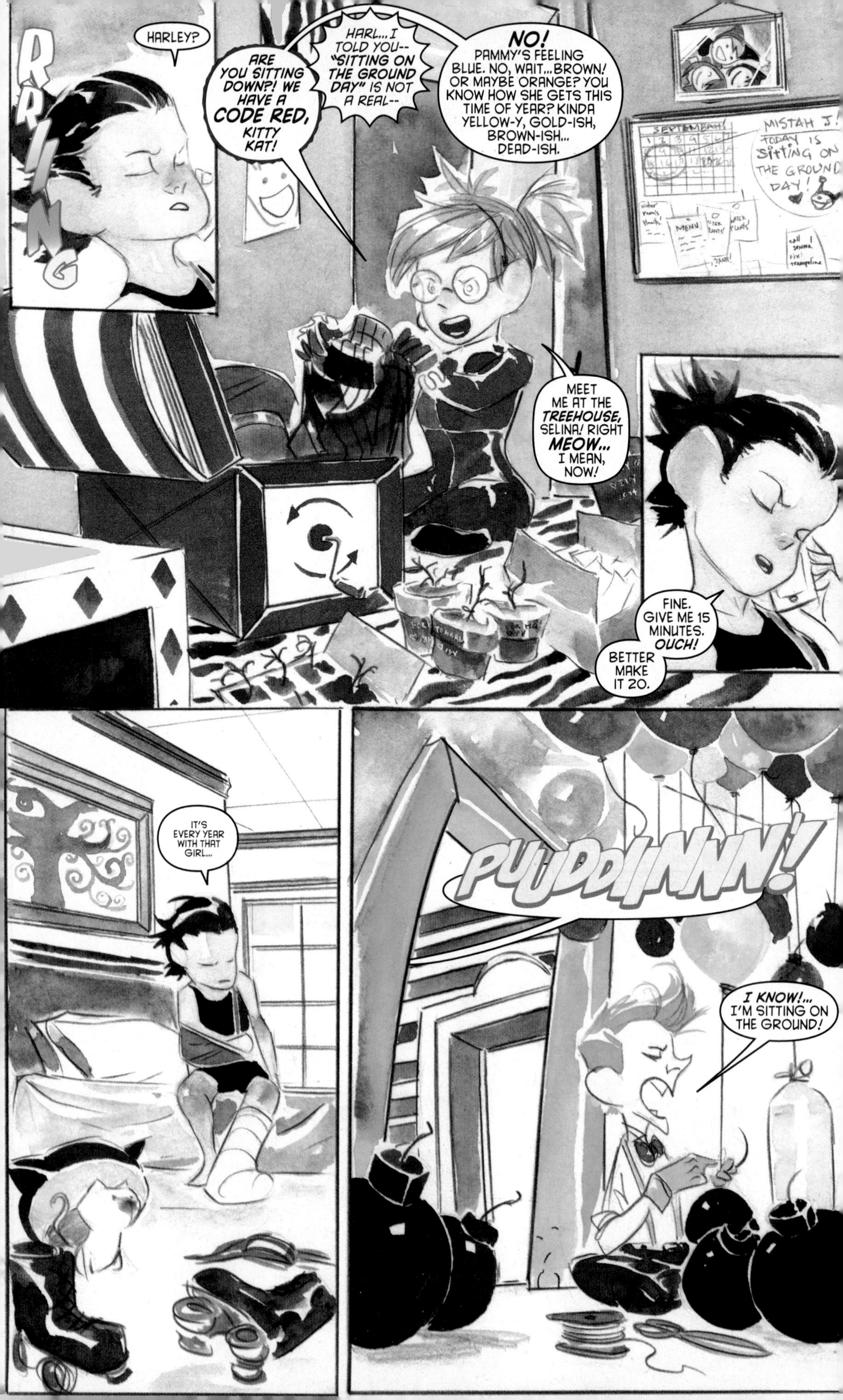
RRIING
HARLEY?
ARE YOU SITTING DOWN?! WE HAVE A CODE RED, KITTY KAT!
HARL... I TOLD YOU-- "SITTING ON THE GROUND DAY" IS NOT A REAL--
NO! PAMMY'S FEELING BLUE. NO, WAIT... BROWN! OR MAYBE ORANGE? YOU KNOW HOW SHE GETS THIS TIME OF YEAR? KINDA YELLOW-Y, GOLD-ISH, BROWN-ISH... DEAD-ISH.
MISTAH J! TODAY IS SITTING ON THE GROUND DAY!
MENU
MEET ME AT THE TREEHOUSE, SELINA! RIGHT MEOW... I MEAN, NOW!
FINE. GIVE ME 15 MINUTES. OUCH!
BETTER MAKE IT 20.
IT'S EVERY YEAR WITH THAT GIRL...
PUUDDINNN!
I KNOW!... I'M SITTING ON THE GROUND!

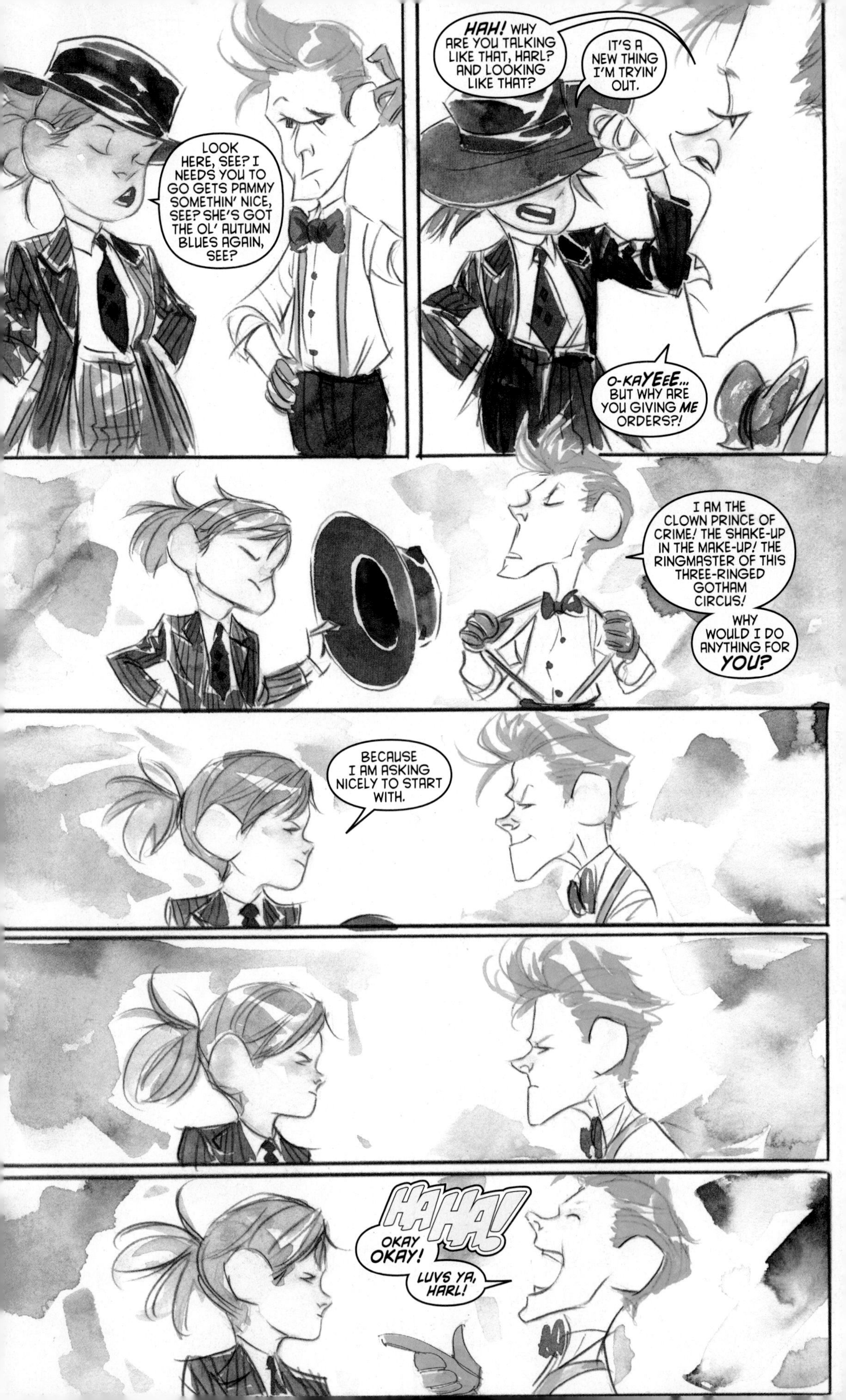
LOOK HERE, SEE? I NEEDS YOU TO GO GETS PAMMY SOMETHIN' NICE, SEE? SHE'S GOT THE OL' AUTUMN BLUES AGAIN, SEE?
HAH! WHY ARE YOU TALKING LIKE THAT, HARL? AND LOOKING LIKE THAT?
IT'S A NEW THING I'M TRYIN' OUT.
O-KAYEEE... BUT WHY ARE YOU GIVING ME ORDERS?!
I AM THE CLOWN PRINCE OF CRIME! THE SHAKE-UP IN THE MAKE-UP! THE RINGMASTER OF THIS THREE-RINGED GOTHAM CIRCUS!
WHY WOULD I DO ANYTHING FOR YOU?
BECAUSE I AM ASKING NICELY TO START WITH.
HAHA!
OKAY OKAY!
LUVS YA, HARL!

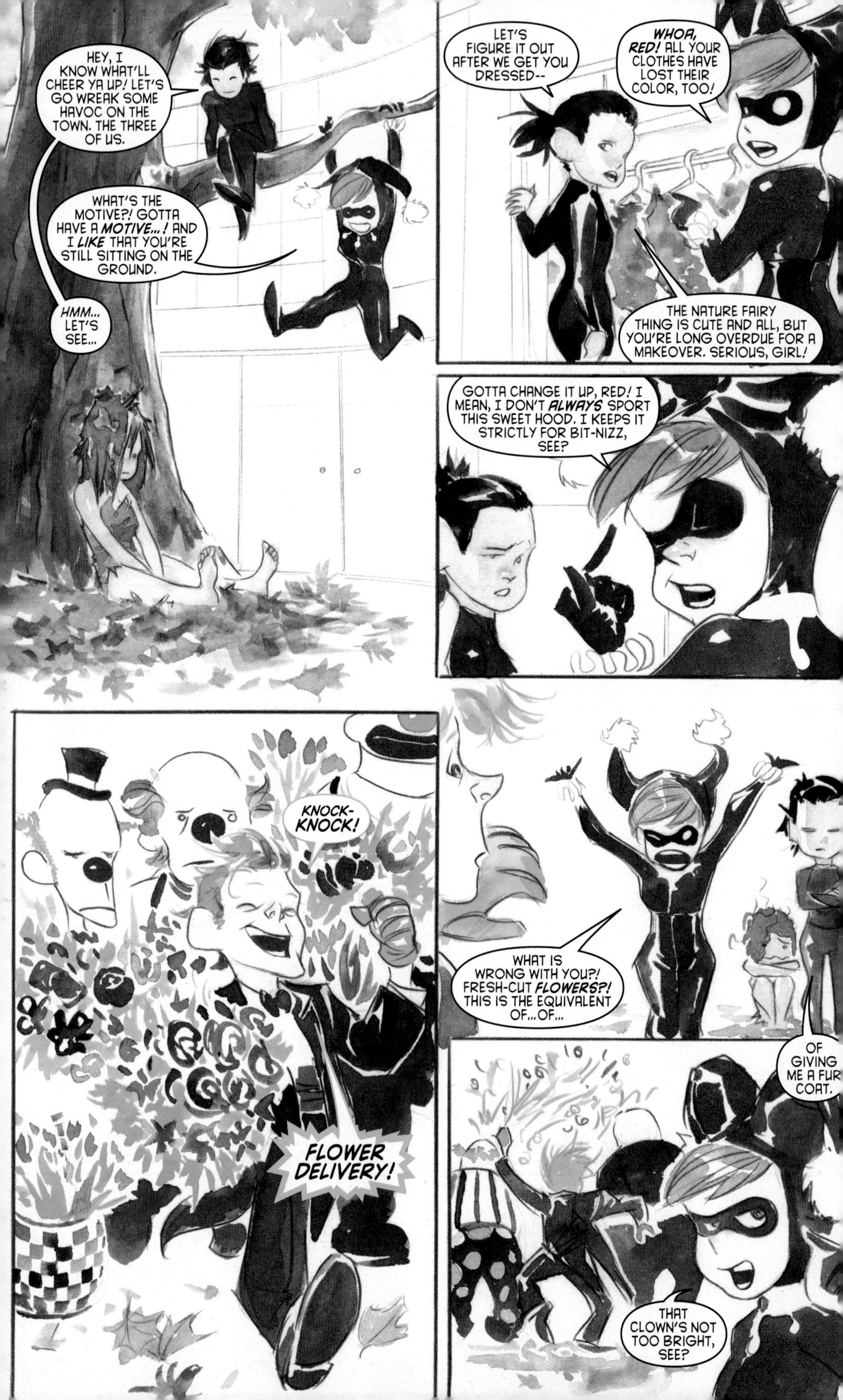
HEY, I KNOW WHAT'LL CHEER YA UP! LET'S GO WREAK SOME HAVOC ON THE TOWN. THE THREE OF US.
WHAT'S THE MOTIVE?! GOTTA HAVE A MOTIVE...! AND I LIKE THAT YOU'RE STILL SITTING ON THE GROUND.
HMM... LET'S SEE...
LET'S FIGURE IT OUT AFTER WE GET YOU DRESSED--
WHOA, RED! ALL YOUR CLOTHES HAVE LOST THEIR COLOR, TOO!
THE NATURE FAIRY THING IS CUTE AND ALL, BUT YOU'RE LONG OVERDUE FOR A MAKEOVER. SERIOUS, GIRL!
GOTTA CHANGE IT UP, RED! I MEAN, I DON'T ALWAYS SPORT THIS SWEET HOOD. I KEEPS IT STRICTLY FOR BIT-NIZZ, SEE?
KNOCK-KNOCK!
FLOWER DELIVERY!
WHAT IS WRONG WITH YOU?! FRESH-CUT FLOWERS?! THIS IS THE EQUIVALENT OF... OF...
OF GIVING ME A FUR COAT.
THAT CLOWN'S NOT TOO BRIGHT, SEE?

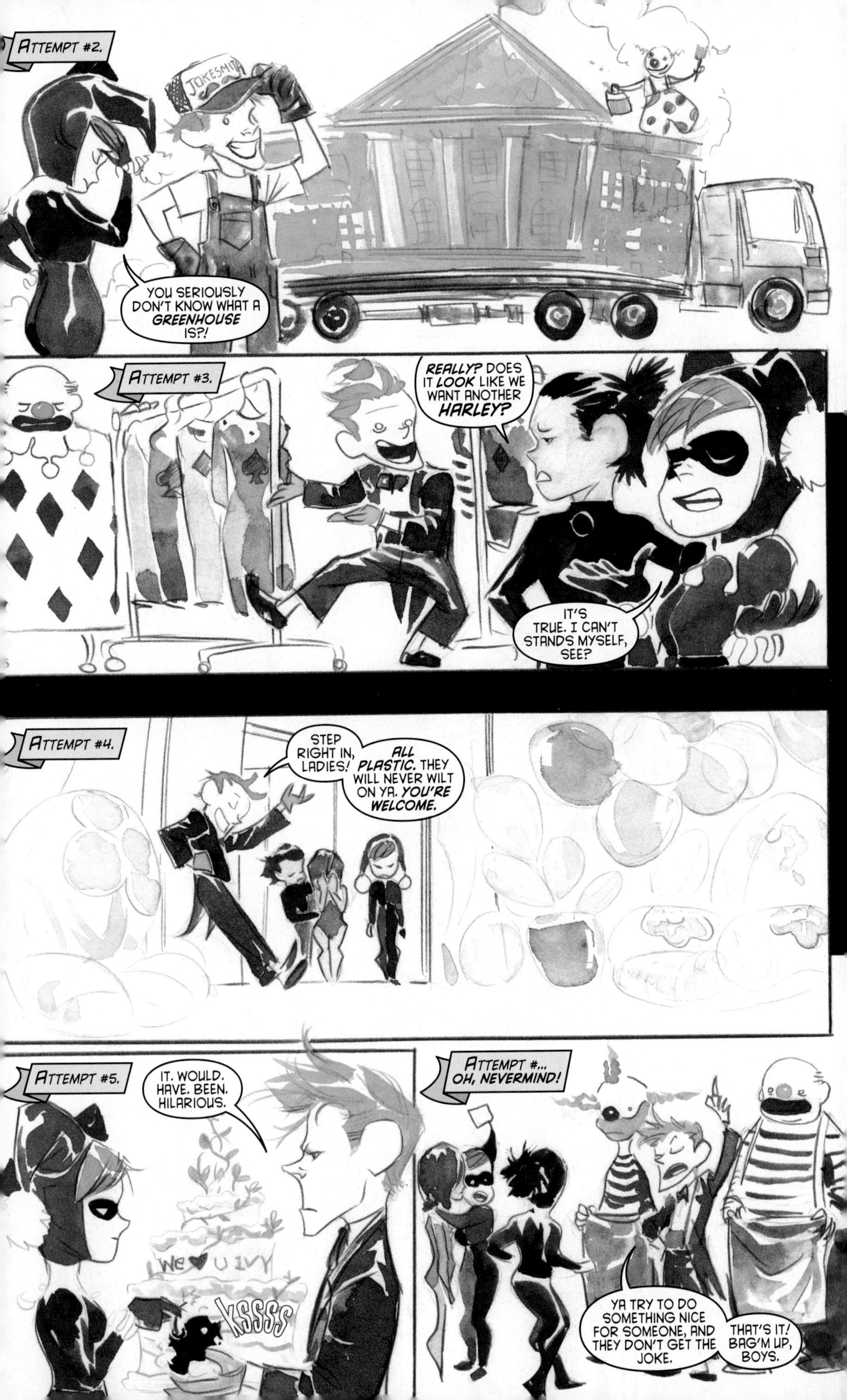

ATTEMPT #2.
YOU SERIOUSLY DON'T KNOW WHAT A GREENHOUSE IS?!
JOKESMITH
ATTEMPT #3.
REALLY? DOES IT LOOK LIKE WE WANT ANOTHER HARLEY?
IT'S TRUE. I CAN'T STANDS MYSELF, SEE?
ATTEMPT #4.
STEP RIGHT IN, LADIES!
ALL PLASTIC. THEY WILL NEVER WILT ON YA. YOU'RE WELCOME.
ATTEMPT #5.
IT. WOULD. HAVE. BEEN. HILARIOUS.
WE ♥ U IVY
KSSSS
ATTEMPT #... OH, NEVERMIND!
YA TRY TO DO SOMETHING NICE FOR SOMEONE, AND THEY DON'T GET THE JOKE.
THAT'S IT! BAG'M UP, BOYS.

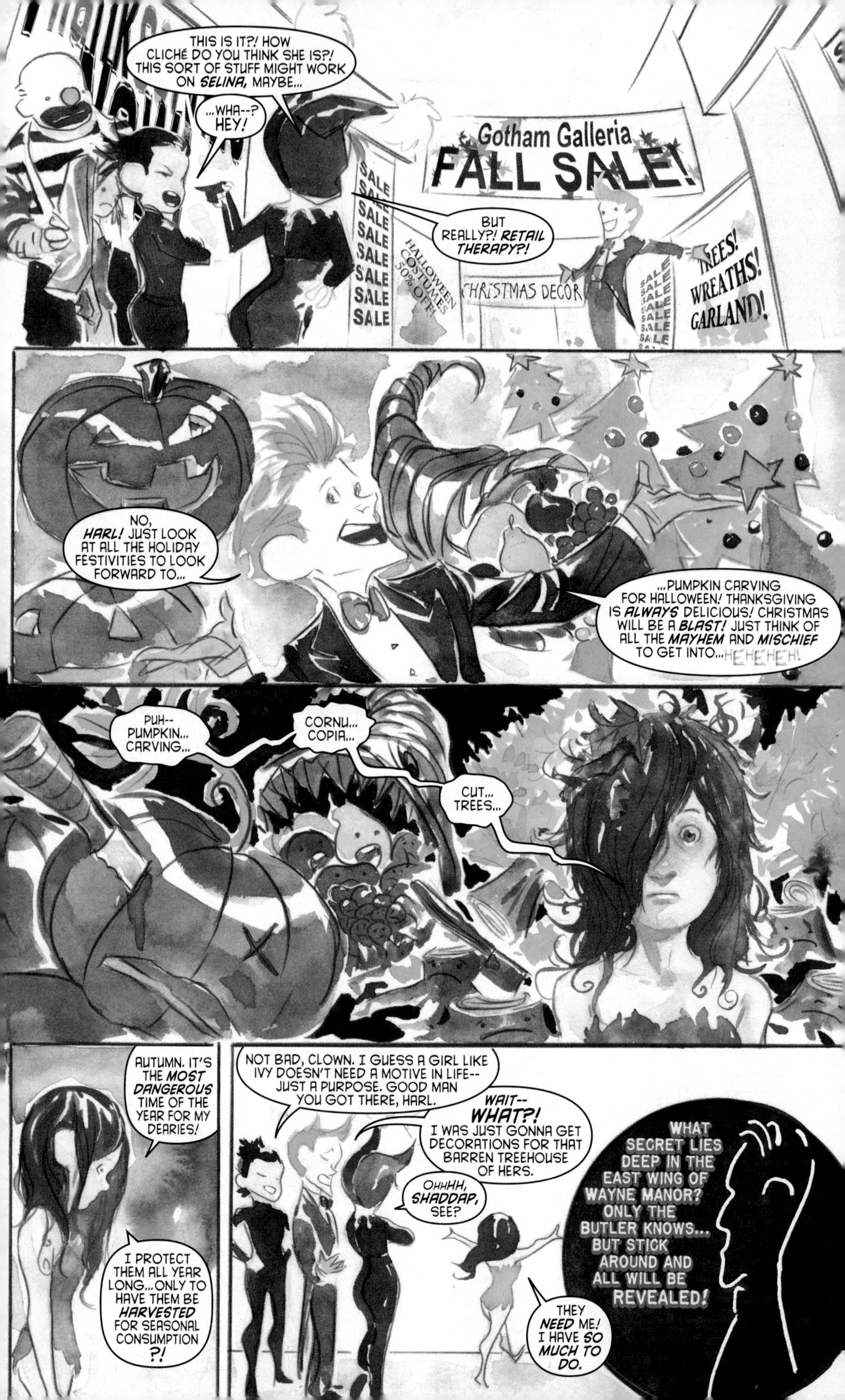
THIS IS IT?! HOW CLICHÉ DO YOU THINK SHE IS?! THIS SORT OF STUFF MIGHT WORK ON SELINA, MAYBE...
...WHA--? HEY!
Gotham Galleria FALL SALE!
SALE SALE SALE SALE SALE SALE SALE SALE
HALLOWEEN COSTUMES 50% OFF!
BUT REALLY?! RETAIL THERAPY?!
CHRISTMAS DECOR
TREES! WREATHS! GARLAND!
NO, HARL! JUST LOOK AT ALL THE HOLIDAY FESTIVITIES TO LOOK FORWARD TO...
...PUMPKIN CARVING FOR HALLOWEEN! THANKSGIVING IS ALWAYS DELICIOUS! CHRISTMAS WILL BE A BLAST! JUST THINK OF ALL THE MAYHEM AND MISCHIEF TO GET INTO...HEHEHEH!
PUH-- PUMPKIN... CARVING...
CORNU... COPIA...
CUT... TREES...
AUTUMN. IT'S THE MOST DANGEROUS TIME OF THE YEAR FOR MY DEARIES!
I PROTECT THEM ALL YEAR LONG...ONLY TO HAVE THEM BE HARVESTED FOR SEASONAL CONSUMPTION ?!
NOT BAD, CLOWN. I GUESS A GIRL LIKE IVY DOESN'T NEED A MOTIVE IN LIFE-- JUST A PURPOSE. GOOD MAN YOU GOT THERE, HARL.
WAIT-- WHAT?! I WAS JUST GONNA GET DECORATIONS FOR THAT BARREN TREEHOUSE OF HERS.
OHHHH, SHADDAP, SEE?
THEY NEED ME! I HAVE SO MUCH TO DO.
WHAT SECRET LIES DEEP IN THE EAST WING OF WAYNE MANOR? ONLY THE BUTLER KNOWS... BUT STICK AROUND AND ALL WILL BE REVEALED!

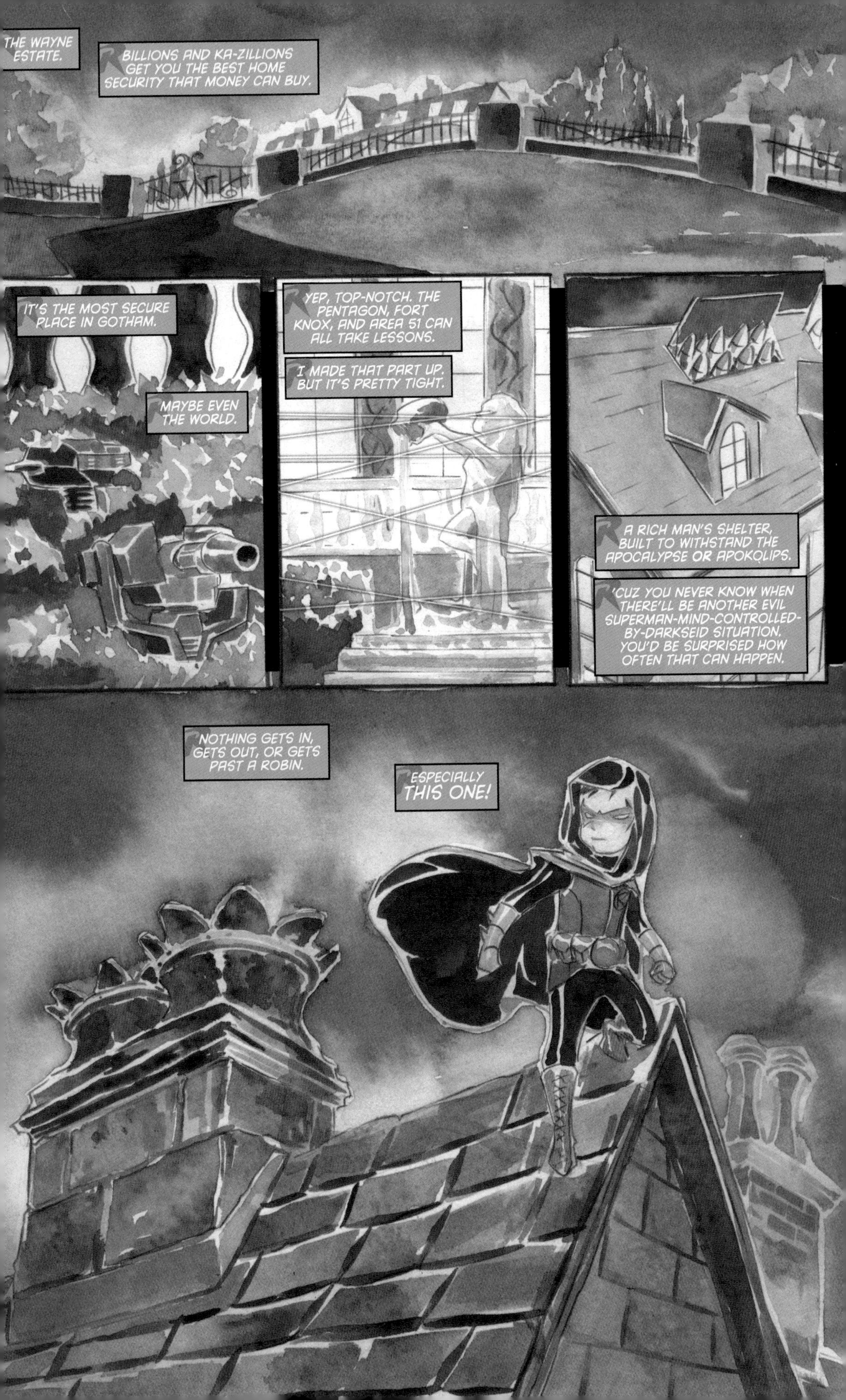
THE WAYNE ESTATE.
BILLIONS AND KA-ZILLIONS GET YOU THE BEST HOME SECURITY THAT MONEY CAN BUY.
IT'S THE MOST SECURE PLACE IN GOTHAM.
MAYBE EVEN THE WORLD.
YEP, TOP-NOTCH. THE PENTAGON, FORT KNOX, AND AREA 51 CAN ALL TAKE LESSONS.
I MADE THAT PART UP. BUT IT'S PRETTY TIGHT.
A RICH MAN'S SHELTER, BUILT TO WITHSTAND THE APOCALYPSE OR APOKOLIPS.
'CUZ YOU NEVER KNOW WHEN THERE'LL BE ANOTHER EVIL SUPERMAN-MIND-CONTROLLED-BY-DARKSEID SITUATION. YOU'D BE SURPRISED HOW OFTEN THAT CAN HAPPEN.
NOTHING GETS IN, GETS OUT, OR GETS PAST A ROBIN.
ESPECIALLY THIS ONE!

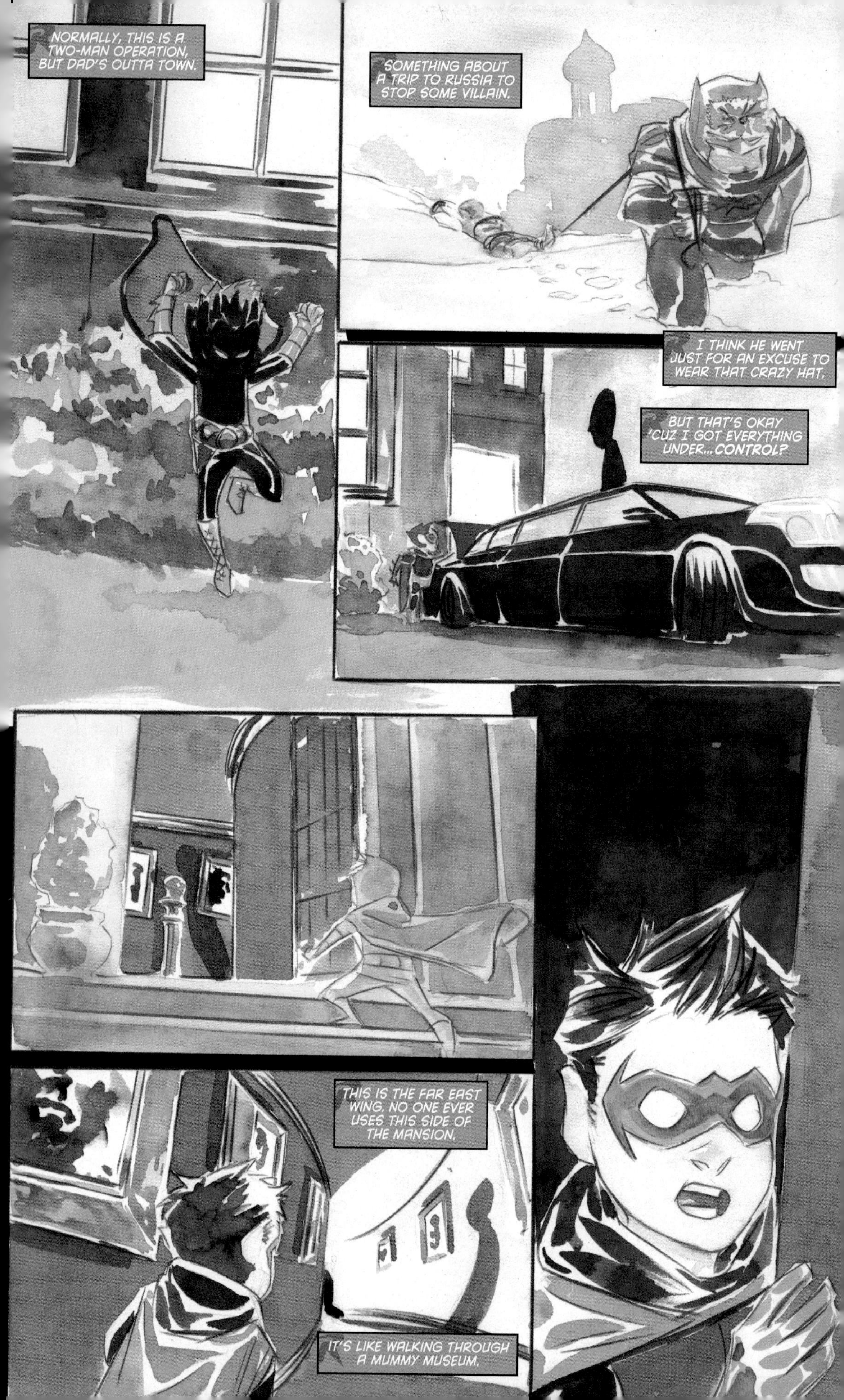
NORMALLY, THIS IS A TWO-MAN OPERATION, BUT DAD'S OUTTA TOWN.
SOMETHING ABOUT A TRIP TO RUSSIA TO STOP SOME VILLAIN.
I THINK HE WENT JUST FOR AN EXCUSE TO WEAR THAT CRAZY HAT.
BUT THAT'S OKAY 'CUZ I GOT EVERYTHING UNDER...CONTROL?
THIS IS THE FAR EAST WING. NO ONE EVER USES THIS SIDE OF THE MANSION.
IT'S LIKE WALKING THROUGH A MUMMY MUSEUM.

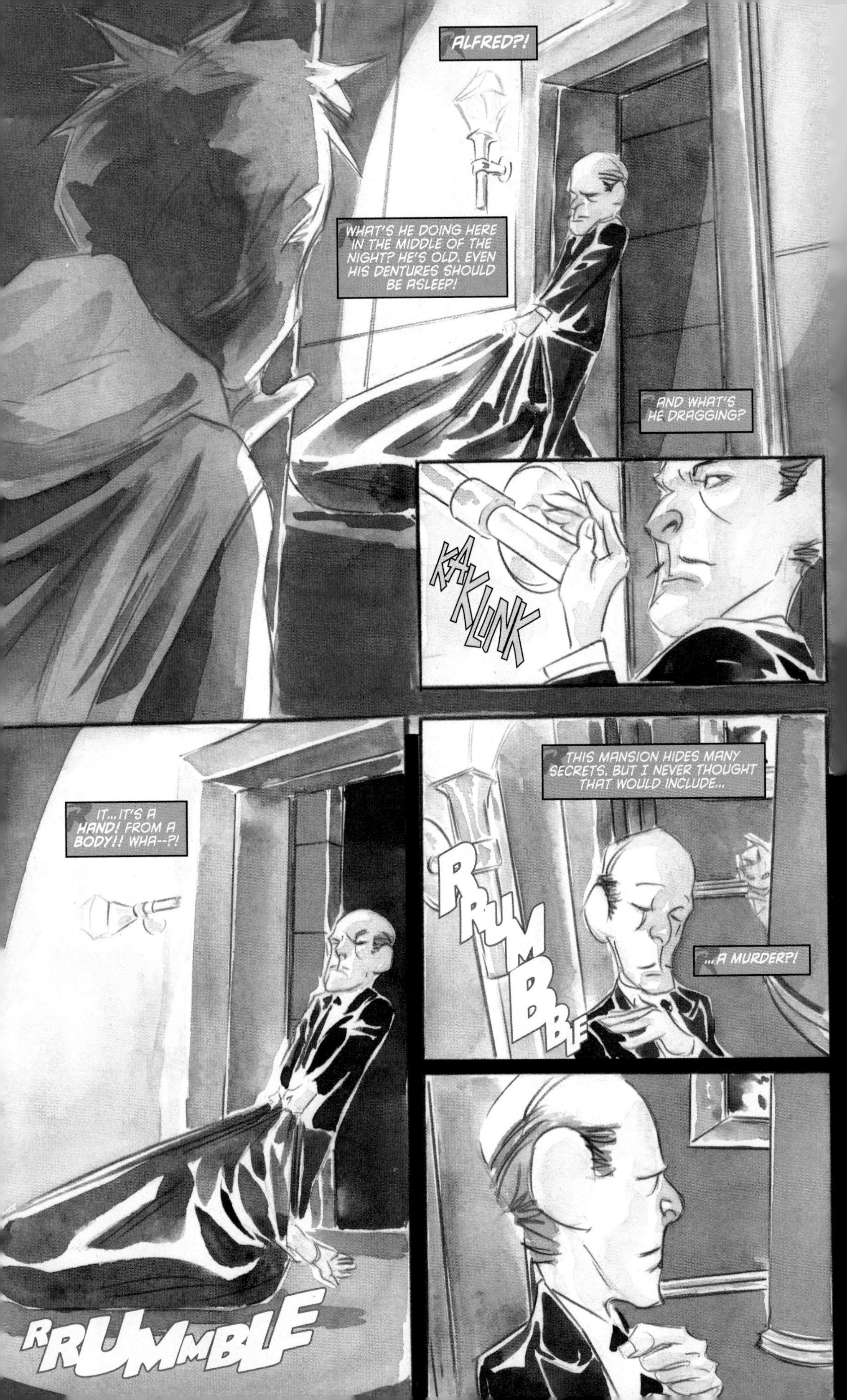
ALFRED?!
WHAT'S HE DOING HERE IN THE MIDDLE OF THE NIGHT? HE'S OLD. EVEN HIS DENTURES SHOULD BE ASLEEP!
AND WHAT'S HE DRAGGING?
KA-KLINK
IT...IT'S A HAND! FROM A BODY!! WHA--?!
RRUMMBLE
THIS MANSION HIDES MANY SECRETS. BUT I NEVER THOUGHT THAT WOULD INCLUDE...
RRUMBBLE
...A MURDER?!

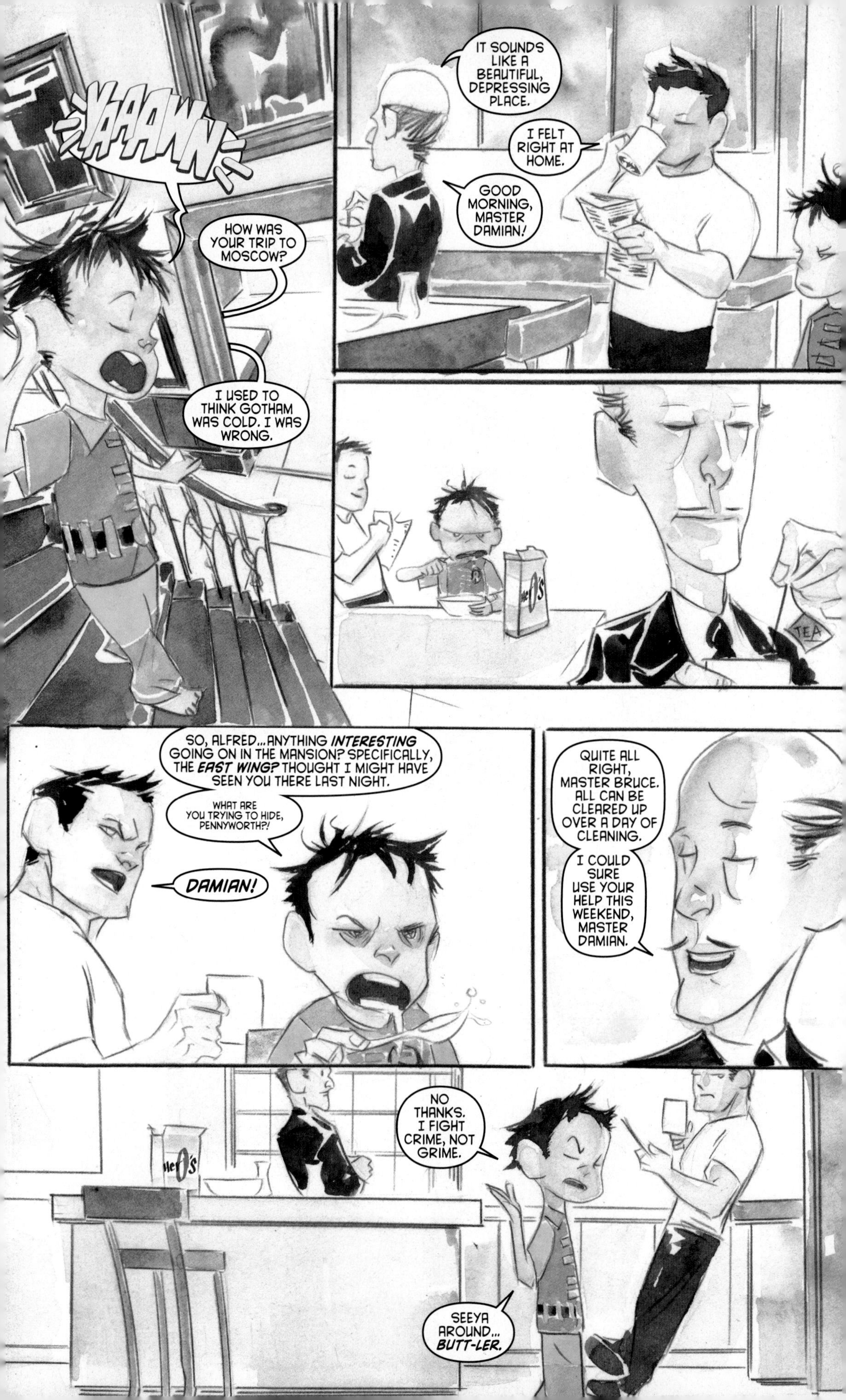
YAAAWN
HOW WAS YOUR TRIP TO MOSCOW?
I USED TO THINK GOTHAM WAS COLD. I WAS WRONG.
IT SOUNDS LIKE A BEAUTIFUL, DEPRESSING PLACE.
I FELT RIGHT AT HOME.
GOOD MORNING, MASTER DAMIAN!
TEA
SO, ALFRED... ANYTHING *INTERESTING* GOING ON IN THE MANSION? SPECIFICALLY, THE *EAST WING?* THOUGHT I MIGHT HAVE SEEN YOU THERE LAST NIGHT.
WHAT ARE YOU TRYING TO HIDE, PENNYWORTH?!
DAMIAN!
QUITE ALL RIGHT, MASTER BRUCE. ALL CAN BE CLEARED UP OVER A DAY OF CLEANING.
I COULD SURE USE YOUR HELP THIS WEEKEND, MASTER DAMIAN.
NO THANKS. I FIGHT CRIME, NOT GRIME.
SEEYA AROUND... *BUTT-LER.*

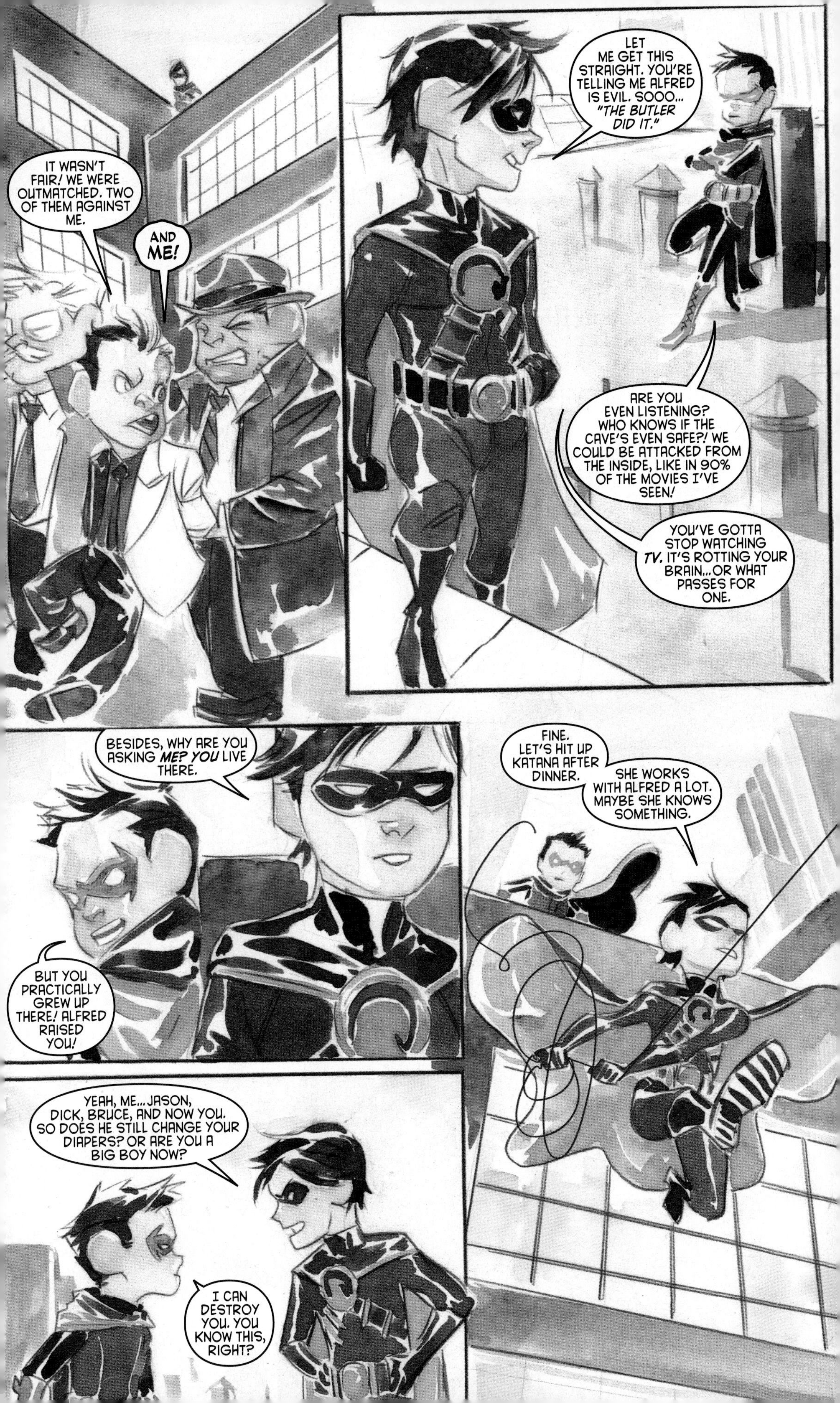
IT WASN'T FAIR! WE WERE OUTMATCHED. TWO OF THEM AGAINST ME.
AND ME!
LET ME GET THIS STRAIGHT. YOU'RE TELLING ME ALFRED IS EVIL. SOOO... "THE BUTLER DID IT."
ARE YOU EVEN LISTENING? WHO KNOWS IF THE CAVE'S EVEN SAFE?! WE COULD BE ATTACKED FROM THE INSIDE, LIKE IN 90% OF THE MOVIES I'VE SEEN!
YOU'VE GOTTA STOP WATCHING TV. IT'S ROTTING YOUR BRAIN...OR WHAT PASSES FOR ONE.
BESIDES, WHY ARE YOU ASKING ME? YOU LIVE THERE.
BUT YOU PRACTICALLY GREW UP THERE! ALFRED RAISED YOU!
YEAH, ME...JASON, DICK, BRUCE, AND NOW YOU. SO DOES HE STILL CHANGE YOUR DIAPERS? OR ARE YOU A BIG BOY NOW?
I CAN DESTROY YOU. YOU KNOW THIS, RIGHT?
FINE. LET'S HIT UP KATANA AFTER DINNER.
SHE WORKS WITH ALFRED A LOT. MAYBE SHE KNOWS SOMETHING.

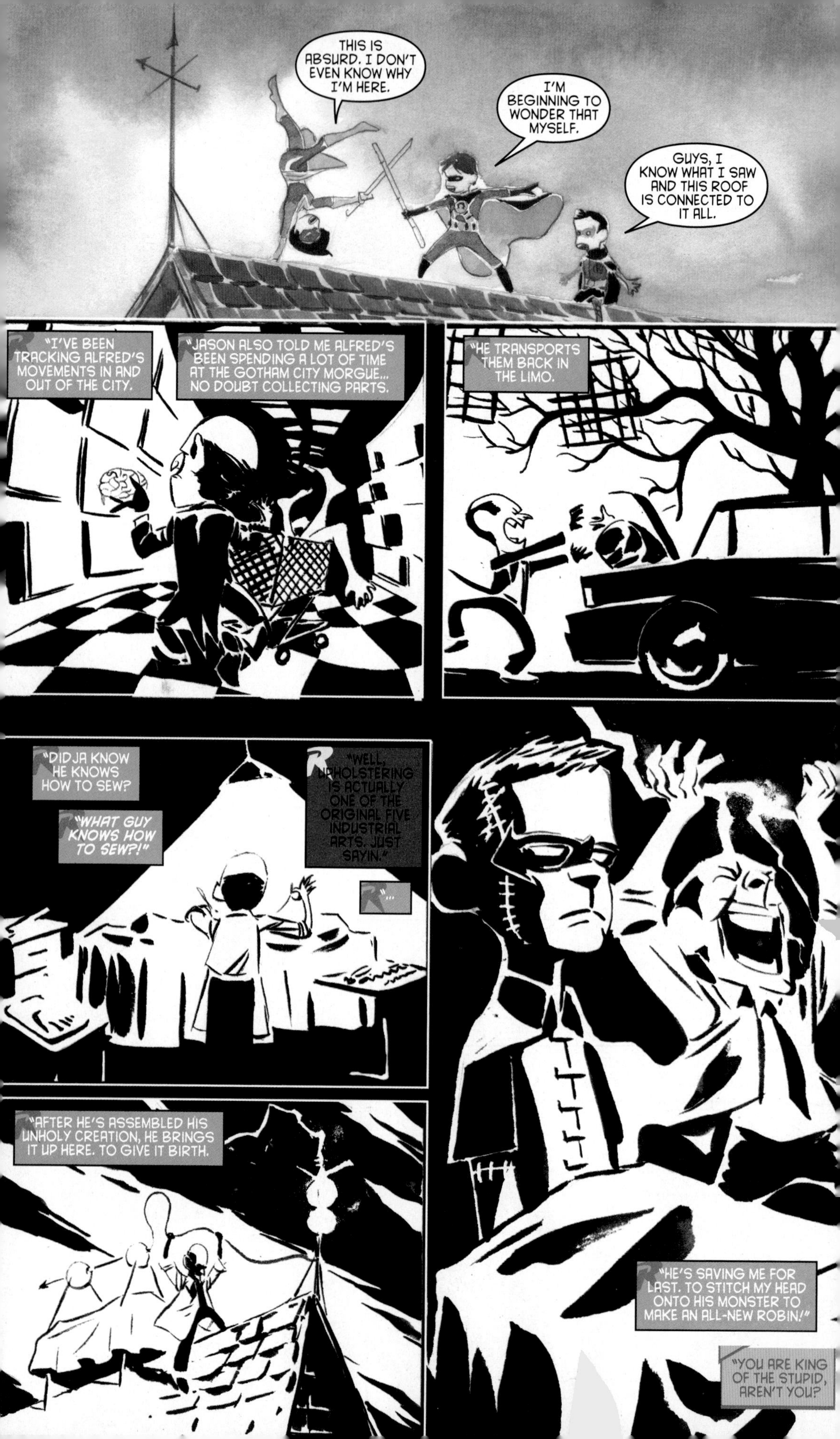
THIS IS ABSURD. I DON'T EVEN KNOW WHY I'M HERE.
I'M BEGINNING TO WONDER THAT MYSELF.
GUYS, I KNOW WHAT I SAW AND THIS ROOF IS CONNECTED TO IT ALL.
"I'VE BEEN TRACKING ALFRED'S MOVEMENTS IN AND OUT OF THE CITY.
"JASON ALSO TOLD ME ALFRED'S BEEN SPENDING A LOT OF TIME AT THE GOTHAM CITY MORGUE... NO DOUBT COLLECTING PARTS.
"HE TRANSPORTS THEM BACK IN THE LIMO.
"DIDJA KNOW HE KNOWS HOW TO SEW?
"WHAT GUY KNOWS HOW TO SEW?!"
"WELL, UPHOLSTERING IS ACTUALLY ONE OF THE ORIGINAL FIVE INDUSTRIAL ARTS. JUST SAYIN."
"...
"AFTER HE'S ASSEMBLED HIS UNHOLY CREATION, HE BRINGS IT UP HERE. TO GIVE IT BIRTH.
"HE'S SAVING ME FOR LAST. TO STITCH MY HEAD ONTO HIS MONSTER TO MAKE AN ALL-NEW ROBIN."
"YOU ARE KING OF THE STUPID, AREN'T YOU?

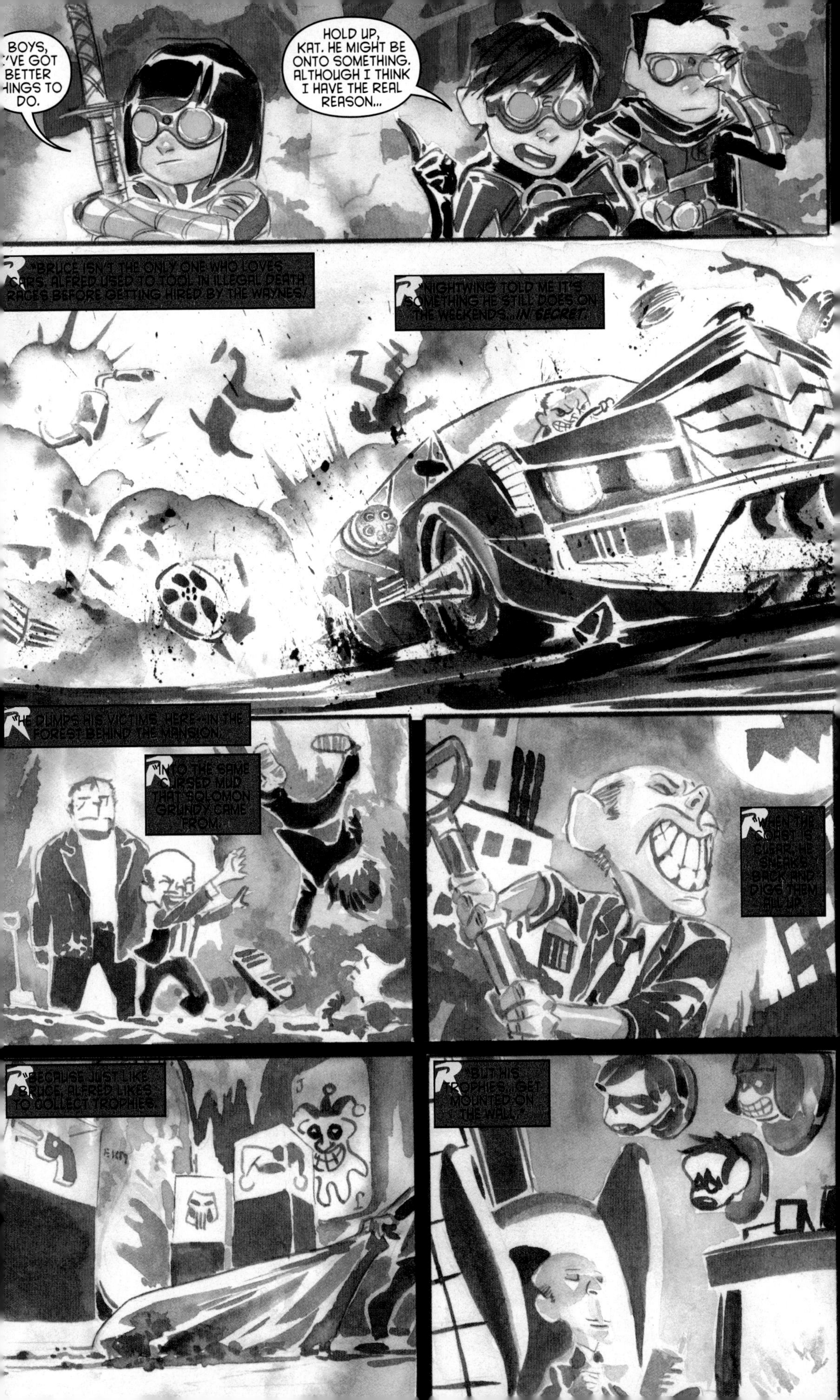
BOYS, I'VE GOT BETTER THINGS TO DO.
HOLD UP, KAT. HE MIGHT BE ONTO SOMETHING. ALTHOUGH I THINK I HAVE THE REAL REASON...
"BRUCE ISN'T THE ONLY ONE WHO LOVES CARS. ALFRED USED TO TOOL IN ILLEGAL DEATH RACES BEFORE GETTING HIRED BY THE WAYNES!
"NIGHTWING TOLD ME IT'S SOMETHING HE STILL DOES ON THE WEEKENDS... IN SECRET.
"HE DUMPS HIS VICTIMS HERE--IN THE FOREST BEHIND THE MANSION.
"INTO THE SAME CURSED MUD THAT SOLOMON GRUNDY CAME FROM.
"WHEN THE COAST IS CLEAR, HE SNEAKS BACK AND DIGS THEM ALL UP.
"BECAUSE JUST LIKE BRUCE, ALFRED LIKES TO COLLECT TROPHIES.
"BUT HIS TROPHIES GET MOUNTED ON THE WALL."

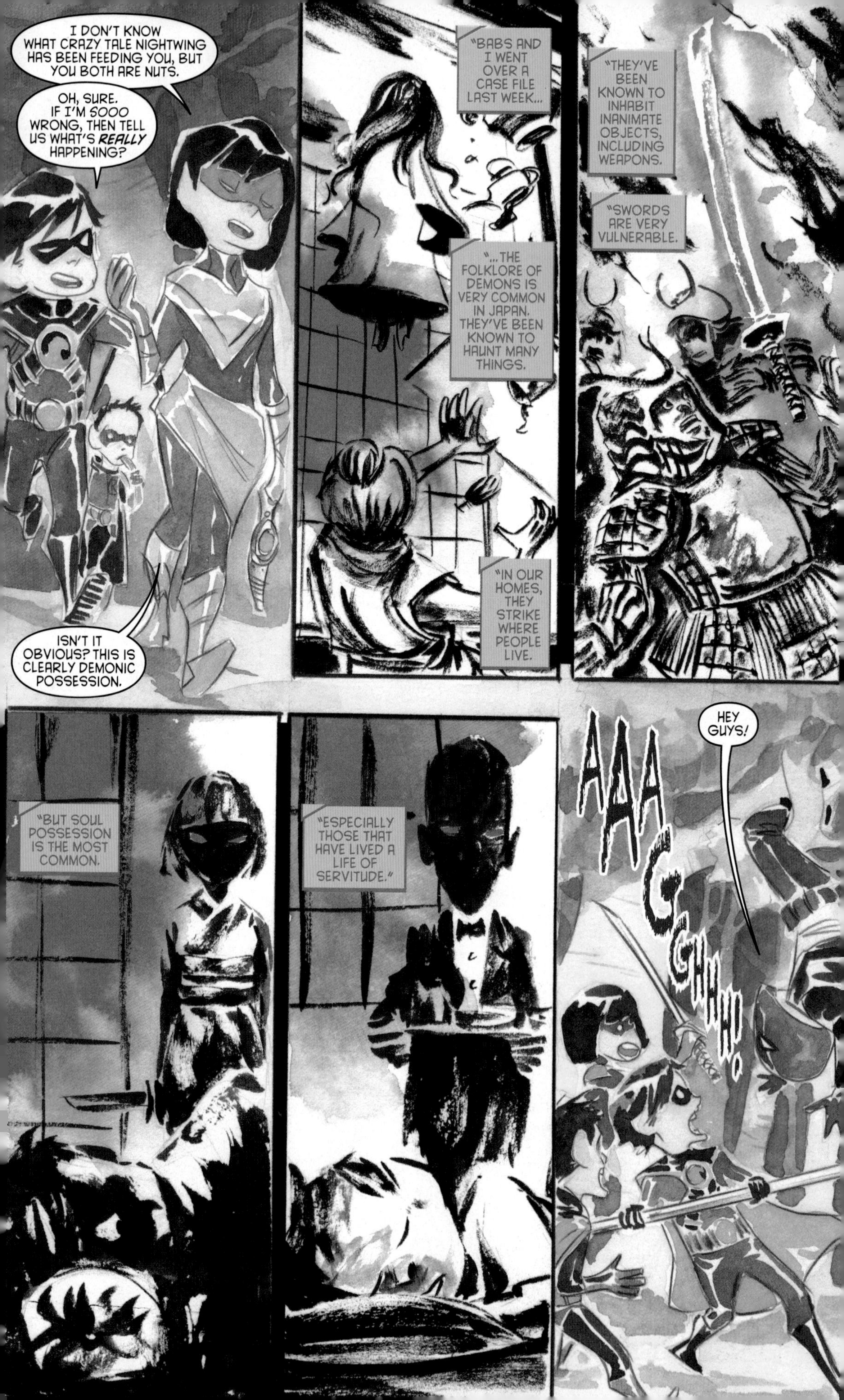
I DON'T KNOW WHAT CRAZY TALE NIGHTWING HAS BEEN FEEDING YOU, BUT YOU BOTH ARE NUTS.
OH, SURE. IF I'M SOOO WRONG, THEN TELL US WHAT'S REALLY HAPPENING?
ISN'T IT OBVIOUS? THIS IS CLEARLY DEMONIC POSSESSION.
"BABS AND I WENT OVER A CASE FILE LAST WEEK...
"...THE FOLKLORE OF DEMONS IS VERY COMMON IN JAPAN. THEY'VE BEEN KNOWN TO HAUNT MANY THINGS.
"IN OUR HOMES, THEY STRIKE WHERE PEOPLE LIVE.
"THEY'VE BEEN KNOWN TO INHABIT INANIMATE OBJECTS, INCLUDING WEAPONS.
"SWORDS ARE VERY VULNERABLE.
"BUT SOUL POSSESSION IS THE MOST COMMON.
"ESPECIALLY THOSE THAT HAVE LIVED A LIFE OF SERVITUDE."
HEY GUYS!
AAAGGHHH!

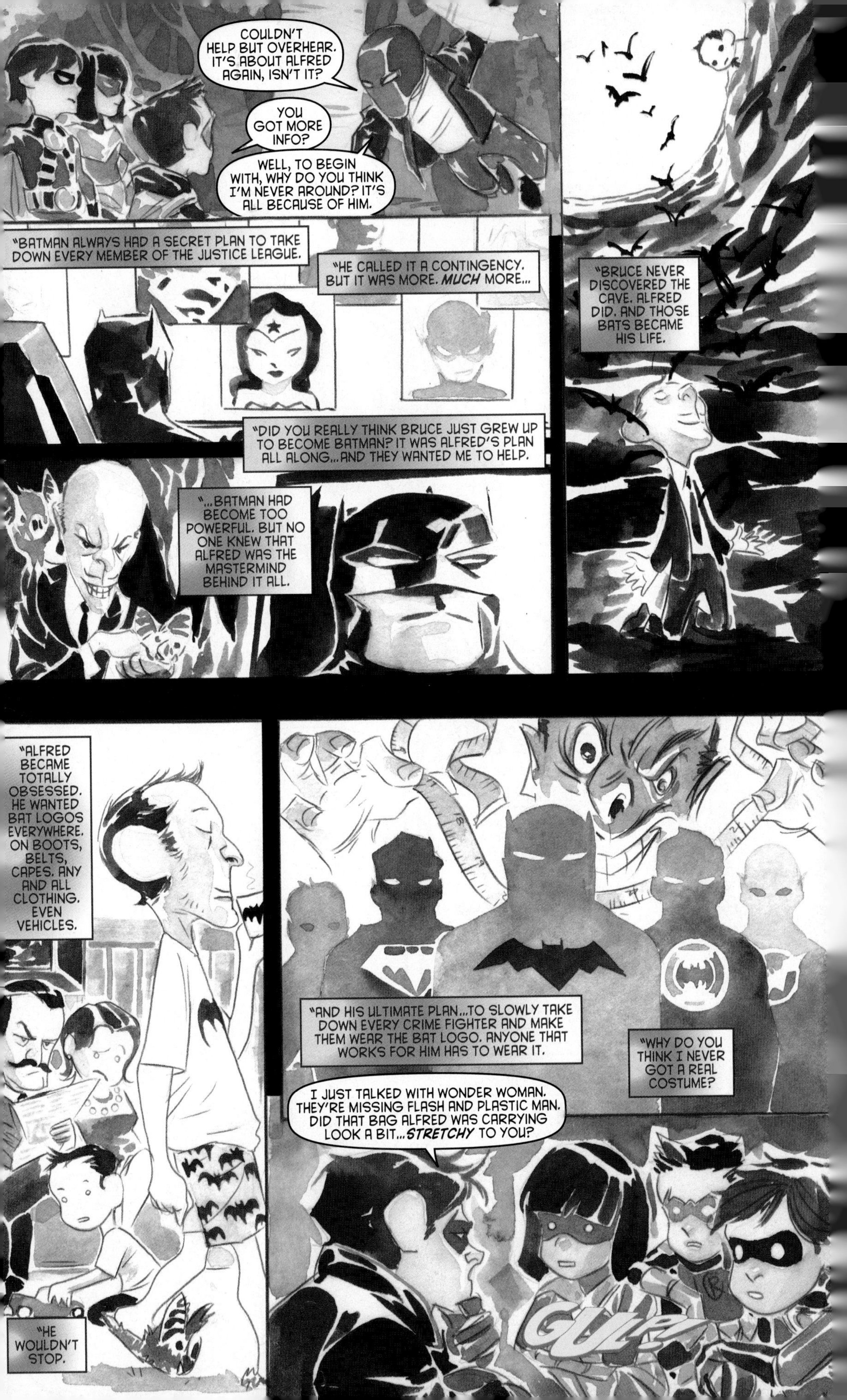
COULDN'T HELP BUT OVERHEAR. IT'S ABOUT ALFRED AGAIN, ISN'T IT?
YOU GOT MORE INFO?
WELL, TO BEGIN WITH, WHY DO YOU THINK I'M NEVER AROUND? IT'S ALL BECAUSE OF HIM.
"BRUCE NEVER DISCOVERED THE CAVE. ALFRED DID. AND THOSE BATS BECAME HIS LIFE.
"BATMAN ALWAYS HAD A SECRET PLAN TO TAKE DOWN EVERY MEMBER OF THE JUSTICE LEAGUE.
"HE CALLED IT A CONTINGENCY. BUT IT WAS MORE. *MUCH* MORE...
"DID YOU REALLY THINK BRUCE JUST GREW UP TO BECOME BATMAN? IT WAS ALFRED'S PLAN ALL ALONG...AND THEY WANTED ME TO HELP.
"...BATMAN HAD BECOME TOO POWERFUL. BUT NO ONE KNEW THAT ALFRED WAS THE MASTERMIND BEHIND IT ALL.
"ALFRED BECAME TOTALLY OBSESSED. HE WANTED BAT LOGOS EVERYWHERE. ON BOOTS, BELTS, CAPES. ANY AND ALL CLOTHING. EVEN VEHICLES.
"HE WOULDN'T STOP.
"AND HIS ULTIMATE PLAN...TO SLOWLY TAKE DOWN EVERY CRIME FIGHTER AND MAKE THEM WEAR THE BAT LOGO. ANYONE THAT WORKS FOR HIM HAS TO WEAR IT.
"WHY DO YOU THINK I NEVER GOT A REAL COSTUME?
I JUST TALKED WITH WONDER WOMAN. THEY'RE MISSING FLASH AND PLASTIC MAN. DID THAT BAG ALFRED WAS CARRYING LOOK A BIT...*STRETCHY* TO YOU?
GULP

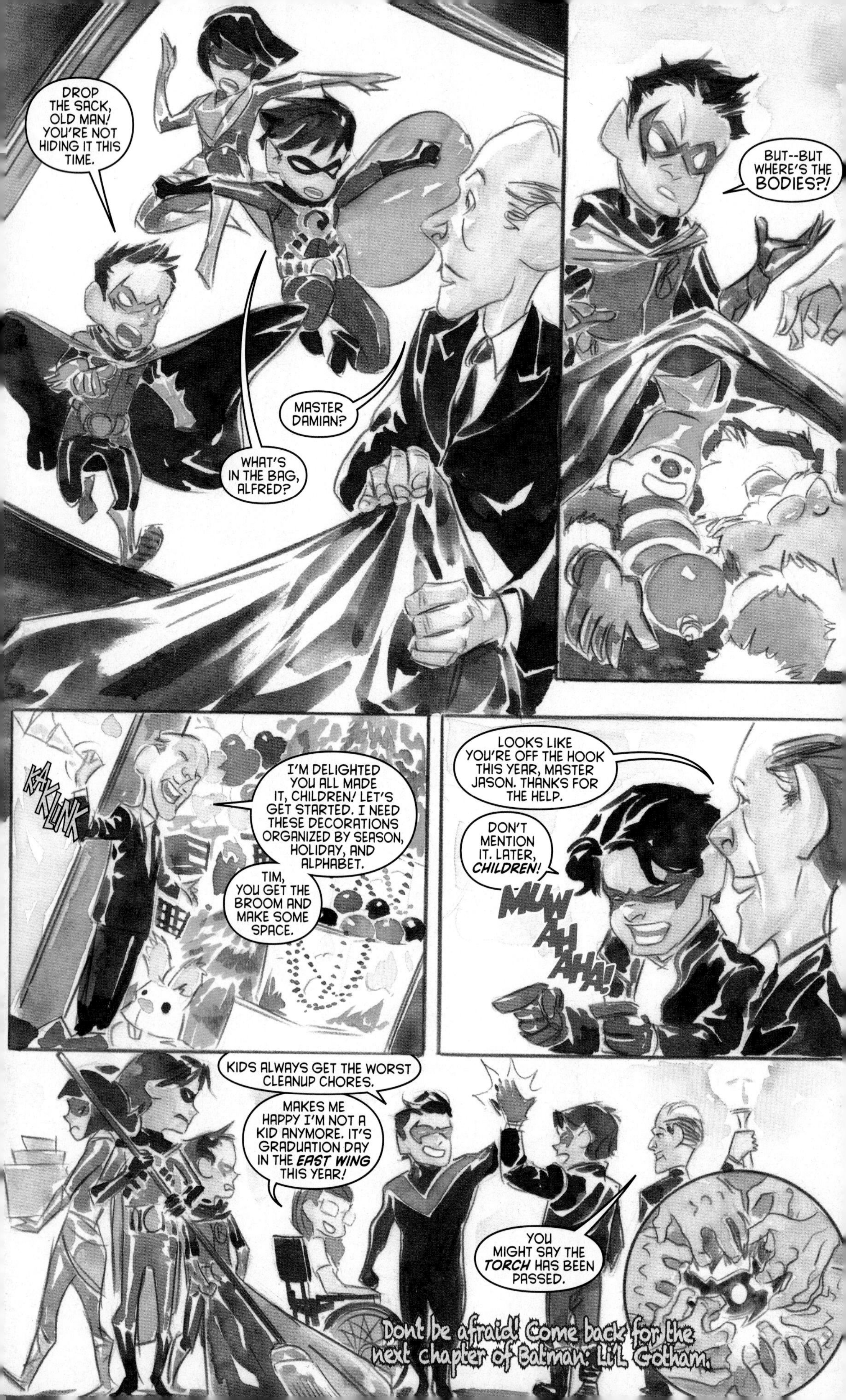
DROP THE SACK, OLD MAN! YOU'RE NOT HIDING IT THIS TIME.
WHAT'S IN THE BAG, ALFRED?
MASTER DAMIAN?
BUT--BUT WHERE'S THE BODIES?!
KAKLINK
I'M DELIGHTED YOU ALL MADE IT, CHILDREN! LET'S GET STARTED. I NEED THESE DECORATIONS ORGANIZED BY SEASON, HOLIDAY, AND ALPHABET.
TIM, YOU GET THE BROOM AND MAKE SOME SPACE.
LOOKS LIKE YOU'RE OFF THE HOOK THIS YEAR, MASTER JASON. THANKS FOR THE HELP.
DON'T MENTION IT. LATER, CHILDREN!
MUWAHAHAHA!
KIDS ALWAYS GET THE WORST CLEANUP CHORES.
MAKES ME HAPPY I'M NOT A KID ANYMORE. IT'S GRADUATION DAY IN THE EAST WING THIS YEAR!
YOU MIGHT SAY THE TORCH HAS BEEN PASSED.
Dont be afraid! Come back for the next chapter of Batman: Li'l Gotham.

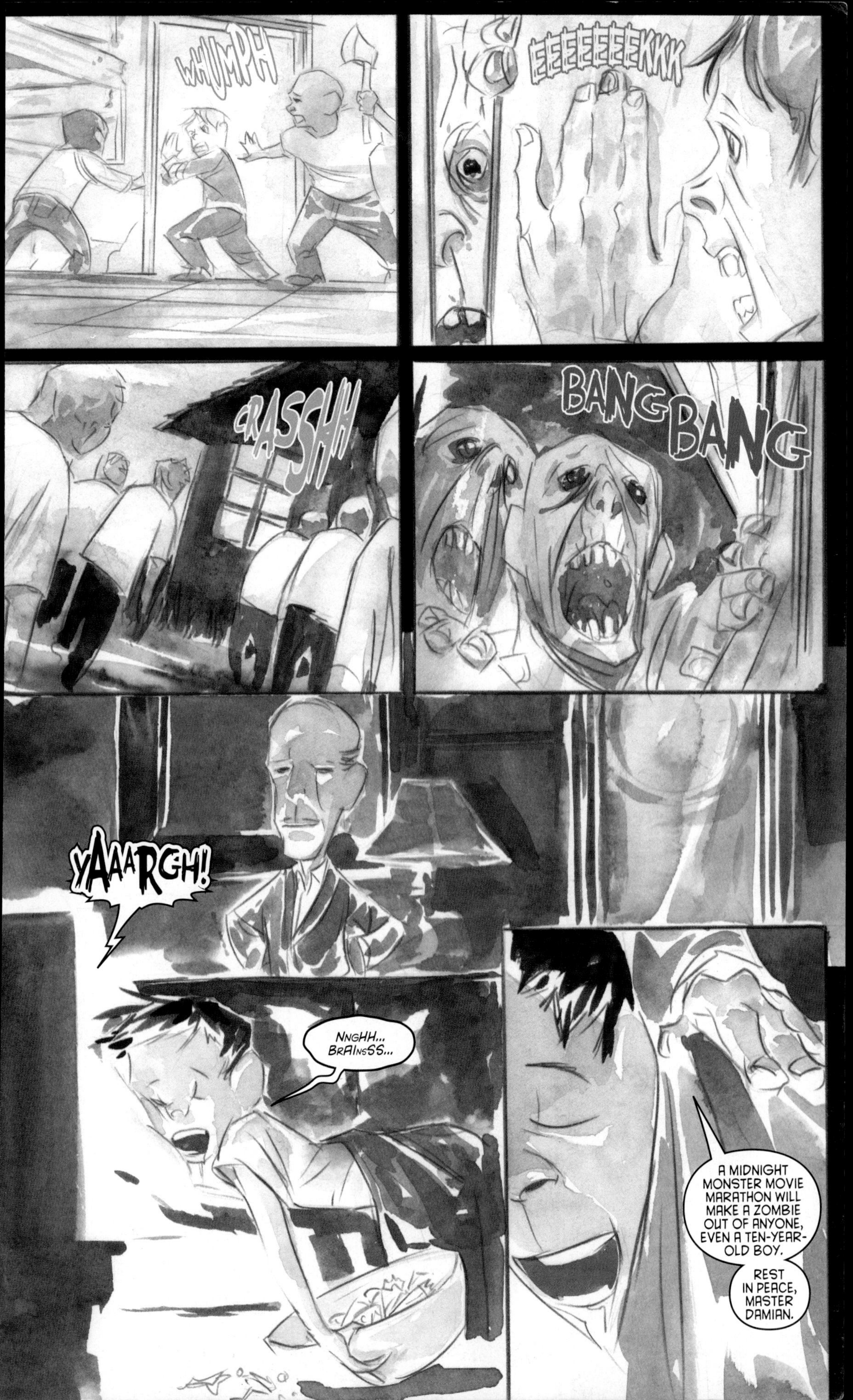
WHUMPH
EEEEEEEEKKK
CRASSHH
BANG BANG
YAAARGH!
NNGHH... BRAINSSS...
A MIDNIGHT MONSTER MOVIE MARATHON WILL MAKE A ZOMBIE OUT OF ANYONE, EVEN A TEN-YEAR-OLD BOY.
REST IN PEACE, MASTER DAMIAN.

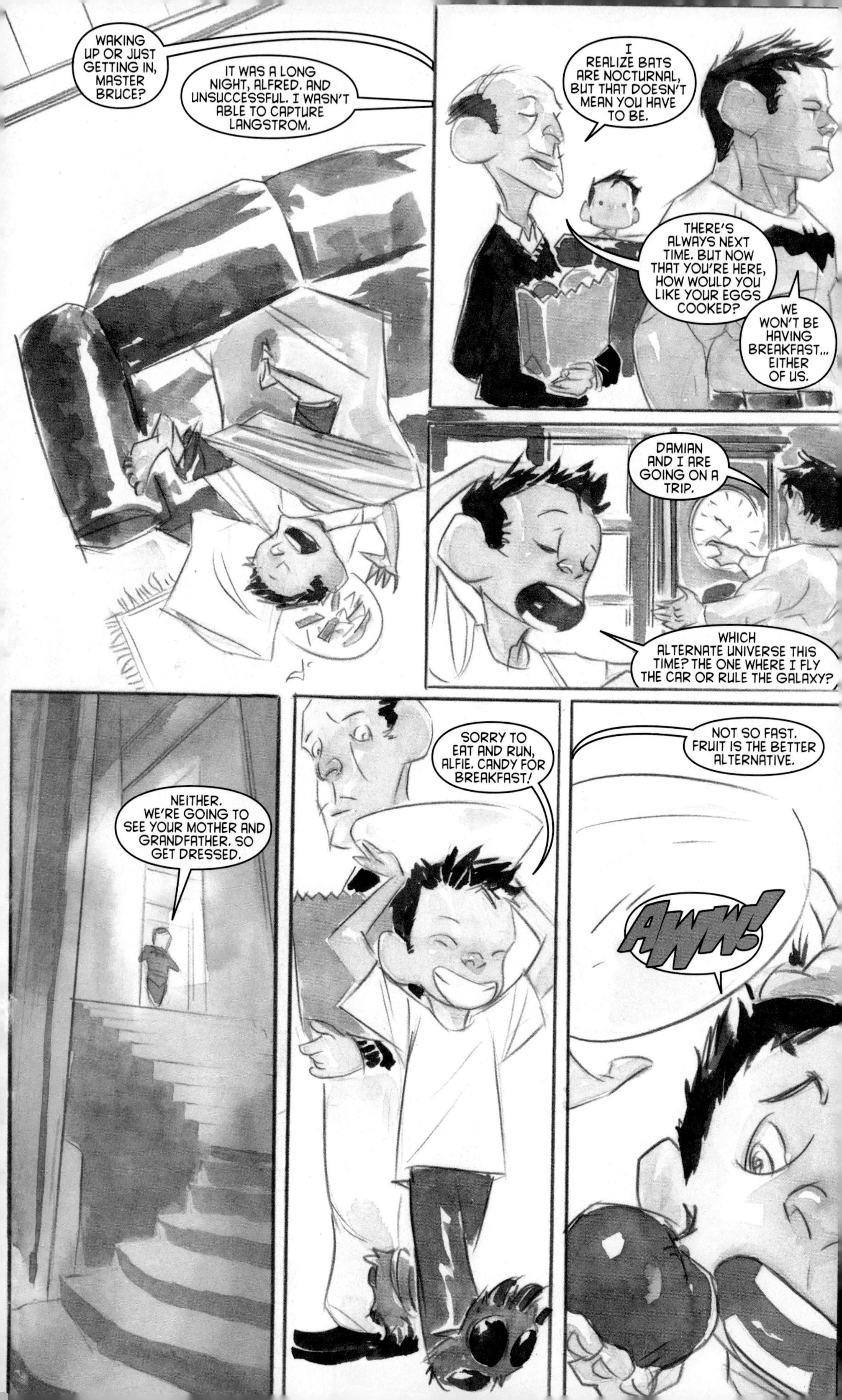
WAKING UP OR JUST GETTING IN, MASTER BRUCE?
IT WAS A LONG NIGHT, ALFRED. AND UNSUCCESSFUL. I WASN'T ABLE TO CAPTURE LANGSTROM.
I REALIZE BATS ARE NOCTURNAL, BUT THAT DOESN'T MEAN YOU HAVE TO BE.
THERE'S ALWAYS NEXT TIME. BUT NOW THAT YOU'RE HERE, HOW WOULD YOU LIKE YOUR EGGS COOKED?
WE WON'T BE HAVING BREAKFAST... EITHER OF US.
DAMIAN AND I ARE GOING ON A TRIP.
WHICH ALTERNATE UNIVERSE THIS TIME? THE ONE WHERE I FLY THE CAR OR RULE THE GALAXY?
NEITHER. WE'RE GOING TO SEE YOUR MOTHER AND GRANDFATHER. SO GET DRESSED.
SORRY TO EAT AND RUN, ALFIE. CANDY FOR BREAKFAST!
NOT SO FAST. FRUIT IS THE BETTER ALTERNATIVE.
AWW!

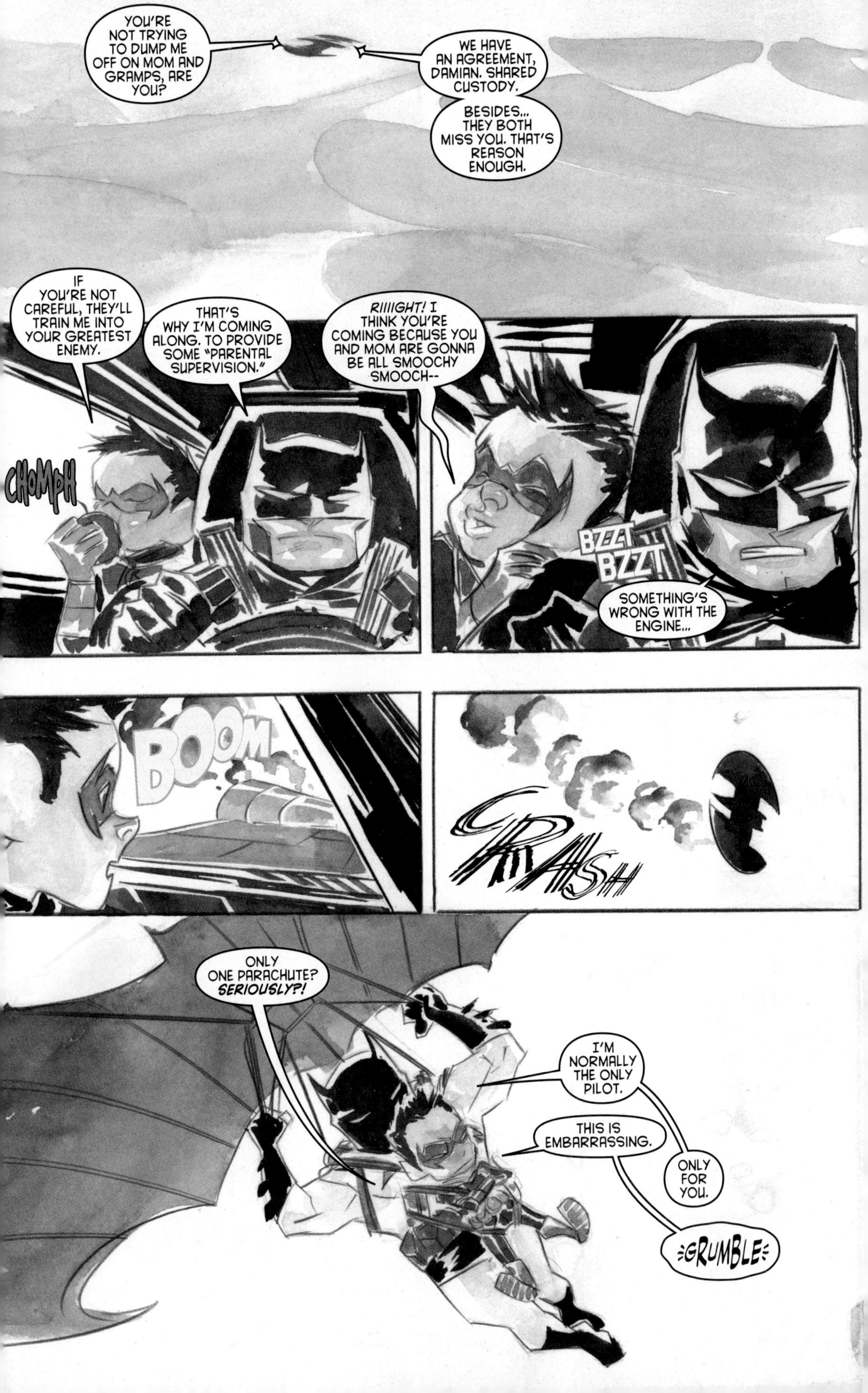
YOU'RE NOT TRYING TO DUMP ME OFF ON MOM AND GRAMPS, ARE YOU?
WE HAVE AN AGREEMENT, DAMIAN. SHARED CUSTODY.
BESIDES... THEY BOTH MISS YOU. THAT'S REASON ENOUGH.
IF YOU'RE NOT CAREFUL, THEY'LL TRAIN ME INTO YOUR GREATEST ENEMY.
CHOMPH
THAT'S WHY I'M COMING ALONG. TO PROVIDE SOME "PARENTAL SUPERVISION."
RIIIIGHT! I THINK YOU'RE COMING BECAUSE YOU AND MOM ARE GONNA BE ALL SMOOCHY SMOOCH--
BZZT BZZT!
SOMETHING'S WRONG WITH THE ENGINE...
BOOM
CRASH
ONLY ONE PARACHUTE? SERIOUSLY?!
I'M NORMALLY THE ONLY PILOT.
THIS IS EMBARRASSING.
ONLY FOR YOU.
GRUMBLE

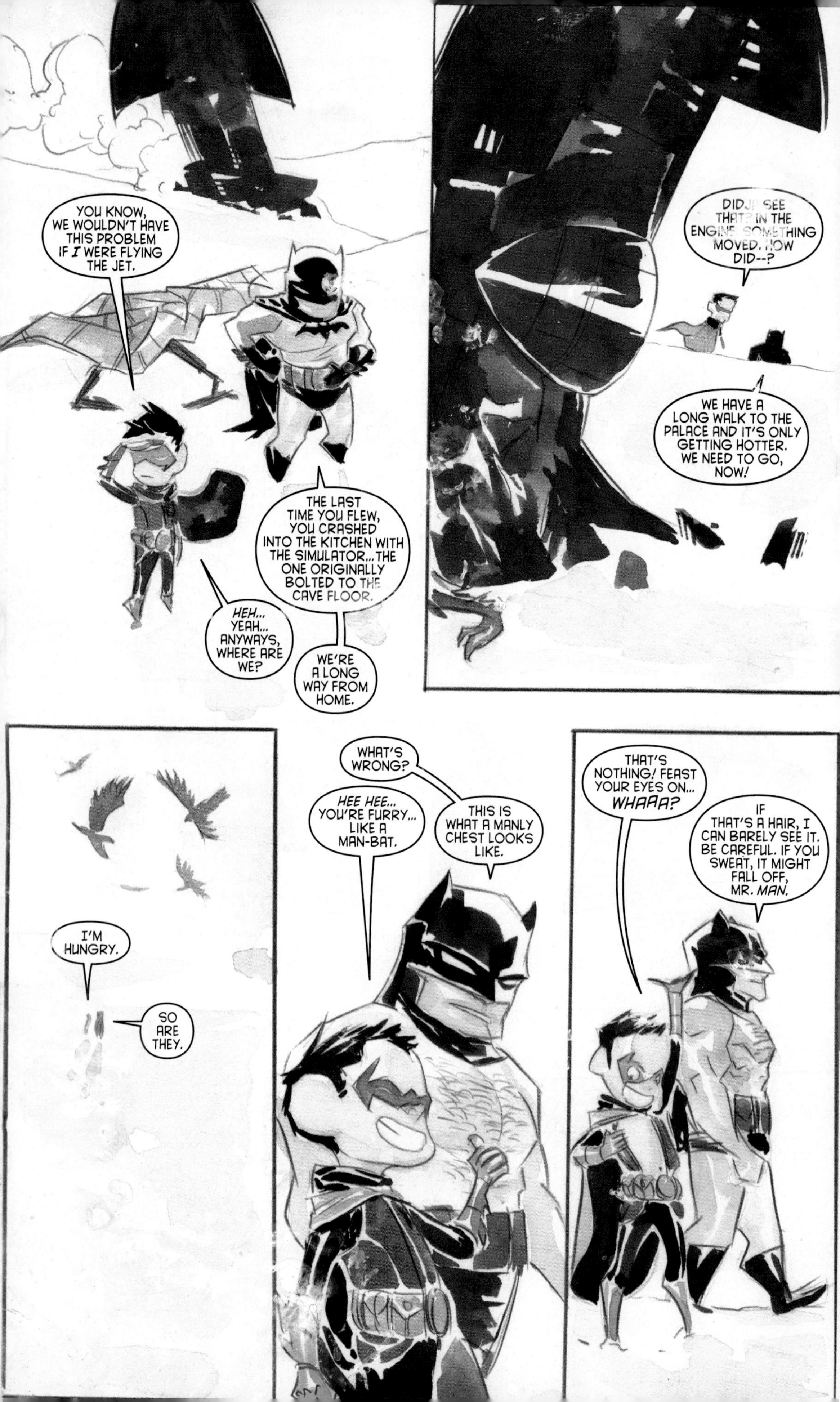
YOU KNOW, WE WOULDN'T HAVE THIS PROBLEM IF *I* WERE FLYING THE JET.
THE LAST TIME YOU FLEW, YOU CRASHED INTO THE KITCHEN WITH THE SIMULATOR... THE ONE ORIGINALLY BOLTED TO THE CAVE FLOOR.
HEH... YEAH... ANYWAYS, WHERE ARE WE?
WE'RE A LONG WAY FROM HOME.
DIDJA SEE THAT? IN THE ENGINE SOMETHING MOVED. HOW DID--?
WE HAVE A LONG WALK TO THE PALACE AND IT'S ONLY GETTING HOTTER. WE NEED TO GO, NOW!
I'M HUNGRY.
SO ARE THEY.
WHAT'S WRONG?
HEE HEE... YOU'RE FURRY... LIKE A MAN-BAT.
THIS IS WHAT A MANLY CHEST LOOKS LIKE.
THAT'S NOTHING! FEAST YOUR EYES ON... *WHAAA?*
IF THAT'S A HAIR, I CAN BARELY SEE IT. BE CAREFUL. IF YOU SWEAT, IT MIGHT FALL OFF, MR. *MAN.*

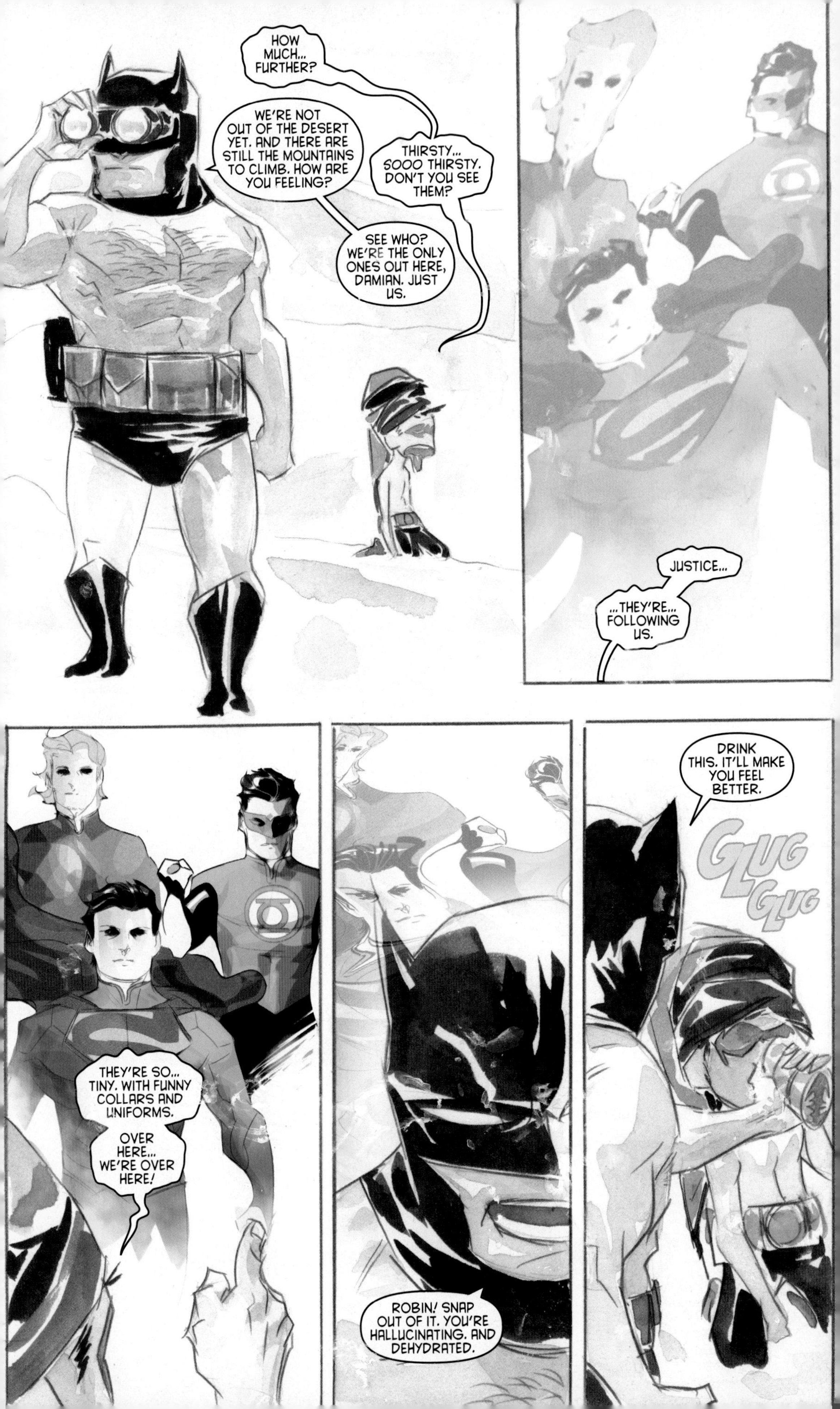

HOW MUCH... FURTHER?
WE'RE NOT OUT OF THE DESERT YET. AND THERE ARE STILL THE MOUNTAINS TO CLIMB. HOW ARE YOU FEELING?
THIRSTY... SOOO THIRSTY. DON'T YOU SEE THEM?
SEE WHO? WE'RE THE ONLY ONES OUT HERE, DAMIAN. JUST US.
JUSTICE...
...THEY'RE... FOLLOWING US.
THEY'RE SO... TINY. WITH FUNNY COLLARS AND UNIFORMS.
OVER HERE... WE'RE OVER HERE!
ROBIN! SNAP OUT OF IT. YOU'RE HALLUCINATING. AND DEHYDRATED.
DRINK THIS. IT'LL MAKE YOU FEEL BETTER.
GLUG GLUG

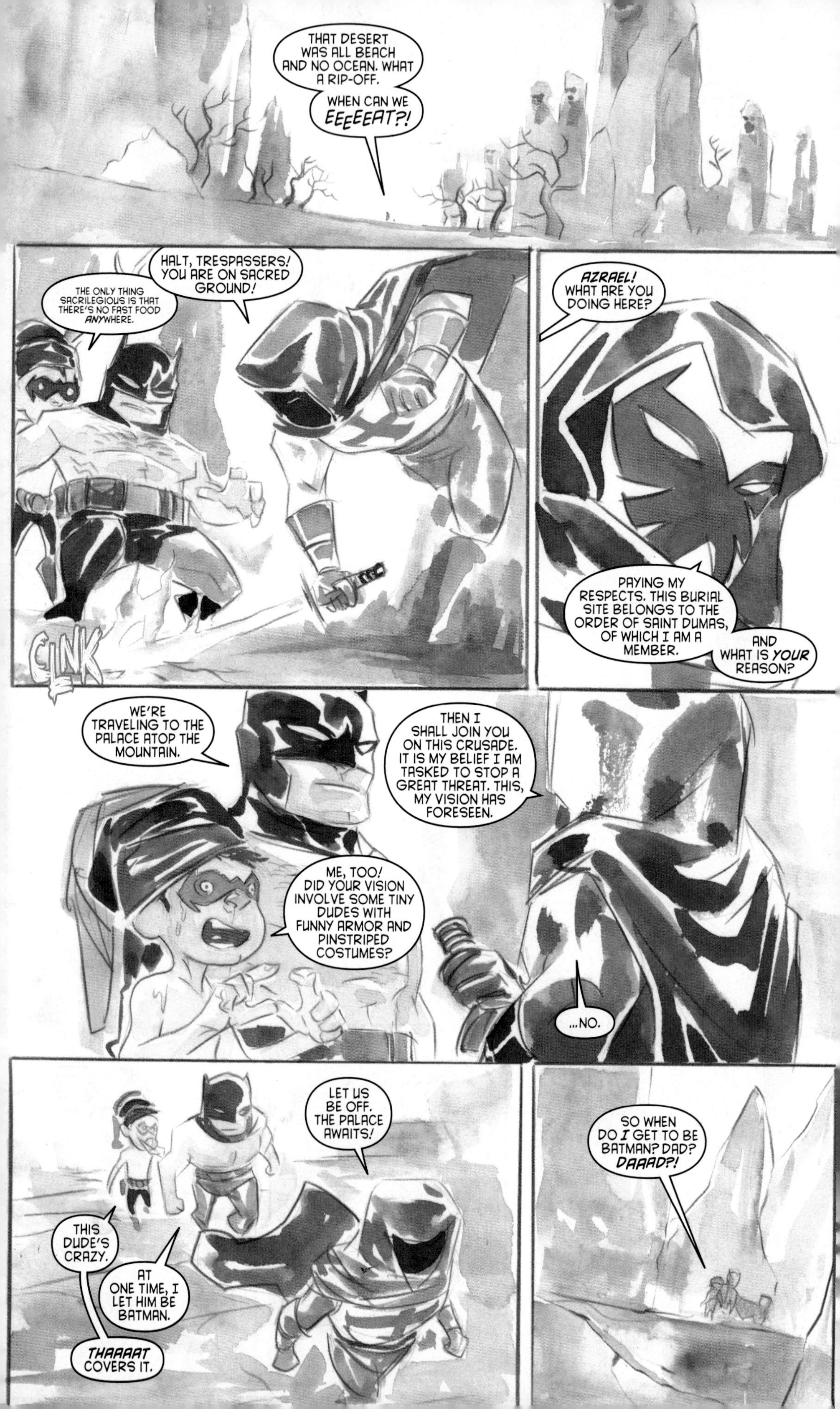

THAT DESERT WAS ALL BEACH AND NO OCEAN. WHAT A RIP-OFF.
WHEN CAN WE EEEEEEAT?!
HALT, TRESPASSERS! YOU ARE ON SACRED GROUND!
THE ONLY THING SACRILEGIOUS IS THAT THERE'S NO FAST FOOD ANYWHERE.
CLINK
AZRAEL! WHAT ARE YOU DOING HERE?
PAYING MY RESPECTS. THIS BURIAL SITE BELONGS TO THE ORDER OF SAINT DUMAS, OF WHICH I AM A MEMBER.
AND WHAT IS YOUR REASON?
WE'RE TRAVELING TO THE PALACE ATOP THE MOUNTAIN.
THEN I SHALL JOIN YOU ON THIS CRUSADE. IT IS MY BELIEF I AM TASKED TO STOP A GREAT THREAT. THIS, MY VISION HAS FORESEEN.
ME, TOO! DID YOUR VISION INVOLVE SOME TINY DUDES WITH FUNNY ARMOR AND PINSTRIPED COSTUMES?
...NO.
LET US BE OFF. THE PALACE AWAITS!
THIS DUDE'S CRAZY.
AT ONE TIME, I LET HIM BE BATMAN.
THAAAAT COVERS IT.
SO WHEN DO I GET TO BE BATMAN? DAD? DAAAD?!

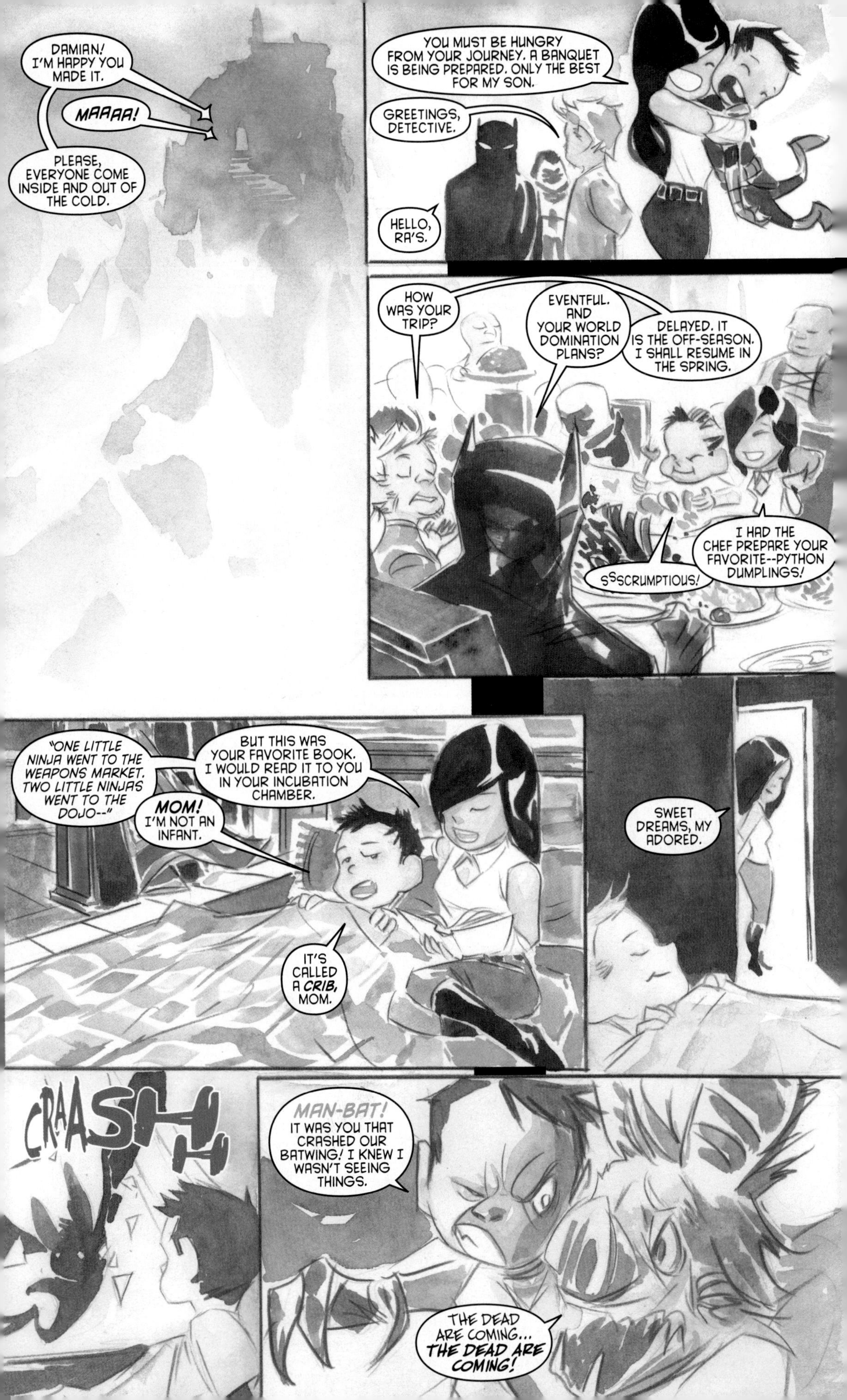
DAMIAN! I'M HAPPY YOU MADE IT.
MAAAA!
PLEASE, EVERYONE COME INSIDE AND OUT OF THE COLD.
YOU MUST BE HUNGRY FROM YOUR JOURNEY. A BANQUET IS BEING PREPARED. ONLY THE BEST FOR MY SON.
GREETINGS, DETECTIVE.
HELLO, RA'S.
HOW WAS YOUR TRIP?
EVENTFUL. AND YOUR WORLD DOMINATION PLANS?
DELAYED. IT IS THE OFF-SEASON. I SHALL RESUME IN THE SPRING.
I HAD THE CHEF PREPARE YOUR FAVORITE--PYTHON DUMPLINGS!
SSSCRUMPTIOUS!
"ONE LITTLE NINJA WENT TO THE WEAPONS MARKET. TWO LITTLE NINJAS WENT TO THE DOJO--"
MOM! I'M NOT AN INFANT.
BUT THIS WAS YOUR FAVORITE BOOK. I WOULD READ IT TO YOU IN YOUR INCUBATION CHAMBER.
IT'S CALLED A CRIB, MOM.
SWEET DREAMS, MY ADORED.
CRAASH
MAN-BAT! IT WAS YOU THAT CRASHED OUR BATWING! I KNEW I WASN'T SEEING THINGS.
THE DEAD ARE COMING... THE DEAD ARE COMING!

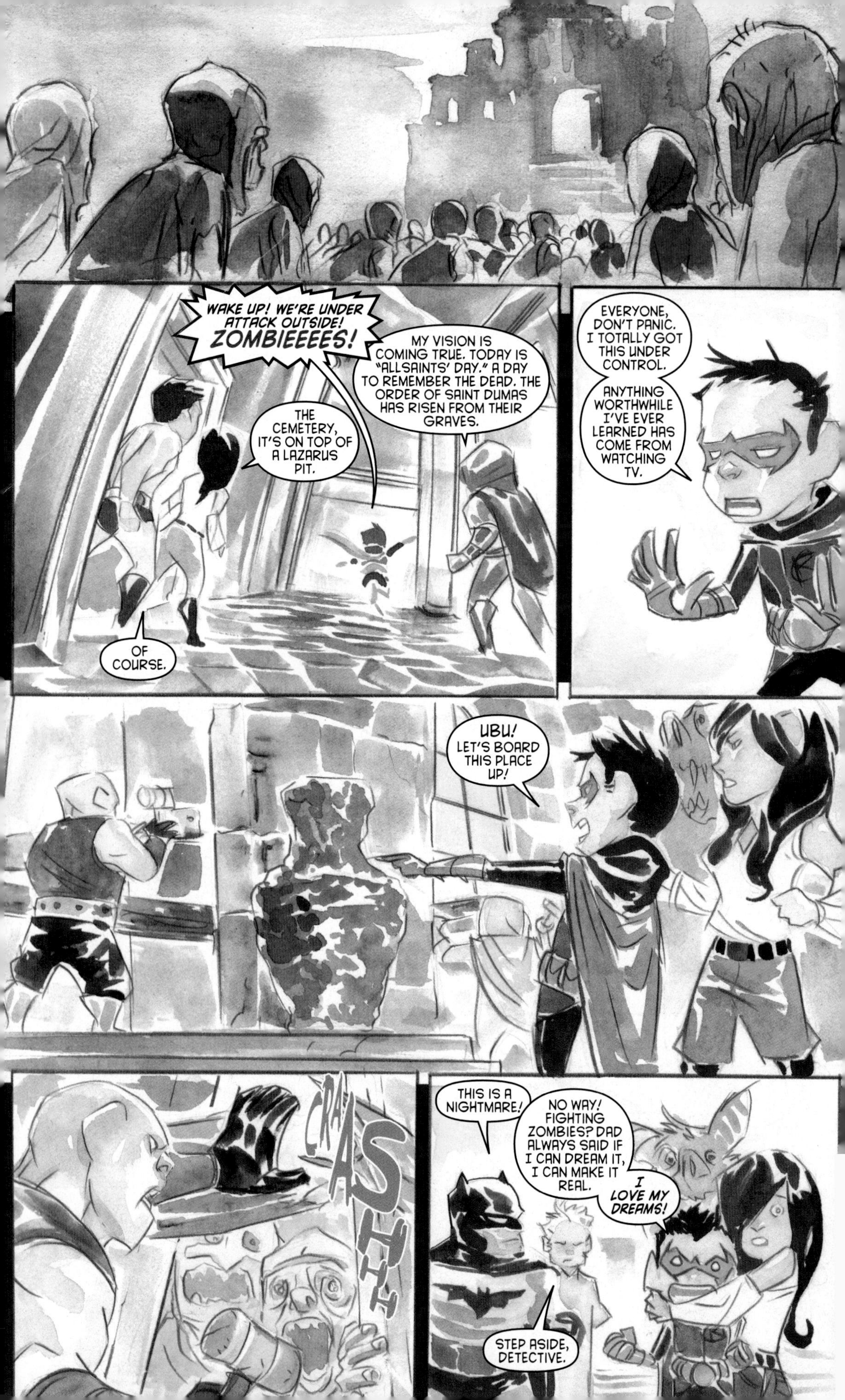
WAKE UP! WE'RE UNDER ATTACK OUTSIDE! ZOMBIEEEES!
MY VISION IS COMING TRUE. TODAY IS "ALLSAINTS' DAY." A DAY TO REMEMBER THE DEAD. THE ORDER OF SAINT DUMAS HAS RISEN FROM THEIR GRAVES.
THE CEMETERY, IT'S ON TOP OF A LAZARUS PIT.
OF COURSE.
EVERYONE, DON'T PANIC. I TOTALLY GOT THIS UNDER CONTROL.
ANYTHING WORTHWHILE I'VE EVER LEARNED HAS COME FROM WATCHING TV.
UBU! LET'S BOARD THIS PLACE UP!
CRASHHH
THIS IS A NIGHTMARE!
NO WAY! FIGHTING ZOMBIES? DAD ALWAYS SAID IF I CAN DREAM IT, I CAN MAKE IT REAL.
I LOVE MY DREAMS!
STEP ASIDE, DETECTIVE.

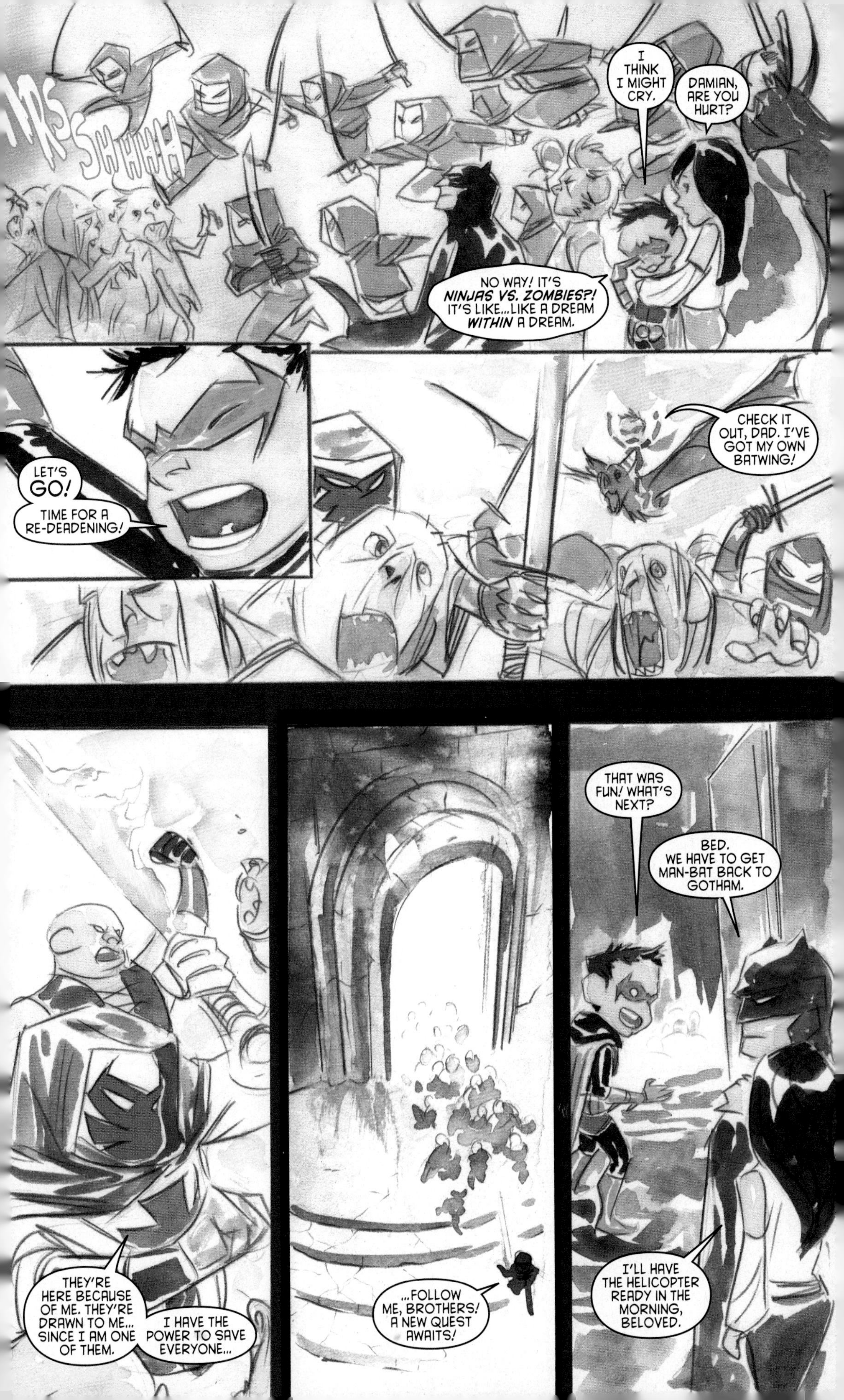
SHHHHH
I THINK I MIGHT CRY.
DAMIAN, ARE YOU HURT?
NO WAY! IT'S NINJAS VS. ZOMBIES?! IT'S LIKE...LIKE A DREAM WITHIN A DREAM.
LET'S GO!
TIME FOR A RE-DEADENING!
CHECK IT OUT, DAD. I'VE GOT MY OWN BATWING!
THEY'RE HERE BECAUSE OF ME. THEY'RE DRAWN TO ME... SINCE I AM ONE OF THEM.
I HAVE THE POWER TO SAVE EVERYONE...
...FOLLOW ME, BROTHERS! A NEW QUEST AWAITS!
THAT WAS FUN! WHAT'S NEXT?
BED. WE HAVE TO GET MAN-BAT BACK TO GOTHAM.
I'LL HAVE THE HELICOPTER READY IN THE MORNING, BELOVED.

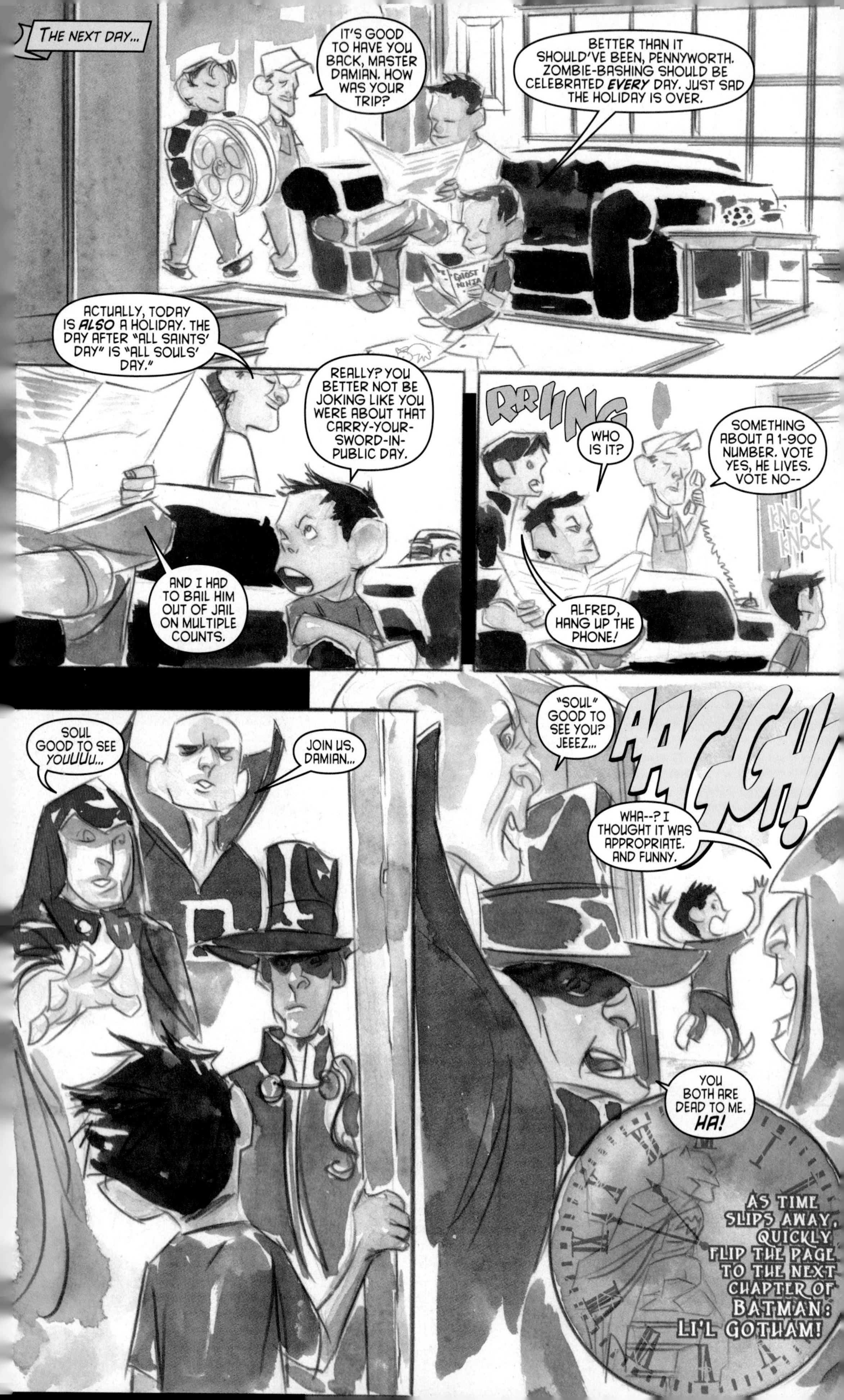
THE NEXT DAY...
IT'S GOOD TO HAVE YOU BACK, MASTER DAMIAN. HOW WAS YOUR TRIP?
BETTER THAN IT SHOULD'VE BEEN, PENNYWORTH. ZOMBIE-BASHING SHOULD BE CELEBRATED EVERY DAY. JUST SAD THE HOLIDAY IS OVER.
GHOST NINJA
ACTUALLY, TODAY IS ALSO A HOLIDAY. THE DAY AFTER "ALL SAINTS' DAY" IS "ALL SOULS' DAY."
REALLY? YOU BETTER NOT BE JOKING LIKE YOU WERE ABOUT THAT CARRY-YOUR-SWORD-IN-PUBLIC DAY.
AND I HAD TO BAIL HIM OUT OF JAIL ON MULTIPLE COUNTS.
RRIING
WHO IS IT?
SOMETHING ABOUT A 1-900 NUMBER. VOTE YES, HE LIVES. VOTE NO--
KNOCK KNOCK
ALFRED, HANG UP THE PHONE!
SOUL GOOD TO SEE YOUUUU...
JOIN US, DAMIAN...
"SOUL" GOOD TO SEE YOU? JEEEZ...
AAGGH!
WHA--? I THOUGHT IT WAS APPROPRIATE. AND FUNNY.
YOU BOTH ARE DEAD TO ME. HA!
AS TIME SLIPS AWAY, QUICKLY FLIP THE PAGE TO THE NEXT CHAPTER OF BATMAN: LI'L GOTHAM!

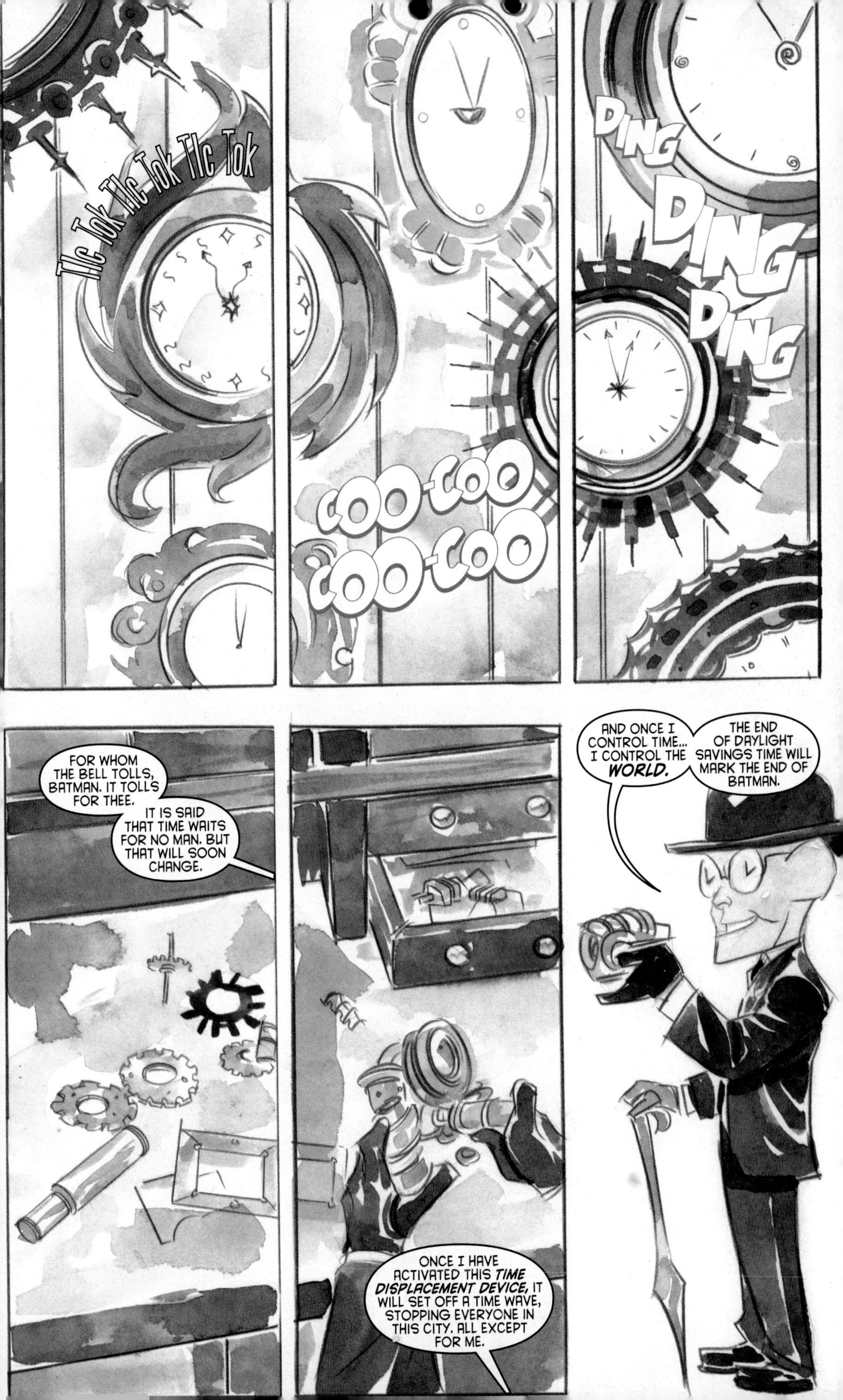
TIC TOK TIC TOK TIC TOK
COO-COO COO-COO
DING DING DING DING
FOR WHOM THE BELL TOLLS, BATMAN. IT TOLLS FOR THEE.
IT IS SAID THAT TIME WAITS FOR NO MAN. BUT THAT WILL SOON CHANGE.
ONCE I HAVE ACTIVATED THIS *TIME DISPLACEMENT DEVICE,* IT WILL SET OFF A TIME WAVE, STOPPING EVERYONE IN THIS CITY. ALL EXCEPT FOR ME.
AND ONCE I CONTROL TIME... I CONTROL THE ***WORLD.***
THE END OF DAYLIGHT SAVINGS TIME WILL MARK THE END OF BATMAN.

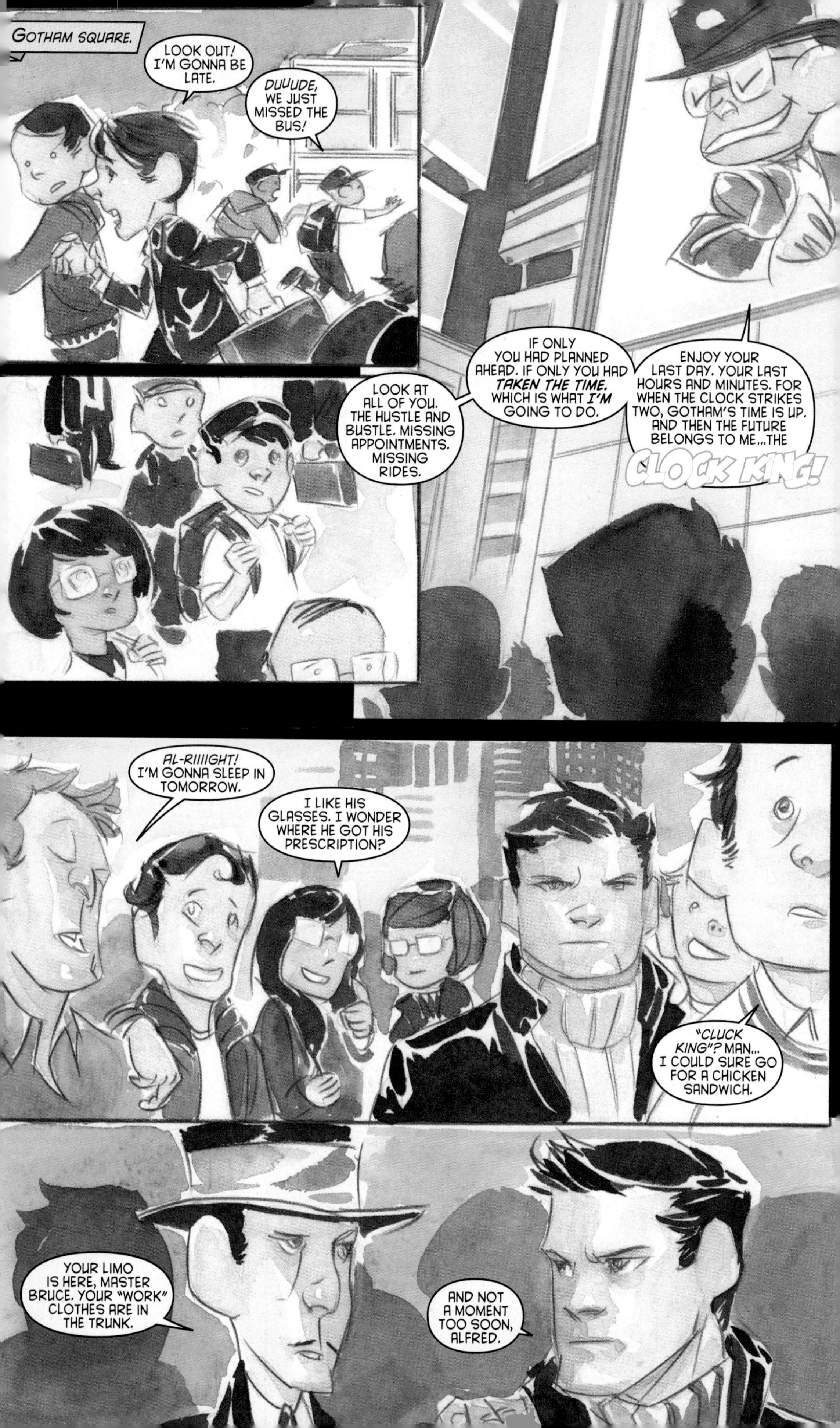
GOTHAM SQUARE.
LOOK OUT! I'M GONNA BE LATE.
DUUUDE, WE JUST MISSED THE BUS!
LOOK AT ALL OF YOU. THE HUSTLE AND BUSTLE. MISSING APPOINTMENTS. MISSING RIDES.
IF ONLY YOU HAD PLANNED AHEAD. IF ONLY YOU HAD TAKEN THE TIME. WHICH IS WHAT I'M GOING TO DO.
ENJOY YOUR LAST DAY. YOUR LAST HOURS AND MINUTES. FOR WHEN THE CLOCK STRIKES TWO, GOTHAM'S TIME IS UP. AND THEN THE FUTURE BELONGS TO ME...THE CLOCK KING!
AL-RIIIIGHT! I'M GONNA SLEEP IN TOMORROW.
I LIKE HIS GLASSES. I WONDER WHERE HE GOT HIS PRESCRIPTION?
"CLUCK KING"? MAN... I COULD SURE GO FOR A CHICKEN SANDWICH.
YOUR LIMO IS HERE, MASTER BRUCE. YOUR "WORK" CLOTHES ARE IN THE TRUNK.
AND NOT A MOMENT TOO SOON, ALFRED.

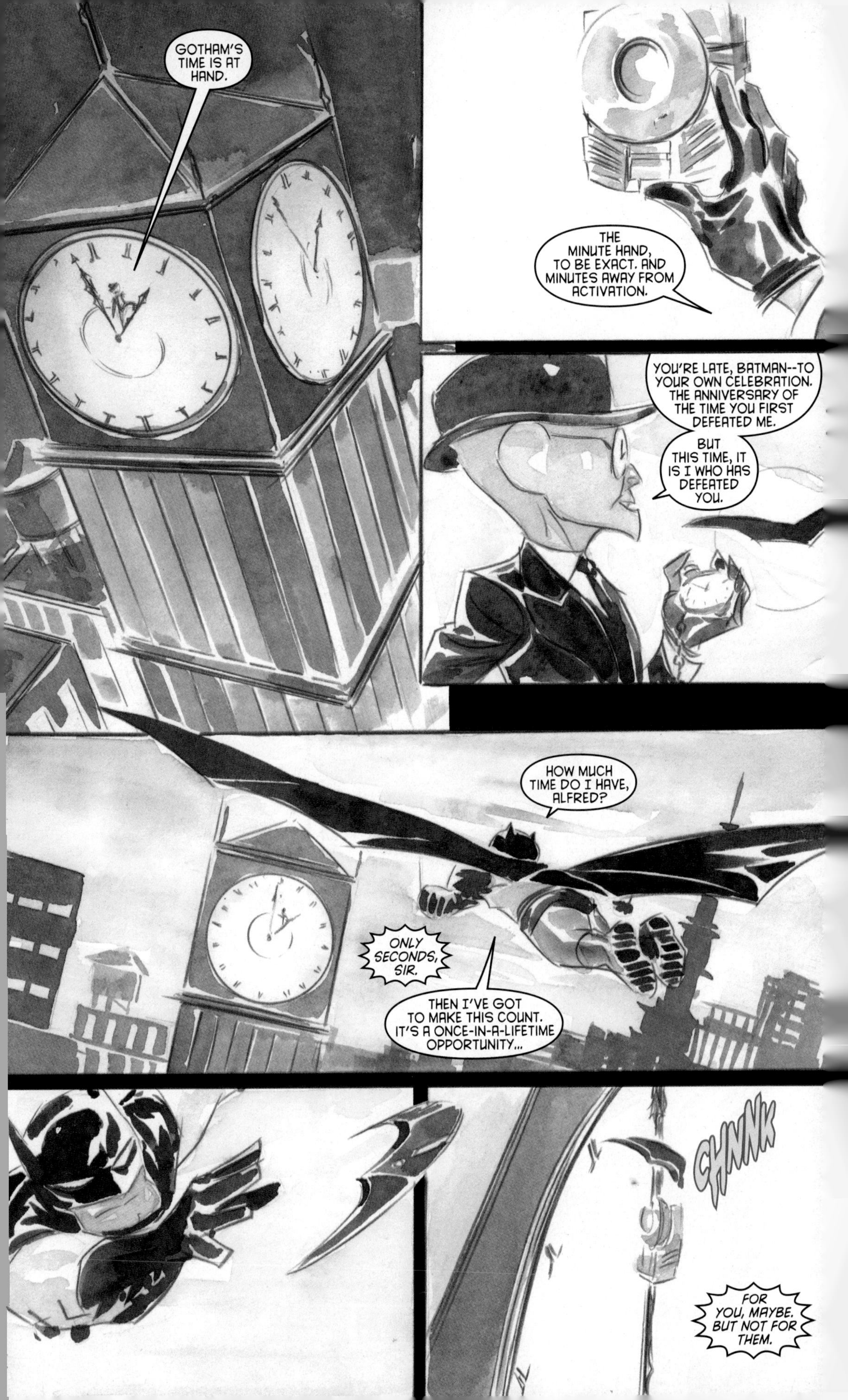
GOTHAM'S TIME IS AT HAND.
THE MINUTE HAND, TO BE EXACT. AND MINUTES AWAY FROM ACTIVATION.
YOU'RE LATE, BATMAN--TO YOUR OWN CELEBRATION. THE ANNIVERSARY OF THE TIME YOU FIRST DEFEATED ME.
BUT THIS TIME, IT IS I WHO HAS DEFEATED YOU.
HOW MUCH TIME DO I HAVE, ALFRED?
ONLY SECONDS, SIR.
THEN I'VE GOT TO MAKE THIS COUNT. IT'S A ONCE-IN-A-LIFETIME OPPORTUNITY...
CHNNK
FOR YOU, MAYBE. BUT NOT FOR THEM.

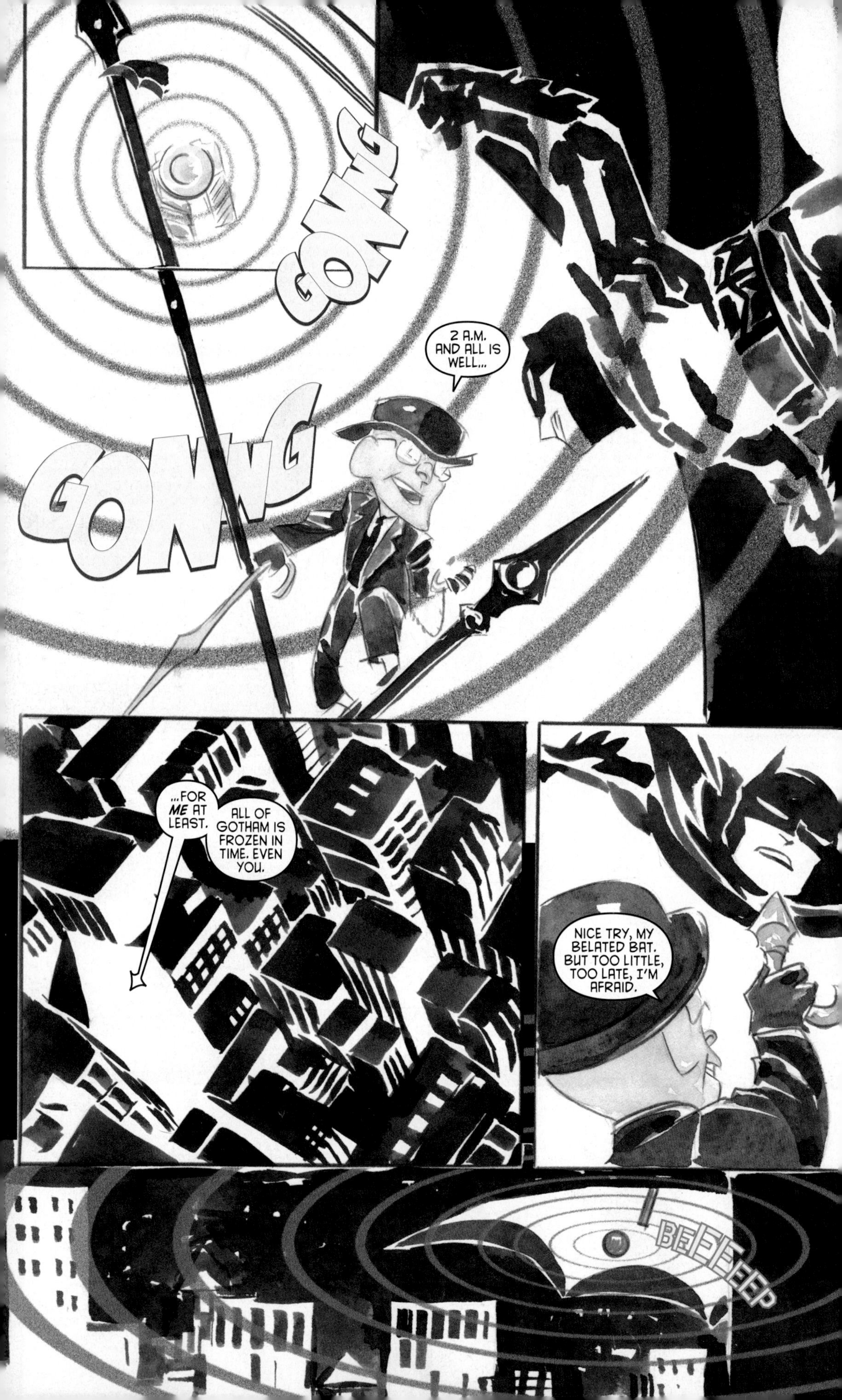
GONNG
2 A.M. AND ALL IS WELL...
GONNG
...FOR ME AT LEAST.
ALL OF GOTHAM IS FROZEN IN TIME. EVEN YOU.
NICE TRY, MY BELATED BAT. BUT TOO LITTLE, TOO LATE, I'M AFRAID.
BEEEEEP

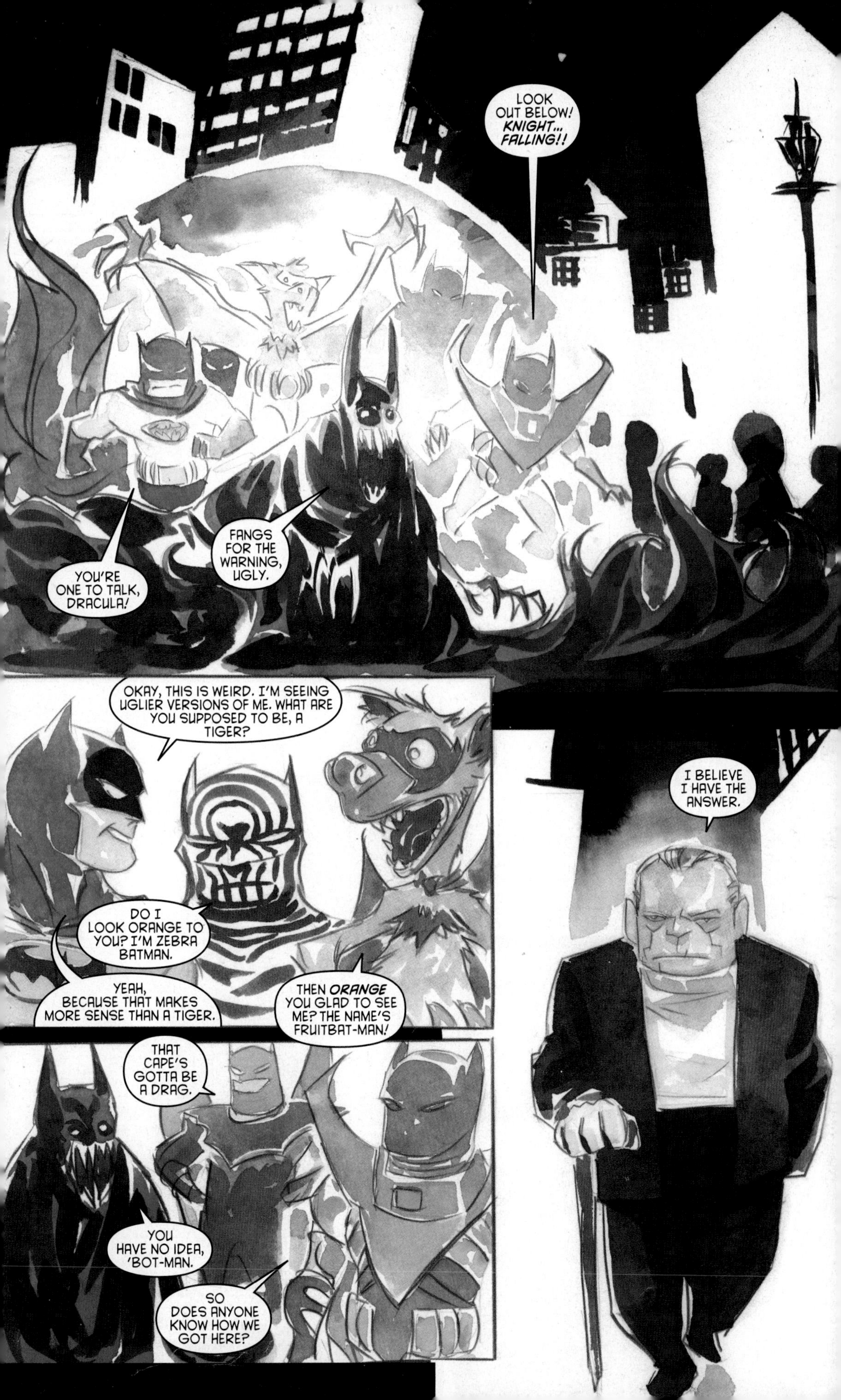

LOOK OUT BELOW! KNIGHT... FALLING!!
YOU'RE ONE TO TALK, DRACULA!
FANGS FOR THE WARNING, UGLY.
OKAY, THIS IS WEIRD. I'M SEEING UGLIER VERSIONS OF ME. WHAT ARE YOU SUPPOSED TO BE, A TIGER?
DO I LOOK ORANGE TO YOU? I'M ZEBRA BATMAN.
YEAH, BECAUSE THAT MAKES MORE SENSE THAN A TIGER.
THEN ORANGE YOU GLAD TO SEE ME? THE NAME'S FRUITBAT-MAN!
THAT CAPE'S GOTTA BE A DRAG.
YOU HAVE NO IDEA, 'BOT-MAN.
SO DOES ANYONE KNOW HOW WE GOT HERE?
I BELIEVE I HAVE THE ANSWER.

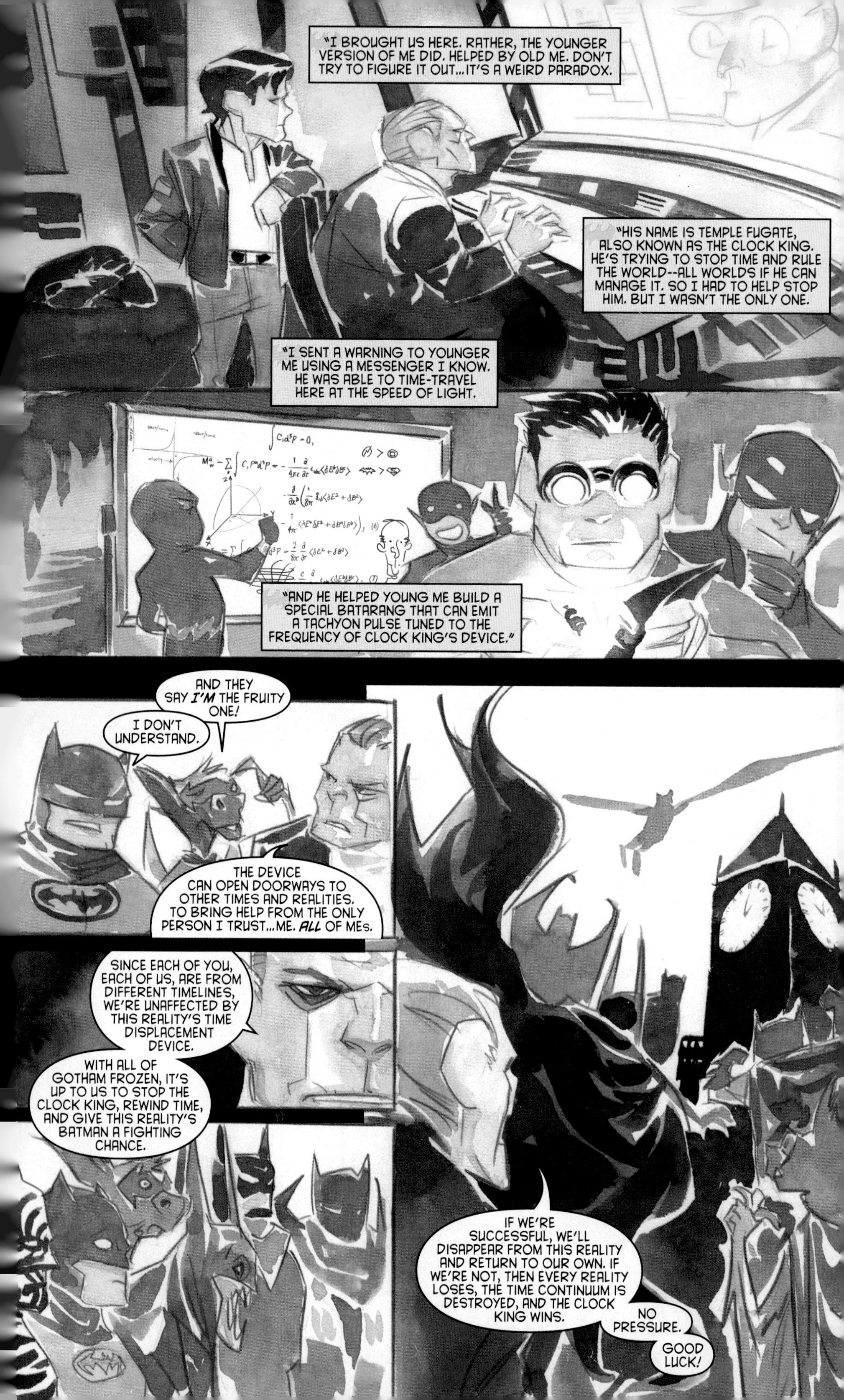
"I BROUGHT US HERE. RATHER, THE YOUNGER VERSION OF ME DID. HELPED BY OLD ME. DON'T TRY TO FIGURE IT OUT... IT'S A WEIRD PARADOX.
"HIS NAME IS TEMPLE FUGATE, ALSO KNOWN AS THE CLOCK KING. HE'S TRYING TO STOP TIME AND RULE THE WORLD--ALL WORLDS IF HE CAN MANAGE IT. SO I HAD TO HELP STOP HIM. BUT I WASN'T THE ONLY ONE.
"I SENT A WARNING TO YOUNGER ME USING A MESSENGER I KNOW. HE WAS ABLE TO TIME-TRAVEL HERE AT THE SPEED OF LIGHT.
"AND HE HELPED YOUNG ME BUILD A SPECIAL BATARANG THAT CAN EMIT A TACHYON PULSE TUNED TO THE FREQUENCY OF CLOCK KING'S DEVICE."
AND THEY SAY *I'M* THE FRUITY ONE!
I DON'T UNDERSTAND.
THE DEVICE CAN OPEN DOORWAYS TO OTHER TIMES AND REALITIES. TO BRING HELP FROM THE ONLY PERSON I TRUST... ME. ***ALL*** OF MEs.
SINCE EACH OF YOU, EACH OF US, ARE FROM DIFFERENT TIMELINES, WE'RE UNAFFECTED BY THIS REALITY'S TIME DISPLACEMENT DEVICE.
WITH ALL OF GOTHAM FROZEN, IT'S UP TO US TO STOP THE CLOCK KING, REWIND TIME, AND GIVE THIS REALITY'S BATMAN A FIGHTING CHANCE.
IF WE'RE SUCCESSFUL, WE'LL DISAPPEAR FROM THIS REALITY AND RETURN TO OUR OWN. IF WE'RE NOT, THEN EVERY REALITY LOSES, THE TIME CONTINUUM IS DESTROYED, AND THE CLOCK KING WINS.
NO PRESSURE.
GOOD LUCK!

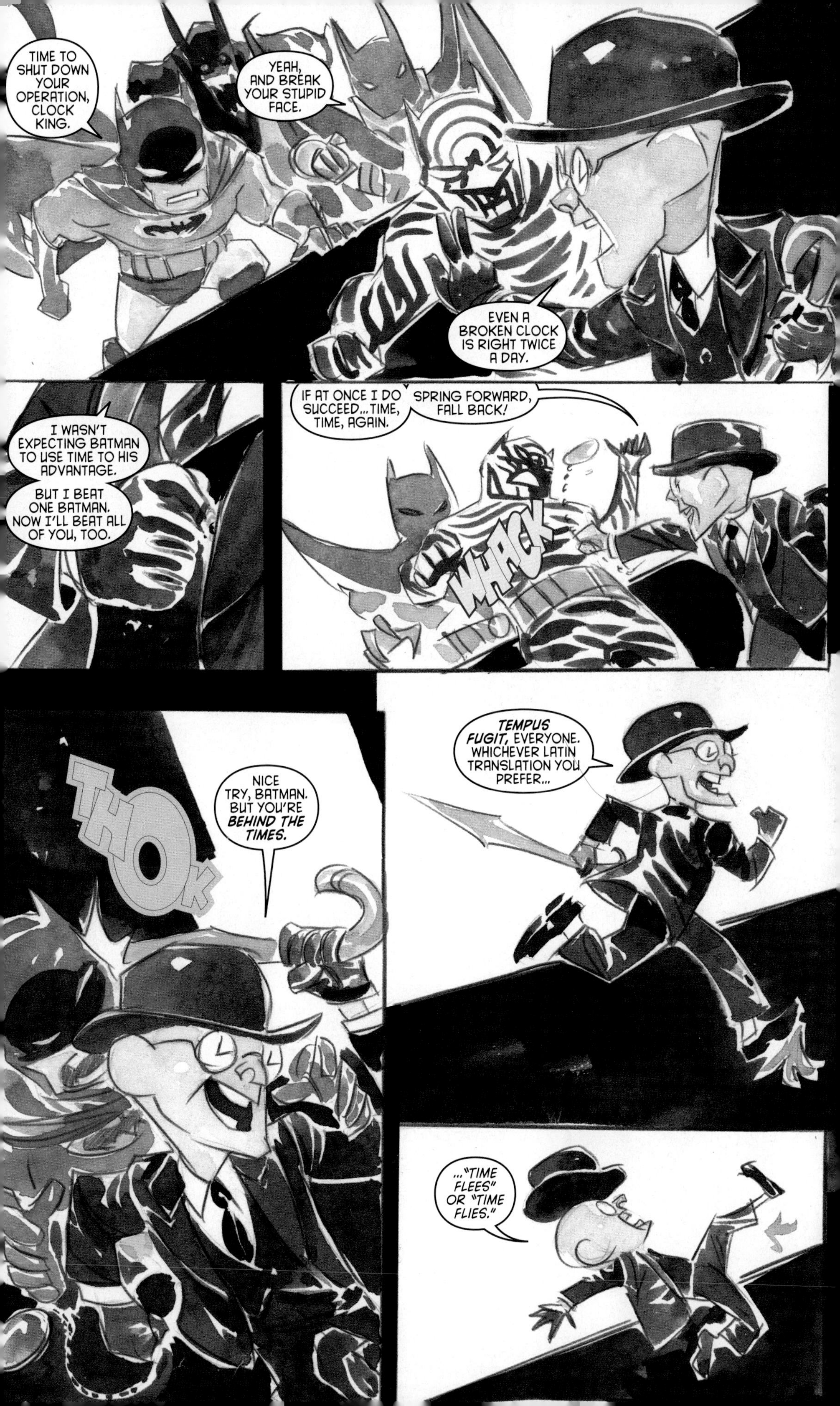

TIME TO SHUT DOWN YOUR OPERATION, CLOCK KING.
YEAH, AND BREAK YOUR STUPID FACE.
EVEN A BROKEN CLOCK IS RIGHT TWICE A DAY.
I WASN'T EXPECTING BATMAN TO USE TIME TO HIS ADVANTAGE.
BUT I BEAT ONE BATMAN. NOW I'LL BEAT ALL OF YOU, TOO.
IF AT ONCE I DO SUCCEED...TIME, TIME, AGAIN.
SPRING FORWARD, FALL BACK!
WHACK
THOK
NICE TRY, BATMAN. BUT YOU'RE *BEHIND THE TIMES.*
TEMPUS FUGIT, EVERYONE. WHICHEVER LATIN TRANSLATION YOU PREFER...
..."*TIME FLEES*" OR "*TIME FLIES.*"

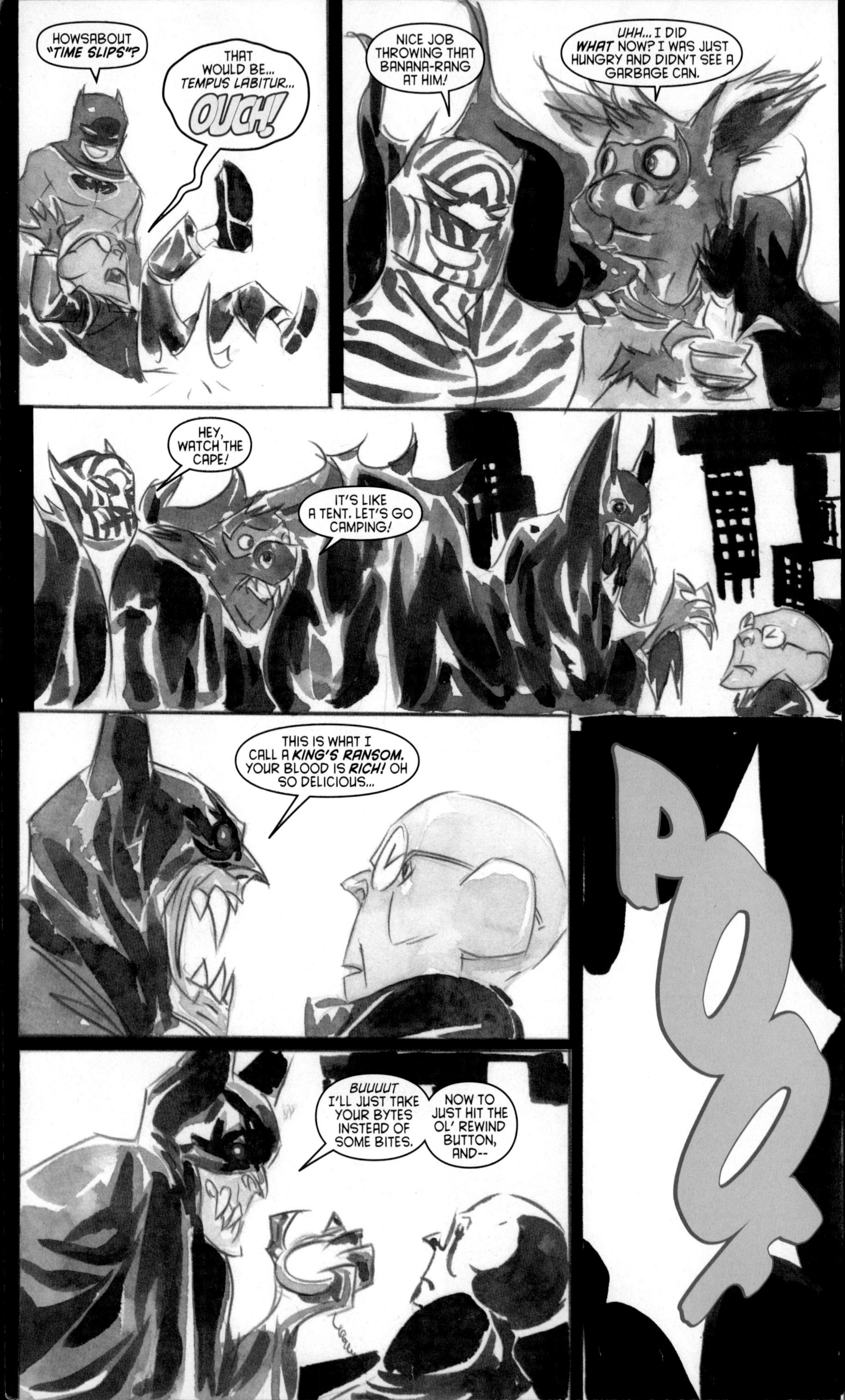
HOWSABOUT "TIME SLIPS"?
THAT WOULD BE... TEMPUS LABITUR...
OUCH!
NICE JOB THROWING THAT BANANA-RANG AT HIM!
UHH... I DID WHAT NOW? I WAS JUST HUNGRY AND DIDN'T SEE A GARBAGE CAN.
HEY, WATCH THE CAPE!
IT'S LIKE A TENT. LET'S GO CAMPING!
THIS IS WHAT I CALL A KING'S RANSOM. YOUR BLOOD IS RICH! OH SO DELICIOUS...
BUUUUT I'LL JUST TAKE YOUR BYTES INSTEAD OF SOME BITES.
NOW TO JUST HIT THE OL' REWIND BUTTON, AND--
POOF

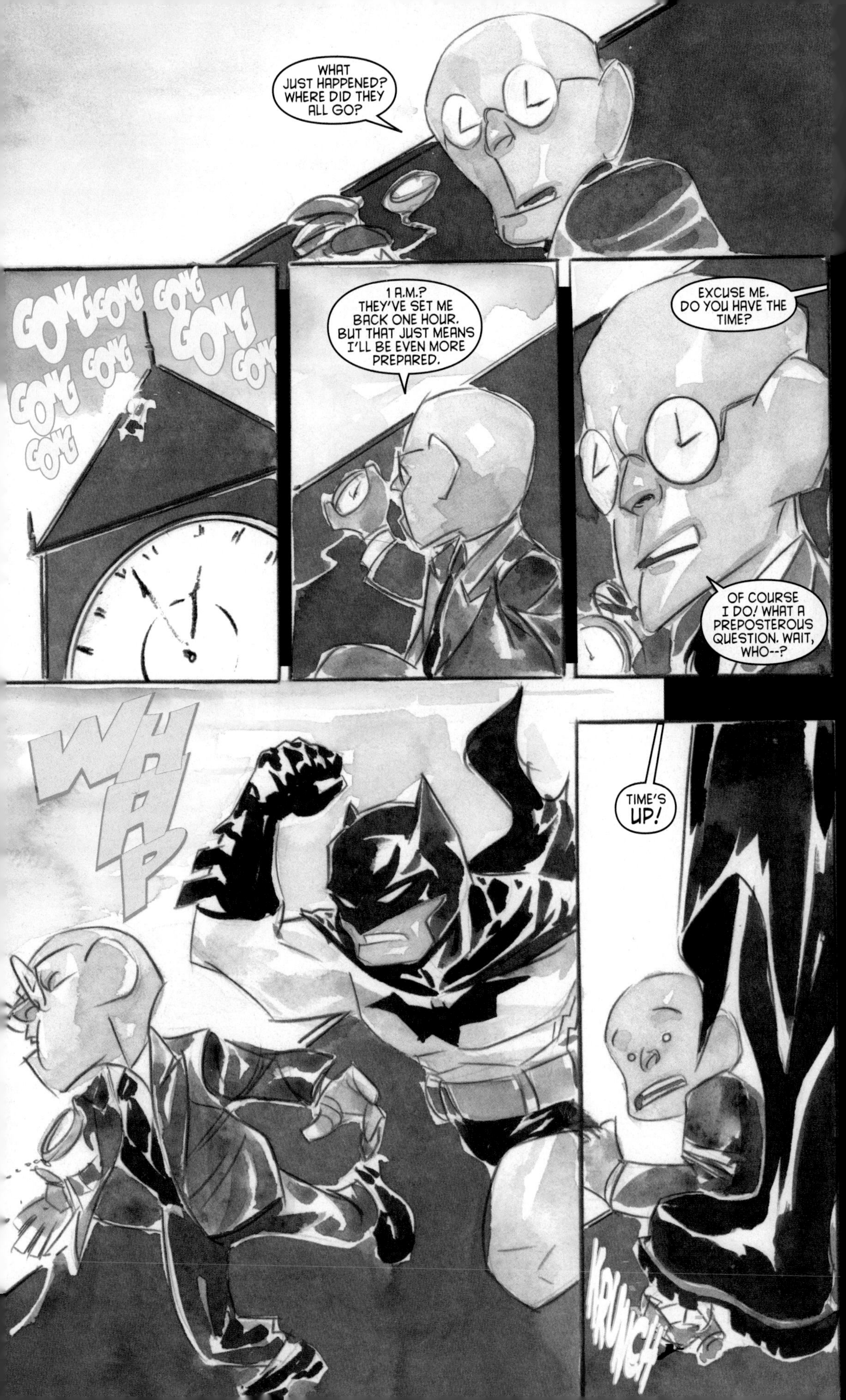
WHAT JUST HAPPENED? WHERE DID THEY ALL GO?
GONG GONG GONG GONG GONG GONG GONG GONG
1 A.M.? THEY'VE SET ME BACK ONE HOUR. BUT THAT JUST MEANS I'LL BE EVEN MORE PREPARED.
EXCUSE ME. DO YOU HAVE THE TIME?
OF COURSE I DO! WHAT A PREPOSTEROUS QUESTION. WAIT, WHO--?
WHAP
TIME'S UP!
KRUNCH

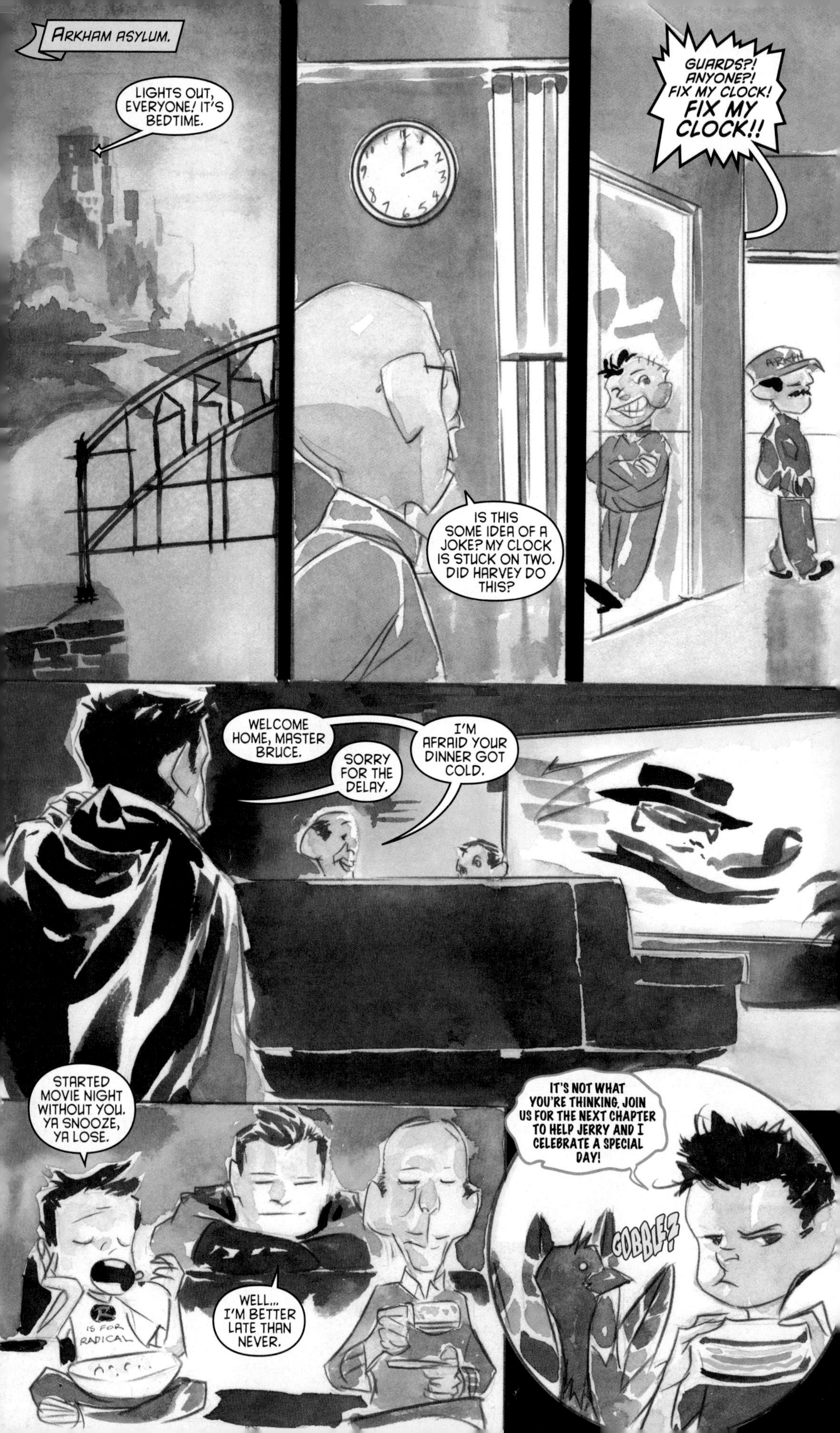
ARKHAM ASYLUM.
LIGHTS OUT, EVERYONE! IT'S BEDTIME.
IS THIS SOME IDEA OF A JOKE? MY CLOCK IS STUCK ON TWO. DID HARVEY DO THIS?
GUARDS?! ANYONE?! FIX MY CLOCK! FIX MY CLOCK!!
ARKH
WELCOME HOME, MASTER BRUCE.
I'M AFRAID YOUR DINNER GOT COLD.
SORRY FOR THE DELAY.
STARTED MOVIE NIGHT WITHOUT YOU. YA SNOOZE, YA LOSE.
IS FOR RADICAL
WELL... I'M BETTER LATE THAN NEVER.
IT'S NOT WHAT YOU'RE THINKING. JOIN US FOR THE NEXT CHAPTER TO HELP JERRY AND I CELEBRATE A SPECIAL DAY!
GOBBLE?

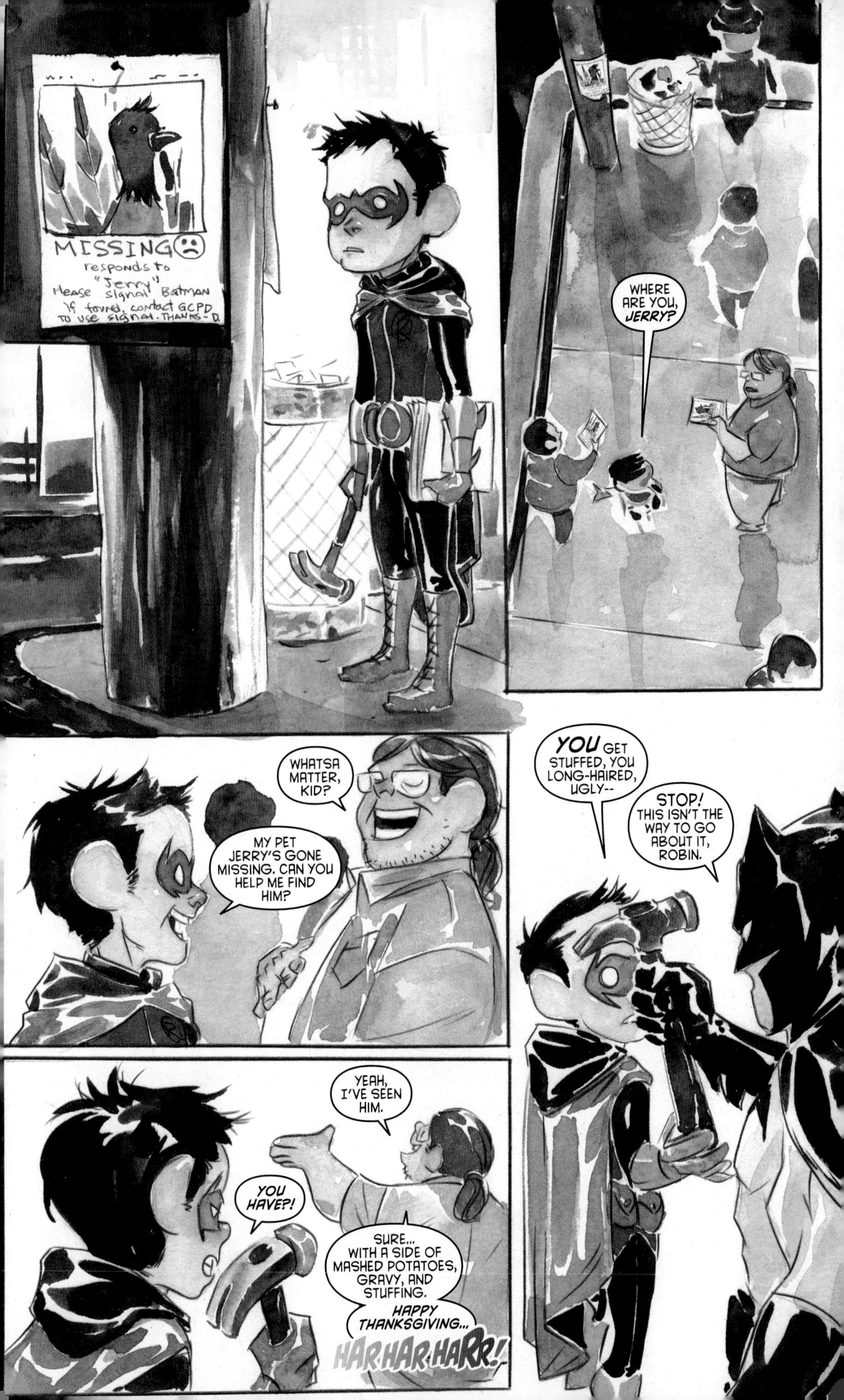
MISSING
responds to "Jerry"
Please signal Batman
If found, contact GCPD to use signal. THANKS - D.
WHERE ARE YOU, JERRY?
WHATSA MATTER, KID?
MY PET JERRY'S GONE MISSING. CAN YOU HELP ME FIND HIM?
YEAH, I'VE SEEN HIM.
YOU HAVE?!
SURE... WITH A SIDE OF MASHED POTATOES, GRAVY, AND STUFFING.
HAPPY THANKSGIVING...
HAR HAR HARR!
YOU GET STUFFED, YOU LONG-HAIRED, UGLY--
STOP! THIS ISN'T THE WAY TO GO ABOUT IT, ROBIN.

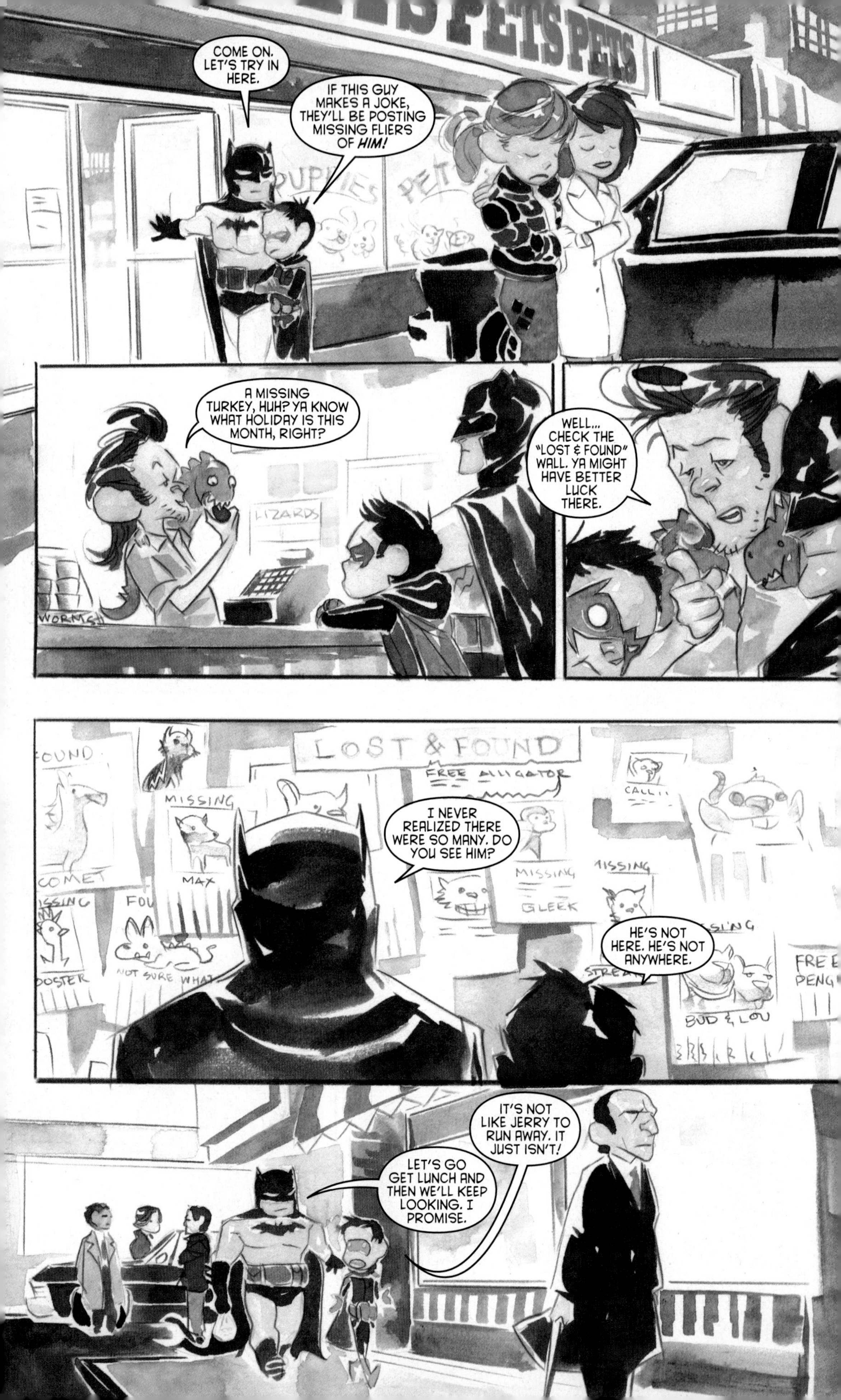

COME ON. LET'S TRY IN HERE.
IF THIS GUY MAKES A JOKE, THEY'LL BE POSTING MISSING FLIERS OF *HIM!*
A MISSING TURKEY, HUH? YA KNOW WHAT HOLIDAY IS THIS MONTH, RIGHT?
LIZARDS
WELL... CHECK THE "LOST & FOUND" WALL. YA MIGHT HAVE BETTER LUCK THERE.
LOST & FOUND
FREE ALLIGATOR
MISSING
MAX
COMET
MISSING
GLEEK
NOT SURE WHAT
I NEVER REALIZED THERE WERE SO MANY. DO YOU SEE HIM?
HE'S NOT HERE. HE'S NOT ANYWHERE.
BUD & LOU
IT'S NOT LIKE JERRY TO RUN AWAY. IT JUST ISN'T!
LET'S GO GET LUNCH AND THEN WE'LL KEEP LOOKING. I PROMISE.

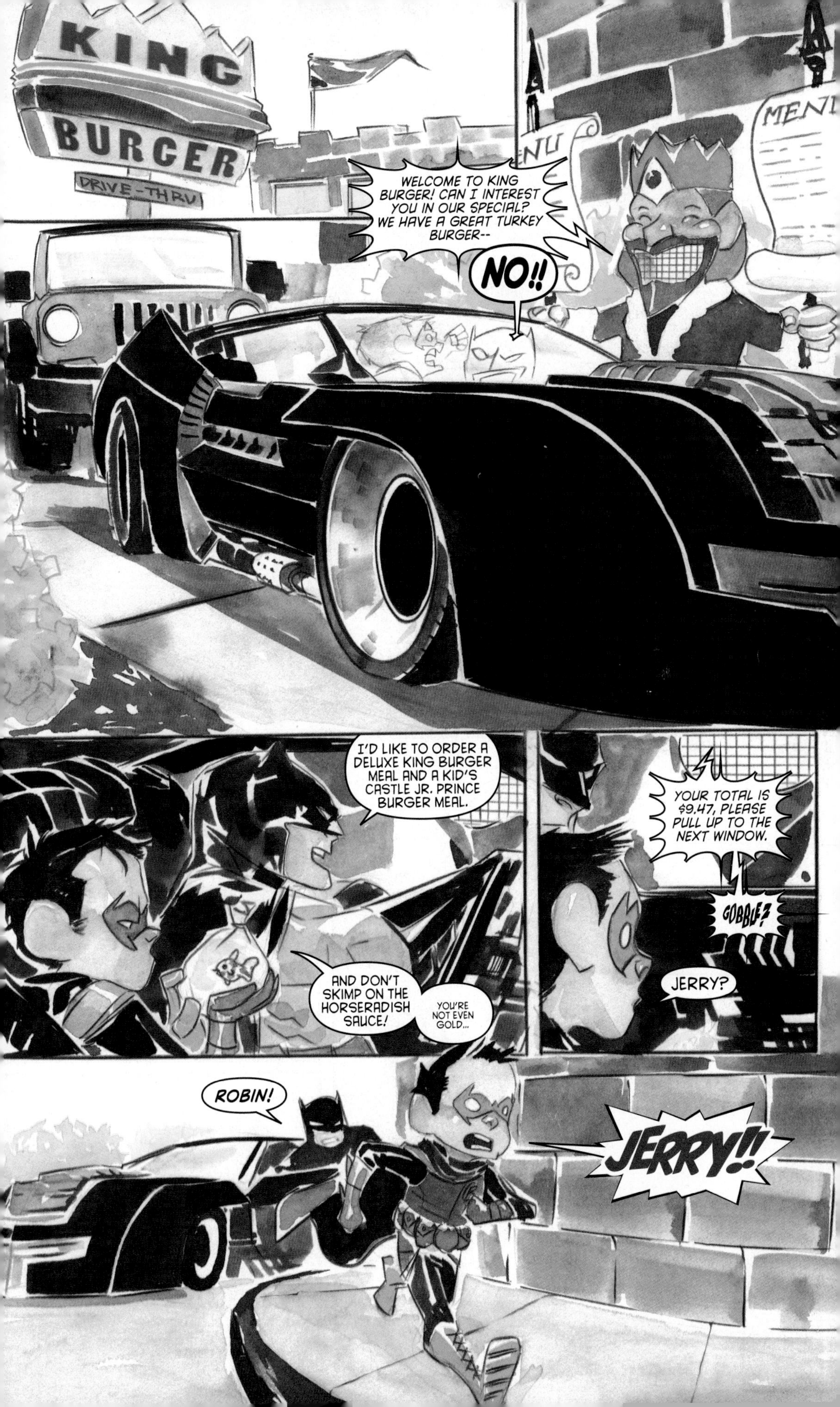
KING BURGER
DRIVE-THRU
MENU
WELCOME TO KING BURGER! CAN I INTEREST YOU IN OUR SPECIAL? WE HAVE A GREAT TURKEY BURGER--
NO!!
I'D LIKE TO ORDER A DELUXE KING BURGER MEAL AND A KID'S CASTLE JR. PRINCE BURGER MEAL.
AND DON'T SKIMP ON THE HORSERADISH SAUCE!
YOU'RE NOT EVEN GOLD...
YOUR TOTAL IS $9.47, PLEASE PULL UP TO THE NEXT WINDOW.
GOBBLE?
JERRY?
ROBIN!
JERRY!!

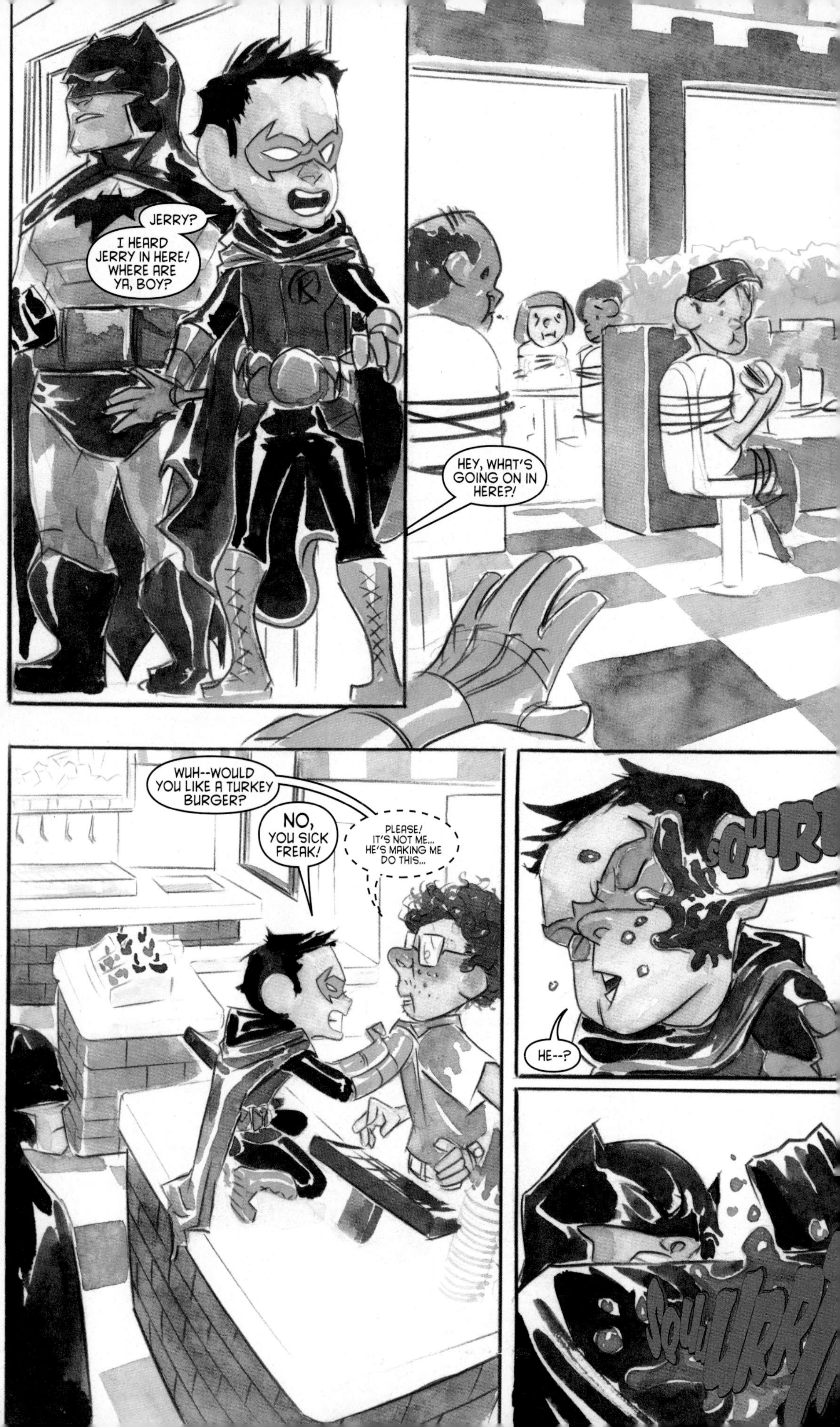
JERRY?
I HEARD JERRY IN HERE! WHERE ARE YA, BOY?
HEY, WHAT'S GOING ON IN HERE?!
WUH--WOULD YOU LIKE A TURKEY BURGER?
NO, YOU SICK FREAK!
PLEASE! IT'S NOT ME... HE'S MAKING ME DO THIS...
HE--?

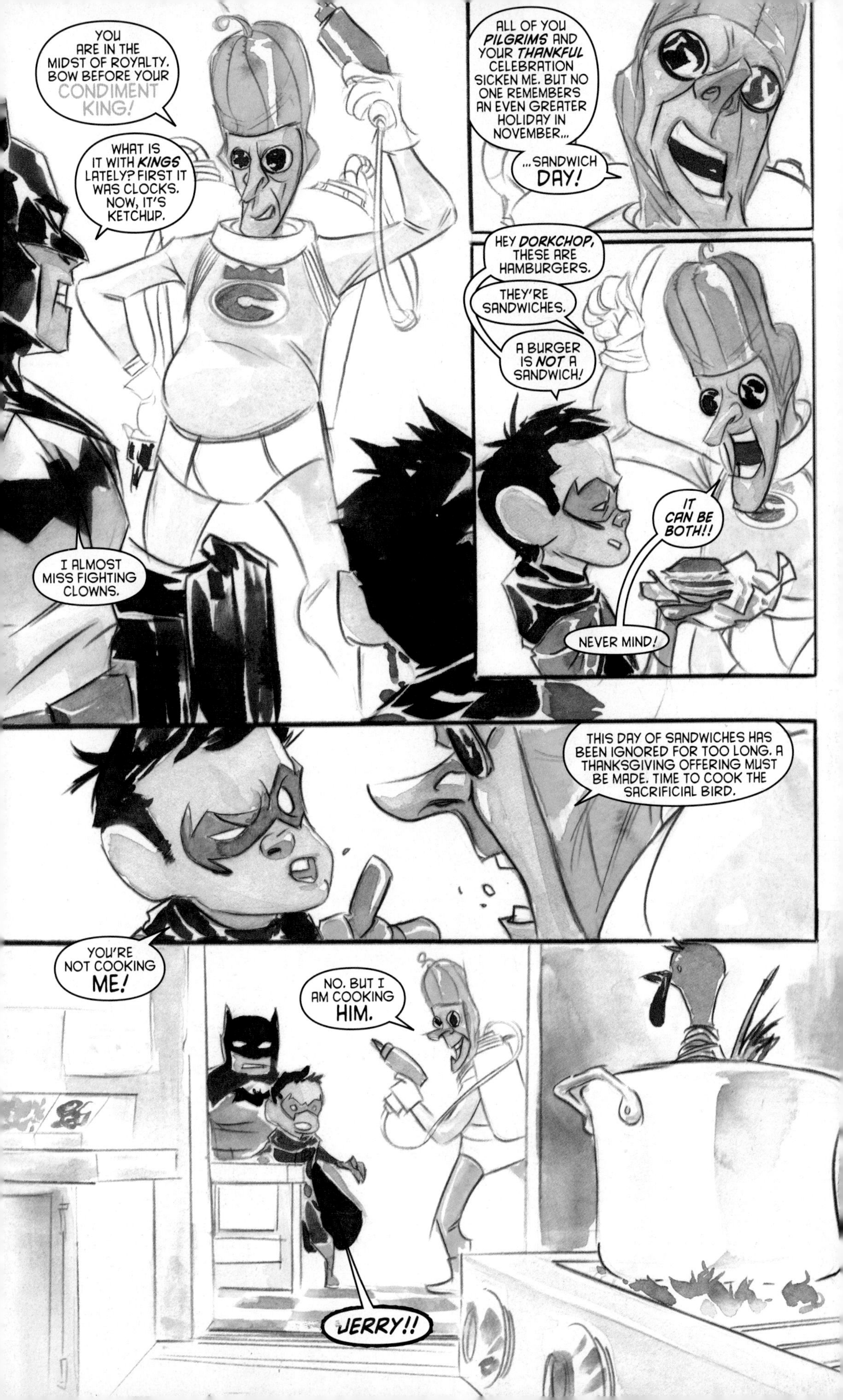

YOU ARE IN THE MIDST OF ROYALTY. BOW BEFORE YOUR CONDIMENT KING!
WHAT IS IT WITH KINGS LATELY? FIRST IT WAS CLOCKS. NOW, IT'S KETCHUP.
I ALMOST MISS FIGHTING CLOWNS.
ALL OF YOU PILGRIMS AND YOUR THANKFUL CELEBRATION SICKEN ME. BUT NO ONE REMEMBERS AN EVEN GREATER HOLIDAY IN NOVEMBER...
...SANDWICH DAY!
HEY DORKCHOP, THESE ARE HAMBURGERS.
THEY'RE SANDWICHES.
A BURGER IS NOT A SANDWICH!
IT CAN BE BOTH!!
NEVER MIND!
THIS DAY OF SANDWICHES HAS BEEN IGNORED FOR TOO LONG. A THANKSGIVING OFFERING MUST BE MADE. TIME TO COOK THE SACRIFICIAL BIRD.
YOU'RE NOT COOKING ME!
NO. BUT I AM COOKING HIM.
JERRY!!

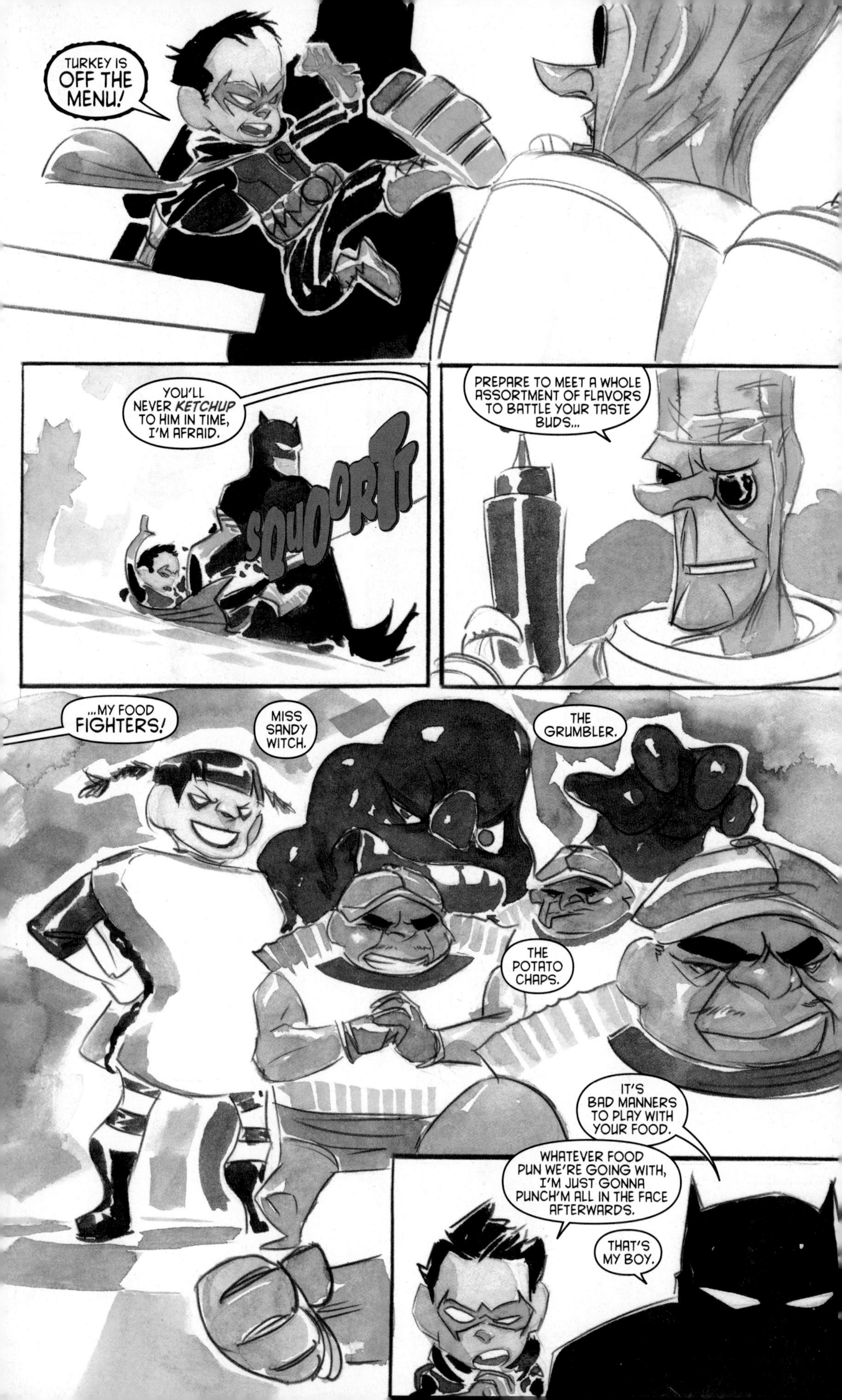
TURKEY IS OFF THE MENU!
YOU'LL NEVER KETCHUP TO HIM IN TIME, I'M AFRAID.
SQUOORTT
PREPARE TO MEET A WHOLE ASSORTMENT OF FLAVORS TO BATTLE YOUR TASTE BUDS...
...MY FOOD FIGHTERS!
MISS SANDY WITCH.
THE GRUMBLER.
THE POTATO CHAPS.
IT'S BAD MANNERS TO PLAY WITH YOUR FOOD.
WHATEVER FOOD PUN WE'RE GOING WITH, I'M JUST GONNA PUNCH'M ALL IN THE FACE AFTERWARDS.
THAT'S MY BOY.

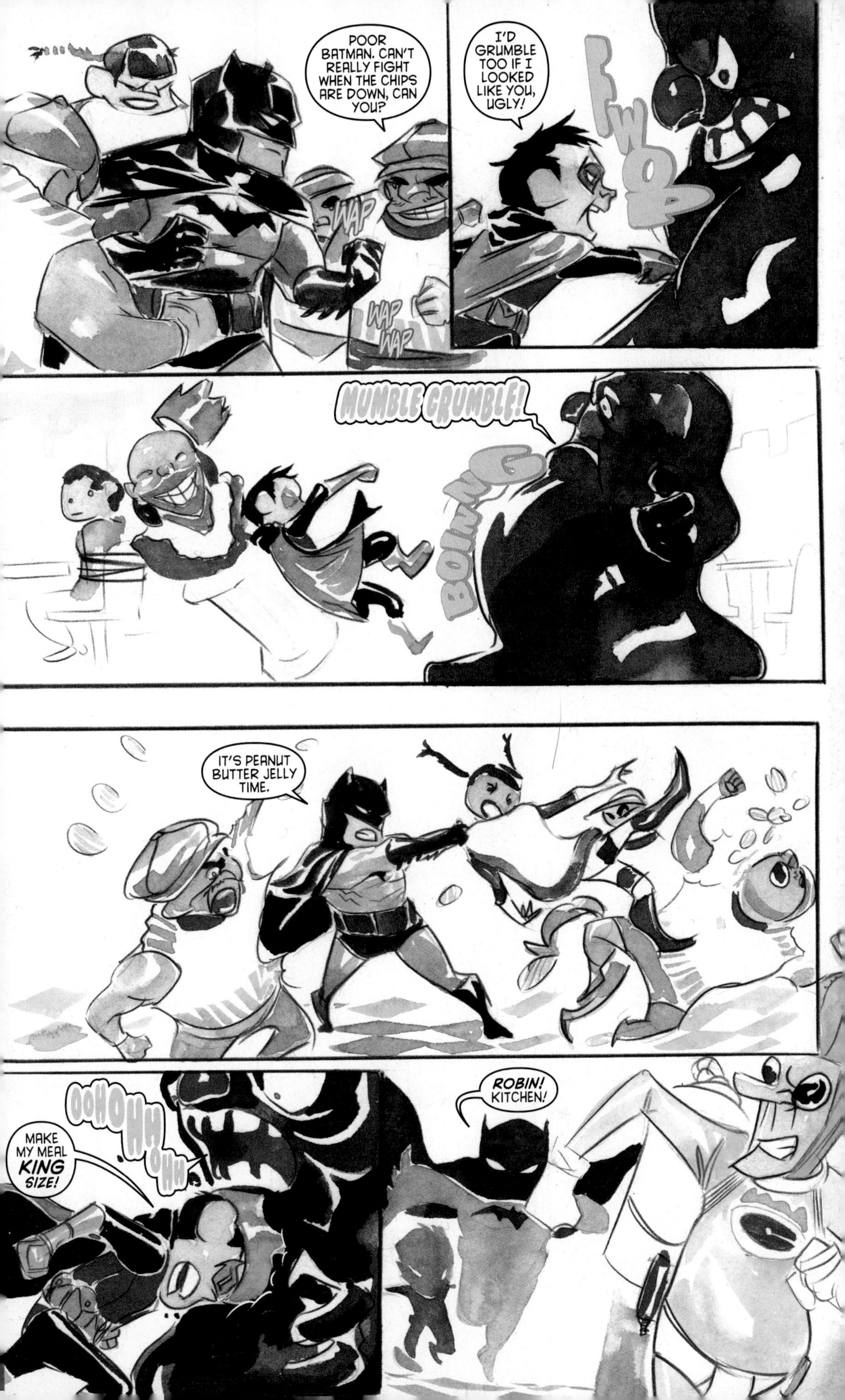
POOR BATMAN. CAN'T REALLY FIGHT WHEN THE CHIPS ARE DOWN, CAN YOU?
WAP
WAP WAP
I'D GRUMBLE TOO IF I LOOKED LIKE YOU, UGLY!
FWOP
MUMBLE GRUMBLE!
BOING
IT'S PEANUT BUTTER JELLY TIME.
OOHOHHHOHH
MAKE MY MEAL **KING** SIZE!
ROBIN! KITCHEN!

TAKE A SEAT AND RELISH THIS MOMENT, MY DYNAMIC DUMPLINGS!

FEELING HOT? YOU SHOULD. THAT'S GROUND TRINIDAD MORUGA SCORPION PEPPER IN YOUR EYES.

SKRAHASSSSSSH

WHAT A SWEET AROMA! I BELIEVE HIS GOOSE IS ALMOST COOKED.

QUITE THE PICKLE YOU'RE IN.

AND NOW, PREPARE FOR MY SPECIAL MOLTEN BBQ SAUCE. THE SECRET INGREDIENT... IS NITROGEN!

AAAAH!

GOBBLE DOBBLE!

SPROOP?

IT BURRNS!

WHO'S THE TURKEY NOW, NERDLOAF?!

GOBBLE

BROTH'D DOWN BY AN INFERNAL BIRD!

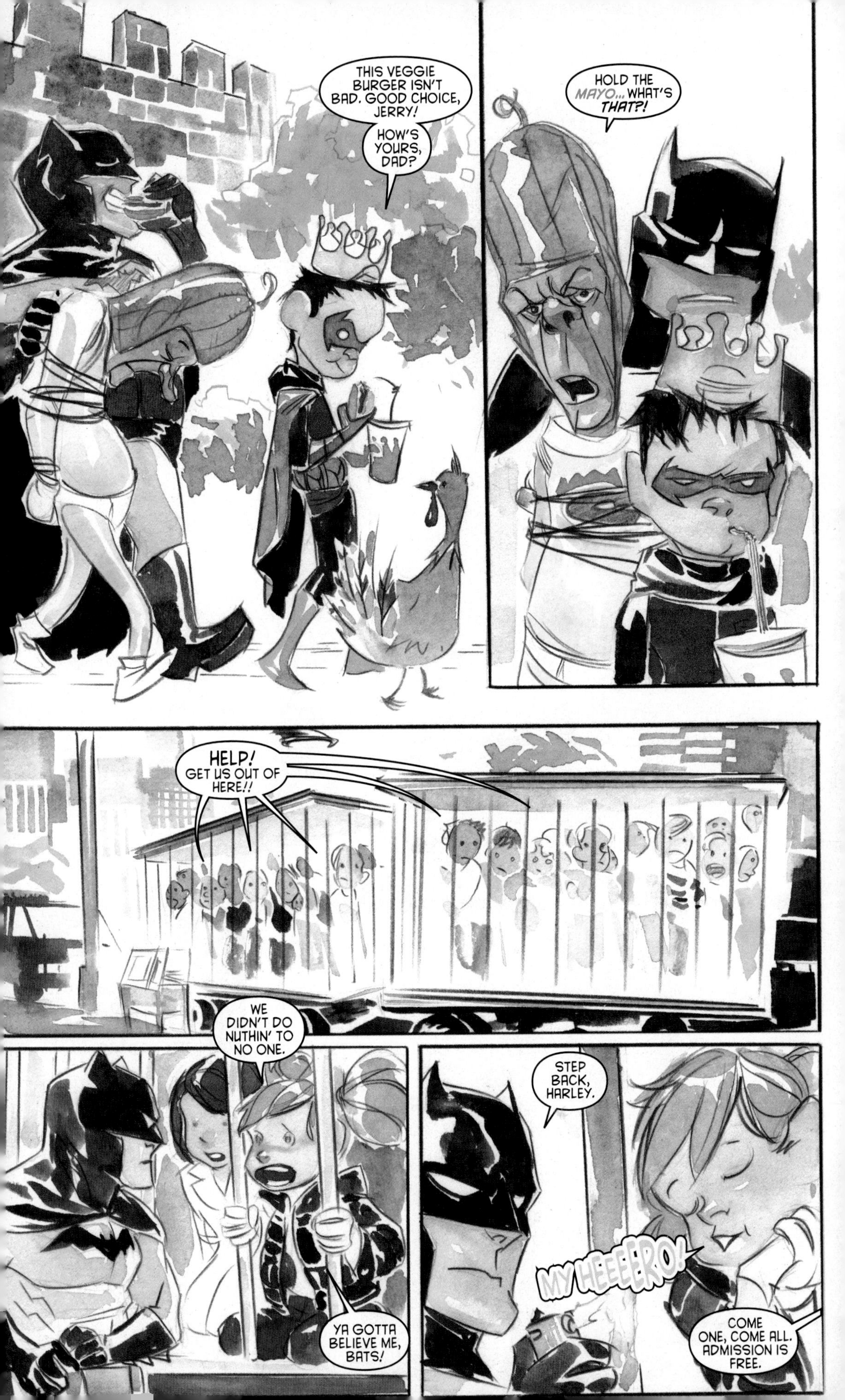
THIS VEGGIE BURGER ISN'T BAD. GOOD CHOICE, JERRY!
HOW'S YOURS, DAD?
HOLD THE MAYO... WHAT'S THAT?!
HELP! GET US OUT OF HERE!!
WE DIDN'T DO NUTHIN' TO NO ONE.
YA GOTTA BELIEVE ME, BATS!
STEP BACK, HARLEY.
MY HEEEERO!
COME ONE, COME ALL. ADMISSION IS FREE.

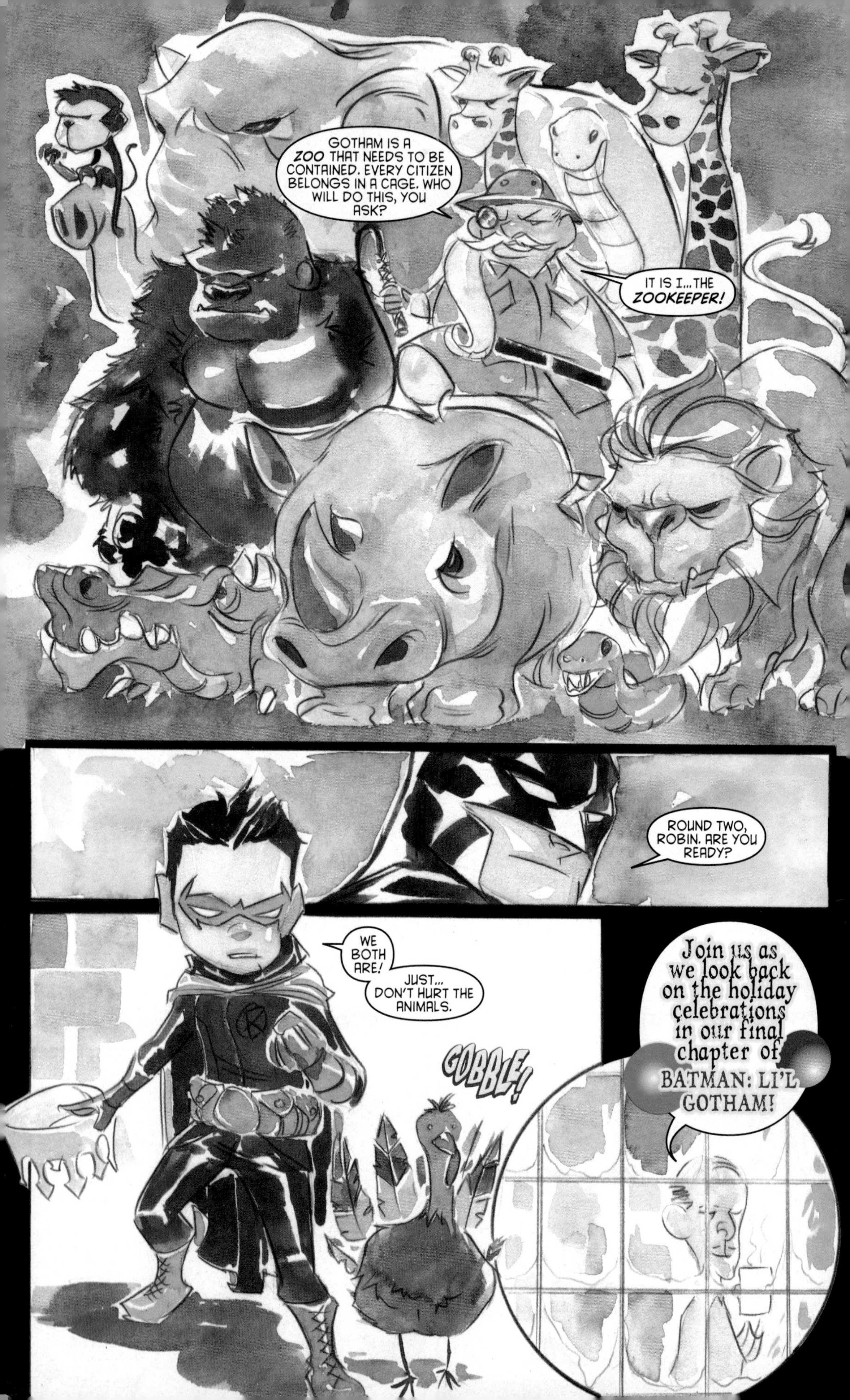
GOTHAM IS A ZOO THAT NEED'S TO BE CONTAINED. EVERY CITIZEN BELONGS IN A CAGE. WHO WILL DO THIS, YOU ASK?
IT IS I... THE ZOOKEEPER!
ROUND TWO, ROBIN. ARE YOU READY?
WE BOTH ARE!
JUST... DON'T HURT THE ANIMALS.
GOBBLE!
Join us as we look back on the holiday celebrations in our final chapter of BATMAN: LI'L GOTHAM!

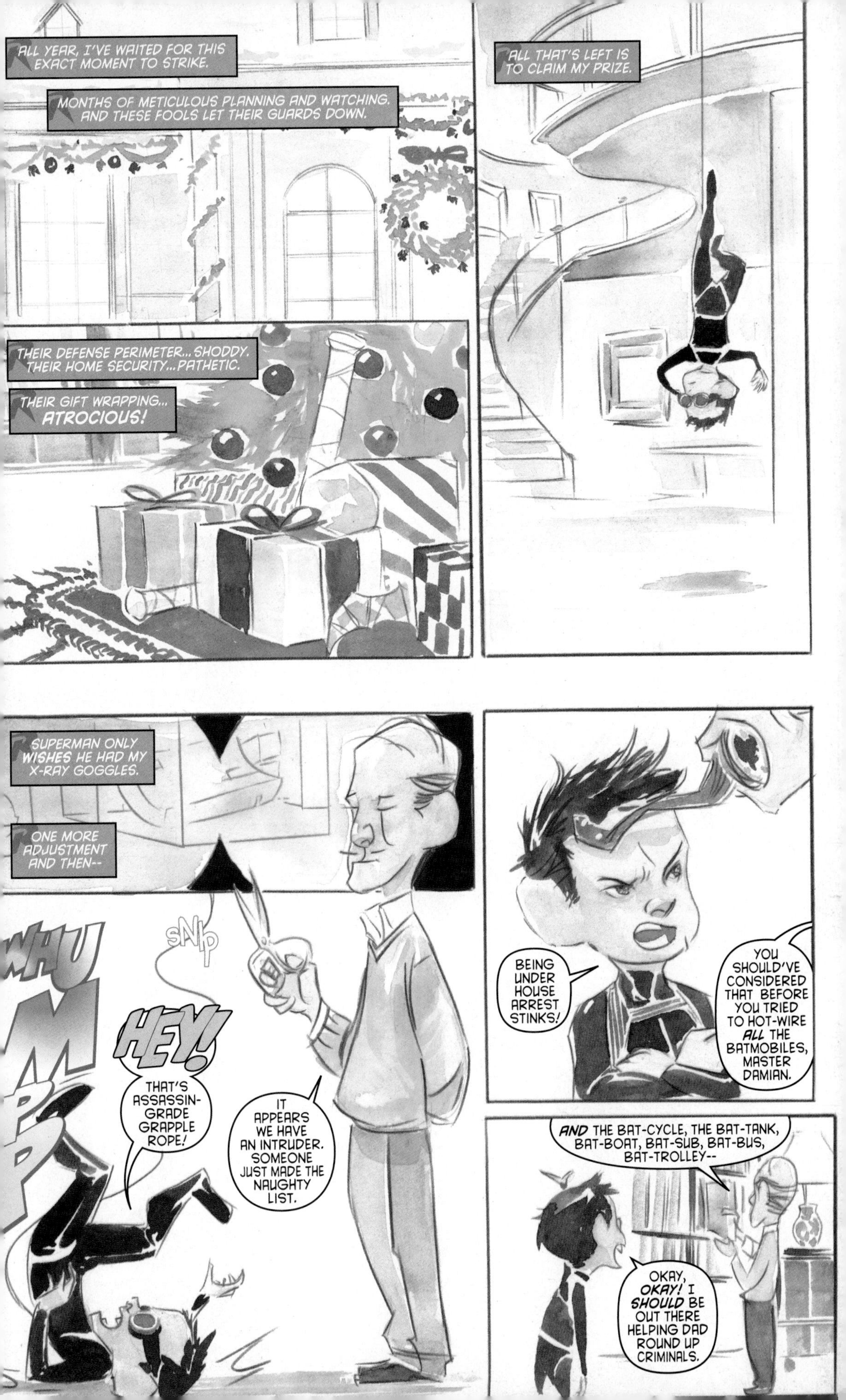

ALL YEAR, I'VE WAITED FOR THIS EXACT MOMENT TO STRIKE.
MONTHS OF METICULOUS PLANNING AND WATCHING. AND THESE FOOLS LET THEIR GUARDS DOWN.
ALL THAT'S LEFT IS TO CLAIM MY PRIZE.
THEIR DEFENSE PERIMETER... SHODDY. THEIR HOME SECURITY... PATHETIC.
THEIR GIFT WRAPPING... ATROCIOUS!
SUPERMAN ONLY WISHES HE HAD MY X-RAY GOGGLES.
ONE MORE ADJUSTMENT AND THEN--
SNIP
WHUMP
HEY!
THAT'S ASSASSIN-GRADE GRAPPLE ROPE!
IT APPEARS WE HAVE AN INTRUDER. SOMEONE JUST MADE THE NAUGHTY LIST.
BEING UNDER HOUSE ARREST STINKS!
YOU SHOULD'VE CONSIDERED THAT BEFORE YOU TRIED TO HOT-WIRE ALL THE BATMOBILES, MASTER DAMIAN.
AND THE BAT-CYCLE, THE BAT-TANK, BAT-BOAT, BAT-SUB, BAT-BUS, BAT-TROLLEY--
OKAY, OKAY! I SHOULD BE OUT THERE HELPING DAD ROUND UP CRIMINALS.

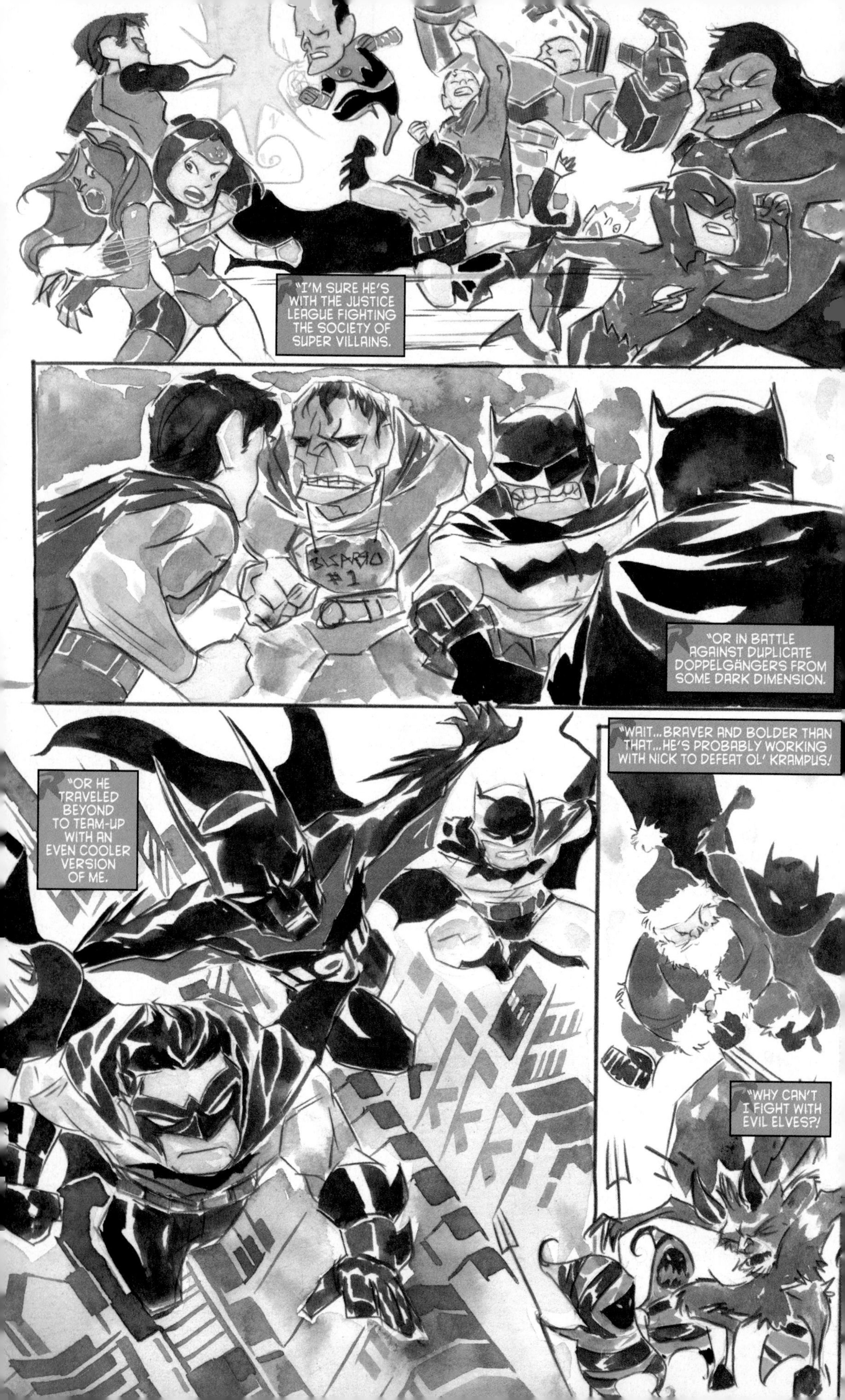
"I'M SURE HE'S WITH THE JUSTICE LEAGUE FIGHTING THE SOCIETY OF SUPER VILLAINS.
BIZARRO #1
"OR IN BATTLE AGAINST DUPLICATE DOPPELGÄNGERS FROM SOME DARK DIMENSION.
"OR HE TRAVELED BEYOND TO TEAM-UP WITH AN EVEN COOLER VERSION OF ME.
"WAIT...BRAVER AND BOLDER THAN THAT...HE'S PROBABLY WORKING WITH NICK TO DEFEAT OL' KRAMPUS!
"WHY CAN'T I FIGHT WITH EVIL ELVES?!

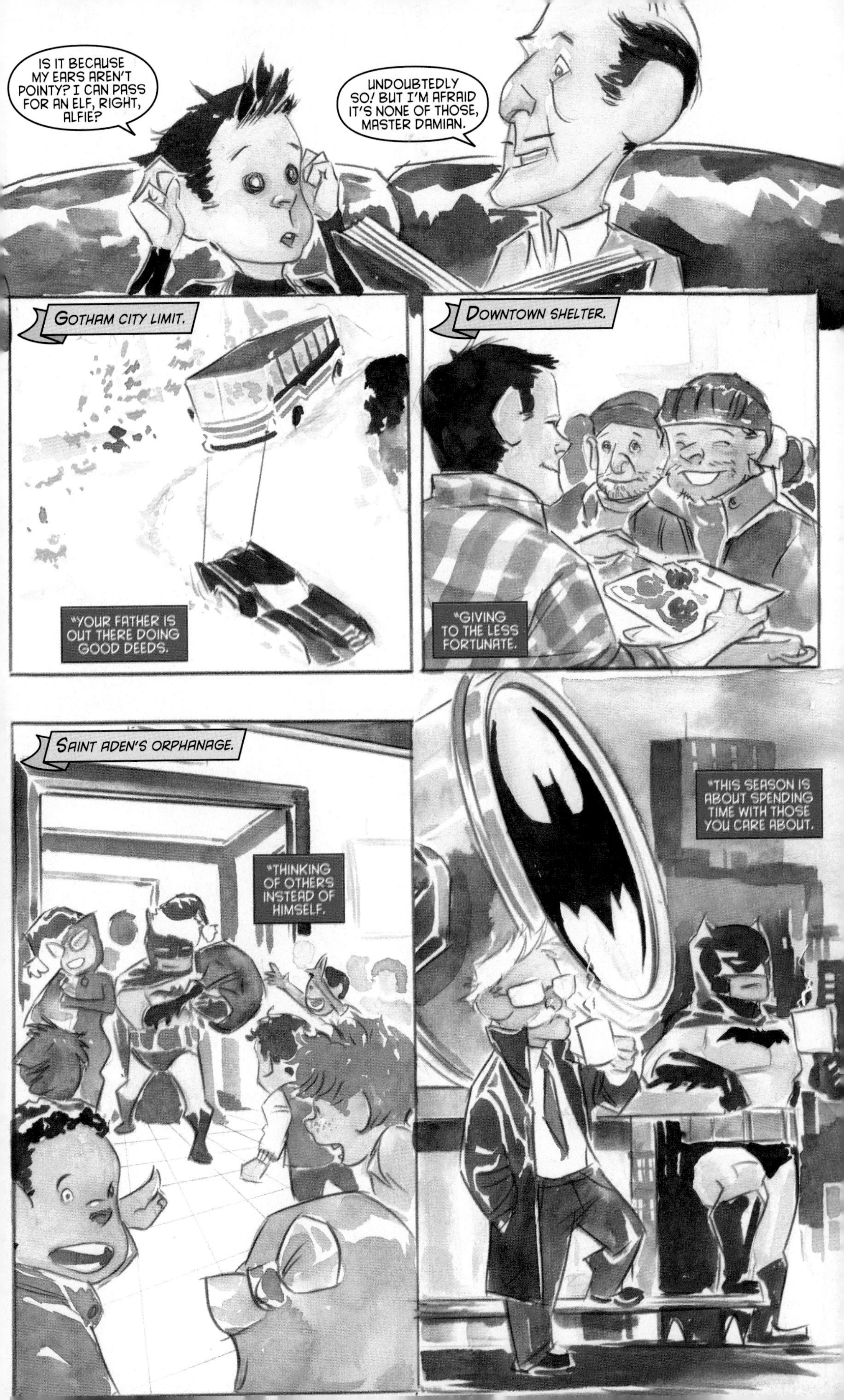
IS IT BECAUSE MY EARS AREN'T POINTY? I CAN PASS FOR AN ELF, RIGHT, ALFIE?
UNDOUBTEDLY SO! BUT I'M AFRAID IT'S NONE OF THOSE, MASTER DAMIAN.
GOTHAM CITY LIMIT.
"YOUR FATHER IS OUT THERE DOING GOOD DEEDS.
DOWNTOWN SHELTER.
"GIVING TO THE LESS FORTUNATE.
SAINT ADEN'S ORPHANAGE.
"THINKING OF OTHERS INSTEAD OF HIMSELF.
"THIS SEASON IS ABOUT SPENDING TIME WITH THOSE YOU CARE ABOUT.

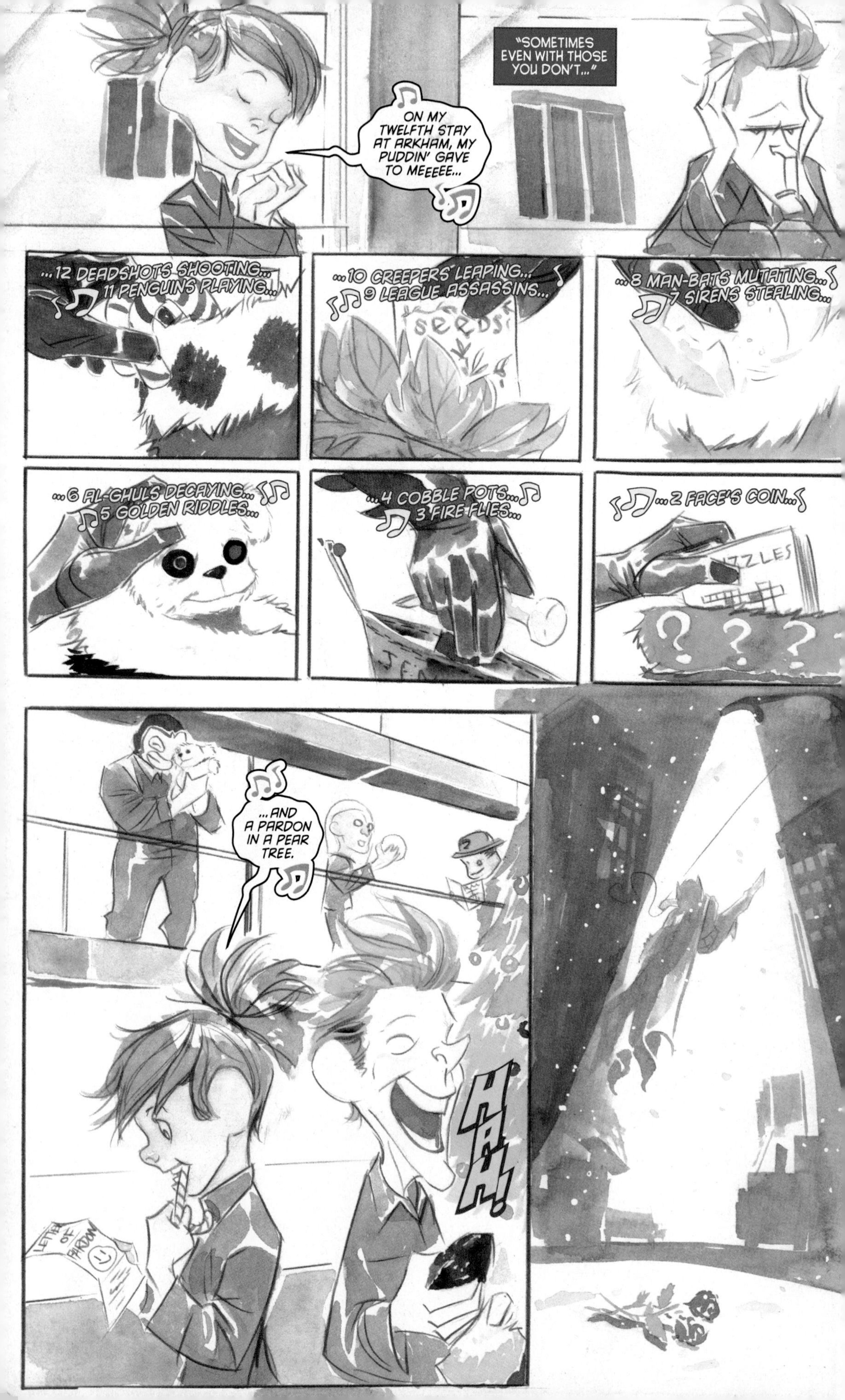

ON MY TWELFTH STAY AT ARKHAM, MY PUDDIN' GAVE TO MEEEEE...
"SOMETIMES EVEN WITH THOSE YOU DON'T..."
...12 DEADSHOTS SHOOTING... 11 PENGUINS PLAYING...
...10 CREEPERS LEAPING... 9 LEAGUE ASSASSINS...
SEEDS
...8 MAN-BATS MUTATING... 7 SIRENS STEALING...
...6 AL-GHULS DECAYING... 5 GOLDEN RIDDLES...
...4 COBBLE POTS... 3 FIRE FLIES...
...2 FACE'S COIN...
...AND A PARDON IN A PEAR TREE.
LETTER OF PARDON
HAH!

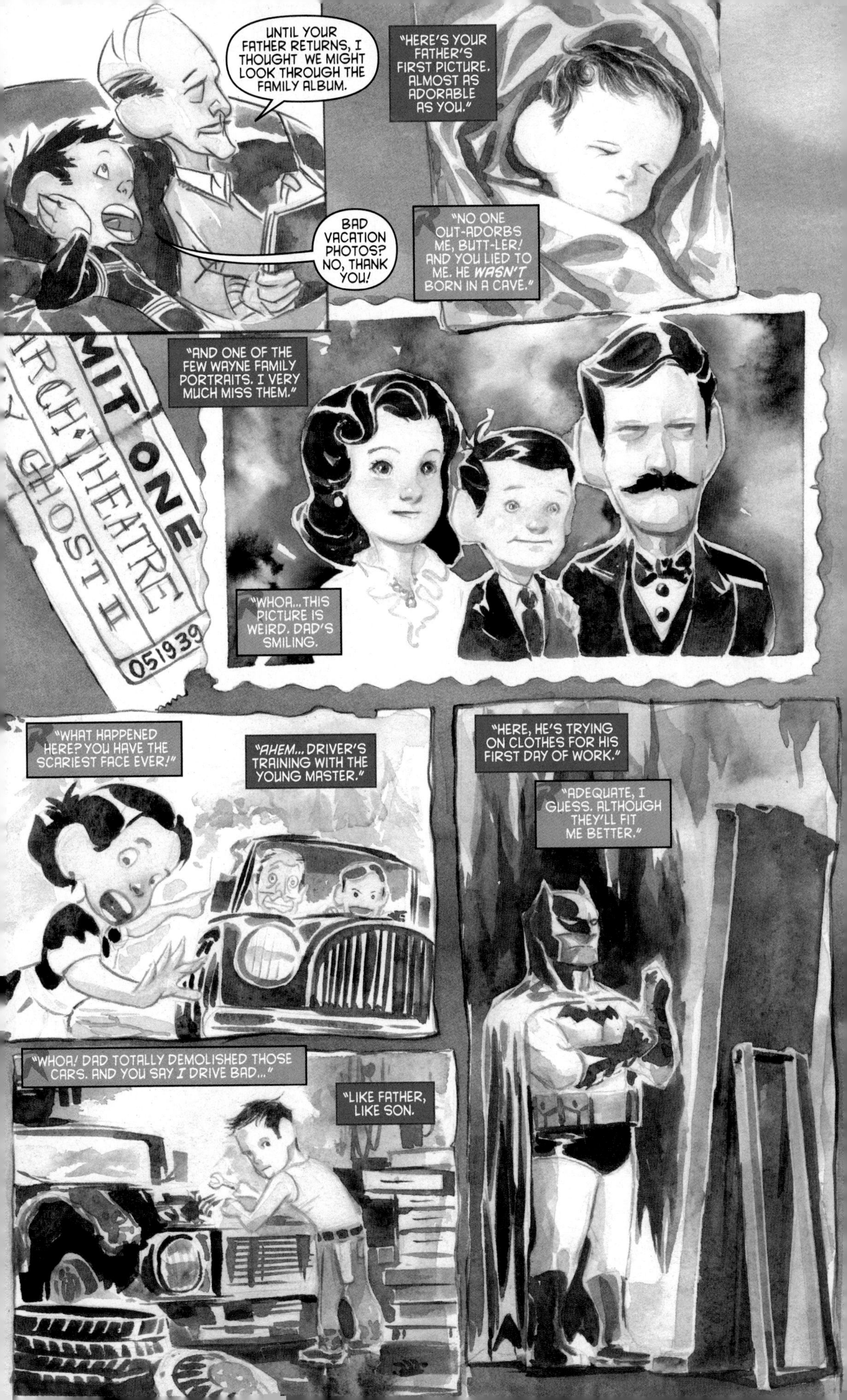
UNTIL YOUR FATHER RETURNS, I THOUGHT WE MIGHT LOOK THROUGH THE FAMILY ALBUM.
BAD VACATION PHOTOS? NO, THANK YOU!
"HERE'S YOUR FATHER'S FIRST PICTURE. ALMOST AS ADORABLE AS YOU."
"NO ONE OUT-ADORBS ME, BUTT-LER! AND YOU LIED TO ME. HE WASN'T BORN IN A CAVE."
"AND ONE OF THE FEW WAYNE FAMILY PORTRAITS. I VERY MUCH MISS THEM."
MIT ONE
ARCH THEATRE
GHOST II
051939
"WHOA... THIS PICTURE IS WEIRD. DAD'S SMILING.
"WHAT HAPPENED HERE? YOU HAVE THE SCARIEST FACE EVER!"
"AHEM... DRIVER'S TRAINING WITH THE YOUNG MASTER."
"HERE, HE'S TRYING ON CLOTHES FOR HIS FIRST DAY OF WORK."
"ADEQUATE, I GUESS. ALTHOUGH THEY'LL FIT ME BETTER."
"WHOA! DAD TOTALLY DEMOLISHED THOSE CARS. AND YOU SAY I DRIVE BAD..."
"LIKE FATHER, LIKE SON.

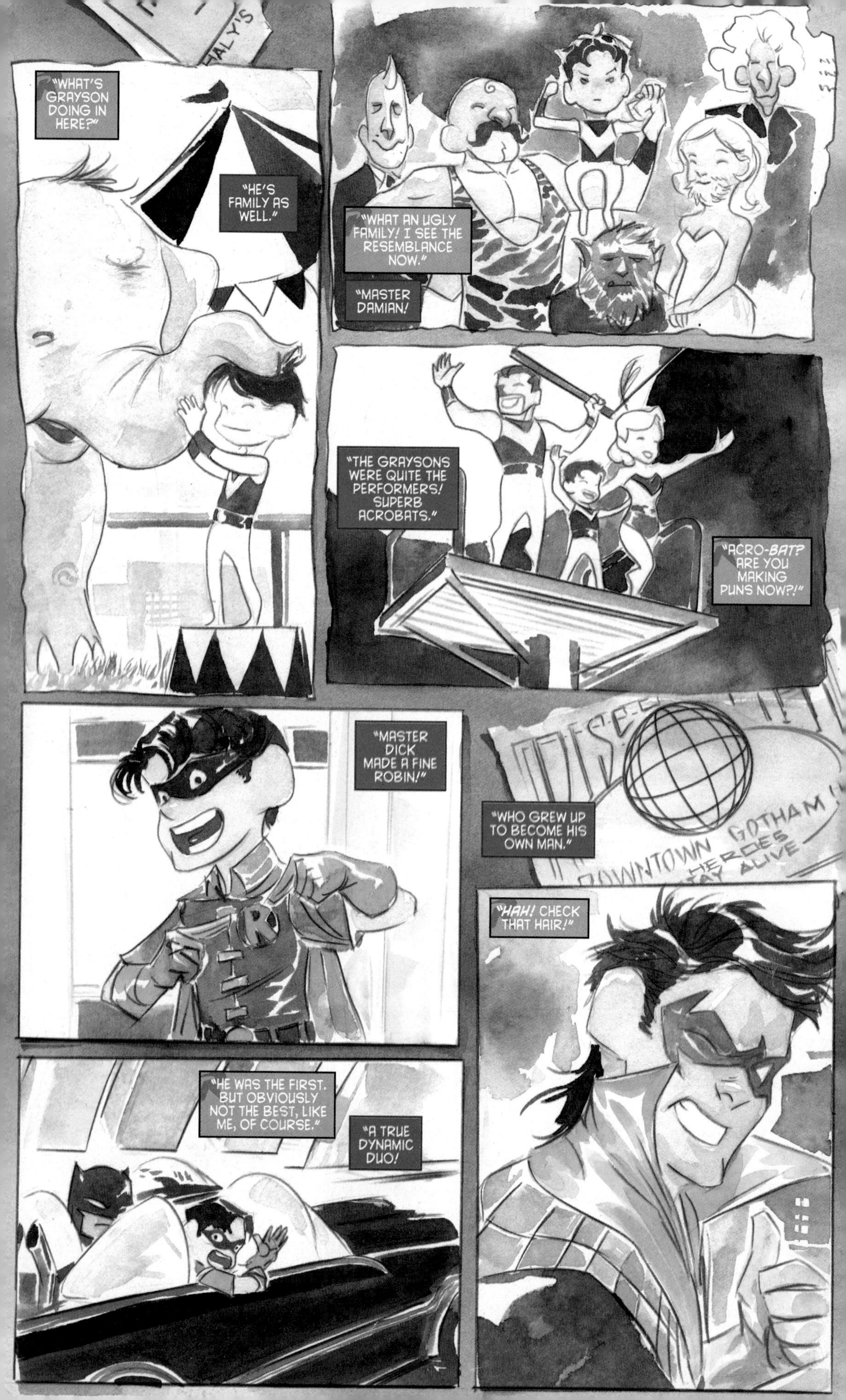

HALY'S
"WHAT'S GRAYSON DOING IN HERE?"
"HE'S FAMILY AS WELL."
"WHAT AN UGLY FAMILY! I SEE THE RESEMBLANCE NOW."
"MASTER DAMIAN!
"THE GRAYSONS WERE QUITE THE PERFORMERS! SUPERB ACROBATS."
"ACRO-*BAT?* ARE YOU MAKING PUNS NOW?!"
"MASTER DICK MADE A FINE ROBIN!"
"WHO GREW UP TO BECOME HIS OWN MAN."
DOWNTOWN GOTHAM
HEROES
"*HAH!* CHECK THAT HAIR!"
"HE WAS THE FIRST. BUT OBVIOUSLY NOT THE BEST, LIKE ME, OF COURSE."
"A TRUE DYNAMIC DUO!

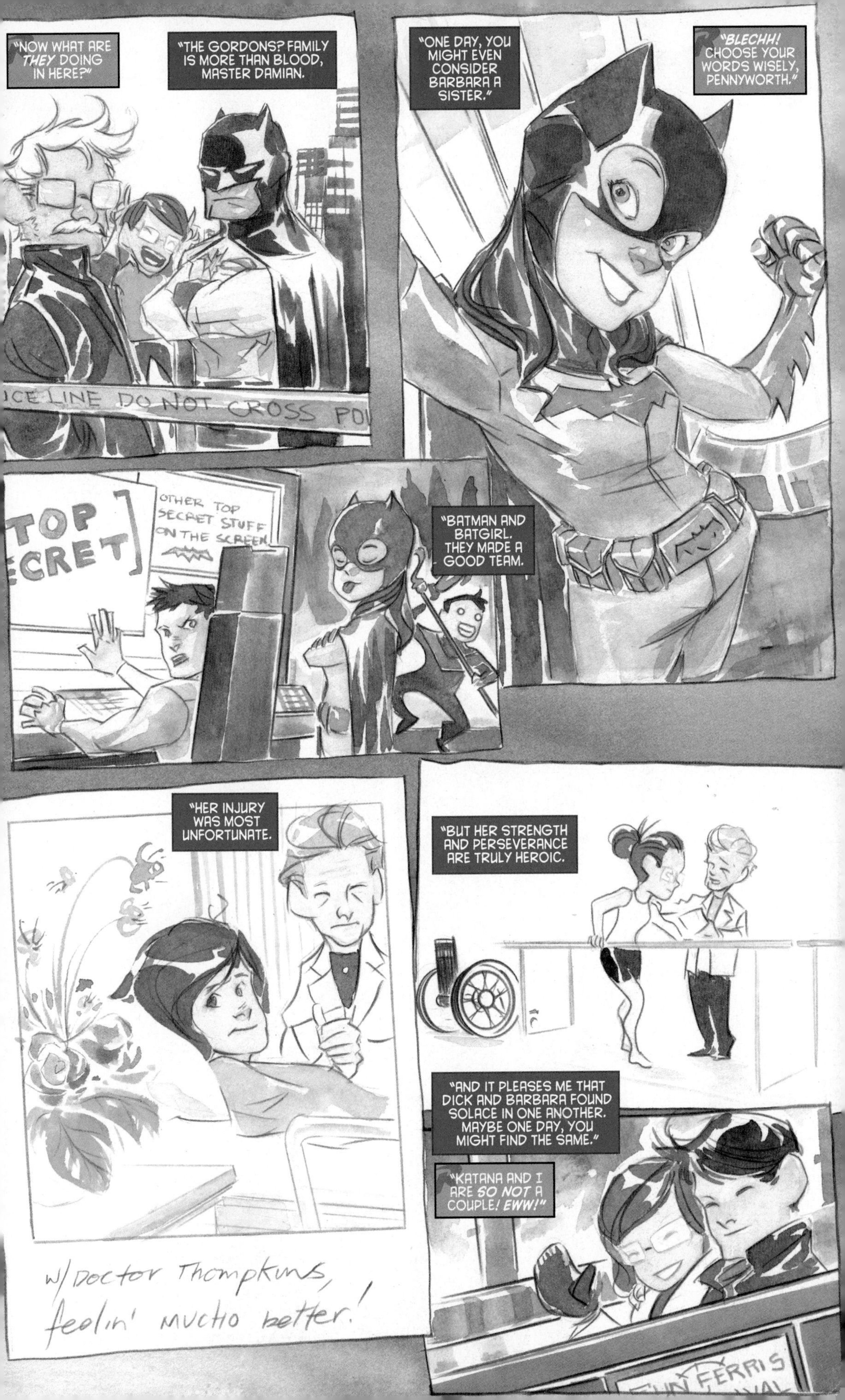
"NOW WHAT ARE *THEY* DOING IN HERE?"
"THE GORDONS? FAMILY IS MORE THAN BLOOD, MASTER DAMIAN.
CE LINE DO NOT CROSS PO
"ONE DAY, YOU MIGHT EVEN CONSIDER BARBARA A SISTER."
"*BLECHH!* CHOOSE YOUR WORDS WISELY, PENNYWORTH."
TOP SECRET
OTHER TOP SECRET STUFF ON THE SCREEN
"BATMAN AND BATGIRL. THEY MADE A GOOD TEAM.
"HER INJURY WAS MOST UNFORTUNATE.
w/Doctor Thompkins, feelin' mucho better!
"BUT HER STRENGTH AND PERSEVERANCE ARE TRULY HEROIC.
"AND IT PLEASES ME THAT DICK AND BARBARA FOUND SOLACE IN ONE ANOTHER. MAYBE ONE DAY, YOU MIGHT FIND THE SAME."
"KATANA AND I ARE *SO NOT* A COUPLE! *EWW!*"
FUN FERRIS

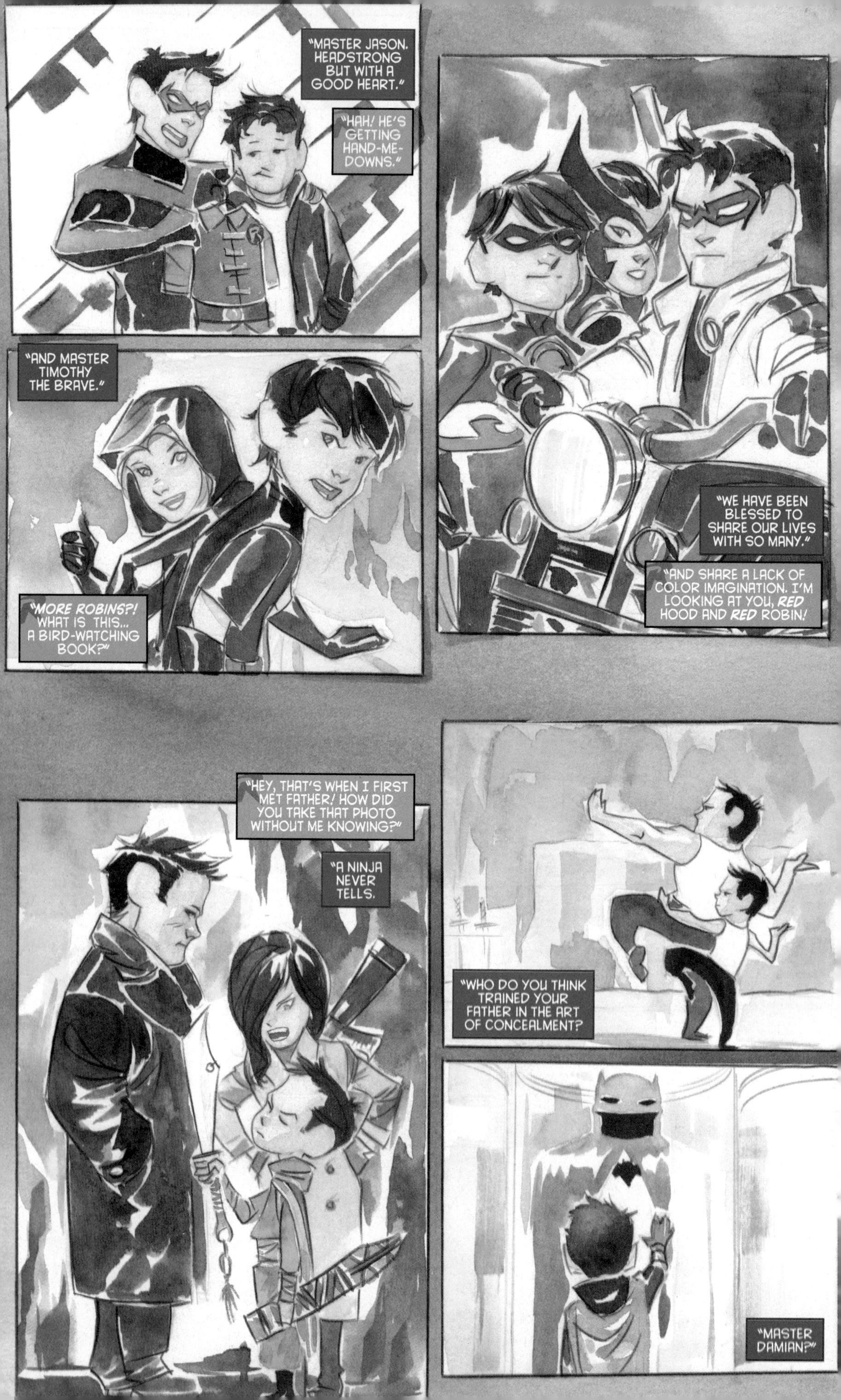
"MASTER JASON. HEADSTRONG BUT WITH A GOOD HEART."
"HAH! HE'S GETTING HAND-ME-DOWNS."
"AND MASTER TIMOTHY THE BRAVE."
"MORE ROBINS?! WHAT IS THIS... A BIRD-WATCHING BOOK?"
"WE HAVE BEEN BLESSED TO SHARE OUR LIVES WITH SO MANY."
"AND SHARE A LACK OF COLOR IMAGINATION. I'M LOOKING AT YOU, RED HOOD AND RED ROBIN!
"HEY, THAT'S WHEN I FIRST MET FATHER! HOW DID YOU TAKE THAT PHOTO WITHOUT ME KNOWING?"
"A NINJA NEVER TELLS.
"WHO DO YOU THINK TRAINED YOUR FATHER IN THE ART OF CONCEALMENT?
"MASTER DAMIAN?"

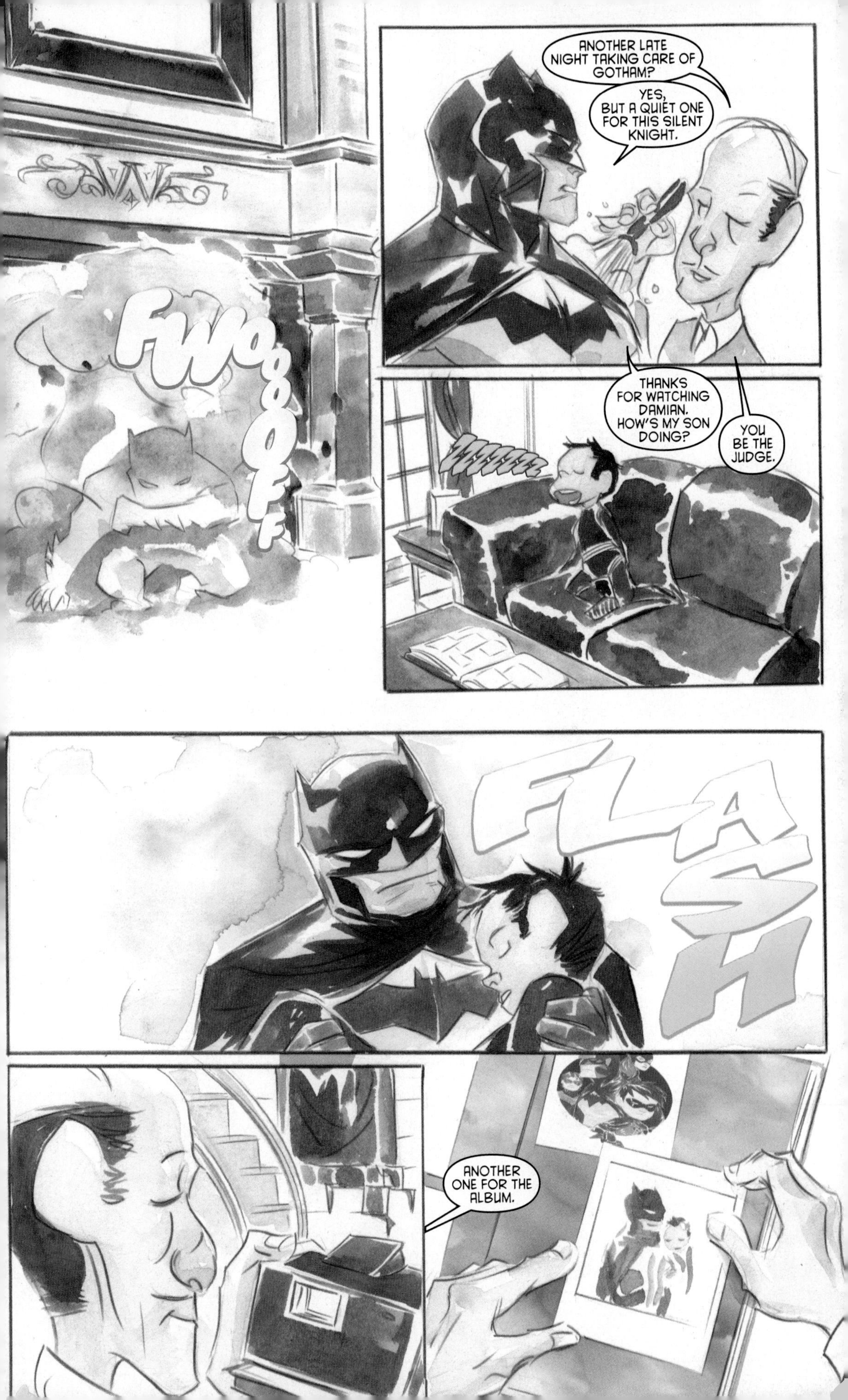
FWOOOOOFF
ANOTHER LATE NIGHT TAKING CARE OF GOTHAM?
YES, BUT A QUIET ONE FOR THIS SILENT KNIGHT.
THANKS FOR WATCHING DAMIAN. HOW'S MY SON DOING?
ZZZZZZZ
YOU BE THE JUDGE.
FLASH
ANOTHER ONE FOR THE ALBUM.

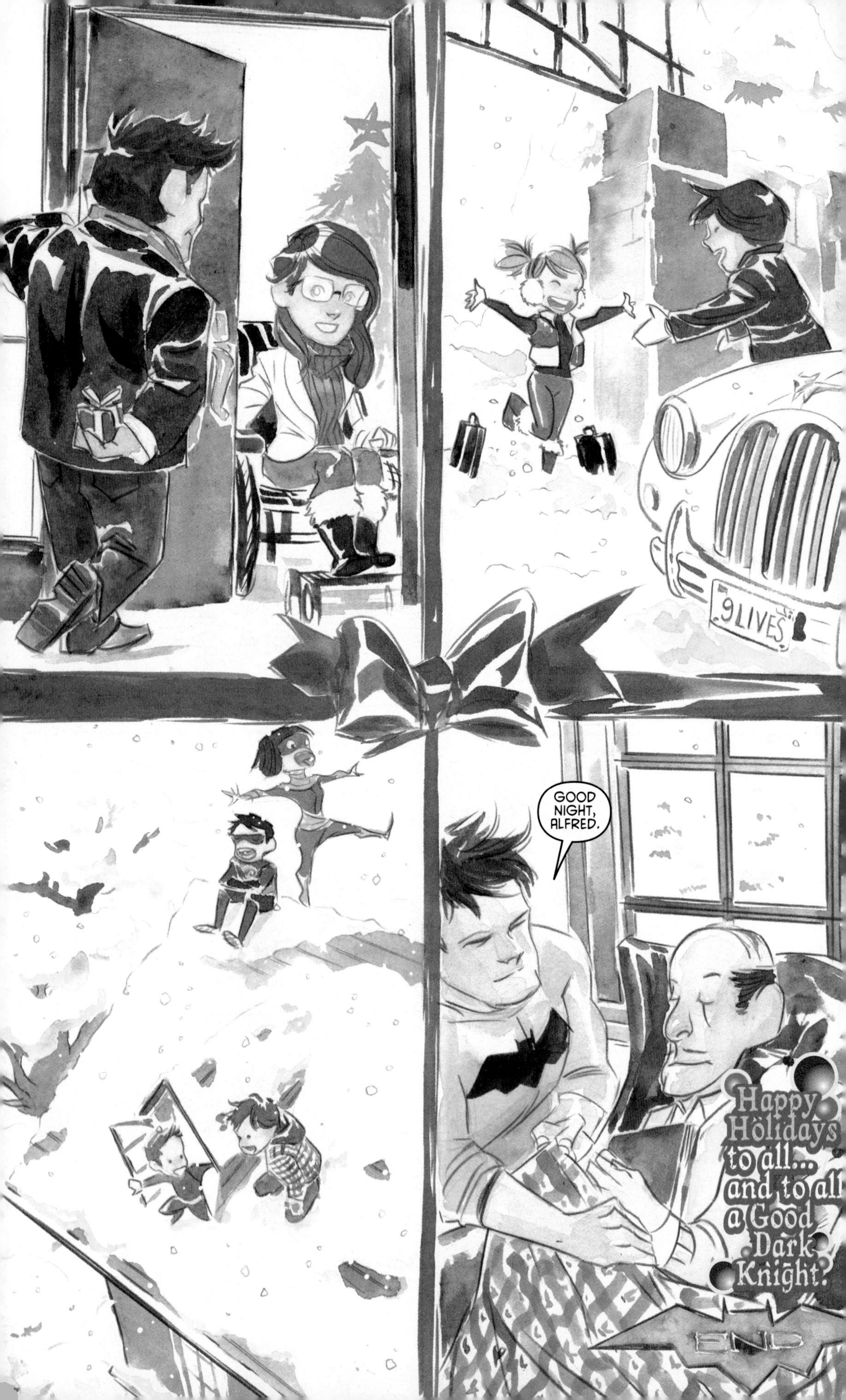
9LIVES
GOOD NIGHT, ALFRED.
Happy Holidays to all... and to all a Good Dark Knight!
END

Batman: Li'l Gotham #7 cover by Dustin Nguyen

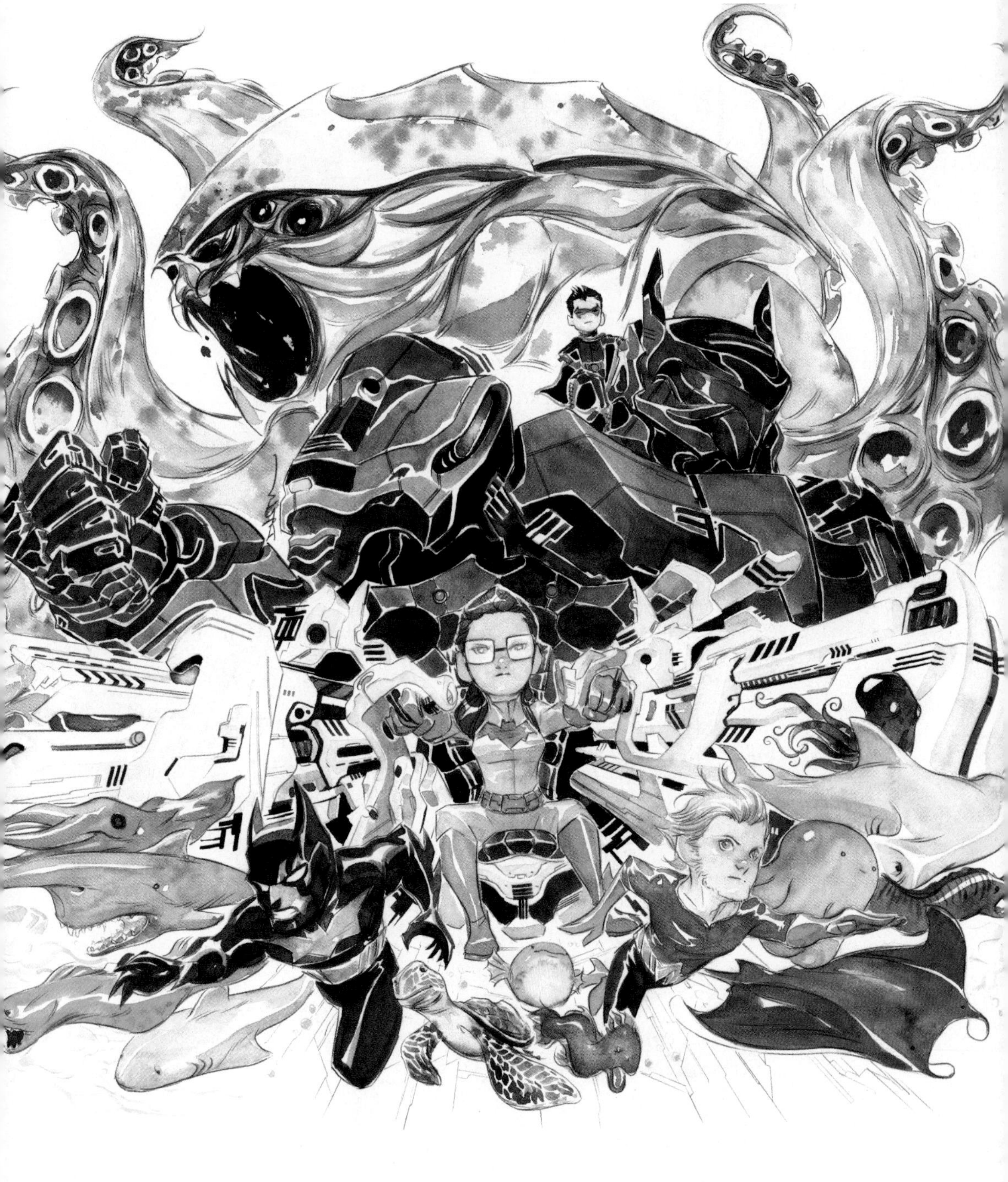

Batman: Li'l Gotham #8 cover by Dustin Nguyen

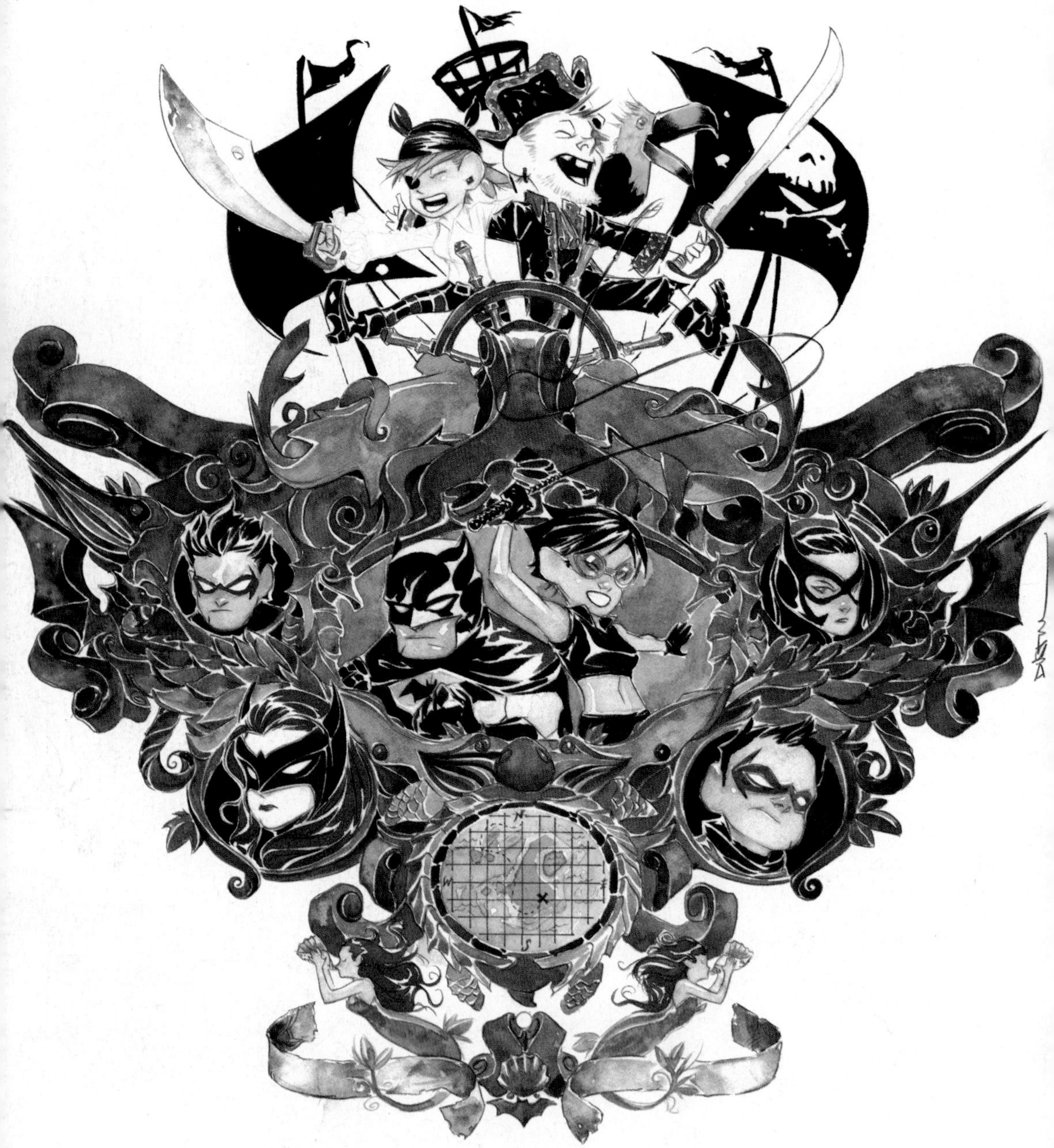

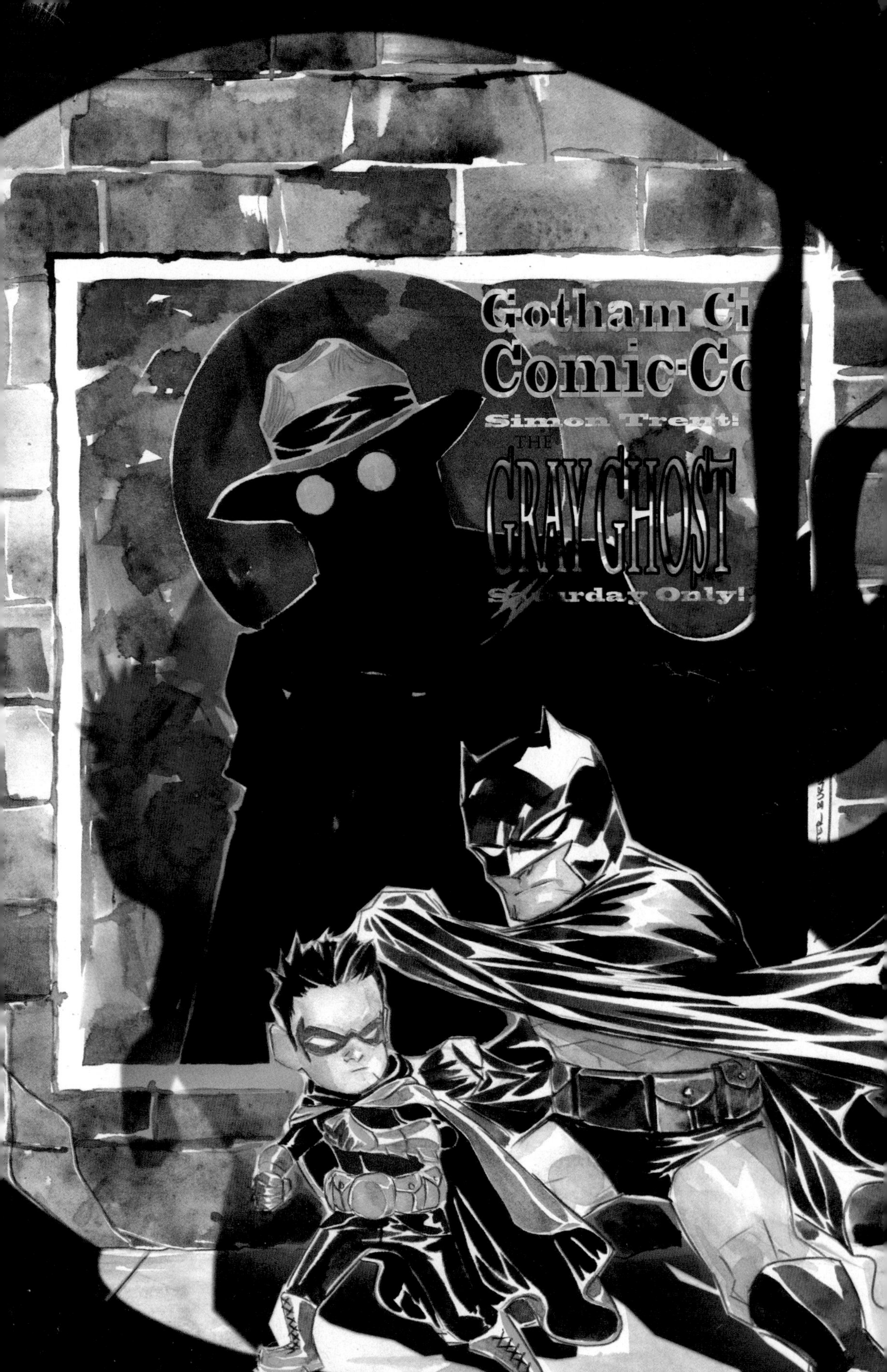
Simon Trent!
THE
GRAY GHOST
Batman: Li'l Gotham #9 cover by Dustin Nguyen

Batman: Li'l Gotham #10 cover by Dustin Nguyen

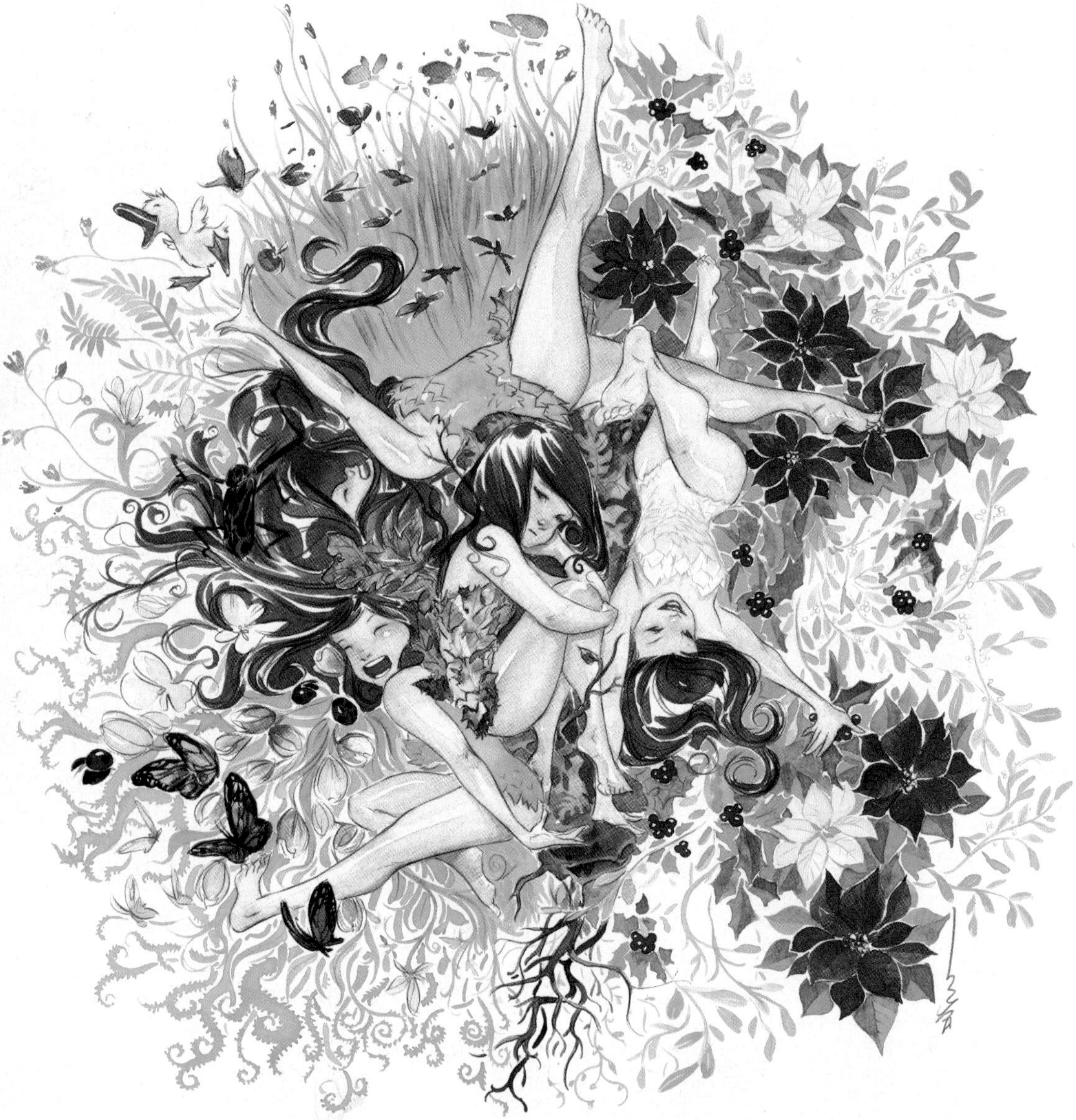

Batman: Li'l Gotham #11 cover by Dustin Nguyen

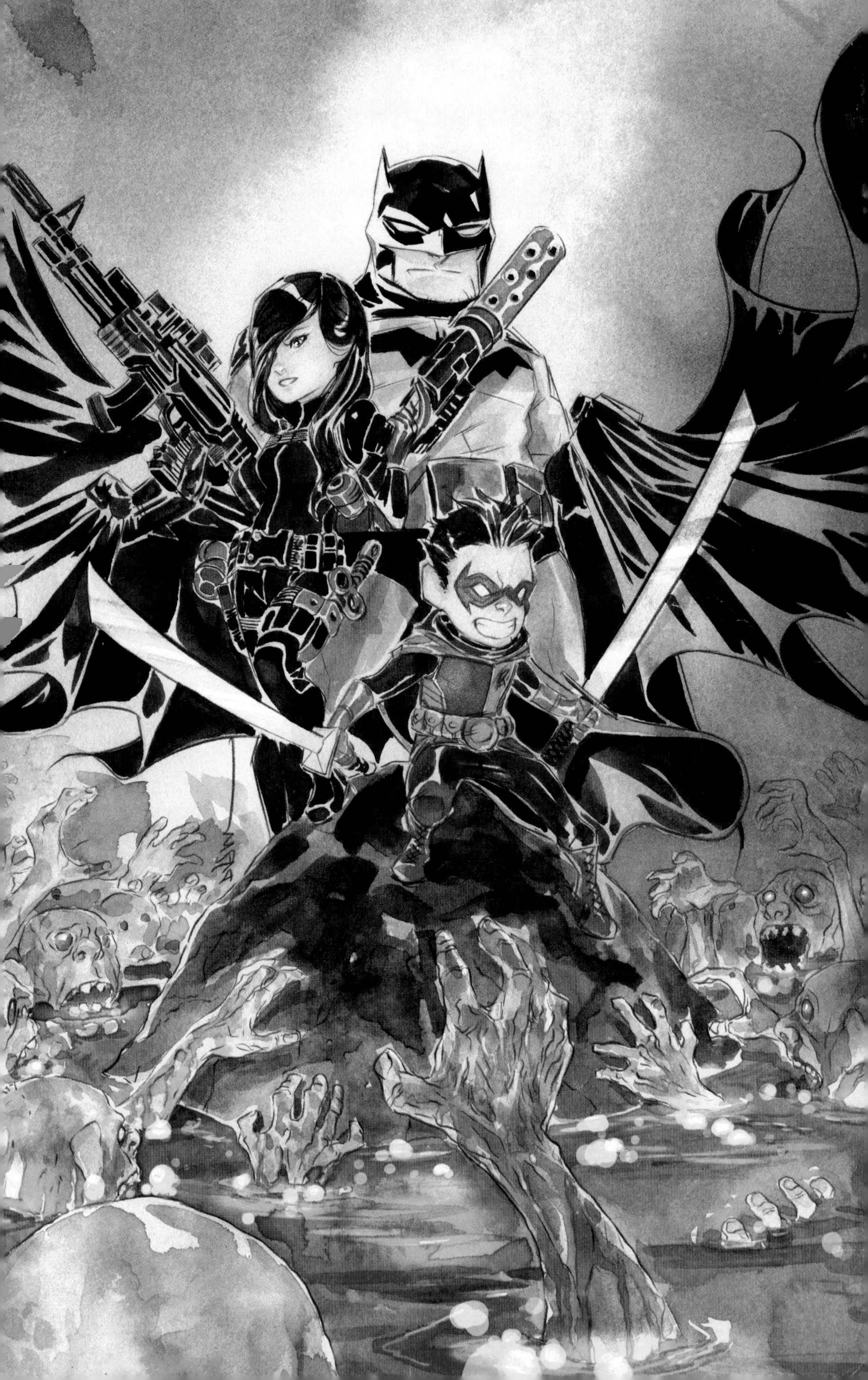

Batman: Li'l Gotham #12 cover by Dustin Nguyen

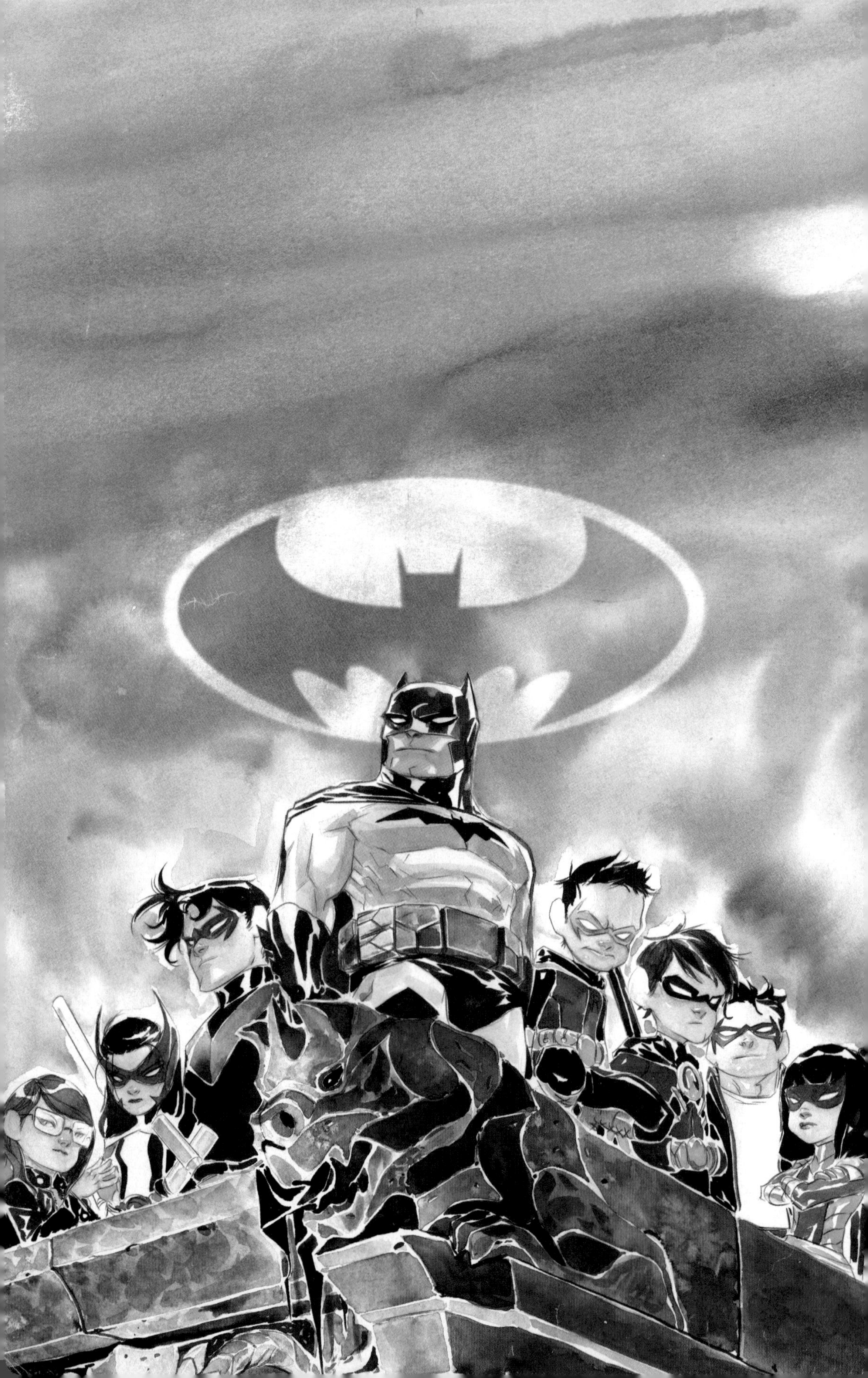